Kate McGill, Romanian Cold Hand

Minnesota renegade Femme Fighter seeks
memorable encounter with animal abusers.

Michael Chechik Sunday

iUniverse, Inc.
New York   Bloomington

Kate McGill, Romanian Cold Hand

iUniverse books may be ordered through booksellers or by contacting:

iUniverse
1663 Liberty Drive
Bloomington, IN 47403
www.iuniverse.com
1-800-Authors (1-800-288-4677)

ISBN: 978-1-4502-4349-0 (sc)
ISBN: 978-1-4502-4350-6 (ebook)

Library of Congress Control Number: 2010912776

Printed in the United States of America

iUniverse rev. date: 08/19/2010

Also by this author:

"This is Your Brain On the Internet"
1995, Ziff Davis Press

Foreword

This book is a chronicle of Katherine Harendt McGill's life from her teens to early twenties. The final chapter took place when Kate entered her thirties.

The phenomenon of the Romanian Cold Hand reflects real life. The U.S. Army invested funding to study the foundations of synthetic telepathy. Remote viewing research was funded by the Defense Intelligence Agency and CIA. Numerous other countries, particularly the Soviet Union, actively research neuroscience hunting for weapons.

You can read more chapters about Kate and her family at www.katemcgill. com.

Table of Contents

CHAPTER ONE
KATE'S GRANDMOTHER AT AGE THIRTEEN TAKES REVENGE

Haganah Harendt as a young teen walked across Europe with her mother Haddassah attempting to survive the Nazi Holocaust. They began their journey in Romania where the Harendts lived for generations. Their family was unique because they were gypsies who were also Jewish. Many years later Haganah would become Kate McGill's grandmother. As you will see, they share an unwillingness to behave like obedient young women.

Spring was still weeks away, but the air felt warm and pleasant to former Adjutant General — now simply Herr — Heinrich Manfreid Massemel, as he set off for his Wednesday morning meeting at the Fleisbeisen town school dressed in well pressed dungarees, white dress shirt with brown tie and a heavy cordoroy jacket.

It had been almost a year since the Great War — World War II — ended with the betrayal of the Third Reich. The defeat still caused Massemel to burn with anger. He had volunteered early for service and rose quickly through the ranks, attaining his final office near the end of the war. Now he planned to live out his remaining days with the quiet pride of a German who had served his country loyally.

Some Americans and even a few Russians still passed through Fleisbeisen, but its lack of vital utilities and the absence of a former military base exempted it from close scrutiny by the American military. Nonetheless, rumors abounded about the prosecution of ex-Wehrmacht, Gestapo, and other patriots for their wartime activities.

Massemel, in keeping with the dignity associated with his family name for five generations, conducted himself as an upstanding citizen. He had resumed his duties in tax collection, served on two local school committees, and intended to continue his family's long history of serving the community.

His wife, Trude, knew that he had participated in certain activities concerning the Jews, referred to as *der Juden*, but who had not? Everyone had responsibilities to fulfill in a war. Yes, it had been distasteful; only a few twisted souls took any satisfaction from the job at hand. Who could enjoy such things? Certainly not her Heinrich.

Neither Massemel nor Trude took much notice of the elderly woman who shuffled past their house just as he set off on his 15-minute walk to the school. Nor did Massemel, sorting out his plans for the day, note the aging pre-war Volkswagen that passed him as he approached the school. He had also failed to notice the same car when it drove by him on the previous two days.

As the Volks pulled alongside him, the old woman in an raggedy rain coat and flowered hat overtook him. The beginning of a courteous smile crossed his face when he registered her presence, but it quickly froze when he saw the standard-issue Luger aimed at his head. He opened his mouth to cry out and felt the Luger jam against his teeth, breaking off part of one and lacerating his tongue.

The woman shoved him into the rear seat of the Volks with a strength that belied her appearance — clearly, she was no crone. As she climbed in alongside him, she kept the gun crammed into his mouth. Massemel realized this was no ordinary hold-up. Jammed up against the small rear seat in a position of supplication, he had a sudden flashback of uncomfortable memories. He attempted to speak, but the woman shoved the gun roughly, making him gag. She raised her left hand in a gesture that commanded silence.

Out of the corner of his right eye he could just barely see her hand, which was completely unwrinkled. She was relatively young. Massemel quickly calculated his options as he had so often done in his military role. He knew this was no ordinary crime; it wasn't money they wanted. They wanted him. And this woman, this girl, worried him because she was young. She might not understand mercy, as he had frequently exercised it when dealing with *der Juden*. Though it was true that there had been times when his staid burgher's sense of values had failed him, and he had experienced a certain delight, a thrill, in carrying out his work. And then there were the very few times, with the young girls, so helpless; he had been carried away before he pulled the trigger.

Calmly, methodically, he rationalized his situation and suddenly understood why the gun was in his mouth. It had been one of his own tactics to terrorize *der Juden* when it was necessary to move them against their will.

And, yes, on occasion, the gun might have discharged. Those were thoughts he chose not to dwell on.

The Volks lurched over bumps, its ancient shocks and springs totally ineffective. Massemel noted a few landmarks, a road sign, and realized they were near the old dam —and the town cemetery. The Volks turned and stopped. They had entered the cemetery.

As the driver emerged from the front seat, Massemel's heart sank. He had hoped his abductors were both women, but the driver was a man, a young and strapping man. Pulling the front seat forward, he motioned Massemel out. The two pushed him across a small path, to the rear of a chapel. They had chosen a secluded spot.

He was sweating profusely. He knew this spot; he had brought people here himself. It was protected from view by trees and a brick wall. They were completely isolated. His eyes were not covered, but the two stood out of view behind him. Abruptly, the woman again thrust the gun into his mouth. He knew why; it was an action that intimidated and overwhelmed a supplicant, and now he was the supplicant.

"Adjutant General Massemel,", she said, "you murdered two of my relatives, two young men, barely out of their teens. You had options, including letting them go or sending them to a work camp, but instead you murdered them on this spot. I witnessed the execution. You may say a prayer if you wish."

Massemel thought he recalled those two. Yes, it had occurred on this spot. One of them had been bawling like a baby, the other quite stoic. Massemel thought that, yes, he might have let them go. Now he wasn't sure why he had not. And clearly, this woman witnessed the event. How unforgivable to have let a witness live.

She said, "I watched you murder my young cousin like cutting down a young tree, without a second thought. I swore then I would avenge his death."

His muscles began to give way, his breath came in short, painful bursts, and he felt a warm stream of urine in his pants. He was losing bodily control. He tried to turn, but the man's strong hands grabbed his head firmly.

"Adjutant General, you gave my cousin no time. We at least are giving you this grace. Are you ready to meet your fate?"

Massemel began to weep uncontrollably. He'd come all the way through the war, and before that the many years in the Brown Shirts. Yes, he'd had to shoot his share, but he never engaged in the torture so popular among the animals. That was why the Brown Shirts had been disb—.

The Luger flashed twice and he fell dead.

The man and woman dragged his body to a newly dug grave and pushed it in. It took them ten minutes to replace the dirt.

In a thick Romanian accent, the man asked, "Haganah, are you all right?"

She didn't look up as she tossed in the last few shovelfuls.

"Perfectly fine. Now we have two to go."

"I thought you said one more?" He did not understand how one so young could hand out this punishment without blinking. She was made of iron.

"No, two — we have two more. I will explain. It is our obligation; that was the pact. I am the instrument of our revenge."

They left the old Volks and picked up pre war Peugot bicycles propped against the chapel wall. The bicycle chains and handle bars were badly rusted but the tires seemed to hold air. They had two hours of riding and a train journey ahead.

As she climbed on the bike she reached in her pocket to make sure her money was intact. She thought, *Can I do this again?*

As they began riding she thought, *There is no other choice.*

CHAPTER TWO

KATE MCGILL SKATES ON THE PATHS

Forty one years after thirteen year old Haganah Harendt handed out the harshest possible justice in Germany her granddaughter Kate at nearly the same age faced a very different and substantially less emotional challenge.

The first story appeared in the Minneapolis Star-Tribune when Kate McGill was fourteen. "This young female skater needs to learn better judgment on our lake paths. But who is she? Minneapolis police report that a young woman on roller blades has been seen burning up the bike paths around Lakes Harriet and Calhoun. 'She can't seem to understand this kind of speed is not for our lake paths,' said Captain Randy Levy. 'We get these complaints occasionally but only this one young woman barrels along so fast. She's a bit the supergirl.'"

A few months passed and with typical Minneapolis hometown pride the Star Tribune asked, "What happened to that lightning fast female skater we were seeing? The Minneapolis police report 'the skating tornado' has not been seen all summer. What gives?"

Sarah McGill read the story and smiled to herself. Katie had been off in Colorado training for two months at a skating camp which meant no more Star Trib stories to worry Sarah.

Then one day in September when schools were back in session Sarah's close friend Buzz Roemer called. Buzz had been like a second father to Katie for the last few years since Paul, Kate's dad, had gone on the road campaigning to save endangered environmentally sensitive land. Buzz was a self made wealthy businessman who collected exotic cars and was thought to be underwriting the rescue of Americans who found themselves jailed unfairly by despotic regimes overseas. In small town Minneapolis Buzz took pride in his rep as righter of wrongs, a guy who helped re-balance the odds against the underdog.. Kate called him The Buzzerator. He even admitted openly to employing mercenary soldiers. Tough ones.

Buzz asked, "Is Katie back home now, Sarah?"

Sarah replied, "Back at Wayzata High, charged up about her computer classes. Talking big as ever."

Buzz responded, "I saw her skating on those new bike paths that interconnect the ski resorts in Colorado."

"And?"

"Your Katie went from superfast to blindingly ballistic. Maybe her muscles, her frame matured more or her instructor's physical training made a difference. Even those macho, muscular tough guy skaters, the ones that use the paths to train for winter skiing were dazzled. When she showed up things came to a halt."

"Buzz, this is good news or what should I think?"

"Sarah, good news if Kate can learn to control her speed. I mean she is not only fast but all that gymnastics, the karate training, the weight training, kick boxing gave her talent for maneuvering around stuff. She also amped up a macha little attitude which didn't hurt. Some ski resort staff helped her create a challenging slalom course where she did spectacular flips, turns, jumps over and around barriers. You know that trick going down escalators backwards on her skates? Well now she does this double flip over a car at this ridiculous... uh, it's a cool trick...."

"Buzz, it's not funny anymore. She refuses to tell me what she did in Colorado. She just says, '...I dreamed up a couple new tricks, mom...' Nothing more but I saw that big scrape on her right hip. Buzz, can't you say something to her? She's getting so crazy about these tricks...."

Sarah felt isolated, the only person who wanted Kate to stop these scary demonstrations. Kate's father Paul traveled incessantly. Kate had such drive to out do herself.

Buzz replied, "Well, Kate's ambition needs outlets so maybe she felt it better to experiment when you couldn't watch every move, you know? I kept an eye on her, Kate pushes the envelope, she always has."

Sarah had constant nightmares of Kate in hospitals, Kate breaking bones. This was way past Kate the Tom Boy. She simply couldn't refuse a challenge.

"Sarah, your girl has talent and guts. She had guts playing hockey with boys, bad odds didn't bother her. Remember when she played those big guys from St. Paul? Man, she could outskate them AND outshoot them!"

"Buzz cool out. You know we had to stop that. She was going to get hurt. The coach kept saying, 'Kate, go easy, you'll get knocked around.' Our daughter just doesn't have the same fears as normal people."

Buzz allowed a moment to pass.

"Uh, Sarah, I guess you should know this, I heard about it, didn't see it. She and two young women were walking through town at night and some drunk guys gave them a hard time."

"And?"

"The word was Kate dispatched them, three of them like they were toys. Tossed three sizeable young men around."

Sarah recoiled. "Buzz. You weren't there, this could be a rumor, right?"

"Sarah, your daughter will not take grief from anyone. It's a fact but that's good in a way. She truly can take care of herself."

Sarah never quite knew what to make of Buzz's speculations. She did know Katie respected Buzz's take charge attitude but she was fifteen years old and still very much a kid. Buzz could also be kid-like including questionable judgement..

Then again, Buzz could also be the man you want in your corner if there is trouble. Which Buzz does a mother trust?

Two Minneapolis police cars pulled up side by side, driver's windows facing each other on a still soft July night. Patrolling around Lake Calhoun near the uptown neighborhood cops could be easily bored. Underage drinking or a little hooliganism was about all the police encountered.

"Quiet for you?"

"Yah, pretty much but this young guy was talkin'.…Supposedly around Lake Harriet or Calhoun at six in the morning a whole bunch of kids are showin' up with brooms."

"Brooms?"

"Yah, he said kids from Wayzata and Minnetonka caravanning down here with brooms. That's the word? It's kind of strange because those two towns always have a rivalry."

"Does 'brooms' mean they are fighting?"

"Didn't sound like it. A big deal about skating, some kid on skates."

"Could be the skating tornado is back?"

"I'll call it in for the next shift. Those guys rarely have much to do."

The sun showed its first summer rays at 5:30 AM. By 5:45 dozens and dozens of high school teens, many up all night, showed up around Lake Calhoun hanging out on the paved blacktop bike path.

Kids excited, kids confused. Most unsure what on earth they were doing at this ungodly hour but everyone was saying, "Man, you gotta see this! She only does it like once!"   Minnesota gets pretty quiet all winter unless you get excited about ice hockey or ice fishing so when summer opens up the tires are squealing, the kids go a little bonkers. Everyone wants some excitement so even a girl on skates could be an event.

Ever since Kate McGill screamed through Ridgedale shopping mall on skates up and down escalators, barreling through the mall aisleways, driving security crazy and then turning up captured in security videos on the evening news her classmates became Kate Fans. When would she do something off the wall again?

Buzz Roemer counseled her to dream up pranks that were useful or educational. "In my day our pranks were just for fun but they didn't accomplish much. You can do better!"

Kate listened to Buzz.

After Ridgedale she topped herself by skating the entire Skyway system interconnecting office buildings allowing shoppers to walk inside in cold weather around downtown Minneapolis. She popped into the Skyway on Earth Day outfitted in a spectacular all green body suit affixed with signs reminding people to recycle or reuse. Again she made the evening news. Skating through the trading floor of a stock exchange upset a few but the police seemed to turn a blind eye.

Pranks With A Point became Kate's trademark. High schoolers liked her gutsy attitude and they wanted to see if she could pull off the next one?

Kate talked a few guys and girls into painting a huge banner with the word "bully!" in flaming pink hanging the banner from two trees across from the home of a local boy who was bothering other kids. He got the message.

Sarah lost it when Kate showed up with a black eye and some bruises after she confronted an adult man who kicked someone's dog. "Kate, you can't do this. Your father and I get nuts when you start pulling this kind of stuff. It's gotta stop!"

Kate promised to think about that.

Not all escapades were about teaching lessons. Kate craved speed and she loved an audience. Kate had been training with an ice skating coach at first but she wanted more speed. Next she started talking to people at the University of Minnesota which led her from the Athletic Department eventually to a specialist on aerodynamics. He offered to put her in a University wind tunnel to optimize her skating stance. Kate doggedly worked on lowering her wind resistance and a skating company offered to build special wheels for her inlines. Kate pushed out to the physical limits.

"Here she comes, look at that over by the boat house! Man, you ever see somebody skate that fast?" Kids excitedly broomed off the blacktop yelling at each other and looking up the path for the Silver Wraith, Kate McGill's new name in town.

Dressed head to toe in a silver body suit with all silver inline skates Kate built up her momentum speeding past groups of kids who gave up a night of sleep to see someone their own age do something cool. Kate tied down her reputation for pushing the limits.

Kids along the path were chanting and screaming, "Go Kate!"

From the side Kate was completely bent forward, her upper body parallel with the ground. Her long arms cut through the air, her fingers grazing the pavement on forward strokes, reaching high behind her on the back stroke. Her legs stretched far behind her and it almost appeared she would simply fall forward and hit the pavement. The wheels made a high pitched singing sound. While concentrating with singular intensity Kate somehow managed to acknowledge the brooms as she passed with a wave.

Beyond pure speed Kate's greatest challenge required hills to conquer. One hill existed between Calhoun and Lake Harriet so Kate started on Harriet with the intention of finishing on Calhoun. Kids began gathering on the connector path as Kate exited the first lake. Not a huge hill but enough for Kate to build up speed, as she accelerated down the short hill Kate performed a crowd pleasing 360 degree airborne turnaround. Upon landing she should have stopped for an intersection but Kate followed the jump by performing a forward rolling flip in mid air over the cross street. No ramp, just thrusting herself high into the air using her speed momentum. She landed and screeched a left hand corner heading out onto the Calhoun path.

Kids talked about that front flip for many years and it again made the news captured on video.

Minneapolis police were getting wind of this little happening and began showing up around the lake. The beat cops thought this was harmless fun.

"We've got her at the south end of Calhoun. This makes no sense but according to our radar gun she's approaching like 40 miles per hour. God she's like a machine, a well oiled machine."

"Officer, you need to interrupt her little party. This is Captain James Peterson and you can't have some nut going that fast on the path. Stop this thing now. You have my orders!" In their cars the police shook their heads. This was hardly life threatening.

Kate began rounding the southwest end of Lake Calhoun.. At her speed, it was roughly equivalent to driving a car at very high speed on a narrow road. The asphalt bike path designed for a bike traveling at 8 miles per hour became a thin ribbon.

Kate wore a primitive head set connected to a walkie talkie system

She heard a young male voice, "Kate, I'm back up at the north end, there's a bunch of cops up here now."

Kate couldn't worry about cops. They purposely started this early so the paths would be empty.

"Kate they're pulling one of the cop cars across the path. I think they want you to stop!"

Gasping for breath Kate yelled out, "Try talking to the cops. Tell them I'm making a movie. Tell them something!"

She focused on the path moving up the west side of the lake. Her speed gradually increased. A police car was now tracking her on the nearby street. Behind the police car a helmeted man rode a tall yellow dirt bike.

"Man, she's just flying. We got her over 35 miles per hour down here too! She is really something to watch!"

"Officers, you have a job to do. Shut down this skater now!"

"Control, this person is moving at high speed. You want me to shoot her in the leg? That would be like wounding a thoroughbred race horse. I'm the guy that shot, what, Native Dancer? Tell that one to the kids over dinner."

"You got a job to do. Do it! You don't have to shoot her for gods sake!"

The young guy acting as spotter got on the walkie-talkie.

"Kate, they got some kind of stun gun, there's a guy pointing it over the hood of that blue car."

"Check."

Kate saw the police car and came up out of her crouch.

Kate rotated on one skate and was now skating backward toward the cops and the stun gun. The officer drew his bead wanting to hit her in a leg, that would bring her down. But he couldn't figure out why she was facing away. ….

Twenty yards out and still rolling at near 30 miles an hour Kate brought her left leg around as hard as her muscles would allow. The left leg came up high, higher and now she rotated her entire body with full force.

The officer looked up. This was not in the equation. She was flying in an arc right at him, one leg leading, skate pointed right for his head. He reared back still pointing the short weapon.

Kate took out the gun with one skate grazing the officer's shoulder. Her rear leg bounced off the car's windshield. She completed the arc landing on her left skate. Kate brought her other skate crashing down ending in a crouch. And she remained in a crouch for twenty yards, losing speed but presenting a much smaller target. Finally she stood up and began building speed.

A few yards off the trail small knots of people were yelling encouragement. Kate pumped up her speed but now she realized she faced losing odds. If she left the path they'd have her easily and her energy was dropping, the most dangerous sign. Ahead she could see more police, numerous red lights. She was cooked.

A male voice, sounding far away appeared in her headset. "Kiddo, I'm behind you. I'll pull you out of this. I'm coming up on the path."

Snorting and growling the Yamaha motorcycle with its license plate obscured jumped the curb and moved in behind Kate on the path. Ahead police lying in wait saw the dirt bike and began frantically communicating.

"Look right, I'm just behind you!"

Kate recognized the voice. Buzz had showed up to watch and now he was pulling her out of the soup.

Then the Yamaha was even with Kate, she looked over.

Kate put her left hand on the rail and with her right hand she grabbed his shoulder to pull herself up on the seat. Her skates clumsily found their pegs. Enough to hold her weight. The dirt bike began accelerating.

"Hang on, we gotta jump this curb. Put your weight on your skates!"

Again Kate obeyed. The cycle jerked back and forth, the front end came off the ground Two police cruisers whipped around on the road to give chase, it was no longer just a girl skating, now laws were being broken.

Buzz goosed the Yamaha hard, accelerating away from the police. Changing lanes putting a few cars between them and the police the motorcycle rocketed away. He brought the bike above 80 to gain space. Buzz and Kate approached the intersection of Lake Street and Calhoun Parkway. Suddenly the big Yamaha slowed dramatically and they cut across traffic, whipped an illegal left turn and headed for Lake of the Isles. Another abrupt right turn and the dirt bike left the street, shot across a grassy area and disappeared up a short hill.

Kate shouted, "Where are you goin', Buzz?"

He shouted back, "It's ok Katie, it's under control." Buzz took them down two streets and then headed into an alley.

Whipping a fast turn the motorcycle pulled into a small garage.

"Hop off, honey. My friend Schon won't mind if we park here for a bit."

Buzz held the bike until she got off. Then he put the bike on its side stand and ran for the garage door pulling it down quickly by hand. Buzz pulled off a leather jacket and helmet.

"There you are kiddo. Problem solved. I'll be outside, you need to put on the street clothes your Mom gave me over on that bench."

CHAPTER THREE

KATE AGE SIXTEEN WEARING
SARAH'S SEVENTIES ERA DRESS

If anyone was surprised at Kate's evolving self image it was certainly Kate. Change seemed to occur daily, even hourly and as a sixteen year old girl, Kate craved a little stability. So even though every other daughter seemed hell-bent on a vendetta with their respective mothers, Kate enjoyed a close, even intimate relationship with Sarah.

For her part, Sarah was thrilled. As a mother, Sarah experienced a serious maternal fear of totally losing her one and only daughter so finding Kate flowing back to her for advice kept Sarah on an even keel...at least most days.

The tradeoff apparently was Kate's distancing from her own peers. Kate had no dislike for her high school classmates, but there was just no common ground. Sometimes, not often enough, Kate's grandmother Helen helped out, either with a little money, advice or the all-too-infrequent visits. Helen ran her companies out in Los Angeles, traveled extensively and always had so much going on.

But Helen loved her grand daughter, doted on her and gradually made a bit more time to spend with Kate. Sarah stood by, tried to help and somehow knew only Kate could accomplish the required harnessing of the emerging "wonder girl". That was the phrase used by reporter for the Sun Sailor, the local suburban newspaper.

The headline read: "Wayzata Junior's Plate Is Overflowing!"

"Already scoring fourth highest on National Merit Scholar exams in this county, young Kate McGill dazzles one and all with her spirited displays of gravity defying roller blading at last summer's Aquatennial. Kate's proud parents Paul and Sarah McGill additionally can witness their 'wonder girl's' exploits as the only high school girl invited to participate in college women's volleyball and if that weren't enough young Kate McGill has been invited to apprentice at Tempered Steel, the respected and quite exclusive computer consulting firm."

The Sun Sailor went on to detail how her teachers and friends perceived Kate's exploits and Kate's future academic prospects. By any standard, Kate McGill was on her way Big Time.

The same Kate McGill who could be found crying in her bedroom the day before the spring prom, totally confused by the same issues any high school girl confronted.

"Mother!!" Kate's bellow emanating from inside the Rat's Nest, as her mother derisively referred to her bedroom, clearly announced Kate's frustration. "Where are my god damn fancy-ass prom shoes? Mother will you please!!"

Sarah found her prodigal daughter sitting amidst dress up paraphenalia, a thoroughly disconsolate teenager. "Mother...how am I supposed to do this? I will not wear that organza mess Mrs. Jensen lent us. I won't and that's that!"

Sarah leaned against the door jam, one hand on her hip. "Katie, I thought you just loved that dress. You said it was 'perfectly retro' or something to that effect. You knew it came from the sixties. It's a period piece. But I thought you...."

"Mother, I look like a throwback in that awful dress. I'm klutzy enough as it is. If it were up to me I'd skip this miserable dance and watch Saturday Night Live reruns."

Sarah bit her lip. If she pushed Kate into going it could blow up in her face. "Katie, look, it's one of only two school deals we expect you to attend. You just had that wonderful piece written about you, your classmates expect you to be there. Now, what's it to be?"

Kate dragged herself up to her feet without answering and stepped over piles of rejected clothes to turn on her tape deck.

"I need Bonzo's advice. You just give me some time."

"Who is this 'Bonzo', Katie? Is that the boy you were going with?"

"Oh, god mother! You were the one who introduced us." Kate whipped around with a churlish little grin.

Sarah had no idea what or who she was referring to.

Then the first unmistakeable bass drum kicks and iron solid snare drum cracks of "When The Levee Breaks" by Led Zeppelin flooded the small room. Sarah jumped a couple inches at the high volume. When Katie listened to music it was unfailingly intense.

"That 'Bonzo', mom. The one you knew," Kate shouted over the crashing cymbals. She referred to John Bonzo Bonham, Led Zeppelin's masterful drummer, an inspiration to two generations of rockers and generally considered a partial incarnation of black evil.

Yes, Sarah had known him, at least in passing, from her years on the road shepherding various performers from gig to gig. She had seen Bonzo Bonham perform his miracle of stark power drumming on stage. No one before him or since seemed to propel so much sheer will and gut wrenching power from a set of drums.

And she'd seen John Bonham mistreat people, act the ugly bully, behave very badly. Sarah fully knew part of his life force derived from this very dark side. At least a few times Sarah had momentarily appeared in Bonzo's gun sights, an object of his visceral desire.

So watching her daughter respond to Bonzo's ministrations, even with him long buried, a victim of his own rocker's excesses, gave Sarah an uncomfortable chill.

Sarah closed the door leaving Kate to rock out with her English pals. Sarah had a flashback to the Oakland Coliseum near San Francisco. She remembered one of the few terrible moments during her rocker days. Led Zeppelin's wretchedly fat and throughly disgusting manager Peter Grant attempting to bully, no just totally intimidate Bill Graham, the famous rock concert promoter in a mano a mano faceoff. Bill was the intimidator normally but these two had a native hate for one another. Grant had his bully boys with him, Bill was momentarily on his own. Sarah remembered John Bonham being the cause of this standoff, a menacing presence standing close by.

Sarah always found him threatening and unpleasant...the drummer from hell.

Sarah could never understand while Bill referred to the group as "Led", almost in an affectionate way. She knew how he disliked their manager.

Sarah was potting around in the kitchen cleaning up after one of Kate's little baking experiments. Kate had developed a thing for lemon meringue pies but she was having trouble actually making one. Sarah looked up from the sink at an apparition before her. The dress was all too familiar, Kate had been digging around in the innermost recesses of her mother's past, way back in a small trunk at the mustiest rear of the closet. Sarah buried her more questionable rock and roll momentos in the trunk thinking her secrets were quite safe. But Kate was nothing if not unstoppably curious.

"This is my prom dress. It's a perfect fit, don't you think?" Sarah had to swallow hard. The "dress" was a two of a kind creation from Granny Takes A Trip in London. The other had been owned by Anita Pallenberg then Keith Richards' inamorata when she wasn't schtupping one of the other Rolling

Stones or another woman or....well, whoever. She was a real looker, God she had been gorgeous. They bought the dresses on the same day. Sarah only knew of her and purely by chance they both showed up in the tiny shop on Kings Road. Like so many boutiques in London or L.A. "Granny" had a moment in the sun. The royalty of rock streamed there for a time, the handmade silk and brocade creations perfectly captured the time.

The dress in question was exotic even then, a sculpted, form fitting ravisher of the female body, molded from the softest deerskin. It required a stunning feminine form, bosomy, a little hippy with a fabulous rear end and killer legs. For a moment Sarah recalled she and Anita staring at each other wearing the twin dresses.

They stood together before a mirror with virtually opposite questions in their minds. Anita couldn't be troubled with cost, her sugar daddy lolled about in the rear of the scarlet Bentley out at the curb. Money wasn't an issue. Anita wanted her still gorgeous flesh to nearly pour out of the dress.

Sarah was almost broke. She'd been flown in to talk with British keyboardist Graham Bond and a few other artists, possibly to handle them on the road. This knockout American road manager now had her own reputation. But once she arrived in England Sarah discovered local rockers prone to outrageous behavior, particularly drinking. She decided to take a local tour and went hunting for one rock momento from her visit. That brought her to Granny Takes A Trip. Sarah could not pass this dress up and shared momentary sisterhood with a rock legendess, only two of these dresses were ever sewn.

Anita flew from the shop with hers, into the back of the Bentley to be greeted by an utterly bored musician who wondered, "Anita darling, would you mind if I, uh....?" Anita never minded.

After Sarah parted with nearly her last pound note and walked out the stupidity of what she'd just done hit her hard. "I've got no money, no gig and I'm stranded in London with no plane fare home." And then she smiled to herself. How perfect.

Kate was waiting for The Maternal Reaction. "So?"

Sarah perused her up and down. "Katie, it's your body and your life. Your body is up to it, I just don't know if you want to inflict this on your classmates."

"Mom, everyone's wearing something wacky to this dance. Good lord, it's not like I'm going nude."

Sarah responded, "Katie, go look in the mirror, you're right at the edge of nude. Turn around." Kate obliged.

"Well, you've got your mother's rear end and it's on display in a major way. Katie, you sure you want to flaunt yourself?"

"Mom! You did it and you told me you didn't even wear a bra. At least I'll do that!"

Sarah marveled at how every statement had an exclamation mark.

"Kate, I was nine years older, it was London in 1972 or was it '71? Anyway it was a different place. Honey, I don't need to remind you that we're still in Wayzata. Far-out here is colored laces in ice skates. You look very, very adult in that outfit, too adult to please me."

"Mom you said you were from the 'If You Got It, Flaunt It School' and...."

"Kate, it was just a different time. This was London or New York or Beverly Hills. Looking like that is normal. A woman could put her self on display back then. It was theatre. Now you're just boobs and a butt to these boys and that's what you're always saying you want to avoid, right?"

Kate was silent. She looked at her image in a kitchen window. "Well then I'm not consistent but I want to do this. It's a family heritage. I got your figure, your beauty, that's what everyone says. So just this once I want to strut it."

"Katie, compared to your classmates, hell, compared to many adult women, you are, uh, well endowed. I know what it means, so was I. It means every man is undressing you in their minds. I wouldn't make it easier for them."

"But, Mom, this is your dress."

Sarah looked away. "Yes, Katie, it's my dress...and it's your choice."

CHAPTER FOUR
LITTER DEPOSIT

Kate and Jeremy Mathias were hanging out down by Lake Minnetonka. A hunky guy with a good mind, an excellent student, one of Kate's few really close friends, he liked to be part of her crazy stunts. Jeremy found Kate exciting and slightly intimidating because of her cocky style. They often met in the park next to the Wayzata marina eating snacks and cracking each other up.

"So Katie, what's coming up in prank-land? I don't mean on skates, you know, real pranks that all the kids talk about?"

Kate hugged her legs up to her chest as they sat on a picnic table. "Well, Jer, you gotta remember there are risks in prank-land. Your family would be upset if you showed up in the back seat of a cop car."

"I don't have to plan around my parents, I want some excitement like anyone."

"Ok, what you doin' around two AM tonight, or I guess that's tomorrow morning?"

"I'm available, I don't have ball practice tomorrow, sure, what's up?"

"I'll swing by to pick you up at two, we'll meet down at the end of your block, ok?"

Jeremy scooted out his bedroom window, tiptoed across a short roof and dropped to the ground. He checked his watch, just a couple minutes ahead of two AM. He took the back alley, crossed a street and waited at the corner dressed in all black as instructed. Right on time a large delivery truck swung the corner. Kate leaned out and waved. He pulled himself up into the driver's cab.

"So you've really done this, I mean drive one of these things before?"
Kate replied, "Yah, no problem."

Kate gripped the bus driver like wheel, checked her left mirror, then her right. She checked her watch. "Uh, got some stuff we're gonna drop off. We gotta drive over to Edina. Sure you wanna come?"

"Sure, sure I do. You think I'm afraid to pull off a prank?"

Kate nodded her head. "Okey dokey, we're off then."

Kate had a big reputation around Wayzata High for gutsy pranks. That's one reason Jeremy liked hanging out with her but she was also unpredictable, given to impetuous behavior.

"Katie, where did this truck come from?"

"Well, I won't get real specific but I asked a friend if he could dig up a big truck for a couple hours. Then we hand painted signs for the side which can be pulled off."

Jeremy nodded . "Where in Edina are we headed?"

"You know that area near the golf course with the big estates. There."

Jeremy nodded again and thought, *Ok, so we're not talking much.*

The truck headed cross town to the toney suburb of Edina, left the freeway, drove into an expensive neighborhood.

Suddenly a two way radio crackled. "Mill City, your eta, please?"

Kate picked up a hand held off the seat and responded: "Two to three. You're in sight. Flash a light."

Jeremy saw a flash light blink off and on twice. He had a funny feeling that whatever they were doing wasn't kosher. Jeremy tried to make out shapes. He could barely see a building or two. There was no moon. Kate slowed, a figure appeared from the shadows and waved her forward once. They drove between two large brick stanyards. Jeremy saw someone holding a fence like it took strength to hold it in place.

The truck lurched forward, then stopped. Kate nearly flew out of the driver's seat.

Jeremy heard voices. Kate opened Jeremy's door. "Jer we're off a bit. We gotta exit faster. Hop out, wait over there."

Jeremy climbed down and walked to where Kate had pointed. He sort of liked the mystery and was a little frightened. The rear door of the truck opened hurriedly. A motor coughed into life inside the cargo hold. It reminded Jeremy of an old fan he used to keep by his bed when it was hot and humid at their house. The noise grew steadily louder. Then a sound like fluttering wings.

Jeremy could see something coming from the rear of the truck. Some of whatever it was blew toward him. He reached down. It looked like paper and cardboard. In the dark the colors were hard to make out but it certainly looked like wrappers from a *Home Food* drive up. Jeremy ate their burgers when he was a young teen.

The motor's pitch rose steadily and the fluttering wings were everywhere. Now Jeremy was sure the wings were fast food wrappers. It took a moment but now made the connection in his mind. *Home Food.* That was their insignia and colors. He looked up at the truck again. The same logos appeared on the door and cargo hold.

Kate ran back to Jeremy, grabbed him by the arm and pulled him back to the truck cab. They both jumped in and Kate carefully backed the large delivery truck out to the road. She turned it quickly and began driving away. Two miles down the road she pulled over again.

"Ok, now we work. Take your side, start on your door, outside, start ripping off all the insignias, they just peel off. Do it real fast Jer. We got maybe 90 seconds."

Kate flew out her door, Jeremy out his. Now he noticed there were "Home Food" logos and banners all the way down the truck panels. He began peeling off the logos fast as he could.

He said, "Katie, they are coming off but it's not super fast!" Jeremy felt the first tinge of fear. They had just done something bad, he was clear about that much.

Kate half whispered from her side, "Just peel it fast, Jer."

He looked both ways on the street, no head lights so far.

He peeled off about half and Kate ran around from her side. She grabbed the pasted on banners and jerked them much harder. They stripped off quickly. She picked up the banners. "Jump back in, Jer. Hurry!"

The big truck lumbered off down the street. Kate swung some corners trying to take a different route home. In another two minutes they could hear sirens approaching.

Kate swung onto the cross town freeway and the sirens faded out.

"Katie, what the hell was that all about?"

She answered, "You just visited Col. Frank Hauser's forty acre spread and we left him a truck full of used *Home Food* wrappers. The Colonel is the majority stockholder in *Home Food Inc.* Not a man who thinks litter is a problem and so stated publicly. We passed the word we needed specifically *Home Food* litter, about six colleges and two universities pitched in, took quite a while to accumulate."

"And what was that strange sound in the truck?"

"We borrowed a large cooling fan, mounted it in the truck. It just blew almost two tons of wrappers all over his estate." Kate turned and smiled.

CHAPTER FIVE

SARAH'S MCGILL'S UPBRINGING

Katherine Harendt McGill grew up in a most unusual household. Her father Paul spent some years of her early life often away from home pursuing a dream to save wilderness and unbuilt land. Paul paid a high price missing part of his daughter's younger years. His absence, in turn, created a vacuum which would impact Kate's development.

Kate grew up very close to her mother partially because Sarah grew up missing her own mother who was obsessed with starting and running her own business. Sarah also had to struggle with a missing father. So Kate missed her father, Sarah missed both her parents at certain times. These absences colored how mother and daughter behaved, their value systems and how each turned out. Sarah briefly would travel in the world but soon returned to Minnesota and remained close to home. Kate, after her, would be the adventurer much like her own grandmother Helen, Sarah's mother.

Perhaps it's not so difficult to understand why Kate, whose father was frequently not around, would develop a strong masculine side and ultimately become a high achiever? Was she making up for the missing male component, was she proving to Paul she could be exceptional? To understand Kate McGill it's instructive to know more about Sarah's upbringing. Particularly, Sarah's own missing father experience.

Sarah McGill born Sarah Harendt never quite got comfortable with her family heritage. Her mother Helen Aray born Haganah Harendt never followed a predictable or normal path in her life. Sarah had been moved around like a gypsy when very young but it began making sense when Sarah came to realize her own mother and grandmother actually came from a gypsy family back in Romania.

Helen and her mother who was born as Haddassah but adopted the moniker Queen Royal Elixir in her thirties did not go out of their way to talk about being gypsies with Sarah. At age eight after insistent prompting from Queen Royal, Helen moved her daughter Sarah to Minneapolis from Los Angeles. For the next several years Sarah had her mother or her grandmother living with her in Minnesota and no father entered the picture. Sarah began experiencing serious emotional problems without a father. Helen traveled to Los Angeles constantly and had established her growing company in Santa Monica, CA. Sarah asked but never received answers about the relocation to Minnesota until her mother simply told her she thought Minnesota was a better place to grow up.

People in their community of Wayzata couldn't help but gossip about this odd trio of females living in a small house just off Broadway. Sarah felt immense confusion as from week to week she wasn't sure which "mother" would be home but very gradually Sarah began making friends, she found a sometime boyfriend and a family from St. Paul, the Roemers, who Queen Royal knew, began visiting and filling Sarah's life with greater joy and stability. By age fourteen Sarah had managed a reasonably normalized existence and the missing male presence was replaced by Buzz Roemer. Not a father figure but a quite mature young man who watched over Sarah. Buzz also had a truly crazy, unpredictable, fun loving side that Sarah adored. Buzz could also be a very intimidating presence being physically large and a voice that could fill an entire room but around Sarah he adopted a fatherly, protective persona. She was the sister Buzz never had.

Sarah knew her grandmother was a real gypsy. As a young teen, Sarah found a library book about gypsies and they seemed to be thought of as dishonest schemers, very odd and not well liked. They looked strange with head scarves and flowing, colorful clothing that looked way out of date. Gypsies preyed on others, utilized clever defenses to outthink non-gypsies, traveled in ancient wagons back in Romania. Sarah already knew she had Jewish parents although she never got a solid answer about where or who her father might be.

Sarah thought, *Hmmm,* Jewish *and a gypsy, that makes me pretty weird.* So she kept it quiet, never talked about that gypsy part of her heritage. Jewish was fine in Wayzata. There weren't that many Jews but they were successful and respected. In her later teens she heard a record by Cher, "Gypsies, Tramps and Thieves" at a girlfriend's house and the other girls were dancing to it and playing they were actual gypsies. Cher's video showed her as a gypsy and Sarah realized her friends thought being a gypsy was quite different and definitely cool. Sarah blurted out, "My mother was born as a gypsy and my grandmother is still one, full blooded!" Her girlfriends definitely had a new respect for Sarah because she claimed to be so exotic. In Wayzata everyone, it seemed, was white, Christian, predictable, middle class and not too exciting.

One month her on-duty mother was Queen Royal, Helen was off in Los Angeles on business. Sarah asked Queen R. to explain what this meant to be a real gypsy. Queen R. gave her a stern, questioning look. "Sarah, honey, I always thought you felt being a gypsy was strange and foreign?"

Sarah smiled, "Yah, well now strange and foreign became attractive with my friends." She explained about the Cher record and video. Queen R. took this all in. Previously Helen remonstrated Queen R. to "...keep all that gypsy folklore under your hat...Sarah lives in the white bread world of Minnesota. Let's not make her life more difficult by playing up the gypsy history...I keep dreading that her father will come calling and then there will be hell to pay..."

Queen R. decided it was safe to trot out some Romanian history, just in dribs and drabs but Sarah asked her to help her dress up like a real gypsy, not a fake one like Cher. Queen R. replied, "Honey, I'll gladly explain the culture I grew up in but you must realize it's not just dressing up, we had and still have an unusual, strong heritage. We were often abused and disliked. Adolph Hitler, the Nazi, wanted to wipe out gypsies even before he got to the Jews in eastern Europe and I grew up with that hanging over my head."

Sarah always felt a distance and foreign quality to her grandmother. Queen R. absolutely had unique, strange ways about her. She did not try to mix with Minnesotans any more than she had to. When she was staying in Wayzata she avoided native costumes except at home. Minnesotans were suspicious of foreigners, that's what Queen R. thought. But now Sarah began encouraging her grandmother to come out of the gypsy closet. It culminated in an afternoon where Sarah almost dragged her grandmother to class when everyone did a show and tell about their family heritage. Sarah sat through a dozen totally identical show and tells about Lutheran blond-haired Minnesotans who had cabins up at Lutsen, owned a boat and loved winter. Even the Lutherans were bored silly.

Sarah was a little older now and more secure so she brought Queen R. dressed up in genuine gypsy clothing and suddenly Sarah went from the little Jewish girl to the exotic Jewish gypsy and her stock shot through the roof. Kids were curious and being so different came off as cool.

Queen R. did an actual show, she entertained and finally she blew the whole class away with a brief demonstration of mentalist talents. Queen R. picked out one girl, an extra pretty, tall beauty named Kristin and began explaining that she, Queen R., knew about Kristin's life and family. Kristin was amused and then Queen R. told Kristin where her big brother was stationed in the army, what movie star Kristin loved and one of her favorite records. The class stopped dead when Kristin turned pale white and nearly fainted. "How…how can you know that about me? Did Sarah tell you? She really doesn't know my family or me all that well?"

Queen R. continued on with a few more revelations and the class could have kissed her feet. How did she know these things, was she reading Kristin's mind? Queen R. explained that part of her heritage involved what she called "light mind reading". These were skills she learned back in Romania. Mrs Stebbins finally had to step in and stop all the questions, her class could not get enough of Queen R and suddenly Sarah McGill was a major star among her friends. Queen R. said she might do one more session but she had rules. Kids only, no adults except Mrs. Stebbins and definitely no older kids. Her powers did not seem to work well with older teens but she did not explain why.

Sarah wore a complete gypsy costume to school for another show and tell. Queen R. had a gift as a seamstress so she designed and sewed a head to foot outfit for Sarah who began waking up to the power of her grandmother's heritage. The kids at school wanted to know much more about Queen Royal Elixir. Sarah now needed plenty of education time with her grandmother bringing them much closer. Sarah's life and perceptions of herself quickly began changing. She had thought her grandmother with the odd moniker was old and stuffy but now Queen R. was the hit of her school.

Sarah insisted Queen R. accompany her on local shopping trips but especially if Queen R. would dress up in native garb. They walked into a local shop called the Foursome, Sarah had been looking for a certain pair of shoes for a dance. Queen R. popped up with "Dearie, go down that aisle, look way down low at the end. Are you size 8?"

Sarah looked strangely at her grandmother. "Grandma, how could you possibly know these shoes would be hidden away down there? Look, here they are, correct size and all! Aren't you looking for anything?"

Queen R. shook her head. "Sarah, I really don't need anything."

"Then why did you ask for me to drive you?"

"I needed to help you find those shoes. I have to be in the store to know."

"Grandma, really? You just knew where they were?"

Queen R. smiled smugly but said nothing. She adored building this relationship with her granddaughter.

Sarah developed a serious respect for her grandmother. Sarah was becoming more certain Queen R. could actually know about events before they occurred. She began testing Queen R., "Grams, I have to take a really tough chemistry test next Thursday. I do poorly with this science stuff, can you help me get better prepared?"

Queen R. knew to be on alert when school subjects came up. Like any kid Sarah was hoping Queen R. could maybe, sort of fudge some answers?

"Honey, I did not do well with school and I never finished high school, we called it something different back in Romania. I will try to help you study for your exam but if what you're asking is if I can give you answers for questions---no, I can't. My limited talents really don't work that way. When adults might meet me and realize I have some mentalist abilities the first thing they do is ask me for answers to big questions like how can they make a lot more money? So I don't do shows for adults. And I also found that older children tend to want the same favors so I stay with younger kids and that works out quite well."

Sarah was disappointed but she began realizing Queen R. had definite ethics and rules about her powers. Queen R. carefully skirted around helping Sarah if it amounted to cheating. Sarah once said, "Grams is it true that gypsies cheat people because you are quite strict about using your talents for honest purposes?"

"Sarah, when I grew up everyone I encountered was convinced that gypsies were constantly scheming to cheat and take advantage of anyone who was not a gypsy. I decided early that I would avoid subterfuge, in other words I would not be cheating people. Honestly that makes it difficult for me when I encounter adults because I dress the way I do it's obvious that I come from gypsy roots. So I tend to stay to myself but in Los Angeles I have a small circle of girl friends who I can relax with. Here in Minnesota, so far, there is only one adult I feel truly comfortable with, Buzz's father Emmanuel. He has a deep interest in my culture and upbringing. He is also very knowledgeable about such subjects as telekinesis. That's the fancy name for mentalist talents so we have plenty to talk about. He also respects my ability and doesn't ask me for favors I don't want to offer."

Sarah gradually accepted her life in Minnesota except for the big, glaring question about her father. Was he alive, who was he? When Sarah asked Helen she consistently put off giving her answers. Helen was not apologetic, she simply told her daughter she would be better off without her father's presence but he did exist. Sarah never appreciated her mother's refusal to talk about her father, never understood her attitude and it created a difficult gulf between them.

Then one day when Sarah turned fourteen someone rang the doorbell at their house. Sarah was eating a sandwich and watching American Bandstand on tv so she was rather distracted when she walked to the door. Her life would have an entirely new dimension after she opened the front door.

Standing with his back to the door on the large front porch was a man in his forties dressed in a severely tailored dark blue suit, his shoes almost shone like bright lights they were so polished. His black hair swept back in a dramatic wave but carefully trimmed to end right at his collar. As he turned around Sarah almost couldn't believe his face. She knew immediately this man had to be her father, his facial structure, particularly the dark, haunting eyes and his nose resembled hers. His teeth and smile were so dramatic, his chin a perfect cleft which completed the unique flow of his face. She thought he had to be one of the most handsome men she had ever seen.

"Sarah, I am your father, Salazar and it's time we were acquainted. Is your mother home today?" Sarah felt frozen in place. She couldn't believe her father was finally visible, present, alive. "You're my father? Why have you not come to visit before? Why could I know nothing about you? I never understood this and it's made me extremely unhappy. I'm home alone but mom will be back pretty soon. Do you want to come in?"

He stood his ground, hands clasped behind his back looking at Sarah, enjoying her beauty. "Sarah, your mother thinks I would be a bad influence on you, that is why she never let me meet you but I finally tired of that game. You are my daughter also and before I get one day older I was going to meet you. I know your mother and how she thinks. Let's just sit out here on the porch, there are a couple chairs. Helen can be very difficult and I don't want to come in without her permission. Can we sit over here?"

Sarah couldn't stop staring at this man who she thought had to be her father and she felt waves of sadness that for fourteen years she had been denied knowing him. Then she looked past her father to see two more men, swaggering and burly who were dressed similarly to Salazar standing almost at attention next to the biggest Cadillac Sarah had ever seen. Their suits and the Cadillac were the darkest, gravest midnight blue color.

"Who are those men?" Sarah asked.

Without turning around to look at the men Salazar responded, "Those men assist me Sarah, they travel with me everywhere. I have homes in a few cities, Detroit, Chicago, other places. I decided this morning I was going to meet you so we drove here from Winnetka, Illinois. Let's sit down, you'll meet them."

Sarah felt dazzled with the newness of encountering her father. She realized he could be anyone but somehow she knew this was the father who had been missing in action all these years. "If you're my father, explain why mother has been so terribly afraid to have you meet me?"

Salazar sat down in one of the wooden chairs on the porch. He carefully unbuttoned his suit jacket, sat back in the chair crossing his legs with precision, ran one hand through his hair and looked at Sarah. "Sarah, look at me and at those men, you tell me what kind of work do I do?"

Sarah almost didn't need to think. "Well, you're a gangster, the mafia, I mean, that is likely wrong but that's how you look."

He smiled and nodded. "Sarah, that is why your mother kept me away. She was afraid I would exert some negative influence. I am a businessman, I deal with people who sometimes carry guns, that does not mean I am a so-called gangster but I have dealings with some pretty rough people. I have interests in businesses that involve gambling which is illegal in many places. I also own nine dry cleaning businesses, I own two resorts outside Chicago, I make a very big living. I have nothing to do with drug dealers or prostitution. Nothing. I now own two television stations. Does your mother talk about me at all?"

Sarah couldn't believe she was finally learning the secret about her father and she had to admit, he looked completely the part of a modern gangster. She wondered if that was all an act? He did not seem to be a gypsy or at least she had never heard of a gypsy dressed so elegantly or driving a fancy Cadillac. As she sat and stared at her father she realized she may have known him many years before but she was very young and her mother may have kept them somewhat apart. The memories were hazy.

"No, she has refused to tell me anything and I never understood why? It was very painful. I'm glad you finally showed up here."

"First, Sarah, my last name and therefore your last name if you chose to use it is very unusual. Torpaydo, it's Greek but I was raised in a Jewish family. Most people say it like Torpedo which is wrong. I'm just sure your mother preferred you use Harendt, her name." Salazar looked away momentarily a pained expression on his face. Then he continued.

"Sarah, I'm going to give you my side of my life in a very simple summary and you can compare my explanation with your mother's. She and I met when we were quite young, she did not want to get married, she always said she cared about me but once she realized I had these so called gangster connections she retreated. Then she realized she was pregnant and for many months we went around and around about getting married. I was perfectly ready to marry your mother but she struggled with the idea. Finally, after months of indecision she agreed to be married and we had a marvelous ceremony, very quiet and private here in Minnesota."

Salazar or Sal as he preferred to be called stopped abruptly. He had not dealt with the issue of separation for some time and his own feelings were welling up. "Sarah, I wanted to be a regular father to you and a regular husband to your mother but she can be very difficult and we never could quite work it out. I lived nearby periodically until you were about four and you may have some memories of me. What I'm explaining is the most difficult thing for me. You may think I look like this hood but I have plenty of feelings about being a man, a father---all of it."

Sarah found this all fascinating, surprising, shocking and wonderfully intimate. She had lived without a father surrounded by children who had their dad around all the time. At times Sarah was just about ready to beat up her mother she was so angry and frustrated. She begged Helen to give her details but Helen doggedly refused and they had regular fights over this divisive issue.

"Dad, like, what did you do then? She didn't want to live with you once I was around?"

Sal was visibly gripped with sadness. "Honey, I came close to killing myself, this was such a terrible problem. Your mother demanded I completely give up my life and businesses, move here, start over, running some small business---I never did know what she thought I would do to make a living. But it's not simple like that for me. I would have had to walk away from years of relationships, trust, understanding with literally hundreds of people. It made no sense to me. So I made the most difficult decision of my life and remained in Chicago with no real connection to you. Your mother and I argued, I hate to tell you how loud and angry we got with each other. Helen took the position that our daughter should not grow up with a father who was 'a mobster'. That is how she referred to my life, I was and still am 'a mobster'. Well I have completely different feelings about that subject but she would not bend an inch. Honestly, to this day, this hour I have never figured out why she had such unbending feelings? Finally we struck a sort of compromise, when you turned fourteen I would be allowed back in your life. This was dreadful but I finally accepted this arrangement. That's what happened, Sarah, it was awful."

Sarah found this explanation fascinating and compelling. Her father made a terribly difficult decision. Sarah could not be sure he made a wise decision but she began understanding both sides. She still felt no less strongly about her mother's unyielding position. She wanted a father, a dad and Helen prevented that from happening.

"Ok, so Dad, what happened after that?"

"Well, there was no point in staying married so we divorced, I pay child support and alimony or did. That stopped. I have tried to remain cordial and friendly which I tell you was often a challenge. Given the circumstances I have abided by her wishes but you deserve to know about me and my family. I have two brothers who live on the east coast and have no involvement in my businesses. My mother lives next door to me outside Chicago. My father is alive but presently lives part time in Europe, mostly in Greece."

Sarah was utterly fascinated and hoped Salazar would talk forever, she had so many questions. "What do I call you? Dad, Sal?"

"Sarah I wish you'd call me Dad or father but that's up to you. Now, your mother will give you various reasons why you and I have not met but let me tell you the most important. I moved out of the country for almost five years. I lived overseas in a variety of places purposely moving around. This made my separation from you even more difficult. When I returned your mother and I talked and I decided staying away was necessary."

"Why, what happened that you had to disappear like that?" Sarah asked.

"There were people who wanted me dead, it's that simple Sarah. It's a potential risk given who I sometimes deal with. So I had to leave. This is when you were age seven to age twelve. I had people running some of my enterprises. Some of the money you live on, by the way, comes from me. Every month, I never fail to pay my share. Ask your mother."

"Do you have other children, do you have a wife?"

"I am now married to Estelle, we have a son and daughter. They all live in the west, I won't say precisely where for the moment. This is a joint decision by Estelle and myself. After my life was threatened we decided it was too unsafe for our kids to live in Chicago. But I see them on a very regular basis."

Sarah replied, "Geez, sounds just like my mother, she commutes to L.A. all the time."

Sal nodded his head. "Yes, I am quite aware that she is gone frequently. We also had plenty of disagreements about her choices. You need to know that her desire to keep you in Minnesota created all manner of problems with me. I complained loudly and argued that you should come live with me near Chicago. We even hired lawyers, lawsuits were threatened, it was not nice."

Sarah had been studying Sal, his mannerisms, body language. "You know, I don't know what a gangster really looks like but you don't sound like some kind of rough and tough guy who murders people. You are well spoken and thoughtful."

His face softened, his manner warmed up. "Thank you Sarah, that means more than you can ever know. I have a part to play in a larger drama, that is why I look and act the way I do. It is expected."

Sarah still couldn't quite believe her real father sat on her front porch. Sal projected an immense confidence, he seemed so self assured. She glanced over his shoulder at the two men and the Cadillac. Sarah wasn't sure if she should be impressed or intimidated by Sal's entourage? But she now had her father!

Sarah was positive her mother would have a completely different vision about her father. Helen could critique a sunny day and come up with some problem. Sarah asked, "Ok, I know you can understand this is all confusing.

But I want to ask you one question, uh, Dad. If you're this wonderful, thoughtful person, why do you keep dealing with all these bad people?"

Sal didn't immediately answer. He studied the wooden deck floor, he rubbed the fingers of his left hand with his right hand. "Sarah, I'm impressed that you're asking me the important questions. Here's my answer: I have often thought about walking away, putting distance between myself and these other business associates. Some of these people are scary, they have terrible judgment and we're all under scrutiny by the authorities. That's all true. This may sound really stupid to you. I like most of these guys, they are like an extended family to me. Even if I could easily walk away it would be hard for me to abandon this life." After Sal gave her this explanation he watched her reactions realizing what he just said might have sounded dead wrong.

Sarah looked distracted. "I guess I need some time to understand what you've been saying. I don't understand why my mother didn't just tell me you're in the...what do you call the business you're in?"

Sal looked frustrated. "Honey, I just run a few businesses. I would never call myself something like 'mobster'. Those terms are so out of date. I work with people, we pay our bills strictly on time. We have offices, we attend meetings, I contributed over two million dollars to charities last year. I'm involved in community affairs, I have thirty eight people on my payrolls and that's not counting the retail employees who number over four hundred people. I am a successful businessman who pays his taxes. I have been audited by the IRS every year since I can remember and they have always honored my tax returns. My people are under orders to be scrupulous, honor the laws."

Sarah responded, "Well, you've convinced yourself it's just like any kind of enterprise but do you have people beat up or killed?" Sarah was feeling a level of empowerment that surprised her. She wanted to know if her "new" father had blood on his hands?

Sal momentarily had met his match. His daughter was forcing him to own up to his own deeds. "Honey, I can't answer that question for all kinds of reasons. One is to protect you and your mother."

Sarah stood up and peered over the porch railing. "Well, here comes Mom."

Helen parked her Mercedes behind the Cadillac and began walking up to the house. Sarah watched her progress. Helen paused at the Cadillac and greeted the two men by name. As she came up the porch stairs she announced, "Well, Sal, you always said you'd just show up and here you are. You can invite the boys up. The more the merrier." She reached out for Sarah, gave her a peck on the cheek and then did the same with Sal. Sarah was surprised she'd be this friendly. Helen kept moving in the front door and disappeared.

Sarah looked at her erstwhile father. "So, she seems to be pretty accepting of your being here."

Sal replied, "Honey, she and I have been talking more recently. This was not out of the blue that I showed up. I wanted you to know me, warts and all. You are my daughter, that is a big deal in my life. Come on, let's go inside." Sal turned to look at his two assistants. One of them waved him on not wanting to be in the house for this meeting.

Sal and Sarah walked in. "Come on, let me show you the kitchen, Dad." Sarah felt a bit unsure calling this man her father but she also loved the idea that she would finally have a real father whatever his calling in life.

Dressed in her typical exquisite fitted business suit, her hair well coiffed and perfect makeup Helen leaned against the kitchen counter drinking an iced tea. She said nothing, the three people stood uncomfortably together in the small kitchen. Helen talked first, "Honey, I guess I owe you the largest apology possible, you should have known your father years back but I won't apologize for trying to protect you. Sal, I have never known why you keep all these gangster connections, you already made some money, just let it go."

Sal felt some discomfort sandwiched in the limited space trying to defend himself. "What can I say, I had to make my peace with my life, my values back when I was a young kid, when I met you as Haganah. This is a choice I made, I can't just walk away from relationships I've had since I was five." He turned to Sarah. "Honey, your mother and I have gone around and around for years over my choices and now you'll have to make up your own mind about me." Sarah nodded. At this point she felt appreciative that she'd have that choice.

Helen looked past Sal to the front door. "Sallie, one of da boyz apparently needs you at the door." Sal turned around, walked to the door, conferred with his so far unnamed associate and walked back to the women. "Well, Sarah, this is part of my package. The FBI just drove up. They shadow me everywhere. I'm sorry, but it's just something I have to live with."

Sarah asked, "Does that mean you have to leave now?"

Sal replied, "Naw, I need to go out and have a little man to man talk. I'll be back in."

Helen watched him go out. "Sarah, this is the choice I made. I hope you can understand my thinking. I loved this guy, I still like him but he remarried, that was appropriate. Actually Estelle and I get on very well. She's a totally mature woman, we both see the same great qualities in your Dad. But she can put up with all the nonsense, the FBI hanging around, the big bruisers with bulges in their suit jackets. It's all so terribly yesterday and like being in some gangster movie from the Fifties. I told her I understand staying with the guy. They have two nice kids but she lives in a city separate from him. I don't even know where she actually lives, they keep it real private. She and I talk once in a while."

Sarah took all this in. Now, perhaps for the first time, she began to understand why Helen had kept her at such a distance from Sal. "Mom, you seem affectionate toward him. I guess I'll never understand why you kept him at such a distance from me?"

They heard the screen door open and shut and Sal lumbered back into the kitchen, his gait a combination of a shuffle and stride. Helen looked up, "So?"

Sal made a gesture with his hand as if to say she should forget it. "It's an agent I run into in Detroit all the time, he got reassigned. These guys know I am operating on the up and up. They have showed up at the office, they ask to check out my car, they stay within the guidelines, so do I. It's a little minuet, each party delicately dancing with the other. They put someone on me all the time, actually it's made my life a bit easier. It's one reason I could live a more normal life. I got the FBI with me constantly."

Helen interjected, "Sallie, how are your kids, how are they holding up?"

"I'm with them three days every week. It's a hassle, I got a private plane to make it easier but now I have someone call the FBI, I tell them where I'm going, which airport, when I arrive. I don't have to but this way they are far less suspicious. So I am with the kids and Estelle, we have worked it out."

Helen looked up from her iced tea, "I wish you'd just shut down, retire, you can walk away now."

Sal looked thoughtful. "Maybe, Helen. Maybe. Let's leave that subject for a little while. We have a daughter I want to know. Sarah, tell me how you're doing in school? Tell me a little about your life here in Wayzata?"

Sarah happily began explaining how she had a good life in Wayzata, who her best friends were, a little about her grades in a few classes.

Helen listened but mostly thought about Sal. *He still looks good, I think he lost weight. Those damn tight suits are so out of date but he carries himself well. Now I wish I'd brought him back into Sarah's life earlier. But the last time I saw him at the Palmer House in Chicago he had all these damn big lunks with him in their fedoras and dark suits lumbering around. I didn't want Sarah exposed to these guys. I will say they are always respectful but they are so obviously mob. It's like right out of a cheap novel and I wanted Sarah to be raised decently. I just know Sarah will never forgive me for denying her father access to her. But what else could I do? Bring the mob into our house? And then I have to deal with all the law enforcement issues myself. As if I don't have enough of that back in California?*

Helen watched father and daughter interact. He genuinely cared about

Sarah. No question he wanted to be a father involved but how the hell would they ever pull that off? He did not have a normal life to begin with.

Sarah had given Sal a nice portrait of herself, who she was and a little about what she hoped to do. Sal took it all in like a very welcome repast. He had waited many years to be any kind of presence in Sarah's life.

He said, "So I want to ask Helen, can I take you both out to dinner tonight. We can go somewhere really posh, a treat on me." Helen watched Sarah's reaction. She clearly wanted to go. "Sal, sure, let's do that, Sarah, you need to get a little dressy. Sal where are you going to stay? I'd invite you but we have only the couple bedrooms."

"Naw, Helen, that's fine, I need to get Tony and Boris rooms, we'll stay downtown. I know the hotels down there. One of my companies sells provisions to the nicer hotels in the upper Midwest. So I know maitre de's, managers. We'll head down there, can we say 7 o'clock, Helen you choose the restaurant, ok?"

Helen and Sarah gave him a little kiss and Sal went out the front door. Sarah followed him and watched unobtrusively. Sure enough two men in a very plain dark sedan were parked across the street. When Sal arrived at the Cadillac one of his assistants or whatever they were called opened the door for him to the back seat. There was a short exchange between Sal's driver and the two men in the sedan. It sounded like the driver told the FBI agents where they were going.

Sarah turned around and Helen stood nearby her hands folded in front of her, uncharacteristically calm. Normally Helen fidgeted constantly. Helen said, "Ok, honey, now you know Sallie, that is your real father and he comes with loads of baggage. He's also a good guy in his own way. I just never got comfortable with his choice of work."

Sarah absorbed her mother's comments. "Mom, about one month ago you told me about some problems you're having at your company. Some of that involved the government in Washington, doesn't it? How is that different than the FBI?"

Sarah stunned her mother. Helen never thought Sarah was listening when she talked about the business back in southern California. "Well, honey, this is quite different, Sal has the FBI tailing him, that's criminal dealings."

"Mom you told me two government agencies, is that what they are called? They were examining your business. I know you're not a criminal but I don't see the difference?"

Helen made a mental note to limit her discussions about her company, *Aray Powersource*, around her daughter. Kids grow up and start paying attention.

"Honey, this could be long and complicated to explain. I run a business but very legitimate. One government agency decided they should investigate our company. We will be exonerated but you have no choice but to play along. I wouldn't worry about it. In his defense, your father has made huge strides in making his enterprises much more like any operation. The difference is he's still surrounded by those bruisers and they all hang out and talk like movie thugs. That is why I would not give in with him. If he was here with us and or we were in Chicago with him dozens of these gangsters would have been part of our lives. That was wrong. Please don't think that decision has not hung over me every single day since. No woman wants to deny a father access to his child but Sal could not bend either. We truly did have irreconcilable differences. We even had an arbitrator come in and work with us. The stupidity of all this was I never really stopped loving the guy. Salazar brought a lot to the party that was wonderful but he also brought Boris and Bruno or whatever their names were. Actually, I should tell you, one of the bruisers turned out to be an amazing, charming and very useful guy to have around. That is Bruno, one hundred percent Italian, thick necked, powerful, dedicated to your father like you can't believe. Bruno Ramaldi, unlike all the other men around your father. Bruno could be rough and tough but he's also smart, clever, surprising. Once, this goes back a few years, when Sal had to be on vacation---did he explain his five year vacation?"

Sarah nodded and frowned.

"Anyway, I needed some help in Los Angeles, your father sent Bruno out and he stayed for a couple weeks, roomed at a hotel. I just kind of needed a guy like Bruno when I was dealing with a tough, uh, customer. Bruno knew just how to behave, what to say, he made my problem disappear. A wonderful guy that Bruno."

Helen looked distracted, lost her train of thought and then continued.

"Sorry, I lost track. Anyway Sallie traveled, moved around, it was rough on him and his whole crew. But he had such trust with these guys they carried on the various enterprises even without Sal and it worked alright."

Sarah asked, "Mom, what actually happened that he had to leave this country?"

Helen had turned to the sink to wash out a glass. With her back turned she threw up her hands and then turned back to Sarah. "Honey, you really don't need to know much but it will help you understand. A very difficult man in Detroit, his name is not important, was really out to kill your father and he tried more than once. Sal backed off further and further hoping someone would find a way to get this guy off his back but it didn't happen. So finally Bruno... Wait, you know what? I can't tell you about this. I really can't. Some day some agent from one of those agencies knocks on your door and wants to know what happened to the guy from Detroit? You have to be able to throw up your hands and say, 'Agent So and So, I have no earthly idea who that man is or what happened to him.' You follow that Sarah? You can't know so many things and that is why your father could not be with us."

"Mom, how does that change now?"

Helen shook her head. "Honest to god, Sarah, I don't know? I could not justify pushing him away any longer, he deserves to know his wonderful child, it's only right. So now we will start the Sal Dance, you and I. We may need to not tell each other things. As your mother that is so upsetting. You are fourteen and have to remember to *not* tell me something. Your father may start disclosing certain details of his life and sometimes you may have to withhold those details from me. Or me from you. And if what's his name, god, what is that guy's name? Oh, yes, Big Donnie. Huge, intimidating man who is actually not a bad guy. But Big Donnie has this terrible habit of telling you about things no one should be hearing and Sal has got to fix that problem. I hate to think how he'll fix Big Donnie. Oy."

"Like what, Mom, this Big Donnie?"

"Sarah, there you are. Right there. Why did I keep you away from your father because of things like Big Donnie. He comes around, tells someone about some guy that got knocked off. These men, they don't think. Now we're contaminated because Donnie tells you some story. Trust me on this, dear. If you start getting time with these guys, if you start hearing some tale about guns or baseball bats just quickly walk away. You can be made to testify in court about this nonsense. It is literally criminal. This is why, honey, I did not want you to do all the double thinking required. You can't just sit and have a lovely conversation with Sal's associates because they may disclose something nasty or illegal and now you're stuck with it. A young girl should never have to deal with that responsibility."

For the first time Sarah could now see her mother's position. Even in a short time Sarah could see her father brought a whole new aspect to their lives, some of it sounded dangerous.

Helen paused and looked pained. "Now, Sarah dear, you will one day have children, you'll make a great mother, no question. Then my dear daughter you'll have your own decisions to make regarding Sal."

CHAPTER SIX
KATE VISITS QUEEN ROYAL IN LAS VEGAS

By her mid teens Kate had grown accustomed to her grandmother's absences in Los Angeles. Haganah Harendt had become Helen Aray and her company was named *Aray Powersource*. Kate had a limited understanding of what *Aray Powersource* did, she only knew they built electronic amplifiers of some kind.

As a grandmother Helen could be demanding, difficult and overly concerned about Kate's choices. Helen was Kate's first experience with a genuinely tough woman. To her surprise Kate began understanding and even appreciating Helen's unrelenting approach to life. And sometimes Kate also came to welcome Helen's absences. Spending hours in the small Wayzata house with a person who never shut down her intensity could be hard to live with.

Meantime, Kate had been waking up to her mysterious great grandmother's unusual life in Las Vegas. Haddassah Harendt had adopted the moniker Queen Royal Elixir and Kate had become intensely curious about Queen Royal who called periodically but traveled rarely. Queen Royal went well beyond mysterious. Kate knew Queen R. conducted seances or something similar and Helen claimed Queen R. could literally see into the future. Then one day Helen dropped a bomb on her granddaughter. "Katie, in the Harendt family my mother's mentalist talents skip me and your mother. You will be the Harendt who receives the legacy."

It took Kate a good four months to swallow that statement.

When Helen called from Los Angeles Kate was particularly interested in what she had to say.

"Katie, it's your grandmother. How are you doing? It's time for you to visit the Queen in Las Vegas. The last time you were with her was, oh, 2 years and

4 months back. you were very young. Do you recall much about that visit?" Helen tested her grand daughter at every turn and Kate now expected it.

"I loved her hotel, it looked like a place in France, that's what I thought. Queen Royal's show room I didn't get to explore, she kept the lights way down. Will I get some time with Queen R. to learn about these family mental talents? You know your Mom called me and began explaining some of this family stuff and even taught me a couple little tricks I can experiment with."

"Katie, that's one of the main reasons you need to visit Queen R. It's time, you're old enough. You may start experiencing the Harendt heritage soon so it's time to get in training."

Kate's breathing caught in her chest. *What? This family deal can just show up and I have nothing to say about it? I have to train for it? For what? I do more than enough training already, three hours every day.*

Helen continued, "So you and my daughter can fly out in two days. You'll have a great time with Queen R."

That was it. Helen's style was telling you what you'll be doing next and then disappearing.

Kate hung up the phone. *She's right about one thing. I want to know my great grandmother and find out what this supposed gift is all about?*

Sarah and Kate were driven from the airport to Haddassah's hotel some blocks off the strip in downtown Las Vegas.

Sarah said, "God, I haven't been here in ages. All these lights. Who pays their electrical bills around here?"

Kate replied, "Her place is definitely on the funky side of the tracks. Oh, look, now she gives herself public billing. I thought Haddassah wanted to stay way below the radar? On that marquee it says, 'Queen Royal Invites You' What changed?"

Sarah said, "Yes that's new. My mother said that since Howard Hughes passed on some years ago Haddassah decided to have a higher profile. Back when he was alive he insisted she stay far out of the public eye."

Kate and Sarah were shown to the Queen Royal suite where they found a note on the bar saying they should join the Queen in her showroom. Sarah injected, "Katie, Haddassah has always been very guarded about her performances. The parents have to wait outside, it's only kids in with Queen Royal and she is strict about it. She says it's the only way to really involve the children, having their parents along spoils the mood."

On their way down in the elevator Kate noticed, "The Queen has now named her showroom 'Queen Royal's Magical Inner Sanctum' and see that sign even says 'Children Only'. I guess the parents are in the lounge and casino down the block?"

An imposing, tall man in a tuxedo greeted them. "Can you ladies kindly identify yourselves, please?"

"We're Kate and Sarah McGill, Queen Royal is my great grandmother."

"Very well, adults are not allowed in with the children but you can observe from a sound booth, let me take you there. You'll be able to hear and see the Queen."

Kate was surprised at his formality. She wondered, *Doesn't he think it's special that Haddassah's grand daughter and great grand daughter are visiting?*

He ushered them into a silent, nearly dark hallway and then into a glassed in room with one row of chairs. He whispered, "Please sit down, you can turn this knob to hear the performance and I'll open this curtain for you."

Kate was impressed with Haddassah's careful preparations. She didn't leave much to chance. When the curtain opened they could see Queen Royal on a low stage and children in rows of seats facing her.

Queen Royal, dressed in a deep purple organza gown wearing a jeweled crown and holding a scepter was speaking with her audience, "Let's see what this young lady would like to know? What is your name, dear?"

"I'm Tildy Regan from Oak Park, Illinois. I read about you in a newspaper and begged my parents to bring me here. I think your Queen's Inner Sanctum is so cool. What I'd like to know is will I ever meet someone famous?"

Queen Royal paused, touched a finger to the side of her head. "Tildy, guess what, you will meet a famous actress, in three years when she comes to Chicago to film a movie. You will meet her in a restaurant downtown on Michigan Avenue when a local radio station has a contest and you win the contest. I can't tell you who that actress is but you will meet her and she will actually be famous. You are so lucky! Now let's talk to this young man. Who are you?"

"Me, I'm Danny Elcher, I live in Seattle with my mom. I've waited three years to come visit you, we had to save our money to make this trip. I'm a good student, will I be able to get into a university? No one in our family ever went to college"

Queen Royal's demeanor shifted noticeably. She walked closer to him and took his hand. She led him on to the stage still holding his hand. She sat on her ornate throne and he sat in a chair next to her.

"Children, now I'm going to say something important. Sometimes I meet a very special person, Danny is one of those. Danny, I know you are a serious and very intelligent student. You will have a challenge in your life. Do you know what a challenge is?"

"Sure, Queen Royal, like a test."

"Danny, I am thinking, you may have been to see a medical person this year."

Danny went wide eyed. "Gosh, how could you know that? Did my mother tell you to say that?"

"Danny, I never met your mother or talked to her. Sometimes I just know certain things about a special child. I am guessing the medical exam revealed something upsetting?"

"Wow, you know that about me? I am so....surprised. What is going to happen to me? Can you tell me?"

"Danny, I bet these doctors talked to you about some tests and that you would spend time in their hospital, isn't that right?"

Danny nodded but said nothing.

"Well, I believe you'll be alright but it will take them some time to figure out your medical problem. So you need to be strong and brave and be prepared to work with these doctors. Your mother is already upset about these doctors isn't she?"

Danny nodded, "Yes, that's why we came here. She wanted us to have a special time together before I see the doctors."

Queen Royal held his hand in a reassuring manner. "Good, you two should have fun on this visit. One more thing, Danny, if you work hard, one day you may be a doctor yourself but it takes many years of hard work."

Danny gazed at Queen Royal admiringly. "Ok, I've thought about being a doctor. Did you know that Queen Royal?"

She nodded. "I had a little hint of that, yes. Danny, you like books, I know that. You should do lots of reading and skip the TV time. You will learn important things if you read books about biology and science. And you need to be careful riding your bike. Ok?"

She walked him back to his seat.

"Now, there is a young woman in this last row. Does your name start with H?"

A girl in pig tails and glasses was stunned. "How could you know that Queen Royal?"

"I sometimes know such things. You need to tell me your name and then come up to the stage with me."

"It's Heather, it starts with H like you said."

They sat down on the stage. "Now, Heather, your parents may want to take you to a big, special city overseas. Do you know if you have plans to go to a foreign or large city?"

Heather replied, "Yes, that's true we'll be going to Paris."

Queen Royal responded, "Heather, when you're there you will want to go to the EuroDisney park like all kids would. But you won't have much time in Paris and I want you to ask your parents to take you to a famous museum instead called the Louvre. In that huge museum there is a room that contains a sculpture by a man named Rodin. Heather, you need to spend some time looking at that large sculpture very closely. It may give you some ideas that will be helpful some years from now. That's my hunch and one day you may want to learn about something called Art History. You'll find it interesting."

Queen Royal paused. "Ok, every time I spend time with children like you I get the same question. Always. I'll show you. Young man in the blue shirt. Why don't you ask me that question, alright?"

"Queen Royal, how do you know that I want to ask you a question?"

"Your name is Milo or Maynard. ask me your question, please."

"Wow, you almost got my name, it's Milan. Well, how do you do this stuff? How can you know our names and all that?"

Queen Royal settled back on to her throne. "Yes, that is the question everyone asks. Here in my answer: I was given a special gift in my family but it only works well with children. I can't really do this with adults. Isn't that strange? Now, your parents will ask you lots of questions about our time together and you can tell them anything you want. What I hope you'll do is treat this experience with respect. If you share what you saw here today only share it with people you like and trust, children who are good kids not those who are mean. Here's why I say that. If a mean child comes to visit me here in Las Vegas they come in to my Inner Sanctum and can spoil my ability to see all of you. So keep this experience special and only tell good children about it. Parents will ask you lots of questions and give them good answers. Ok, to finish up this afternoon I'm going to introduce you to someone who is so incredibly special to me. Actually two people because we have two guests watching, the only two adults I allowed in to my Inner Sanctum in many years. My grand daughter Sarah and great grand daughter Kate. You know her as Kate McGill, she's been in some magazines and on tv."

The children immediately got excited, started jumping up and looking around trying to see Kate.

"Kate and Sarah, my assistant Dinardi is waiting for you at the door, go out and come into the main room, please."

The two women stood up and walked back down the hall entering the Inner Sanctum and walked to the stage as they were directed by the elegantly dressed Dinardi.

Haddassah walked to them as they entered and hugged both women and then took them by the hand up to the stage.

Some kids began shouting greetings to Kate and saying they thought she was wonderful. She acknowledged their responses and then said, "Ok, you guys need to help us and quiet down. I'll be here afterward and can meet all of you, ok? Now let's give Queen Royal your full attention."

The kids instantly quieted down.

"Children, this is easily one of the happiest days of my life. Having my grand daughter and great grand daughter here with me on stage has never happened. You might ask why have I not invited them before? Even Kate, I'm sure, has wondered why? Well, we have a real gift in the Harendt family, that is my real name, Haddassah Harendt and it is passed on to Katherine Harendt McGill. No one knows why but it passes through two generations so that is my daughter Haganah and Sarah, here, my grand daughter. I grew up in a little village in a country called Romania. I am old enough to remember when there were no cars and certainly no TV sets. We made our own clothes. Only little Trudee down here in the cute little hat makes her clothes. I know that. Today you'll see something that has never been seen. Ever. I am going to sit with both Sarah and Kate and all of us together are going to explore a new frontier, we've never done this. But guess what? All of you here in the theater are going to help us. This is an experiment. It's the first time. Are you kids ready to help us?"

The children nearly went crazy saying they wanted to help and it took a minute for Queen Royal to quiet them down.

"Ok, here we go everyone. We have three chairs here and we'll sit in them with Sarah on one side of me and Kate on the other. Now we need all of you to be totally quiet and very calm. We are going to think some thoughts, sometimes these are called visions. And because you kids are so helpful these thoughts may touch you. It's possible you'll see the vision also and young minds can make that vision bigger. Now very important, listen carefully, all of us including we three adults need to stay away from bad images, things that are scary or dark. It can happen sometimes but today we want to have fun and see wonderful, happy thoughts. Let's all relax, open your mind, push out all the busy images and look for a quiet place."

Kate had begun experimenting with mental techniques that Haddassah explained to her over the phone but they had never sat together. Haddassah explained that Kate had to be a bit more mature for the visioning to work but now at 17 Kate could be ready. She was terribly unsteady using her mind for this awkward, foreign visioning but her family encouraged her at every turn.

Haddassah, Sarah and Kate joined hands, the lights were lowered and Haddassah began speaking quietly to the children. Kate found herself almost immediately floundering because her thoughts were not exactly happy and fun. In fact Kate was besieged by thoughts about how unfair the world could be. People who had no money, animals that were killed for sport, unfair and sad stories in the newspaper every day plagued Kate. Haddassah began encouraging the children, bringing them along with ideas but Kate felt feelings welling up that she had never dealt with.

"Katie, relax, don't fight the flow, think about experiences that make you happy like skating."

Minutes passed, Haddassah coached the children who were so excited to be brought along in this new experience.

Sarah tried to only imagine quiet, friendly, natural outdoor images but she could feel her daughter struggling. Something dark and haunting was emerging. Haddassah considered stopping the process after a few more minutes. Apparently Kate was wrestling with difficult thoughts and they were pouring out. When Kate attempted to vision on her own the images barely surfaced if at all but with encouragement from her mother and great grandmother and now a roomful of very willing young brains the normally hidden visions were overtaking Kate's ability to control them.

Haddassah had not anticipated anything like this. Kate had apparently been working intensively to learn how the visioning might work as the power of her images was flooding the theater. Children were starting to react, Haddassah knew it was time to terminate the experiment.

Haddassah spoke up in a loud voice announcing they would be stopping now but the children wanted no such end. Kate felt her psyche hyper powered by 34 young minds who found the scary imagery fascinating.

Haddassah whispered to Kate, "Honey, cut it off, we have all these vulnerable kids here. You must stop!"

Kate was trying to stop but her connection with the children was overwhelming her intellectual decision making. Kate felt the runaway train powering to some unknown uncontrolled destination and in desperation she had to re-direct their youthful energy. Mostly out of fear Kate grabbed on to an idea that she once dreamed about.

The Nevada State Gaming Board marked this particular afternoon as the penultimate unexplained event in its entire history. Owners of casinos within a few blocks remembered the date far more graphically in their financial records. At precisely 2:55 and 38 seconds in the afternoon hundreds of slot machines simultaneously and ever so noisily all paid out their maximum jackpots.

CHAPTER SEVEN
KATE SEES THE EARTHQUAKE COMING

Kate and Sarah were visiting San Francisco. Sarah took Kate briefly out of high school at age fifteen on a long weekend to perform a skating demonstration at the Palace of the Legion of Honor on the far west side of San Francisco. Overlooking the bay just outside the Golden Gate Bridge, the museum had a sweeping front lawn and gardens. Kate on skates was asked to invent an artistic use of the walks and parking lot surrounded by sculptures.

It was only ten minutes of routines but every minute took almost an hour to figure out. Kate entertained an audience of a few hundred, she was not yet in the news, most onlookers found her skating and tricks to be an odd amusement. While nearly at the end of her routine Kate suddenly felt a strange vision shoot through her mind and it so disrupted her she nearly lost her composure. She struggled to the end, was applauded and skated back to a bench to take her inline skates off. While bent over removing her skate another shaft of light shot through her mind followed by yet another more colorful vision.

Kate had recently spent time with her great grandmother Haddassah who tried to explain how many years previous as a teenager she also had experienced such disturbing light shows in her head. Haddassah said, "My dear great grand daughter, you have heard us speak of this family trait, the visions, the sometimes blinding lights. I had them when I was your age. And then one day I actually managed to see a picture or vision. It was what my father was experiencing that very day, a fight with another man. I saw it before it happened. That was how it started my dear. Very upsetting, I had no one to help explain it."

Kate realized that maybe now she would have these strange visions. It certainly disturbed her balance and coordination. Kate thought she'd leave the skates on and just roll around for a few minutes, maybe that might help?

Kate rolled around the sculptures trying to clear her head. It seemed better, she began to relax and then as she bent over to read a plaque she saw something. It was the water adjacent to the museum, the bay. But Kate was facing the opposite direction. What the hell? The picture remained stationary in her mind. Now this was certainly odd? Then something changed, it looked like a big wave. Then Kate got it. This was a tsunami a few feet high sweeping in from the ocean toward the Golden Gate Bridge.

She whipped around. Bad idea. She got a blinding flash through her brain.

Don't move fast. She looked out to the real bay. No tsunami. She very cautiously turned back the other direction. The image of the huge wave returned. Now what?

She stood there witnessing this wave. Then Kate experimented with the image, could she pull back? Yes, now she saw people in the parking lot. She turned again. These people were all different. She returned to the image which now wavered. A man was looking at his watch. He said, "Honey, it's almost 3, we have to get going."

Kate warily brought her arm up. It was 2:14 PM. The tsunami was coming in 45 minutes? And then one more vision popped up. Buildings in the Marina a few miles east and they were on fire and toppling. An earthquake. Kate had seen pictures of earthquakes. The buildings often fell over.

What could she do? Start screaming there would be an earthquake or a big wave? She felt panic rising in her throat. Her mother was waiting for her at a friend's house in the Marina and was to pick Kate up after the demonstration.

She calculated the time. Her mother was in the marina. "Hell, I can just call her, tell her to get out of there." Kate reached for her cell phone in the small backpack, punched in the number and got a busy signal. "Shit, mom, get off the damn phone!" But three more tries as Kate fended off well wishers she got a busy signal. "Damn it, I've gotta get down there. How much time do I have?"

She had 22 minutes to reach the house in the marina. "I'll never make it on blades and mom took the car. I'll hitch a ride!" She asked a few people, it got very confusing. She said, "I just need a ride to the marina right now, it's urgent!" But people had excuses, couldn't go, tied up, weren't sure where they parked.

Kate thought, *God, I gotta get there.*

Kate began skating, moving through the crowd eventually reaching a street that ran downhill. She began picking up speed.

At her best pace it would take fifteen minutes to reach the Golden Gate Bridge, another fifteen minutes or more to skate downhill and then across the flat of Chrissy Field and then into the Marina. "I am screwed, I need help."

As if by magic she caught sight of an aging Land Rover going her direction. The original SUV with square fenders looked really beat up but it was heading toward the bridge. It had a heavy metal bar on the back holding on a spare tire. Kate accelerated and caught onto the bar. The Land Rover was not traveling fast but faster than Kate could keep up her fastest pace. She hung on and then wrapped her hands around the bar. This was perfect as long as the Land Rover took her to the bridge. From there she could skate the rest.

Kate could not see the driver or passengers as the spare tire blocked her vision. That meant they likely could not see her as well. "That's fine, I need a fast ride, I don't want to be best friends."

The Land Rover began picking up speed heading toward the Golden Gate Bridge. Kate hung on tighter. "Geez, take it easy buddy, this old wreck may not hold together." But the Land Rover sped up again, then more, then faster again. Kate guessed he was driving 50 and this was approaching the limits of her leg strength and the roller blade wheels to roll comfortably. Faster yet and Kate realized she either had to let go right away or take her chances. She was getting there much quicker but her blades would not handle the bumping and bruising at these speeds.

She made a judgement call and decided to lift her blades off the pavement clinging to the metal bar. "If this thing lets loose I am totally screwed." But the bar held steady and Kate braced her blades against the back bumper of the Land Rover.

"How the hell fast is this guy going?" She looked to the side, the old SUV was flying almost literally. "Jesus, this is completely scary. If I let go now I'll be traveling so fast I don't think I can keep my blades grounded.

She craned her neck to look backwards. No cars were behind them. The Land Rover started shaking and rattling. This guy was driving way too fast for such a beatup vehicle! But if anything, the speed rose and now Kate was completely committed. Wherever this joker went, she also was going.

Kate was becoming deeply frightened. What on earth had she grabbed onto here?

The Land Rover rocketed under the overpass leading to the Golden Gate Bridge and careened around the corner opposite the bridge parking lot. Now it was downhill and Kate guessed they were going 50 or maybe faster. She began beating on the rear window but it was like no one could hear her.

"This guy will not make the next corner, it's sharp right hand turn, this wagon is gonna flip over and I'm going with it, I gotta get off this thing!!"

Kate looked around, she had a few seconds, the Land Rover was plunging down a hill toward the turnoff for Fort Point. "No god damn way this'll make it, oh my God!!!"

Kate dropped her blades to the pavement. It sounded like the wheels were being ground down to nothing and her legs were beaten by the road surface. She had some wrist protectors, knee cap protectors, no helmet.

She had no choice and let go. Immediately her speed dropped substantially but fighting the speed brought her down to her knees and almost over backwards. Kate was terrified. She was hurtling like a literal rocket and in fifty yards she had to handle the right hand turn!

She saw two bumps approaching, she couldn't handle them in a crouch so she fought her way up to a semi standing position. This helped, her speed dropped again but she was still way over forty miles per hour.

Every ounce of concentration went into the moment. She began leaning right pushing the blades left. She was reducing speed, she might make the corner. The centrifugal force was heavy pulling her out from the corner but she kept all her muscles bent right and she whipped around the near ninety degree corner like she was a waterskier on a long, fast rope. Somehow her force of will and trained muscles held steady. Immediately she was faced with a fast decision. The little road down to Chrissy Field was a steep left hand turn down and one way the wrong way!

Kate plummeted down the narrow road praying that no cars or bikers were coming up. But again her luck held, she screamed down the road, ran through an intersection and slalomed out onto the road through the old world war two airfield. Her speed had dropped to a manageable level. Kate's legs and hips were like wet spaghetti but she was holding it together.

Ahead a flat, straight road led to the Palace of Fine Arts and the Marina district adjacent. She yanked out her watch. It looked like 15 minutes. "God, that Land Rover got me down here in no time and I didn't crash and burn."

She moved into an aerodynamic crouch and even with weakened legs began skating for her goal. Suddenly a thought shot through her mind. *Where had the Land Rover gone? It was there, she let go, it shot ahead. And........where did it go? Maybe it made the corner? Maybe it went off the steep hillside? Maybe it disappeared?*

Kate managed to pull out her cell phone, punched a coded button and this time reached her mother. "Mom, I'm five minutes away on Crissy Field. Yes, I'm coming your way. Listen to me, I can't say much. Walk out the front door, walk over to the park where they play volleyball, just opposite the

Exploratorium. We'll meet at the park. Run, Mom, get over there it's a couple minutes from you!"

Kate was having trouble breathing but kept up a strong pace. She passed the military PX and in two minutes arrived at the meeting place. Moments later Sarah ran across the street and they fell into each other's arms.

"Katie, you were on TV. Channel 2 had all of it on tape including that forward flip but what's the big rush, you sounded upset? Where are we going?"

"Trust me, mother. Now come on!"

Sarah ran to keep up with Kate heading for the St. Francis Yacht Club. Dozens of ultra expensive cruisers and yachts were berthed at the club.

They ran toward a large ocean going twin engine cruiser about 60 feet long. Kate skated to a man cleaning stanchions. "Mister, in six minutes there will be a sizeable quake, it will impact the water here in the bay. Please drive all of us out into the bay, it will be much safer."

The man looked at her quizzically. "Are you crazy? How could you know that?"

Kate realized she must sound ridiculous. All she had was the strange vision back at the Palace of Legion of Honor. "I'm, uh, I am just positive this will happen. If I am wrong you will waste fifteen minutes and I'll feel really stupid. If I'm right you will be alive."

"Look, you seem like a nice girl. But how could anyone know such things?"

He glanced at Sarah. Standing behind her daughter Sarah summoned up her best look of certainty, her jaw conveying total belief in Kate's words. The man took note. A mature woman who seemed awfully determined.

Kate repeated, "I am telling you the absolute truth. This will happen. What's your name?"

"Sam. Samuel Irvine."

"Sam, I'm Kate McGill, you really must listen to me. I am not nuts. There will be a small tsunami out beyond the gate and a much larger quake right here."

"You want me to believe this?"

She was on the edge of hysterics. "Yes, I'm telling you, in under five minutes this quake will pound right through here."

Dressed in expensive sailing gear, wearing a little leather cap, an experienced sailor and yachtsman Sam considered her story. He saw there was little to lose in believing her and maybe something big to gain.

"You're saying a quake will happen right down this corridor and create a wave in the process?"

"Two waves, one is going to appear out there. It could be heading in to the bay right now. Then in under five minutes a quake will occur. It will dump a huge wave back in on the shore."

The man wasn't looking at Kate now. He strained to see out toward the Golden Gate Bridge but the water out there was not visible. Then he did a fast mental calculation about changes in water levels if there were a quake as she described.

"You had some kind of vision?"

She nodded.

"Ok, we do it your way. Pull up those ropes and your friend should go back there, just loosen the ropes, throw them off."

He jumped up to the navigating pulpit, turned over the engines, looked around quickly to ensure he had room to back out the boat. His neighboring slip mate on a 30 foot sail boat asked where he was off to. "Out into the bay, it's safer, earthquake coming." The neighbor shrugged his shoulders and went back to polishing brass fittings.

It took almost two minutes to throw off the ropes and begin the backing process.

Kate stood unsteadily on her skates nearby Sam. "Can you go any faster?"

"Trying, trying, it takes a minute. Where are you trying to get to?"

"If we could be a few hundred yards out, that would do it. I don't know why but 200 yards seems right. Just away from these other boats and the piers."

Kate realized she was still on skates. She quickly sat down and unbuckled them.

The boater cut some corners, hurried the large boat in reverse, nearly collided with a neighboring craft. All around them were moored expensive racing boats, splendid cabin cruisers and the odd small craft.

No one pulled out of the St. Francis Yacht Club moorage in a hurry. Sam was hurrying and people nearby and even well down the jetty were taking notice. Heads turned, quizzical looks given.

Sam headed into the channel toward the bay. They had to travel 200 yards, make a turn to port and power out into the bay. Normally the rule calls for no wake, creeping along at under 5 knots.

Sam pulled back on the power and headed down the channel at 15 knots. People began yelling and gesturing for him to slow down. Sam knew this could ruin his status with a bunch of serious sailors.

He tapped the throttles up higher. They cleared the main moorage, motoring past the Wave Organ, round the tip of the little peninsula and into the bay itself.

Sam had almost certainly altered the tone and texture of his life. If the quake happened he was clean. If the quake failed to appear he would have major explaining and apologizing and even then, inside the St. Francis, well, tough going...."

"How long now?"

Kate checked her watch. "I've got, under two minutes. Listen, you're the sailor, when this thing hits, what happens?"

Sam was checking gauges, watching the water surface, taking stock of the wind conditions, the relative tides. "If it comes from southeast to northwest the water could be sucked out with the force---out a ways, I can't really say for sure. Then, well, if that other one is coming in. God, I don't know, they could meet or, well. I just really don't know."

Kate looked west to the Golden Gate. She couldn't really see anything, some boats bobbing in swells, one good sized cargo vessel making for Richmond just emerging from the bridge. Suddenly the cargo ship rose up some feet. It was terribly sudden like a huge hand pulling the vessel into the skies.

Kate blurted out, "Ok, I'd say we have trouble coming this way. That cargo boat just leaped out of the water."

Sam whirled around with a frozen expression. "That Korean cargo hauler, you saw it jump out of the ----oh, shit. No wonder, it's a tsunami, I've seen them overseas. This is what you said would happen?"

Kate nodded and looked over at Sarah. "Sam, what do we do? Just hold on?"

Sam began turning his vessel bow first into the approaching wave. "Both of you, get those life vests on immediately. Then, you have a choice. Tie yourself onto that rail or just hang on."

Sarah asked plaintively, "And you will do what?"

"I just hang on. I don't like being tied on. Now when it gets ---."

Sarah's scream drowned him out. Her face radiated abject terror, she was pointing toward the shore. Sam and Kate whirled around again. "Oh, lord...." is all Sam could manage. Kate was simply dumbfounded.

Looking across the marina green toward downtown San Francisco they could see a procession of collapsing structures falling like dominos. The progressing wave of a quake dragged building after building down across the marina approaching the waterfront. Not all houses literally fell, some simply swayed, others kneeled, still others disappeared. Smoke and fire could be seen leaping among the destroyed buildings, sirens commenced their wail, people were running across the green in fear utterly unsure where to go.

And then black gunk sprayed up out of the green. The marina district built totally on bay fill liquefied and a layer of black, ugly liquid emerged in the green lawn. Now a stream of gunk shot skyward.

Sarah watched the momentary spout. "That is like watching hell present itself. God that is awful looking!"

Kate hung onto a wooden rail and watched the incoming wave. "Sam, we're going to face it head on?"

Sam grunted as he tied on his life vest. "Now listen, both of you I'm going to run up the power, this has two big engines. If we're flipped over or whatever and you end up in the water try to move away from the boat until it settles. Then clamber on it. It will keep you up for a while."

Sarah tried to remain calm but bile welled up in her throat. The wave wasn't moving all that fast which seemed to make it even more ominous.

Sam had been concentrating on positioning the boat for the incoming wave and then he looked backwards for a moment.

"Oh Jesus Christ. The quake is sucking water out of the harbor. It's just like you said..."

Literally Sam was stuck between the devil and the deep blue sea. The unnatural wave forming behind them in the harbor was going to be much taller and potentially far more damaging.

Sarah could see people pointing and screaming on the shore. She decided to fling herself up on the boat's roof where she could hold on to a railing and another grab bar. Kate found a small alcove alongside the boat's door but Sam had no choice but to stay at the wheel.

He now experienced what legends say could happen. Tiny snippets of images from his childhood did actually flash through his mind. He watched the tsunami and realized it was gradually losing force and one more glance backward told him in a few seconds the weird wave from the shore would reach them. He clutched the metal wheel and then threaded both arms through it figuring he'd stay with the boat longer.

Both women simply shut their eyes. Sam watched until the last second, measured distances and decided to apply more power just as the remainder of the tsunami hit them. Then he also shut his eyes. There was no point in trying to watch he and his new companions being crushed by the water.

Sam's last conscious thought proved strangely omniscient. "She told me 200 yards offshore. Why?"

The roller from the bay, now perhaps 5 feet tall, hit them first. The boat obediently powered right up the wave which had lost its sharp edge. Sam had been right, more power was working.

And then their stern rose and rose again and now the bow pointed down 30 degrees. Sam knew if they went more vertical the whole sixty foot ketch would be plunged down into the bay.

It rose another few degrees and Sam opened his eyes. He knew this was idiotic but it felt like the two waves had created a liquid plateau as the bow now began returning toward horizontal.

An amateur picture and video taken from shore would later confirm, Sam's boat was momentarily poised atop the two waves.

And then they crashed down. If the trip up was disorienting the trip down was terrifying as the boat dropped like a stone, the conflicting waves crashed together tossing the boat higher and allowing it to plunge. Sarah and Kate screamed so loud it hurt and Sam took a hit in the face from the steering wheel.

But moments later there they sat just like nothing had happened. The waves effectively cancelled out each other's raw energy although as Sam struggled to his feet he could see a large ripple heading toward Sausalito.

Sarah relaxed her grip and opened her eyes. There was Kate hugging Sam, they both were crying and laughing. Sarah's body felt like it been through that mangle machine her mother used to use to iron sheets at home. She walked forward unsteadily and clutched both Sam and Kate.

They separated finally turned to look shoreward. Sirens were everywhere, smoke rose from four fires. Sam looked around the boat but saw no obvious damage. "I need to head in, there's gonna be hell to pay at the St. Francis."

He motored slowly toward the inlet. As they drew closer the oily black tar could be seen on the lawns of the marina green.

"Oh my god, look at this mess!" Sam shook his head and nearly wept again. Dozens of ultra expensive sail boats and cruising yachts were flung into one another and a few had crashed up on the shore looking like broken toothpicks. You could hear the crying and screaming as people discovered their formerly pristine vessels destroyed like scattered tinker toys.

Sam brought the boat to idle scanning for a place to berth his own vessel. Finally he spotted a niche down at the end and crept for the space. Police cars were arriving and teams of EMT's were already at work extracting crew members from crushed sail boats.

Sam brought his boat to rest in a corner of the small harbor. "I gotta get off of here, Sam, my legs are just not seaworthy any more, nor is my brain. " said Sarah.

Sam slumped on the captain's chair. "Ladies not sure if I'm gonna be seaworthy for a while either. But Kate, if you hadn't picked me I'd surely be over in the mess of broken boats. I owe you my life."

"And we owe you Sam. We would have been in deep trouble."

As Sarah stepped off the boat she glanced at the stern. Sam's boat was called "The Miracle Worker".

It was October 17, 1989.

CHAPTER EIGHT

KATE MEETS PETER IN CHICAGO

Sarah spent two years after finishing her college degree traveling, exploring and finally working as a road manager in the music business. But after two years she realized she was ready to get off the road and some days after arriving home she woke up and felt different. It didn't take long to figure out she and Paul were going to be parents.

Now 23, Sarah struggled with her willingness and preparation to be a mother but any doubt quickly passed as a rush of maternal instincts overwhelmed any reluctance. She had found life on the road and the rock life style left a lot to be desired. She and Paul had big plans for buying a house until it became clear between them they had limited money. She called Helen and in that conversation her mother said, "Honey, for right now, why not keep this simple. Our house is just sitting there, I'm not going to be in Minnesota all that often, my life is tied up in *Aray Powersource* here. Your grandmother will not leave Las Vegas all that willingly, she is pretty rooted in that little theater she's built. Why don't you and Paul just take our old house. You can always sell it and buy something larger."

Sarah liked the house she grew up in, she didn't feel cramped by all the visions of childhood. After her few years of travel she was quite happy to be home and Sal could get to Minneapolis frequently. The years passed quickly raising their baby girl named after Katherine Hepburn, Sarah's favorite actress. By age 7 it was becoming obvious, Kate McGill had inherited genes from both Helen and Sal. Kate was strong willed, motivated and smart. Kate began developing physically even before becoming a teenager and her parents found themselves in an endless cycle of athletic explorations driving their daughter to training camps and contests all over the state. Kate tried almost every conceivable sport finally settling on martial arts, particularly Judo, skating,

51

biking and gymnastics. Kate would be physically stronger than most young men her age. Like her grandmother Kate demonstrated a strength of will and determination early combined with surprising physical coordination. By age twelve Kate became a young star in any sport she attempted.

Where other teenage girls could only think of clothes, makeup and dating, Kate's entire devotion focused on physical conditioning. When she entered skating competitions or judo demonstrations her competition could only be young men as teenage girls could not muster the strength to stay up. Even the young men were rarely competitive with Kate.

By the time Kate was a teen Helen could no longer stand in the way of Kate learning about Sal's world. Kate's innate talent for learning far outstripped anyone's ability to control what she could absorb anyway.

Kate's physical development certainly included femininity and she now had to deal with clothing choices and how much she revealed of her body. Kate inherited her mother's curves but her conditioning dramatically heightened the whole package. Kate looked more like a well developed young woman even at age sixteen. After a short campaign to convince her parents she could take the train alone to Chicago, Kate stepped off the train at Union station dressed in her normal jeans and a work shirt to be met by Sal and Bruno. Kate knew Sal surrounded himself with men in suits. She didn't realize until that moment that "the suits" were not normal sized men. Bruno occupied a large space, when he walked in a crowd Bruno couldn't be missed and Bruno soon felt protective of Kate.

Sal was determined to separate Kate from his collection of bruisers and enforcers but Kate developed an instant fascination with Sal's guys. She watched every available *Untouchables* tv episode she could find, she knew the names of Chicago gangsters going back to the nineteen twenties. Sal realized Kate was actually very much at home with tough guys. She wanted to know what made them tick. The men found her utterly exotic, a young woman who could handle herself physically and was unintimidated by their attitudes and language. Sal thought he'd show his granddaughter the bright lights of Chicago but Kate wanted to hang out with "the muscle". Now Sal had a more disturbing problem. Kate was blossoming into a sexy young woman, at sixteen and Sal saw these men eyeing her like any man would.

He put out the word that any man who even thought about touching Kate was history but Kate recognized the problem and made sure she didn't send out the wrong messages. It became a tricky balancing act and Sal had to answer to Helen who took a decisive position: "Sallie, our granddaughter finds your boys fascinating but I will not tolerate her involvement with any of them, none of them. Out of the question. I don't want her alone with any of them ever. She deserves to know you but you make it very clear that she is far off limits."

"Helen, Bruno is so protective of Kate, he sees that potential and has taken steps to ensure nothing inappropriate can occur. These days are passing anyway, I'm handing off the old business to others. I think it's better to allow her curiosity to be satisfied."

"Sal, this is not optional, keep Kate free and clear of those guys. She can talk to them but that's it. I don't want a sad tale coming out of her visits to Chicago."

Sal offered to take Kate to a Chicago Cubs game. Kate had limited interest in baseball but most of "the boys" were attending so Kate wanted in. They rode out to Wrigley Field in two extra long Caddy limos. For the first time Kate got a strong dose of Sal's other life, moving in public with eight men surrounding him, two occasionally walked backwards keeping an eye out behind. Kate found herself sandwiched between Bruno and an even larger bodyguard, Carlo. Sal walked just ahead of her and he was flanked by two more men. As the group proceeded a wide gap opened before them as local fans made way for the phalanx. Kate couldn't believe her own eyes. It was like a legion of Roman soldiers accompanying their leader pushing through the crowds with an intimidating power surge. As the only female Kate got eyed by everyone around them. She couldn't decide if she liked all the attention or was simply embarrassed by it?

Once they arrived at their box seats Kate noticed there were two uniformed Chicago police stationed very close by. The Cubs had been playing fairly well so the crowd at Wrigley was close to being capacity but Sal's seats were surrounded by a ring of empty seats.

Kate leaned over to Sal. "Granddad, why are there these empty seats around us? Every other seat is filled."

Sal popped peanuts in his mouth while sipping a ballpark beer. "Seats, oh, yah, I buy these seats so we can have privacy. I'm a local low key celebrity so it's easier if we just don't have people on top of us."

Kate counted the empties. There were twelve nearby empty seats. She added up the likely cost. It was hundreds and hundreds of dollars to give Sal and company insulation. Kate tried to look around, watching nearby fans. People were clearly giving Sal's party a mental buffer but especially women couldn't help but check out the gangster crew. It was Kate's first experience with sustained public exposure where she could watch the watchers. She found it stimulating but a little confusing. She saw people giving Sal's people not so friendly looks. The game down on the field held little interest for Kate and she even thought Sal wasn't all that interested but he seemed to enjoy being in the crowd, just being a fan out for a day at the park.

Kate stood up at the end of the fifth inning. "Sal, I gotta visit the little girl's room. I'll be back." This caught Sal offguard. He motioned to Bruno to accompany Kate but she held up her hand. "I don't need anyone to come with. I'll be fine." Sal watched her leaving and thought she carried herself with real authority given her age.

Bruno leaned over to Sal, "Sal, she's something. That girl's got guts, a lotta spirit and she doesn't flinch at anything. When the guys starting carryin' on, a few swear words she barely notices, I think."

Sal glanced back over his shoulder a few times. "Bruno, I'm not so sure this is all good for her, being around our guys, she's getting' a major dose of tough guys and they can be pretty, I don't know, primitive. These are not ballet dancers."

Bruno laughed, "She's perfectly at home with all of us. And the guys give her every courtesy. Frankly it's much better with Katie around. They watch their language, they talk with a little tact. It makes them mind their manners. Did you know she was arm wrestling Antonio yesterday. I thought he was layin' down for her, cuttin' her slack but she kept him at the table, she couldn't beat such a big guy but she almost kept him to a draw. I was very impressed."

Sal looked concerned, "Bruno, that could be dangerous, she's a sixteen year old girl. She has no business tryin' to beat him."

Bruno laughed, "Boss, she almost whipped him. He was caught way off guard. She has muscle that girl and amazing balance. After a minute he had to really work to beat her."

As Kate came back down the stadium steps people watched her with great interest because she was with Sal's crew. She had become a truly attractive, self confident young woman. Kate loved all the attention even though being with these guys was a bit peculiar.

At the top of the ninth Sal's crew rose as one and began making their way up the stairs. Bruno did not want to be caught with the entire crowd leaving together. He said, "I'd really rather stay until the Cubbies win this one but it's not good being stuck in the crowd."

Kate found the Chicago crew totally fascinating. With the exception of the two Roemer brothers, most men she encountered were square, predictable working stiffs, particularly in Minnesota. Kate wanted more. She called Sarah and asked for an extension which Sarah agreed to but now Sal had to make absolutely sure Kate was safe and secure.

"Dad, it's Sarah, you know Katie wants to hang around with you for a few more days in Chicago, that ok?"

Sal replied, "Sarah, it should be fine, it's very quiet in our business right now, she'll have someone with her all the time."

On the fourth day of her visit, Kate sauntered into Sal's main office, a warehouse off Armitage in the Old Town district. A former storage facility, Sal had new windows and skylights created, an antique pool table dominated the room, in the corner two pinball machines lit up with ringing bells. Toward noon the whole warehouse took on the pungent smells of Greek or Italian food, Sal often taking the chef role. Outside the neighborhood had been filling up with alternative lifestyle, former hippies and the first smatterings of young adults starting to earn a living. Prosperity poked up along the street.

Kate lolled around the warehouse for twenty minutes but in this context she was out of place, the men had work to talk about and she could not be any part of those discussions. Kate was starting to realize that some or maybe all of these guys might be committing violent acts. That didn't square with the friendly, family-like reactions she found with the guys. She wasn't yet sure if she should take them at face value or start reacting to the mob overtones? Sal walked down to the ground floor to check on Kate who was shooting pool with Carlo. The men still eyed her but she was becoming part of the family if a little awkwardly.

A young man entered the building, Sal spotted him and called out, "Hey, Peter, someone for you to meet over here." The young man approached, Kate glanced up from the billiard table. In an instant an electric current zapped between Kate and Peter. She watched him approach, he was different, more poised and very handsome.

Peter introduced himself and Kate heard the words but her mind was elsewhere. *Who is this guy? He's so cute, I love his hair, no I love more than the hair. Wow, we need to get acquainted. He doesn't seem like all these other guys who work with Sal. Well, he couldn't be, he's my age. Right, my age. I wonder if he thinks I'm cool?*

The son of a close friend of Sal's, one year older than Kate, Peter Scalissi looked every inch a full blooded Italian with olive skin, a grand head of very black hair, a well built physique, dressed in jeans and a t-shirt similar to the way Kate dressed. Most important, Peter's radiant smile and dark, romantic eyes brought her to a halt. Peter extended his hand, she took it looking him straight in the face. This was not your typical mob wanna-be. All the other guys were from the heavy duty street type mold but Peter looked more poised and interested. "So you're Katie. I've been hearing your name for days and hoped to meet you." His whole being sent out friendly and distinctly non-bully vibes. She liked his voice with a decided lightness and a twist of cleverness thrown in. She hoped he'd keep talking.

Peter tried to be a bit oblique, purposely kept his eyes above the shoulders but she had this way of looking at you, a smirk or was it just friendly? He could tell her body was better developed than the average teenage girl. She stood with shoulders back, her stance radiated strength and preparedness. Kate sent a ray of awareness so directly into his eyes, she was unafraid---that was it. There was none of the normal teenage girl reluctance or coyness. This girl had cajones and Peter could not resist a girl with strength.

They began talking about Chicago, then Minneapolis, then music, he knew something about blues and that just took off because Kate had been studying Muddy Waters and a harmonica player named Little Walter. Peter knew their music, the record company, Chess Records, and now the whole dialogue picked up even more speed.

Sal stood with his fingertips touching the edge of the pool table not watching either young person, his body leaned against the table. Sal saw it happening immediately, these two kids were strongly attracted and it was like a little magic. The others in the room could just as easily not have been there. Bruno watched the two also and knew Sal would have a whole new problem. This charming Peter with his good looks, a smart kid and no eyes to be one of the crew, he was Kate's kind of boy. That meant Kate's grandmother would be riding herd on the two kids even from California.

Kate turned away to find her fanny pack and Peter's eyes followed her body as she turned and reached. Peter knew this was not even thinkable, this was Sal's granddaughter, there would be no hanky panky. Sixteen years old, way, way too young but as she stood back up he realized she had the presence of a much older person. Yes a teenager but not like any teenager Peter had ever met.

Kate purposely kept it moving along but she thought Peter put out such a nice, comfortable and very cool vibe and cute with a capital C. His hair lay across his forehead, such thick, rich hair and no girl could resist wanting to just touch that bushy mop.

Sal stepped in, "Kids we have work here, Carlo has to take me over to La Salle Street. Peter, you are assigned to take care of our girl here, she needs to be back at our house in about three hours for dinner, you're invited, your Dad will be coming. Oh, wait, you can't drive can you?"

Peter brightened up, "Mr. Torpaydo, we'll take the bus, it's easy from here and Katie can see the city." Kate smiled, "Sure, great, it stopped raining, no problem."

Carlo watched the scene unfold and knew Peter couldn't resist young Kate.

Peter and Kate left the warehouse, as they walked out onto the street people from the neighborhood gave them a careful once over. Kate immediately felt the focused looks.

"What's the deal, if you walk out of that building they all check you out?"

Peter waited until they were a bit further from a few people on the street. "Katie, you know who your grandfather is, his reputation?"

She watched Peter's face as they walked. "Yah, sure, he's in charge, these are mob guys, right?"

Peter nodded but didn't smile. They walked another half block and then he took her arm and steered her across the street. "Katie, I don't know how much you know about Chicago but this is the land of the Daley family, this is serious syndicate territory, we always seem to have a governor in the slammer. The mob, here, means big time power, influence, serious manipulation of the system. I don't want to start telling you about your grandfather but let's say he's respected and also feared. That's the truth."

This slowed Kate down. She enjoyed hanging out with these big oxes but she always knew they were not tame. "So, uh, he has people killed, beat up, like that?"

Peter shook his head, "I can't say, I read the newspaper, I hear gossip from people my age, our age. I have known him since I was a kid. He and my father go back, way back."

"Is your Dad part of Sal's deal?"

Peter smiled, "Only in this sense, my father is a lawyer, very connected here in Chicago. But they are also boyhood friends so it's complex. There is a mature, adult respect between them and my Dad seems to look out for Sal, tries to be a friend when he is needed."

"But he's not a mob guy?"

Peter nodded. "Kate, the truth is I don't know what all my Dad does but I believe he stays out of Sal's business. They're just friends."

Peter directed her to a bus stop, they stood side by side as cars wooshed by. Kate found him distinctly different than others her age. Peter had poise for 17 years old and an outgoing friendly disposition. "Peter, so you like Pete or Peter?"

"Kate, you like Kate, Katie, Katherine?" They both grinned. Kate had never met up with a young guy who she had an actual attraction for, not just because he was cute but she liked his attitude, intelligence, opinion. Sarah's voice bounced around her mind. "Honey, you're gonna encounter some cuties, just make sure they don't take advantage....There are good guys, plenty but guys want to score, you know what I mean? Guard yourself, be careful." Kate eyeballed Peter, he returned the interest but he could feel Sal's presence lurking around them both. Peter also twice encountered Kate's grandmother Helen. Peter knew Sal, they often ate dinner together and Sal had that tough guy, macho presence but treated Peter with a hands-off respect. Not, Helen. She could actually scare Peter. She had a determined, hard edged look when she wanted you to pay attention. Unlike Sal who rarely used his muscular presence for leverage, Helen almost pried open conversations, leaning in to the table, her face contorted for emphasis, her words precisely chosen for their impact. Peter definitely thought Helen had the more domineering, forceful presence. But then you couldn't beat Sal's boys to add old fashioned physical brawn.

The Chicago transit authority bus arrived, the two teenagers stepped inside and took two seats in the middle. Peter began a pleasant, informative description of the local sights, he explained how Old Towne had become the hip hangout back in the sixties, he pointed out where a local club, Big Johns, had once operated. Kate knew about some of the musicians who got their start in their neighborhood like Paul Butterfield and Michael Bloomfield. Kate playfully punched Peter's shoulder wrinkling his leather jacket. Peter chuckled but the hit hurt just a bit.

Peter pointed out more landmarks, they passed a sign announcing Lincoln Park Zoo. Peter asked, "Hey, we could jump off at the zoo, what do you think?"

Kate's answer surprised him, "Uh, a park is fine, Peter I'm not too comfortable at zoos. I heard your zoo is very good but I get very strong vibes from the caged animals. They are definitely not happy in those cages, I know that for sure. Sometimes, you're gonna think I'm odd, but I can really feel what the animals feel. I went to a zoo with my Dad up in Madison and when I get close to the lions or elephants they are very unhappy in those cages. I'm sorry to be such a downer but that's what I really feel. I know zoos need to exist but if it was up to me I'd take all those animals back to their native haunts and let them go."

Peter listened to Kate and thought, *Boy, this is one very unusual young lady. She understands what animals are feeling and thinking? Ok, can't argue with that. Maybe she does? Never heard anyone talk like that. She is so pretty but she has opinions.*

A number of teens boarded, quickly got loud and raucous. Peter felt protective of Kate, gave the teens nasty looks but the sound got louder, a few seniors stood up and moved away. Then two of the kids began scuffling with each other and accidentally fell into two of the seniors. Peter jumped up and ran to their assistance but one older person got her wrist twisted, the driver couldn't immediately help. The loud teens kept up with their disturbances. Peter was upset but had to shrug his shoulders, "What are you gonna do with these goons?"

Kate observed the continuing shenanigans, some passengers got off early to avoid the thrashing kids. Kate stood up, Peter reached for her hand but she slipped away. She moved down the aisle, as she walked the look on her face became almost serene but very determined. Peter had seen that look before. Helen had that look when she meant business.

Kate stood in front of the noisiest teens and said nothing. One looked up, "Hey little missy, you never seen Blackstone Rangers before?" Heads on the bus swiveled, the Blackstone Rangers were respected and feared in Chicago. She didn't break her stance and gave them a very slight grin. The young man speaking stood up standing nearly a foot taller than Kate. "Missy, back it down, you on our turf here." She still said nothing but gave him an intent stare. They were two feet apart standing in the aisle. Her challenge was irritating him. But he couldn't deny this girl had him thinking twice about making trouble.

She calmly said, "I'll arm wrestle you for who backs down, big guy."

She gently reached down, took his right hand in her right hand, brought them up to eye level. He had the clear advantage, his weight and height were vastly superior. Then she applied tension and he had to react. They had an audience now. Kate braced herself against a bus seat, her nemesis realized this was actually happening and had to react. He also braced himself. This young woman was starting to overpower him. He thought, *This shit can't be happening, this is crazy!*

He began powering back, she lost the advantage, her arm began gradually bending down further and further. Then suddenly from out of nowhere she started coming back reaching into some reservoir of strength. The young man realized something weird was happening. This girl, this teenager was nearly as strong as he was and now she was powering up, her stance toughened, her arm began bringing his up to the center and she was actually forcing his much bigger, thicker arm into submission. Peter watched Kate's face. It was definitely *that Helen face*, beyond determined, calm but totally resolute. Kate had to reach a good foot higher just to keep even yet she gradually, steadily brought his arm back, now almost parallel to the ground and then even further. He looked in her eyes. Whoever she was, she had some devilish mojo working against him. He didn't give up but she had him, his arm almost bent to his waist.

She didn't crow in victory or say anything smart alecky. She barely smiled but allowed his arm to return to vertical. Then she said, "You're a super strong guy." That was it, she could have made him feel stupid which he did anyway. Then she brought his arm around and twisted her grip so they were actually shaking hands.

She said, "What's your name?"

He saw what she was doing. This would not be a victor and the defeated. She was making it easy for him to return to normal. "I'm Marlon, you're incredibly strong, no one's every beat me arm wrestling."

Now she smiled, "Hey, it happens, you never know who has the upper hand, do you. Nice meeting you, Marlon."

It ended. The tension in the bus subsided. Kate walked back and slid in next to Peter. She made sure there was no victory jubilation on her face. "Hey, I'm starving, take me to find a good sandwich, ok?"

Peter just nodded and let out a deep sigh. *Ok, that was quite a little scene. Did she really beat that guy fair and square? Whoa that was something.*

Read about a young Buzz Roemer meeting Sal Torpaydo at www.katemcgill.com. Look under the "chapters" heading.

CHAPTER NINE

KATE MEETS THE MULE

At age sixteen Kate could finally drive but her mom's VW Jetta, fun as it was, fell short of Kate's ideas. She wanted to master anything on wheels not because she cared about the cars as much as the idea of mastering the machines. Kate liked to be in charge.

She had extracted one solemn promise from Buzz Roemer: *When I'm legal and I can show you my license you'll take me to your garage and let me try out a few of those crazy contraptions.*

Buzz Roemer traveled the world at one time bringing back all manner of strange collector's cars. A small German armored troop carrier, a Russian truck with two reverse gears, an early Italian tractor from the company that became Lamborghini, a beatup but still useable BMW motorcycle built in 1938, and a few dozen more---all relics of world war two.

In recent years Buzz experienced an almost meteoric rise in his financial fortunes. Further over in the garage resided a delectable array of sports cars from an early Porsche 911 to an Aston Martin DB3 completely rebuilt. The Ferraris started with an early Lusso, then a Dino, then a Testa Rossa. Parked in a corner of the garage a plain appearing Audi bearing a few dents and two large wings, one in front, one in the rear.

Kate's magic day arrived and Sarah showed up with Kate and her newly minted driver's license at nine AM on a clear spring morning. Buzz had pulled out a few of the stranger vehicles but he encouraged Kate to try the simpler ones like an aged VW bug from the early sixties.

"Katie, this is a four speed, it's in an H pattern and the reverse is ----."

Kate cut him off. "Got it, I've studied the bugs. Let's go, I can do this."

And so she did, one after another and they were soon riding in the German troop carrier jerkily crawling around Buzz's large parking lot. After more military vehicles, all oddities, they broke for lunch. She'd been burning to drive the Porsche 935, a strictly built for racing streamlined coupe with a long tail. Porsche's of this breed could reach one hundred eighty miles per hour and were not to be trifled with. Second gear would break most speed limits in America and if you were strapped for speed just shift to third gear.

"No, Kate, first it's not licensed for the street and second, this is built for racing drivers with experience driving fire breathers."

Kate had learned how to lobby Buzz. Her insistent, never say die approach generally wore him down.

"Katie, now listen. The Porsche is a legendary race car. It took me a year before I even considered driving it myself. I had a highly experienced pro driver train me, direct me, I took courses and went to a driver's school. It is blindingly fast and can snuff out your young life in a split second of inattention. I'll take you for a ride at some point."

She saw the odds, pretended to play along until her moment arrived.

They ended up putting the 935 on its trailer and hauling it forty miles out of town to an abandoned airfield Buzz admitted to knowing about. After more education Buzz began making a two mile circuit around the airstrips. After fifteen minutes he returned to the trailer. Then she started lobbying again. She could handle this, she would be strictly careful. and it just kept going. He responded, "Now listen, this is over seven hundred fifty horsepower, the gearbox will be lunched if you jam the gears so just ----."

But she held up her hand, jumped out, ran around entered the driver's door and plopped into the driver's seat. Buzz reluctantly accepted the passenger's seat. She looked over the few gauges, the strangely shaped gear shifter, reached for the foot pedals buried deep under the steering wheel and without Buzz explaining it turned the key, hit the starter button and a metallic jumble of very expensive cams and gears exploded into life in the Porsche's tail. She figured out the gear selector and brought the revs up. The magnificent Porsche motor literally breathing some fire shrieked up and down as Kate tapped the gas pedal.

Off they went out onto the unused concrete slabs down one runway, back up another, Kate steering the Porsche like the overgrown go-kart it was. On the third time around she brought it up to six thousand RPM in fourth and they touched one hundred thirty five miles per hour. The monstrous disk brakes brought them down to a crawl.

"I'll never get past third gear in this baby will I?"

Buzz shook his head. "Katie it's a thoroughbred racing machine. It's still waiting for you to put your foot down but don't even think about it. Kate, men wait years, if ever, to handle a machine this evolved. You'd be better off in the mule. That was built for rallying, it has a turbocharged five cylinder, it's a little road rocket, can handle any terrain. The Audi Sport Quattro was built to win brutal road rallies."

She turned and smiled sweetly at Buzz. "Can I drive it on the regular roads?"

Two hours later back at the garage Kate sat in the mule's fiberglass and metal driver's seat that clutched her in its grip. "Man, this thing is ugly inside but it's all business." Only the essentials remained of the sparse interior. Two bucket seats with six point racing harness, full roll cage in case the mule turned upside down, just a few gauges and fastened down on the floor a sawed off shotgun. Kate gripped the small leather wrapped wheel. This felt like her. Real essentials, built to do a job, kind of primitive and angry if you pushed on the gas.

Buzz felt the need to instruct her. "They only built a couple of these, then it became the S1 Quattro Sport, even in this version you have to hit the revs between 4000 and 7000 to find the power. Now listen, you were ok in that Porsche but we were on that airstrip. This is every bit as as dangerous if you step on it too hard." She was listening with half an ear but trying to figure out the strange ignition system and finally realized it had a kill switch, just a large red up and down metal handle. She put it in "on" and pushed the starter. The cacaphony was like the Porsche but in front of them and it sounded jagged and uneven. The exhaust note sounded like a ripping metal. She eased it into first and the Audi lept forward.

"Whoa, this baby's full of herself!" Kate exclaimed. It took fifteen minutes hunting around to feel out the steering, the gigantic disk brakes and most of all the powerplant that simply burbled power. Up through third into fourth Kate came up behind a slow moving RV. She sneaked a peek around the boxy RV and then steered into the oncoming traffic.

"Goose it you got a truck coming," Buzz advised.

Kate stepped down hard on the mule and the resultant lunge threw them both back into the seats. She topped one hundred in a flash as the turbo charged motor cleared its throat and then screamed up to one hundred thirty mph.

"Holy shit, this is a total beast! I love it!"

Buzz kept his thoughts to himself as Kate brought it back down to eighty five in fourth, the mule barely working hard. "This is the one Buzzer. It's just so ugly brutal. I can see how that smuggler must have loved taking this through the mountains."

Buzz added, "It's got two extra sets of driving lights, the second ones, on this switch are aircraft landing lights. Turns night into day. By the way that smuggler, he's doing time in France. They caught him with pounds of cocaine.

That's how I got this thing. He needed cash fast. He gets out in five years and wants his car back, he told me."

Kate nodded lost in her own thoughts. Somehow she had to talk Buzzer into loaning her this mule.

"It has Nova Scotia plates. That was the only place I could get it licensed. It's not really legal in the states. All the smog nonsense. The smuggler needed a car that attracted zero attention. It was really designed for rallying in Africa under miserable, awful conditions so it doesn't complain much but I change the oil every twelve hundred miles."

Kate was absorbing the history but her deeper attention traveled down her arms to the solid rubber like wheel. Her fingers could feel the road, her rear end could feel the engine talking to the rough cut gears in the transmission, the brakes were so astonishingly powerful that stopping was not about slowing down. It was about watching in your mirror to make sure nothing was too close. The mule could stop so incredibly fast.

It was a true Q-ship. Kate knew that term from reading about World War II.

Q-ships were well armed killer boats disguised as freighters. Q-ships sneaked by the enemy looking like a waste of time.

The concept appealed immensely to Kate. Walking right by someone who was looking just for you and missed you hiding in plain sight.

She waited until they got back to the garage and she parked the mule. Kate never thought she'd love a car, particularly one that looked so beat up but she loved this mule.

"Uh, Buzzer, what's the chances of a long term loan? This car has my heart beating in it."

"Kate you can come out and drive it but you gotta finish high school and get accepted at a college. Then we'll talk about it."

Some sixteen months later Buzz found himself standing at the edge of his office and garage compound in an early summer delight of humid cricket chirpings and songbirds greeting the sun.

"Katie, I guess I wasn't really expecting you to take me up on loaning out the mule. I, uh, well, wasn't expecting this, you know."

Kate leaned against the left front fender of the mule one hand absentmindedly fiddling with her hair. "Buzz I just need this mongrel. It's like me. Hacked together, awkward, incomplete. But a strong heart. Actually my mom said that about me. So..."

Buzz couldn't help but fall for her pitch. He never really could say no to Kate.

"Alright, here are the rules. Let's see. Honey, listen to me, I let you get away with murder way too often. But I do it because that's how you'll learn fast. So the only rule is, uh, don't get stupid. This innocent looking beater will carve grooves in the pavement. It accelerates like a modern Corvette and those tires can clutch the road like a hawk's talons. Kate you can kill yourself by pushing it too hard. Can I trust you with this?"

Kate had one habit Buzz disliked. She'd make like she wasn't listening and just shrug. She did that now. Buzz was getting a bit steamed with her. Suddenly she jumped toward Buzz, threw her arms around his neck and hugged him.

"Buzzer, you're not making a mistake. I'll take care of this mule like it's my child. Believe me!"

Kate Age Seventeen Testing the Mule under Rally Conditions

If you were standing near five hundred forested acres owned by a certain Andrus Johansen eight miles from Shakopee, Minnesota you'd see a small white and red car airborne twisting and sliding up, down and around a crude dirt and gravel path wide enough to be a primitive road. The two door Audi Sport Quattro sedan, a car originally built for economy and rugged dependability was shrieking when not making odd popping sounds. From behind there were streams of belching fire shooting out of the exhaust.

Farmer Johansen, a long ago veteran of European auto rallying, where drivers fling cars around primitive roads at speeds beyond human calculation taking chances with outthinking gravity and missing large trees by scant inches had wisely herded his livestock to a spare field on his acreage. Now he stood atop an aged and leaning water tower with binoculars tracking the progress of the mule. With him stood Buzz Roemer intently staring at his boots while attempting to talk with the driver on a two way walkie talkie fed into his head set.

Buzz said, "Katie, don't worry about the Audi, it's designed for this abuse. Worry about trees, fences and rocks!"

Through his head set he heard squawking and squeals as Kate apparently mastered or abused the hybrid car. Inside Kate was attempting to apply the lessons learned from Andrus while circling the acerage on roads designed by Andrus to replicate his native Sweden. Andrus drove rally cars in the seventies before Audi had much of any presence in the sport. His rally car of choice was a Saab 96 radically re-engineered, one of the original rally legends.

Inside the Quattro Kate rounded a right hand ninety degree corner, the mule was thrown into a high speed slide spewing dirt and gravel in a rooster tail behind, the five cylinder turbo charged engine blipping up and down the audio scale as she used the power of all wheel drive to accelerate.

Her hands and legs performed a comic opera of intense, fast movement as she shifted gears, stabbed the brakes, rammed the gas pedal all in lightning quick order.

Clearing the corner Kate used the more than four hundred horsepower slingshotting back up to one hundred miles per hour then briefly braking and tossing the Audi into an uphill left hander at over eighty skittering across gravel and patches of icy soil. Over a hilltop, all four tires broke free of the earth, the Audi sailed into thin air descending like a landing airplane. Even before arriving at the next downhill right hander Kate threw the mule toward the corner apex bringing it into a power slide culminating in a tight s-shaped corner. Kate momentarily jerked up on the hand brake bringing the rear end around, dropping the brake and screaming off up through four more gears.

The two men observed from their perch. Andrus nodded up and down as the little rocket touched one hundred twenty five miles per hour on a short straight stretch and as quickly the oversize disc brakes brought the mule to a stop. The men descended a ladder and approached the idling sedan. Kate uncinched a full face helmet and gradually removed nomex driver's gloves one finger at a time. She uncoiled her body from the six point seat belt harness and emerged from the driver's seat shaking her shoulder length hair out.

Kate shrugged her shoulders staring directly at Andrus. "So?"

The ruggedly built athletic man with a square jaw stared back. "You're taking too many chances approaching turns, you don't need to get sideways that early. You're running the revs too high as you reach for shift points accelerating. There is more low end push, the torque curve is powerful and most of your useable power comes in the lower range. I will say, you are extraordinarily smooth. I never could have guessed a young person could drive like a ballet dancer. That is your immense strength."

Kate's face lit up like a christmas tree. She had finally discovered something to do with a car that made sense.

CHAPTER TEN

KATE SAVES THE ANIMALS

"Mom, he's one of them, he's a Mathias and they reek of money but he's cool about it. He's nice, pretty rugged, doesn't try to tell me that I shouldn't do things, he argues logically. Jeremy Mathias. And he's not embarrassed by what I wear. He thinks learning all these martial arts is great, doesn't think I'm weird to worry about vulnerable animals. He's a year older, hasn't tried to kiss me yet."

Sarah asked, "So, is he cute, do you like him?"

Kate cocked her head. "Uh, sure, every girl thinks he's adorable. I think he wants to be some kind of cop. That's weird, huh?"

"But you don't---I mean think he's really cute?"

"Mom, I'm not marrying this guy. He's a friend and if I don't scare him away maybe we'll go to the movies or canoeing."

"Katie, how are you planning to scare him off?"

"Just stay down. Stay down and I'll look, alright. I've done this before."

Kate got Jeremy to keep his head down while she scouted the perimeter. She normally did this alone because she was unsure how anyone else would react to her behavior. They lay in the dirt behind a small hill surrounded by maple trees overlooking a farm yard. Two large arc lights bathed the yard in yellowish light, the whimpering of dogs could be heard.

"Kate, where the heck are we?"

She shushed him and kept scanning with the night vision glasses. Yes, they were there alright and so were the animals. But Jeremy was tiring of this little game. He got up on his knees.

"Kate, what is the deal here? What's going on out there?"

She sat back down in the dirt and pulled his upper arm toward her, then she half whispered to him, "Over there are some guys, they've been rumored to be training dogs to fight each other but the cops can't keep up with them so I did it instead."

"Jesus, Katie, what are you going to do? This can't be legal, you're not the cops!"

"I was out here before. I want to get their license plates and nail their asses. They have a couple dogs over there right now and I'm going in. Now you stay here."

"What?? I stay here and you're going to fight them alone? Kate, first of all that's why they have police, they do the fighting and arresting, don't be cuckoo. You're not armed, they may be and ----.""

But she was up and gone having pushed his face into the dirt. By the time he was up she had covered twenty yards. That's when he noticed what looked like some kind of pole in her left hand. Kate had been extremely particular about where exactly she brought them. She must have stashed the pole out here, he thought. Or maybe she brought it and he hadn't seen it?

He felt like a complete idiot. She was seventeen years old and was going in to challenge these bad guys? Could this really be? She could get hurt, roughed up or even raped if these guys were so terrible.

He noticed a slight fragrance. He sniffed. It was Kate, her hair. She smelled wonderful.

He followed her, keeping low, tracking her. Truly this was nuts. If kids at school knew she was up to this, oh my god....

There were three young guys and they had two big dogs. Jeremy couldn't see all that well but she was walking right in to a sort of farm yard, there were two bright outdoor lights, a couple cars. He could see and hear the animals whining, they sounded scared or hurt.

She walked right up to the three men who looked maybe early twenties.

Kate said in a loud voice, "I have been out here before, I've seen how you abuse these poor animals for your amusement. I made videotapes of your madness. It stops right now. I want to see your drivers licenses!"

Jeremy thought she was completely looney tunes. Three against one, two of them were big. What is she doing asking for their damn drivers licenses?

"Well, if it isn't Joan of Arc. This is none of your business and you just walked into big trouble here. Maybe you'll get a taste of what these dumb animals get right smart!"

Jeremy could not believe what he was seeing. They were going to take her down and do god knows what to her. One large guy strode toward Kate with his arm raised to strike her.

Suddenly she sprung like a coiled steel trap, the pole came whipping around and hit the big guy across his face and neck. The pole reversed and hit him behind the knees with a vicious crack. As the second blow landed she whirled, ducked a blow from a second guy and rammed the pole directly into his face. Blood and shredded skin flew everywhere. She whirled and turned hitting the second man hard across the chest knocking him to the ground. The third man pulled out a knife to defend himself but Kate was on him clobbering him across the head so hard he completely left the ground.

The dogs were whining louder and growling but one of the men made even more noise. "You god damn bitch, you broke my nose, I am going to rip you apart!"

He staggered to his feet and Kate's pole hit him across the neck and ear and she followed the blow with a kick to his groin lifting him off the ground.

"I have proof you have been killing innocent animals you putrid pieces of human crap. I should rip off your nuts!"

Jeremy could not believe his eyes or ears. Kate McGill was seventeen, a junior in school. She looked like a prom queen.

She reached down her leg and lifted a strange looking phone out of a long pocket.

The phone crackled. "I'm done here. Can you get the cops in. Right away."

Kate walked over to one of the animals which jerked away at first but finally let her touch it. Jeremy couldn't quite see but she had turned away from the men and he thought that was a big mistake. Worse, he had no idea what he was supposed to do? Help her, stay out of it?

One man started to get up holding his face which was dripping blood. When he talked the words were hard to make out but Kate heard him and turned around.

Jeremy only caught five words "...you're going to regret ever..."

Kate left the animal and walked toward the man. He was six feet and burly. Even bleeding he was a large menace. She stopped a few feet away. "If they don't put you in jail I may come finish the job."

Jeremy was stunned. The voice dripped icy determination and sounded much older. It was Kate's voice but it was like hearing a movie actor promise some threatening retaliation.

The man suddenly struck at Kate. She parried the blow sufficiently so it missed her body. She spun into a defensive crouch and then the pole struck his abdomen and Jeremy could hear the helpless exhalation. He also heard something break. Maybe more than one something. The bloodied man staggered, tried to scream in pain but she attacked him again with a blow to the legs and he went down.

The first man was half way up pulling out some kind of chain from his jacket pocket. Kate spun again in a fury and the pole creased his face on the other side. Teeth exploded from his mouth.

Jeremy could not understand how this young woman and what appeared to be a six foot pole could inflict such damage.

Jeremy climbed over a fence and began walking toward her but Kate saw him and held up a hand to stop him. She motioned "no" with her arm and her head. "No. Don't come closer." Jeremy stopped in his tracks. She was right, he wasn't needed at all. Kate walked back over to the second dog and tried to pet it but it was freaked and confused. It backed away. She tried again and the small animal relented. It was shaking terribly. Kate was down on her knees attempting to comfort the animal.

Behind her the middle sized man was up on one knee taking all this in. He could not see Jeremy, all he saw was this girl. He realized she had devastated all three of them. His reaction was ridiculous shame for having been beaten by a girl and it welled up inside of him. He mustered all his energy, his anger drove his body forward. He floundered but managed to stand and throw himself at her.

He began screaming things, how he would tear her apart and worse things. He was covering the forty or so feet between himself and Kate. The smaller dog tried to run but fell down. Kate turned but remained in a crouch putting herself between the man and the dog.

Jeremy watched her. She waited for the attacker and it seemed to Jeremy to take forever. The attacker was expecting the pole again or maybe a knife but instead she momentarily eluded his grasp, looped a nearly invisible wire over his head and yanked. As she learned in judo his momentum did the rest. Like a large fish on a line he flopped to the ground. The wire tightened painfully and suddenly he could not breathe, his oxygen supply stopped completely.

Kate got a good look at the strangling young man. She thought she recognized him, not by name, but he attended school in Orono, he played football and at present he was dying by asphyxiation. She looked down at him and watched him writhe in frustration.

The sirens started and red lights appeared on the road. She remained standing over him, his eyes were bulging, he was flailing at the wire but couldn't actually seem to loosen it. He was sure he was dying. She stared down with seconds ticking by. His color was changing, the sirens were bouncing off nearby barns.

She reached behind him and with one finger loosened the wire noose. He began gasping for breath. She glanced up toward the road and knew she had a few seconds to run but she wasn't quite ready to leave the choking boy. He was the one who threatened her, cursed at her, who likely lead the other two.

He looked strangely innocent now. Their eyes met, that was what she wanted. He had known total fear, his own mortality. That's what counted.

Kate reached into a bag on her belt behind her and removed a small package placing it next to the animals. She hurriedly turned and ran from the yard with her pole. She grabbed Jeremy on the fly and pulled him with her.

He could hear the animals crying and one of the men moaning. The police were arriving, one squad car and a backup truck. .

"Why aren't you staying, Kate. Holy shit, after what you did."

They were both running. He was amazed how light on her feet she seemed to be.

She didn't reply until they reached Jeremy's car. She pushed him into the driver's seat and whipped out the phone. She apparently had some cohort helping her. "Can you patch into their network? Good, I only need a second."

Jeremy began driving fast. She reached over and put a hand on his arm "Slow down, drive casually. It's ok. Turn down at this corner, you have to go right, then stay on the road. Don't speed."

The phone crackled again. "Is this an officer in the barnyard with the three men and the animals?"

"Who the heck is this?"

"Officer, there's a package on the ground. Please pick it up, it's evidence of what they have done to other animals. I shot it with a night vision attachment. It's useable as evidence in court."

"Who the hell is this?"

"I did what you see there. Those men are criminals and dangerous. They mutilated animals and need to be prosecuted."

"Who are you lady. You sound young."

"Did you find the package. It is two identical videotapes. Are they there?"

"Uh, oh, yah, yes. Listen, we need to know ----."

She cut him off. "What's your name?"

"Lieutenant Gallardo. Gallardo. I'm a county sheriff."

"I'll find you. Please safeguard those tapes. I almost died making them."

She hung up.

"Kate how did you almost die?"

"It was literally killing me to video that but I was told we needed evidence. The animals were nearly dead when I got there but I got enough."

"Jesus christ almighty Kate. I can't believe this. All of this....How, how did you find out, I mean, who tells you about these people?"

"Jeremy, I can't tell you anything. Nothing. Look, I'm really, really sorry

I dragged you into this but I needed some help and I was hoping you're tough enough to go through this with me. I know you don't know me very well."

He laughed a puny giggle. "Yah, well, that's a major understatement. You're just beyond belief Katherine McGill. No I don't know you. Where did you learn to handle that pole or whatever it is?"

She felt the energy seeping out of her and she was worried that she had made a huge mistake dragging Jeremy out there. "Jeremy, I train a lot. Look, I'm sorry for getting you involved but you didn't do anything wrong at all. You drove the getaway car."

Now he laughed louder. "Boy, I'll tell you this. I will not forget this night ever. Never, ever. You were so unbelievable. You have such guts, Kate. Such guts."

"Jeremy, can you keep this all to yourself. Please. This is something I had to do. Look, I'm not even all that sure why, ok? When I heard about abuse of this kind I just go haywire, I can't sleep. These men, they're so sick, I just...."

Now he reached over and put his hand on her arm. She was obviously very upset.

"Kate, what I saw you do, that changed my life, honestly. I saw you walk in there I was sure you were dead or worse, you know what I mean? You were just this banshee woman. I don't know, you were just scary in a great way. So I don't tell anyone. You just pushed me around a corner. If you can do that--what I saw, holy shit!"

They drove for a few minutes. She gave him directions until they arrived at the 494 freeway. "Jeremy, cruise, speed limit. Use the second lane, they don't touch anyone in that lane."

"Come on Kate. Where did you get that line?"

She waved off a reply. She was sinking fast. The adrenalin rush required had totally exhausted her supply of energy.

"Jeremy can we just drive home, I'm sorry you had to go through this."

"Are you kidding? Not go through this? This may have been the best experience of my life! You sleep, I'll get you home."

As he drove and Kate keeled over in the passenger seat he replayed what he had seen. Kate was five foot ten tops. One hundred forty, maybe one hundred forty five pounds? She handled herself like a total pro. Jeremy had been sure she was going to just get wiped out.

He thought, *God, what would have happened if I had run in there?*

CHAPTER ELEVEN

SARAH AND KATE ON THE ROAD TOGETHER

Kate spent part of each summer on the road, skating at shopping centers, entertaining kids in hospitals, giving demonstrations at baseball games and festivals. And when she wasn't skating she trained with weights, did aerobic workouts and bicycled long distances. Kate loved to train and develop her physique. She grew to appreciate what body builders did but found herself turned off by the eventual result. Kate became conscious of developing each range of her body up to a point where she looked extra healthy and well filled out. The true hard core body builders looked so extravagant, so overdone and very unnatural. Kate wanted strong but not freaky, muscled but not bizarre.

A year short of being a legal driver, Kate had created an income stream over fifty thousand dollars, saw North America and had fun as the gymnast on skates, the hotshot daredevil with moves that amazed onlookers and a young woman who floored the guys.

A summer of touring with Sarah always in the wings built Kate's self-confidence enormously. The young teen who got her kicks as a street performer sneaking into shopping malls, showing off by skating up the down escalator or skating backwards on one leg down the corridors dodging shoppers while being pursued by security guards soon turned pro. Why not earn money? Why not cash in on her skills and enjoy it as well?

Sarah greased the skids on the road. Compared to road managing on the Joe Cocker Mad Dogs and Englishmen Tour back in 1969 and '70, managing her daughter looked pretty easy. Kate loved the travel, kept in training, carried weights along to work out every morning. Sarah was delighted they could work out together. It was almost idyllic, mother and daughter sharing time and common purpose. Mom handled the schedules and books, Kate did the performing.

When interviewed Sarah said, "Kate is a treat to work with, she knows what she needs, we really don't often conflict. She acts like a pro on the road." Mothers and daughters who saw the interview were envious of this supportive, well-aligned relationship.

The offers had been trickling in, then became a small torrent. From her early teens Kate became sixteen, she did TV appearances and even a movie cameo as the amazing roller skating wonder girl. Kate loved appearing before small town audiences, they were the most appreciative, the least jaded. Sarah began avoiding the carnivals which could shuffle her daughter in with displays of two headed calves. Kate found a level where she felt comfortable, she kept her leotards modest, concocted outfits that allowed her body plenty of freedom without over emphasizing her curves. Kate took immense pride in her physique but not in her ability to turn heads as a sexual object. But, at sixteen Kate began realizing her physical appearance did have an impact and she had to admit it gave her satisfaction.

Gradually the mother-daughter relationship became more like two adults and Kate was to discover a new side to Sarah. But that discovery brought with it a revelation for Sarah as well.

On the road, Kate age seventeen.

Sarah sat on the edge of her bed in their Budgetel motel room. Kate had disappeared early in the morning for a run or ride and Sarah was feeling down, she wasn't even sure why? She turned on the television, clicked through the usual morning shows, then shut it off. The motel room was stark with few amenities, two beds and not much more. Sarah felt restless.

Suddenly Kate burst through the door as was her custom with a bright smile and dripping sweat. Sarah looked up, happy to have some company. Kate looked at her mother and became concerned. "Mom you don't look so happy. What's doing?" She waited for an answer not quickly forthcoming and then walked over to one of the suitcases and began digging around for a pair of special socks she liked for skating.

Sarah slowly responded, "Well, I'm just kind of working something through in my mind, that's all honey." Sarah heard herself say those words but her mind wasn't buying it. She thought, *Oh, this will pass, we've been on the road, maybe I'm a little worn out?*

Kate stood up holding some socks in her hand and looked closely at her mother. "Mom, you're upset, does this have to do with me, did I do something?"

Sarah had been fighting a serious issue for a long time but she had purposely held it back from her daughter. "Honey, it's fine, I don't know, sometimes I really feel like I got the wrong end of the stick. Paul is gone all the time, my father doesn't show up in my life until I'm fourteen. You know what, that really was awful. God, I'm realizing, here I get this wonderful time with you but I'm mad at both of them, your father and my father and sometimes my mother who was constantly traveling. I sometimes feel so abandoned!"

Sarah felt it building fast. She was angry, she stood up, her fists clenched at her sides, the frustration was welling up in her. Kate dropped the clothes in her hands and rushed to her mother wrapping her arms around Sarah. This was not the usual Mom, the accepting, friendly, warm woman Kate counted on.

Sarah burst into tears, sobbing, her body shaking. Kate tried to comfort her and this wasn't about to stop. Sarah continued crying, heaving, clutching on to her daughter. Kate was becoming worried. Was this a much bigger issue? She knew her mother had struggled with the men in her life being absent so much.

Finally after five minutes of the two women hugging, Sarah began recovering, her composure. Kate unwrapped her arms and held her mother's shoulders with both hands looking Sarah right in the eyes. "Mom, if I forgot you or, I don't know, maybe this is too much time on the road. I hate seeing you unhappy."

Sarah began wiping her eyes with both hands and shook her head. "Honey, no, no, this time on the road with you is what I crave, this is wonderful. What you don't know is I've given your father an ultimatum, this just happened before we left Wayzata. I told him he either gets off the god damn road or he finds a new wife. I let him have it with both barrels. I'm just reacting to this whole deal, I guess. That took a lot for me to level with Paul. And you don't know this either but I did the same thing with my Dad, it was a couple years ago. I surprised myself. I asked him why wasn't he more assertive contacting me? I don't care what the hell my mother told him not to do. Screw that, I'm his daughter, I deserve a father. And Katie, so do you and if you get married you deserve a husband who is present. You have to cut them some slack but you also need to talk about your needs. Frankly, I didn't when I was younger. I want you to know about all this, I guess. I don't want you to feel left out like I have been."

Kate wasn't totally surprised, she had wondered how Sarah dealt with all these absent people in her life. "Mom, uh, I really want to be the kind of daughter that is there for her mother. That is so important to me. So you read the riot act to both Paul and your Dad! I never understood why Dad had to travel so much, it bothers me but I also felt you had enough to deal with tracking me. This means a lot for you to unburden yourself. I'm just learning how relationships work. While we're on this subject, I think you can also raise hell with your mother. That's my opinion, I know she was absent as well and she is so demanding when she is around. So you should kick her butt too, if you ask me!"

Sarah now wrapped her own arms around Kate and held her close still crying but more tears of bittersweet joy. "Katie, this means so much to me, we've both had men missing in action and I'm finished with this nonsense. I had a mother who was always gone, a father I didn't really know and now Paul is out saving the world. Forget that crap, I want a husband or I start shopping for a new model. That's what I decided."

Kate began laughing and pulled out of Sarah's hug. "Alright, Mom, this is a big lesson for me to hear my Mom standing up so strong and telling both these men to behave. Honestly I've wondered why you didn't get pissed off with Dad? I need to tell you something now that I kept to myself. About six months ago he and I were off hiking in a park, one of those too rare times I got him to myself. Basically I read him the riot act, same issue. We were in the woods and this just welled up inside me and I told him how upsetting it was for me to not see my father!"

Sarah clutched her fits to her chest. "Really? You did that? Oh, Katie that is so great. Paul is such a wonderful guy but he is sometime so incredibly clueless. It is so important that you tell people how you feel. It's taken me way, way too long to get off the dime and get what I need. I feel so energized by this."

Kate moved back a few feet feeling relieved that her mother was recovering her normal self. "Mom, is this happening because we're on the road, is that why?"

Sarah smiled, "This is my lifeline, you and I traveling together. But it's time for me to get my situation fixed. Let me ask you when you talked with Paul, what did he say?"

Kate laughed, "We spent an hour sitting on a picnic table, he actually cried, he was all fit to be tied and he was stunned that I called him out. He talked about your dissatisfaction and said he had to work on being more present for you. And then, well, we went on to some other stuff...."

Something in the way Kate used the word "stuff" bothered her Mother and Sarah's face darkened, "Stuff, what kind of stuff, Katie?"

Kate hesitated. "Just things about me, how I'm living, It got worked out."

Sarah was having none of this evasive explanation. She walked toward Kate with a firm, steady gaze. "Katie, what did you talk about? I need to know?"

Kate's buoyant mood stopped. "He went after me about, uh...he is worried that I am going to get in trouble. You know, you talked to me about how you and your Mom often had to keep things from each other once you realized who Sal is, what kind of business he is in. You told me that more than once, remember?"

Sarah took Kate by the hand and sat her down on the bed. "Katherine, what are we talking about here? Tell me, honey."

Kate realized she had opened a difficult door to close. "Mom, I thought it best to not tell you about everything I did or was concerned with. Just like you and your Mom. You know, if I did something that was maybe a bit outside the law, well, you shouldn't know so the authorities couldn't accuse you of hiding anything. That is just like with you and your Mom. She kept things from you for a reason."

Sarah was rapidly losing her composure. "My dear daughter, this is just you and I in this room right now. What are we talking about?"

Kate began crying, Sarah wrapped an arm around her shoulders. "Mom, you know I have very strong feelings about animals being abused. Well, I am not comfortable just talking about it, I want to take action. Dad and I have talked a few times. You know those couple times when I took off for a few days this last summer? I drove down to Iowa because I learned about two men who were harming animals, really hurting them for some twisted pleasure. And, I, uh, beat them up. A guy I know told me about what these men were doing, he even had a short video tape that was just excruciating to watch. I went down there and beat the crap out of them. Just me, alone."

Sarah couldn't believe what she was hearing. "Katie, I know you have all these strong feelings about animals and now you talk about these wealthy people who waste their money. But you really did that, you tracked them down? I mean, how, uh, these are two men, how the hell can you physically do such a thing? You weren't using a gun or some weapon? Oh, God, Katie, that is so dangerous, I mean...."

Kate stood up from the bed and walked to the window looking out on the parking lot. "Mom, you know I'm quite strong, I always have been since I was a kid. I have gradually built on my natural strength. All these years of weight training, judo, all of that. I'm able to do this, I found them at a farm, confronted them, one guy threatened me so I reacted, I don't carry weapons. Not like real weapons. I carried a kind of long rod, a piece of wood. I learned how to defend myself with it, then I learned how to use it as an offensive weapon. It's an old tradition, in other cultures it can be called a Kwan Dao, a Nagamaki, Silambaum is another term, there's lot of names. That teacher out in Roseville first showed me how powerful a pole or stick can be. I've refined it. Mom I know you don't want to hear this and that's why I've not told you. But my teacher said he'd never seen anyone use this technique so effectively. You would be proud of me, I can cut a big man down to size with just a wooden pole."

Sarah now stood up and then felt disoriented. What to do? "Katherine, you can get killed, it only takes anger and a gun or knife, you can be dead on the ground. Oh my God, this is so upsetting. You are my only child, oh, that must sound so selfish but you're all I have Kate. I can't bear the thought of losing you."

Kate turned and walked to her mother. "Mom, listen to me, I never wanted to bring this up, I realize I'm your only child. All these years of training, getting up at 5 in the morning, hours of training, the three masters I've studied with. I can take care of myself. My judo master, Mr. Kudohara told me 'Miss Katherine, that's what he calls me, you have a gift, a genuine talent. Use it for a good purpose, that is your mission.' That's what he said and that's what I'm doing, Mom. I don't lose my temper, I am very judicious in approaching these problems but there are people out there who deserve to be punished and the police can't get to all of them. Now, just like you and your father, you and I can't really talk freely about this. I take the greatest caution but at least for now, I will occasionally step in to right a wrong. Just as you had to walk away from hearing what Sal's guys talk about, you and I need to keep this off limits with each other. I am so fortunate to have this gift, I can't fix the world but I can act when appropriate."

Sarah gazed at her daughter through tear filled eyes. Her little daughter had become a young woman but with a mission that went far beyond a mother's understanding. Sarah verbally stumbled, "Katherine, you are telling me, uh, you took aggressive action? I mean, have you done this more than once? Good heavens, this is like opening a closet and finding a whole other person inside. I know you are capable of unusual physical actions, but, uh, just how often have you pursued this tactic or whatever you call it?"

Kate stepped away, walked to her suitcase and pulled out two pictures. "I may regret showing you these but I want my mother, the most important person in my life, to know what her daughter can do when required. This picture, this took place in Iowa, and this one, uh, it was here in Minnesota two months back. I did what you see and I carried a camera to document what occurred."

With trembling hands Sarah accepted the two black and white snapshots. "Katie, you did this, you're saying? How the hell did you take these pictures, then?"

Kate stood hands on hips half regretting what she was doing. "Mom, I have trained since I was eight. All this martial arts preparation, the gymnastics, the emotional preparation allows me to take action. My teachers, well, they don't endorse my actions but all three ultimately try to stand with me. When it's over I snapped two pictures, that's all. These men weren't in a position to attack me after our altercation. I have met a few other women who can exact such punishment. We have a little society, the few of us."

Sarah examined the two pictures. She said, "You did this with just a stick, that's two men? And this, what occurred here? I can tell by the expression on your face now, you are proud of what you pulled off aren't you?"

Kate nodded her head in the affirmative and replied, "I confronted that man over his treatment of animals, down just below Hennepin County he was known to mistreat animals. I paid a call on him, went to his front door, I asked him questions. He got enraged, this is what came of it."

"My God, weren't you hurt, touched. I mean, what happened? He looks bloody and bruised."

"I don't let them touch me, I am well prepared, I don't start these things casually, I study the situation, I am methodical. You need to know I am tough. I realize you will struggle with this but I'd rather you know what this is all about."

This went well beyond where Sarah could have dreamed of going with her offspring. "Katie, this is crazy, this is scary and crazy. You know that don't you?"

Kate nodded her head but her face expressed committed determination. Sarah looked at her daughter staring back at her like an armed soldier. "Oh good heavens, do you know who you look like right now? My mother, that is exactly the look she has when she is determined to finish a task. I've seen it a hundred times. My mother acts like a soldier in war when she's on a campaign. When she would not tell me about my father, even when I threw a shit fit that's how she looked. You got this from my mother, it's running through your veins. Oh, God help us both. You are a fighter."

Kate stared down at her feet and then looked back at her Mother. "Mom, it's true, I have discovered a mission in life, I know it sounds weird but this fits me naturally. I am at peace with this inheritance from Helen if that's where it came from."

Sarah shook her head, "Katherine, people that meet you, they'll never know about this hidden part of you. And, that is exactly the way it must be. You cannot betray this soldier side to the outside world. Out of the question, this must be our secret."

Kate walked to her Mother and embraced Sarah. All the necessary words had been said.

CHAPTER TWELVE

CORY MADIGAN DISCOVERS KATE

Her eyes parched from a diet of videos and photos, Cory Madigan granted herself one slothful saturday in the beach house at East Hampton, totally alone, without time demands. Her marketing mavens made it plain the sought after *GloryDays* perfect woman must materialize or the entire campaign for the Gold line had to be scrapped.

Cory had no appetite for scrapping months of planning. Her presumptions about capturing their *GloryDays* girl had proved illusory. "Nothing should be this ridiculously difficult. Where is she?" Cory mused to herself.

She curled into a fetal ball, hugged the one Absolut vodka gimlet she permitted herself and soaked up the spring sun pouring onto the patio. One hundred fifty feet distant, the Atlantic softly broke onto the sand. She dozed, the drink sat untouched, her mind withdrew, and she finally detached sinking into deep sleep. Her faithful companion, an aging Sony TV broadcasting a music channel burbled in the background.

You could speculate that Kate would have been spotted someday anyway but fate provided an electronic whisper playing across Cory's unconscious at a moment when her ambition to complete the first big *GloryDays* puzzle had been thwarted.

"...upside down...now backwards...Bob have you ever seen anything quite like her...." If the announcer had said "it" instead of "her" Cory might never have sailed back to semi-awareness. Deep in her unwakeful mind, a thought about "...not another amazing whatever...."

But reluctantly releasing her hold on blissful peace, Cory worked her way back to awareness.

Applause could be heard. Cory was thinking, "It's in the other room, it's effort, it will be some high school senior in a fringed cowboy shirt from Wichita doing clever little tricks on skates."

What did it was "Bob, she's just stunning but look at those muscles, I've never...." Cory was up, knocking over her drink and knowing that was the last of the vodka. This little skater better be worth....

Cory crashed into a night stand, half out of blurriness, half out of surprise.

"Oooh." Her first glimpse of Kate was a muscular back upside down as she plunged off a low wall but when her body lands it's in a karate inspired kick, that spins into "...how the hell did she get to that position....?" Cory wondered. "That's counter to gravity, how on earth....?"

Cory was waking up quickly.

"Tape, tape, where's the god damn tape?" Not daring to remove her eyes from the screen, she rummaged blindly through a drawer, found a tape, jammed it in her VCR and stabbed record. "Work you piece of Japanese junk. Work!" She was aware of the ricocheting sound of her voice in the empty room.

Still riveted she frantically grabbed near the night stand, found a cellular phone, uncocked it, punched numbers hoping it was the right sequence and it rang.

"Be there you little putz, be there..." It rang four, five, six times and then he picked up. Having admitted he was there, he was stuck hearing her yell, "Damian turn on TV, channel 35, the stupid Nashville one...can you get it?!"

The price he paid for signing on with Cory included this. She was incapable of restraint in work. Call it an obsessive compulsive side, desire to win or just greed, Cory transcended all normal limits or any others for that matter.

"While Cory has a semblance of personal existence, pushing past barriers in her business activates an elusive hormonal essence of Jewish existential satisfaction."

That's how Damian analyzed Cory's mania for succeeding. While Cory herself was equally incapable of analyzing her own drives. Damian accepted her neurotic passion for achievement, even when he paid a personal price.

"Cory, we can get video tape from them, they're happy to do that because... just a second, where is the remote...what, 35? Ok, hang on..........oh, Jesus, I see her. Oh, she's just delicious...."

A few moments passed. Each party could hear the other's TV in the background. He spoke first. "Cory, she's obviously no model. Look at her shoulders. And her body is luscious. We've talked about offending our target 35-50 women. Serious body envy...that's the risk we're running here. Our ladies need a subtle 'schvitz' of the actual athletic experience. Beyond that, I'm sorry, Cory, but we're in the danger zone. Envision our gals in the checkout lines squeezing their admittedly trim buttocks while reviewing National Star stories about Andre Agassiz's problem with fitting his schlong into those tight tennis shorts. Our gals relate to true athletic excellence in Andre's shorts."

What even her old pal Damian, born Sidney David Weinstein, had never grasped was Cory's essential theme. Her Life Movie was not "How To Succeed In Business Without Really Trying". Over her five year search for herself, Cory recognized that as Marilyn Hertzberg became Cory Madigan, to accomplish her particular dream, her value system required total uprooting and replanting. Out went the "nosherai" of her upbringing, in came Arnold Schwarzenegger harnessing empirical feminist thinking by way of Taos New Mexico rebirth.

It had been a painful chop and channel of her soul. The wonder of Jewish transmogrification, wherein any personna is attainable, albeit at some price, allowed Cory to step up from Buick LeSabre to Mercedes to chauffeur driven limo. Why even set goals your parents could relate to? Aim so high it seemed implausible. Then aim higher yet.

Instead of Barbra Streisand in *Funny Girl*, Cory strove for the cinematic creator Barbra became with *Yentl*. But Cory's ideas grew in proportion and intent. Cory had plans for campaigns to change womens' entire gestalts, not just their pants.

She cut him off. "Look, the nose and mouth. Maybe it will be wrong up close but her features are so...oh, what's the word? Pronounced...prominent... Christ, I don't know...I love her face!"

Damian examined the skater intently. "Well, I've personally never seen anyone doing such maneuvers. That's different." His phrases fairly simmered with the promise of an effeminate lisp that never quite arrived.

"Cory, she's got to be a teenager, no more than 17."

Still transfixed by the promise of securing The Right One, finally, Cory had no sense of age or potential problems. She had seen the one she wanted. That's what mattered.

"Damian, she is our consummate athletic specimen: gymnast, street performer, ballerina. Now she just has to be a lot smarter than your average teen."

An announcer commented, "You know folks, we've waited weeks to bring this to you. This young gal, Kate McGill, asked we have special seating for handicapped kids...."

A female commentator cut in, "Not 'requested', Bob, 'demanded'. I know the organizers were running around trying to satisfy her list of demands. For a young girl, she knows where she's going, I'll tell you."

Cory cracked a tiny smile. "Yesss."

The first commentator continued, "...and this whole rig you see out on the floor with the jumps and braces, she designed herself and it's trucked in from Minnesota.......She's an original. I've covered sports for 18 years, never saw one like her."

Cory was nodding her head, hugging herself. "Yes, she could be ours. Our eagle."

Kate could be seen accelerating up a long ramp approaching bleacher seats from behind. The camera caught her lanky body stretched into a sling shot, tautly strung. She approached the uphill's apex unfolding her body into a 360 degree spin, graceful and languid.

"She can't make it!" zinged through Cory's mind. Along with the audience Cory thought she'd absolutely kamikaze on the steep stadium steps below. Having practiced her landing 50 some times and having crashed a few of those, Kate was ready landing on one skate joined by the other, her feet, ankles, calves, knees each accepting the jolt in a ripple. Her skates held and she bounded down the last few steps.

Cory loved her finish. Not a pirouette, not a dramatic hands over head applause magnet. Kate flew off the stairs onto the concrete floor rolling backwards hands on hips, head high, cool as ice. "Oh, she's just makin' me craaazy," Cory said under her breath.

"Damian, we must contact her. We must find this girl."

"I will find her Cory. I need a few hours."

Cory hung up and prayed she'd actually taped the broadcast. In common with most mortals, taping on her VCR was Rocket Science.

The tape ran, the images were there and Cory grinned. She pushed some marketing materials onto the floor with one hand and sat on her bed, one knee pulled up to her chest.

"My god, she is a muscular goddess, just perfect. And the face is ideal. Not a model's face but real, large features, sensational eyes. Oh jesus, she is our girl!!!"

It took Damian more than a few phone calls to find Kate McGill. She had no actual agent, her appearances were apparently booked by her mother... who, it turned out, had some music business connections of her own. After cashing in a few small favors Damian was given a number in Minnesota. The man who answered had been sleeping.

"I'm sorry, you are with what company?"

"*GloryDays*. We create women's fashion and athletic gear. We're interested in talking with Kate or whoever represents her."

"*GloryDays*? I know that name."

Damian was afraid he'd be talking to a flyover ignoramous off the farm. He was startled.

"Madigan...Cory Madigan...I have a friend in New York who knows her... used to be at Esprit, right?"

"Yes...yes, how do you know that, if I may ask?" Damian drew himself up to his full professional stature.

"Cory helped fund a small ballet company up in New Hampshire my friend started. And apparently she...."

Damian was startled. "New Hampshire...that must be the Black Swan, yes, I helped arrange the funding. So you must know Avery Brown?"

"That's my friend," Paul McGill responded.

Damian shook his head, "Boy, talk about small worlds. I had visions of talking to some ice fisherman."

"Oh, we have plenty of those and people who never left their hometown but I live part time in New York, well, I travel a lot and contribute to a struggling dance group here in Minneapolis. I'm Kate's father, Paul." Paul felt a pleasant rush of fatherly pride in saying it.

"How did your daughter learn to skate like that? She's just so confident and easy about it."

"Mostly hard work since she was 7, I schooled her in ballet, tap, modern dance...but she always was poised. Her mother is a natural dancer, Kate inherited that I'm sure and some god-given talent plus lots of guts. Kate has no fear like most of us."

Damian drank it in. Cory would go nuts to hear this.

"Paul, do you travel with her or...."

"Some, a little, her mother and I don't see each other all the time as I travel fund raising for endangered land. Sarah, Kate's mom, and I work closely. We support Kate, keep track of her."

"I must tell you, my boss, Cory, is just dying to meet Kate. We'd like to bring Kate and both of you to New York, or, or we'll fly out to meet her. Whatever can work. But Cory is an utterly determined person and you wouldn't believe the number of young Kates we've considered."

"Well, Damian, we can arrange it. Just be aware, our daughter has very definite feelings about endorsements. She's turned down lots of offers."

"Paul, we're after more than an endorsement. We need a girl like Kate to carry the banner of one whole line. She'd appear in numerous ads, likely multiple campaigns. I don't know your circumstance but this can be lucrative, quite lucrative."

Paul mulled over his words. "I'm not going to say the money wouldn't come in handy but you should know Kate is strong willed."

Paul went off to locate the women, Damian triumphantly called Cory. "I found her father. Here's a real twist, he is friends with your friend Avery

Brown. Kate's father helps fund a dance company Very likeable man, I'm sure we'd get along."

"Damian, what did he say, what was his attitude?"

"Positive, they're not well off, money would be a factor but he says this Kate has a strong will. Said that more than once, Cory."

"Damian, she's our girl. The one I want needs a brain, needs opinions for this to work."

"Cory, she's 17 or 18. Opinions? On what?"

"I'm not sure but my instinct is vibrating loud and clear."

"Well, Cory, shut off that vibrator until we can get them here."

Cory let the innuendo slide by. She and Damian had history between them.

Three days later, Kate found herself in the largest luxury suite she'd ever seen--- at The Plaza Hotel. She and Sarah were enjoying a breakfast of fruits and breads which Sarah knew must have cost $100 minimum when Cory and retinue showed up.

Cory dressed down for the occasion. She left a tangle of discarded dresses in a heap at home, "Not this...too clingy...not this...too formal...this one too much skin...come on got to be something...." finally settling on a low key, unadorned Donna Karan in muted steel grey, toned down makeup, modest heels, quiet jewelry. Cory thought, *She's the show, seventeen years old, midwest, don't push it.*

As Sarah opened the door an armada of five swept into the suite. Handshakes, introductions with Cory, Damian and three staffers. Kate purposely wore jeans and a t-shirt. She stood up from the breakfast table to shake hands singling out Cory immediately. Cory's eyes radiated calm purpose, her walk was more of a strut. Kate watched her face carefully. She thought, *I see why she's so successful. She's got that determination.* Kate had seen that look before in athletes.

Small talk, some coffee for the adults. Sarah watched Cory warily. She had a reputation for steely negotiations, Sarah read that in Vanity Fair.

Cory kept her distance, purposely gave Kate plenty of space. Kate fielded questions about her routines, where did she come up with them, how did she get started, what else did she like? Kate wasn't ready to sit down, she wandered, picking up pieces of cantalope, her beta carotene staple, drinking orange juice, eyeing Cory.

Kate mentioned she loved volleyball. Cory's ears perked up. Volleyball was on the rise. A near perfect sport for clothing tie-ins although the public was just waking up. But Cory had had her feelers out there, she knew a few names.

She asked Kate if she had ever played against any of the pro players?

Kate shook her head. "I'm not that disciplined. That takes tons of practice, a real regimen. I play for the jolt. I love the blocking, getting in close and the teamwork but I'm not into it for money."

Cory saw that theme. This was not about money, not yet.

"I play pickup games but I'm usually welcome. I play hard."

Cory knew she'd be competitive.

Kate wandered to the window looking down on Fifth Avenue. "I've been invited to play in something called just the Large Game. It's just a few people, the real fanatics playing for the pure joy. This year I'm told it will be near Telluride in Colorado.

Cory was ahead of her on this one. She pretended to be engrossed in her muffin but she was totally tuned in. Cory had been told about the legendary Large Game. It was the volleyball World Series but with no spectators, no media, held in a remote site which was never pre-announced. Only by invitation, only for insiders, only for the truly committed. No commercial anything. Just for the sport.

Anything that unique appealed to Cory.

"Kate, you must be quite good to be invited. I've heard of that event."

"I'm ok. They invited me because I go in committed. I'm not that great but I love playing at 110%"

People finished their coffee and pastries. Cory wanted to get started. "Kate, let us show you some stills and videos about our lines, ok?"

Kate nodded. For half an hour, Cory walked Kate through their brief history, brought out large scale reproductions of the *GloryDays* lines, explained who they marketed to. Cory downplayed sales and marketing talk. Played up their concern with athletic image, staying close to designs that worked for the body, explained how they hoped to spin off into more fashionable niches. No mention of her deeper aspirations.

Cory warily watched Kate and Sarah. "Are they getting this? Is it registering?" she wondered.

After half an hour Kate was obviously restless. She excused herself and walked into the bedroom. She returned buttoning her jeans and said, "Look, Cory, this is cool stuff, you're impressive, I'm kind of surprised you'd think I was right for *GloryDays*. I am what you see here. I like jeans, I'm not into sexy posing, I'm no Cindy Crawford or Anna Lee what's her name. I do this stuff because it's exciting, challenging. I'll work with you but you can't make me look like some New York runway model. I have a problem with my physical image. I'm overdone on the butt and boobs side but in my mind it's what you think about that matters. So you gotta somehow not push the chest out there. You want me, you show me for real but you have to give me some protection also."

Kate picked up a glass of juice, drank some, casually placed one hip on a table and started peeling a banana. For the first time Cory got her real magnetism. This seventeen year old girl had the cool of Humphrey Bogart AND the grace of Lauren Bacall. *How does this young woman come off so utterly guileless and completely at ease?* Cory was thinking. She also thought she could be a genuine sex symbol, not for her body but for the way she seemed to think. "She will drive men crazy."

Kate ate part of the banana, no one else was talking, waiting on her next statement. Kate sensed a pregnant moment. "So we can do some stuff. I like learning. I've turned down some things because it seemed like male fantasies about boobs on wheels or whatever. What are you expecting me to look like. What do I wear?"

Kate stopped. She'd said what she had to say.

Cory had been afraid of a physically gifted teenager with no mind, no moxie. Now her pulse raced, she was perspiring. *Don't blow this Cory, reel her in slowly. Be patient.*

At that moment only Cory had the vision but for her Kate embodied the elements she needed.

"Kate, Sarah, Paul," Cory needed to draw them in. "You know a little about us, our clothing, our company. What I'm after is a campaign that will start this way: Straight forward pictorials, graphics, videos relying on primarily on your physical skills, your obvious talent. Just exactly what anyone would expect having seen you skate. Put on our clothes, skate before the camera, be amazing like you already are, be our physical image. Maybe that's as far as we go."

Kate stood up and walked to a chair. "So, wear the clothes, do fashion shoots. What's your view of my body? Am I sexy, am I a mannequin?"

Now Cory stood up and walked around the couch pausing directly behind Sarah, placing her hands on either side of Sarah's shoulders. It was a purposeful pose. "Kate, what do you want? What are you comfortable with?"

Kate replied, "Do I have a say, some choices?"

"Kate, on a typical shoot a good art director or video director or still photographer tries out ideas, hopefully interacting with you. When we make final choices your sensibilities will be integral to the selections made. I've seen you in a workout leotard, you and your mother both have gorgeous figures. American women would kill for these bodies."

Cory emphasized her point by gently squeezing Sarah's upper arms. Sarah was surprised by Cory's gesture. But she liked it.

Cory continued, "Kate, we sell clothes pure and simple. If you can help us sell clothes, that's what we pay for." Cory wanted very much to go further but knew she must wait.

Kate was not satisfied, "So we're talking about *GloryDays* clothes, nothing more?"

Cory knew this could open the door or slam it shut. "Kate, there's more but we're just beginning, starting out together. I have many more ideas along with my staff but right now I'm concerned that you are comfortable with us, our company."

In a gesture like a young kid, Kate spontaneously dropped to the floor on her butt, legs straight out, then folded her legs and slowly began stretching. Like most things she did, her transition was effortless and unadorned with social grace. These people could have been her high school buddies, not powerful businesspeople. Cory adored her lack of concern.

Stretching her back muscles Kate responded, "Cory, I'll call you Cory if that's ok?" Kate was not looking up, she simply made the statement. Sarah was holding her breath. "My mom and I have read about you, read the Vanity Fair article, the one in Forbes, the New York Times one. You say things about the world, you have opinions. What about that stuff?"

"Kate, I certainly do have opinions, strong ones but I thought it premature to have that kind of discussion. Because you are...."

"Why, because I'm seventeen? I have a couple ideas. I'm not bashful. You said in the New York Times deal that you thought the Benetton campaign, the one with poor people and the car burning in the streets was a waste. Is that right?"

Cory's heart was racing. This was more than she could have asked for. This was four years early.

"Exactly, pictures of poverty and disruption. It was misdirected. I hope to create images that are positive, strong, purposeful using your gymnastic skills. Now, if we could surround it with low key but clear cut words about solving problems in our world, that would be icing on the cake. Yes I do have attitudes about what needs fixing but I was not presuming that you'd be concerned with----."

Kate cut her off. "Cory, here's my deal: Make some money from this, do some neat stuff, see some cool places. I don't want to be a butt in a pair of jeans or some guy's fantasy about sex with a teenager. Maybe I'll even want to take off my clothes but not now. I don't even know what I'm about yet. So I'm interested in statements. Your statements. I don't feel like I have a statement yet."

"Well, you're catching me offguard, that's the truth. I hadn't expected to have this discussion now. But, I'll say this, you want to hear my fantasy, it's this: You could represent younger Americans right now, your athleticism, your looks. I think our country is in trouble, has been for many years. Way too many people making rules, way too many lawyers writing complicated documents, way too many people in our governments trying to solve problems by passing laws. If I had my way, I'd make statements about those problems."

Kate had her head down near the floor in a stretch. She came up to speak. She sought out Cory's gaze. "So you're saying less lawyers, less government rules? Is that where you think our problems come from?"

Cory walked around the couch to the food table. "Kate, I believe it will be the biggest theme in America during the 2000's and beyond. It's the only roadblock we're likely to break down. It's not the only place our problems come from but I believe it's the next problem we must tackle. Lawmakers are killing this country. Strangling our ability to go forward. It's truly criminal. The rules no longer help us."

Sarah was thinking, "Whew, this is pretty heady stuff. She's not just after a pretty face." Sarah stood up to get some coffee. As she walked she asked Cory, "You're talking about controversy, not just selling clothing, is that correct?" Paul was nodding affirmatively at Sarah's question.

Damian was taken aback. He'd never really known Cory's plans included the political statements. He thought it was just Kate's exceptional acrobatics and appearance.

Cory responded, "You're right, I think we can make some statements that Kate's generation will feel kinship with. I will be quite satisfied if we can retain Kate as our physical image. I'm after a young woman with adventuresome spirit, guts, unusual athletic ability. Not just posing, that's what's been missing in our search. We found attractive young women. I wanted a woman whose actions make statements. That's Kate, in my mind."

Sarah look at Cory carefully. "So do you want this political spokesperson as well?"

"Absolutely up to Kate or anyone like her we work with. I'm not about to insert statements in ads featuring your daughter if she can't embrace the idea being presented. That's a given, here."

Kate sprang up from her stretch, arched her back, hands on hips and walked toward Cory. She extended her hand.

"Sounds cool to me. When do we start?"

Cory was flooded with feelings of relief and excitement. "Kate, Sarah and Paul, we'll draw up an agreement." Cory uncharacteristically grabbed Kate's shoulders and drew her into a bear hug. "And I'll shake your hand as well," taking Kate's hand.

Kate went back to her favorite window. "Cory I do have one question, it comes out of those articles about you. Where did you go for those five years?"

Cory had to moderate her elation, put her mind back in gear. "Well, Kate, in those years I went to find myself, find purpose, direction. My roots are in fashion but my soul is in helping alter our world. I've seen all the nonsense about living on a lesbian commune, becoming a cloistered nun, taking psychedelic drugs, living with a rock star. What you need to know, in my opinion, is I went out into the world to be educated and transform myself. It was a long journey, not always fun. It wasn't like going back to school. It was starting over for me and I was 31 when I left. I came back and started the company that became *GloryDays* so I'm 46 now. *GloryDays* is nearly 10 years old. I feel strongly we're here to do something useful. I'm about trying to figure out what I can do that is useful."

The room was very quiet.

Kate turned from the window. "Cool, I'd like to hear about those five years some time. Well, if we're done I'd like to go skate in Central Park. Cory, I know you have roller blades. It was in the Vanity Fair piece. Wanna come?"

Suddenly Cory arose. "Everyone, *GloryDays* staff, except for Andrea, please leave us." Four people obeyed quietly. Cory turned to Kate, "Can I see you undressed?"

It was directed to Sarah but intended for Kate.

Kate looked at Sarah quizzically. Sarah just rolled her eyes. "Cory, why do you need to see Kate undressed?"

Cory met her gaze. "I'm sorry not totally nude, underwear is fine, I need to see her whole frame without clothing. Can we do that?"

Kate thought about it for a moment. "Sure, why not?"

Kate left the room and reappeared moments later in bra and panties, no shoes. Cory's mouth dropped.

"You are the most stunning physical woman I've seen. My goodness, how much weight training are you doing?"

For ten minutes Cory and Kate exchanged ideas about correct training, how much was too much, what foods worked best. And then Cory reached behind her, released the catch on her dress and was also standing, facing Kate now both in just their underwear. Kate thought it was either the most self conscious act she'd ever seen or the most un-self conscious act she had witnessed. She wasn't sure which. Sarah examined her body. Flawless, for a forty something woman, just amazing. Flat tummy, perfectly rounded rear end, modest bosom but the shoulders and chest were like a sculpture. It was how she stood, half defiant, half on display. Sarah thought her hair was so perfectly matched. Very dark, almost black but looking completely natural, a hint of grey but it was shaped like a helmet but attractive and very sensual. Really brought focus onto her high cheekbones.

Kate still only saw eyes.

Sarah couldn't resist. "Cory, I read that you've had no help, no medical procedures. True?" She knew what the answer would be.

Cory's eyes powered in on Sarah. "Yes, Sarah, just loads of work, lots of time spent. I have to set a standard. That's one of my goals. At least until it all falls." Cory's laugh came from her insides. It was throaty and deeper than you'd expect. And Kate thought it made her much more human.

CHAPTER THIRTEEN

KATE AT THE UNIVERSITY OF CALIFORNIA, BERKELEY

Kate traveled as she grew up including visiting California with Sarah where her mother showed Kate all the places made famous in the sixties. They spent a weekend around Berkeley, exploring the campus and Telegraph Avenue. At the end of two days Kate found herself feeling like this could be her place to attend college. She knew it was still ranked high especially in both technology and liberal arts. Most of all Kate wanted to try living in California.

Sarah forewarned her about Berkeley being so different from the midwest. With a deep tradition of dissent, Berkeley literally attracted every major and even the most minor special interests. It contained a large existing population of homeless people, a large black population, a well represented Asian community, a huge and very vocal gay/lesbian community.

Kate had certainly been a bit shaky about this move out of Minnesota. She also had concerns about moving west as she and Peter would not be together except, perhaps, during the summer. She knew they didn't have a full blown romance yet but she cared for him. He had chosen to attend a university in Illinois. Both knew their separation was part of growing up but that didn't make it easier. They shared a tender parting moment when Peter put Kate on the train for California at Union Station in Chicago. They hugged and kissed, both knew this was young puppy love ending and their lives as adults were beginning. She watched him disappear as the train pulled out. Kate was excited and scared about her future. Sarah and Paul both thought Kate would profit by living away from Minnesota.

On her own in Berkeley, Kate vacillated between feelings of extraordinary first time freedom and being personally threatened. This was a long way from Minnesota. In the heat of August as she prepared to begin classes, Kate explored Berkeley. While always a walker and biker, Kate took advantage of her unusual skating abilities to sight-see. She might spot the occasional roller blader on a Berkeley street, only Kate attempted to climb the Berkeley hills on 'blades. And climb she did all the way up to Grizzly Peak Blvd, the road that traced the backbone of the Berkeley hills south to Castro Valley.

For a woman in good shape, the climb was strenuous, for most people nearly undoable. Kate enjoyed the challenge but in the heat she had to break one of her own rules about clothing. Since her early physical development, Kate recognized her well proportioned body attracted attention. Except for swim suits where she could not hide the curves, Kate normally kept fairly covered up.

This day, as she struggled up Cedar Ave. heading toward the hilltops Kate was forced to shed clothing to beat the heat. By two thirds the way up, Kate was down to shorts and a tank top and still sweating heavily. Northern California summers are hottest in August and September.

She became aware of a car somewhere behind her and stayed to the edge of the road to let it pass but the car hung back. Kate wore a tiny bicyclist's mirror clipped to her sun glasses so she could monitor traffic approaching from behind. The mirror was too jumpy to make out exact images but she could see a few youthful faces in an aging Cadillac. Part of the Berkeley culture was multi-racial. White women in Berkeley got used to plenty of Mexican, Asian and black faces. Berkeley, like its next door neighbor city Oakland, was well integrated. Kate decided to stop and let the car pass. Instead, the car pulled up alongside. Inside were three young men, one Latino, one African American and one white.

Kate was instantly aware of being more uncovered than she wished to be so she pulled the shirt draped over her shoulders down to at least partially cover her chest. The young guy sitting in the passenger seat talked first. "How ya doin'? Say we're little lost up here. Tryin' to find Tilden Park. Got a big picnic this afternoon."

Kate was wary but the vibes were not bad, "Just stay on Cedar, it will run you right into the park. Maybe a half mile."

She studied the faces carefully. Two had on sunglasses but so did she. Eyes could tell a lot and they were hidden.

"Say, missey, we're lookin' for some feminine company. This will be a fine, fine picnic. Drink, maybe some smoke. BBQ. What about it?"

"Thanks guys but I have to meet my boy friend, in a few minutes. He's coming back from football practice right now." Old trick she learned back in

Minnesota although there she might have said he was a hockey player. Right now she wished she had said he was a mean cop.

Still, no bad vibes to speak of. Kate knew quite well, when she signed on for California there would be occasional encounters and she was confident about taking care of herself.

The driver leaned over, "What can we say to get you into it, missey? We need company and we'd not like to ask again."

Kate watched the vibe meter. It was headed the wrong way. As she answered she pivoted her body as if to lean over and talk to the driver more directly. In fact, she was repositioning her feet so that she could push off downhill with her rear foot. On skates you're greatest vulnerability was in the first 1 or 2 seconds when you are moving slowly. Even with her unusual leg strength, Kate was helpless standing still. As she bent over she knew her cleavage would be obvious but she needed the crouch to be ready.

"Sorry guys. I'm spoken for. Gotta head home."

The person in the back seat now spoke. "Honey, you gots some kind of very fine lungs there. I got somethin' fine and lar....." As he spoke he fondled himself and his friends laughed.

Time to go. This was not an acceptable conversation. Kate did not hear much after "lungs" as she was headed back down Cedar Ave. Inside the car, the mood turned dark as the three young men realized their failure. The driver decided to get a little payback and follow the female skater down the hill. Cars were faster than skaters.

Kate quickly calibrated her position. On the street, if they pursued her, she was clearly an easy target. There were sidewalks to get her off the street but there were often more obstacles and much less room to maneuver. Kate built up speed immediately, as she skated she pulled her long sleeve shirt on and double checked her wrist guards. If she fell at speed the wrist guards covering her hands and wrists at least helped protect her. Skaters mostly worried about broken wrists. Due to the heat she had no knee or elbow pads on. She was poorly protected for trouble if she had to really hammer on skates.

After hitting half her potential top speed Kate wheeled around on the skates so she was now skating backwards at close to 20 miles per hour. That would be top speed for most skaters and only a few skaters would have the confidence to skate backwards on a city street in traffic. Kate felt tentative but steady enough to sustain the speed.

Her experience with urban skating gave her a big edge. She could maintain good speed backwards almost indefinitely, even with bumps and traffic and she could do most of that by using her little mirror to see oncoming objects. Average skaters were really bothered by cracks or bumps in the surface, Kate could normally absorb their interruptions.

"Oh Shit," she muttered to herself, "I got company." The dark blue '85 Eldorado was pursuing her and catching up fast. She looked quickly over her shoulder, judged some distances and turned to face the car again.

The Cadillac pulled up next to her. The three men were amazed. This woman could really skate. She was cool, confident and not panicking. They couldn't know what Kate felt in her stomach. Wafting out from inside the car she could smell a mix of liquor, cigarette smoke and marijuana.

"Hey missey, we weren't finished chattin'. We don't appreciate your takin' off on us. You understand?"

Kate was very busy making calculations. She could stop at a house and seek help but that seemed awkward. It was the middle of the day, broad daylight but no one was walking the streets in the middle class neighborhood. Kate remembered Buzz's gift was hanging off her fanny pack, a compact Fujitsu cellular phone. It was a calculated risk...could be an affront and cause more hard feelings or could scare them off....

Kate glanced quickly over her shoulder. She was approaching an intersection and stop sign but it was still 30 seconds away. As cooly as she could, she pulled out the cellular phone. Inside the car there was wonderment. "This bitch is somethin' else! Backwards skating, now she's makin' phone calls!"

"This is an emergency. I am on Cedar near Marin and I am being harrassed by three men." It could piss them off. It could scare them off.

"Hey Missy. We're not tryin' to rape you. You causin' us trouble and you in no position to give us trouble!" The faces were definitely unfriendly.

Fifty feet to the intersection. The car could swerve and drive her into another car parked at the curb or just ram her. Kate wheeled and thrust forward on her skates. She wanted to draw them deep into the intersection before she made a move. The driver accelerated to catch her, his heart racing.

Kate pulled them into the intersection. Just as she was about to leave the intersection she defied physics and did a spin turn to the right. As she hoped, the car was nearly on her and with all her musculature, she propelled herself off the straight line course and made the 90 degree turn.

The car traveling 35 could not turn or stop and hurtled further down Cedar. For a few moments Kate could breathe. They were gone. Kate then realized the good news/bad news of her situation. She had left Cedar and was now on Marin. Marin was easily the steepest downhill in Berkeley. Maybe even more precipitous than any hill in San Francisco across the bay.

If they gave up she was fine. Kate could handle almost any hill, even with obstacles like oncoming cars. If they turned around and came after her that could be even more than Kate could handle.

Now Kate was screaming down Marin, a street that cuts through the upscale Berkeley hill residences. A tree lined street where each intersection was like a catapult launcher to Kate. As she entered each intersection the street would momentarily flatten and then given her high speed the street would fling her into the air as the roadbed dropped away into the steep hill.

She could stop and try to hide. She could take a side street if she could slow down enough to make the turn. She was hitting 40 miles per hour and on skates that's flying. Kate took a monumental risk and rotated to skate backwards again. The jeopardy for her was enormous. If she fell backwards at this speed without a helmet or protective gear she could destroy her body.

The blue Caddy appeared two blocks above her trying to negotiate the hill at speed. "Those assholes. They're still coming!" Kate's heart pounded, she was really scared. She could skate urban obstacle courses like very few people in America but she never did it while being pursued by a car.

Kate could only hope they had no guns. Firearms were commonplace in poor communities. Many people had them purely for self defense. Young black men were cut down nearly everyday in Oakland and Berkeley. It was part of life. The young man in the passenger seat had a pistol in his hand although he had no intent of using it. A small 32 caliber but it could do damage.

The car hit the first flat intersection. The entire frame bottomed out, sheets of sparks flew and all three passengers were first thrown forward, then back. And then the street threw the two ton machine into the air. The driver wet his pants. This was more than he bargained for. The passenger holding the pistol momentarily forgot what he was holding and the gun went off sending a bullet through the floorboards.

Kate heard a shot not knowing where it went but her reflexes caused her to duck anyway. If she wasn't hit by a car driving peaceably through an intersection and if her assailants didn't either ram her or shoot her and if she didn't lose her nerve and sprawl on the pavement tearing her skin from the bones...if none of that happened she might be able to bring her speed down.

Skating backwards made it difficult to use the rubber stops on the 'blades to slow her down. So Kate was forced to pivot again, taking her eye off the speeding car and then jam the rubber stops into the pavement with all her might.

By now the driver was on the edge of losing it. Halfway down the second hill and fast approaching another flat intersection where the car would try to drill itself into the pavement, the driver had all but forgotten about the skater.

Kate said to herself, "If I can keep going that big Caddy will lose control but I gotta turn off onto a sidestreet!"

The driver saw it coming. An older car, not in the best of shape, the brakes were weak and poorly adjusted. As he jammed his entire leg against the brake pedal in a vain effort to slow their progress they flashed past Kate and once again bottomed out on the next flat intersection.

But this time physics could not be controlled and the careening car flew off the next landing at an angle and when the car collided with the pavement it was angled 20 degrees off course. Kate whipped through the intersection now behind the Caddy as it plowed into the road and then began a slow yawwing action that caused the front end to slide right and the back end sliding around to the left.

In a flash as the tires lost adhesion, the car flipped over and commenced a plunging roll downhill. The occupants were torn from their seats, the driver's door ripped open and the driver thrown out then under the mass of steel and glass.

The front seat passenger with the pistol lost his grip, grappeled to hang onto first the roof line, then the door handle, then nothing as he was projected through the windshield while the car rolled for the fourth or fifth time. His body tossed like a child's toy toward the curb.

The back seat rider was luckier in that he wasn't thrown out of the Caddy but instead endured a literal pounding as his muscular body was first plunged to the roof, then to the floor, then back to the roof as the car rolled and soared in the air.

No residents were walking on Marin so the Caddy missed pedestrians but destroyed two parked cars finally coming to rest half up on someone's property. Marin was littered with pieces of the Caddy, torn bumpers, fenders, window glass strewn across the road.

The driver lay bleeding, his neck sliced open. The front seat passenger slumped across the remains of a car door massively bleeding but alive. As Kate finally managed to slow and then stop, completely destroying her rubber stops that normally would last three years, she nearly fell over the rear seat passenger who was thrown from the car on its last roll.

Kate stood ten feet from him. One arm was twisted under his torso, his face turned toward the sky, one leg torn at a ridiculous angle. She skated to his body, her glasses had long since been torn off and their eyes met.

Kate's heart pounded so loud all she could hear was her own body. She was not sure what to do. Neighbors were pouring from their houses, some older women laboriously working their way up the hill from below. Stunned and shaking Kate stood still, her legs feeling like melted rubber. The young man gasped for air.

Kate realized she must be in shock. Her whole body felt disconnected, her legs would barely support her, her breathing came in uncontrolled spasms. Then she looked around her. All three passengers from the car were either in the wreckage or partially covered by pieces of the Caddy. Neighbors ran up to the scene, two of the passengers were moving, one was crying, the other moaning but no one knew what to do?

An older man said, "We've go to do something to help these poor men!"

Kate blurted out, "They were trying to run me down...." She stopped. It didn't matter why this had happened, now they were just victims.

Suddenly adrenalin kicked in again, Kate rushed to the nearest man in a white t-shirt and tan pants, his left arm and leg were wedged under the car frame, blood leaked slowly from his leg. The section of the Caddy weighed far too much for her to move, she yelled, "Here, help me move this fender. I need help!!"

First two women, then a man, then two teenagers rushed to her side. They attempted to lift the metalwork, grunting and groaning they heaved it and then the twisted metal gave and Kate dragged him from underneath. She nearly slipped twice balanced on her inline skates. The man remained immobile but his leg seemed to be ok.

She skated around the car wreck to the second man, the one who had been talking to her back up the hill. She began pulling on his shoulders, he was twisted in the door frame. Now others rushed around, by lifting on a door they freed the second man enough that he could crawl back a few feet.

One wheel of the Caddy still spun lazily. Liquids dripped onto the pavement. Most were black and dirty. Some were vibrantly red.

Then Kate felt like she would be sick. Not from the blood and mayhem but from the injustice and her own anger. She couldn't stop herself saying, "Goddammit, these guys were trying to run me down, I barely escaped with my life and here I'm pulling them out of the wreck? What am I doing?"

Kate looked down at her body and legs. Her tank top and shorts were streaming in blood from the two men she pulled out, her skates were stained red and one hand was dripping blood and partially covered with what looked like torn skin.

A woman ran up to her saying, "I live across the street, I'm a nurse, were you in this car?"

Kate suddenly realized she was about to completely blow her top, she was trying to save these jokers who moments earlier were threatening her.

She said to the nurse, "These three jerks chased me down the hill in their Caddy, the car crashes, they could have run me over and now we're trying to pull them out? Where are the cops when you need them?"

Kate hadn't heard the police car siren moments before. Now a second policeman arrived.

She heard a voice, "Right here miss, I'm a Berkeley police officer. What happened here?"

Two ambulances screeched to a halt, EMT's began scrambling out with stretchers to help the men in the wreck.

Kate looked around totally confused. She blurted out, "Oh, man, they were chasing me down this hill, I was terrified...." She looked over to the man from the back seat sprawled in the street ten feet away. He half spoke, "We's jest havin' little fun. No harm meant. You a fine lookin' woman. Nobody thinkin' nothing bad for you."

His eyes closed involuntarily. Then reopened, but only half way. His breathing became more labored.

Kate's face fell. She looked at the cop, back to the man on the ground and said, "Man, these guys should be prosecuted, they were irresponsible and dangerous." Her face softened. "But they're paying a price, I guess. This is so screwed up. I'm terrified, but they're beat up and bleeding. It could have been me instead---but it's not."

The policeman asked, "Miss, you can certainly press charges against them, if they live."

Kate shook her head, "Yah, maybe, maybe I will. Right now I almost don't know what to do."

The policeman put a hand on her shoulder. "You don't have to decide right now but I need to take a report from you. The district attorney will be consulted on this."

Kate sat down on a curb side stretching her legs out into the street. She felt like she'd pass out but then her breathing slowly smoothed out. She watched the medics and two firemen treating the three men lying in the street.

The policeman approached her to get details on the accident. Kate began explaining, "I was skating up Cedar, these guys in this car stopped, tried to hustle me into their car, I told them I would not and I took off on my skates. They followed me aggressively, I turned down Marin and ended up skating like a bat out of hell. I had no idea this street was this steep."

He asked, "Were they threatening your life, did they try to run you over?"

She replied, "They were actively chasing me in that car, one of them had a gun, I think, I heard a shot. Then the driver lost control, this is what happened. They were definitely chasing me, I'd say that was threatening on this steep hill."

The policeman replied, "Let me talk with a few other people."

A bystander spoke up, "I was working in my side yard over in that green house and I certainly heard a gun go off. I saw her and the car. I have no idea how she even stopped, she was literally flying."

The officer asked Kate, "How did you managed to stop on skates? That is surprising."

She replied, "I skate in demonstrations, I have a lot of training skating in urban settings, I could handle this hill but not with a car chasing me. I couldn't imagine what these guys were thinking hurtling down this hill in that old boat?"

The nurse reappeared with some first aid materials. "Miss, you scraped your face and arm, let me clean it up for you." Kate thanked her and sat still for the treatment. The nurse asked, "Are you pretty upset, I sure as hell would be, these guys chasing you down this hill like that. I think you should nail these asses in court, they were acting dangerously."

Kate nodded and thanked the woman. While Kate waited for the policeman she called Buzz and explained what happened.

Buzz said, "Katie, you should think about filing charges against them. I will help you find a lawyer out there. But just know, depending on who they are I wouldn't be surprised if they filed charges against you on some trumped up basis just to slow you down."

Kate reacted, "Buzz, that's crazy, I was trying to save my life, they were chasing me."

Buzz responded, "Katie, honey, just don't be surprised. They get a lawyer, they come into court all bandaged up, they may sue you for medical damages. Get the names and phone numbers of witnesses without fail. I'll have a lawyer for you by tomorrow. Katie, this is the real world, this shit happens, it's not fair or right. You can become the victim all over again when lawyers get involved."

Half an hour later she was free to go. Kate unsteadily prepared to skate down Marin, then thought better about it and chose a side street. She began skating slowly while thinking, *I am not forgetting this little incident. This is just so unfair, now I see how victims really feel. It is so screwed up.*

CHAPTER FOURTEEN

DEPOSITS

Two young men in their early twenties walked together along the breakwater at Cesar Chavez Park on the San Francisco Bay in Berkeley. As they walked both glanced around while trying to remain unobtrusive. The path overlooks the water, wind commonly blows in from the west, in the distance the Golden Gate Bridge and San Francisco stood in the fog.

First Man: "Have you ever actually met her?"

Second Man: "Yah, twice. We found each other through a conversation group on campus but she's rarely around. I know she's struggling to stay up with classes."

FM: "So, does she look, you know, amazing?"

SM: "She goes out of her way to not attract attention, like, physically. She is really nice and pays attention when you talk. But it's weird, I've seen her pictures all over---it's just odd to then be talking to her like she's normal. Just one of the girls. But something happened to her recently, I don't know when but she was chased by some guys, there was an accident, it was in the Berkeley Gazette, not sure about the Daily Cal? Anyway, I guess she's ok now?"

FM: "I didn't hear about that? I saw her picture in one of those slick magazines about California. Why is she going to school at Cal? I mean, why not like San Diego or Santa Barbara? She could cruise through those places but Berkeley is tough. It's tough for me."

SM: "Yup, me too. I was told they accepted her because she's who she is, really exceptional athlete, smart person. I will say, I know a woman who worked with her on, like, NT systems administration and she said Kate knew that stuff. She had real aptitude. You can't fake the technical knowledge."

FM: "But, why this, doing this with us? This is scary and high risk and,

101

you know, not legal at all. She is taking a big chance connecting us with these charities."

SM: "She tracked them down, found some way to screen the people at each nonprofit, she is not in the line of fire. But if we get busted she's involved that's for sure. There she is, coming our way down the path."

Kate approached them on a broken path adjacent to the water. The winds and breaking surf created desired noise making any conversation difficult to overhear or record.

"She will stumble a bit and we help her up."

As the parties converged Kate suddenly stumbled and fell onto the grass. She reached down and grasped her lower leg.

"Did you hurt yourself?" was said loudly.

The men kneeled down next to her. "So, we know two operations were successful and …."

The other young man shushed him. "No names, no nothing, these could be eavesdroppers around us."

The first man acknowledged being warned with a look and then said, "Ok, two done, right?"

She replied, "No, three, two day care centers and a medical clinic in Maryland. Really deserving and flat broke."

The second man added, "That second one was our friend down in Los Gatos, venture capital and real estate. What we moved he'll never even miss. He had the reputation for being stingy. Now he's not."

Kate asked, "And our friend in Texas?"

"We found a way in to our friend's place in Houston and he graciously supplied a suitable amount. Charlie the Gonnif, he screwed people around taking their assets, wiping out jobs in the process. That was a personal pleasure."

The first man shushed the other. "No names, nothing." The other acknowledged the comment with a grimace.

Kate whispered to them, "Ok, then we're complete. I'm very happy we could all pitch in. It pays to know good hacks. Thanks guys."

The first student asked Kate, "I saw you were involved in some chase, an accident here in Berkeley. Are you alright, did you get hurt?"

She smiled ruefully and shook her head. "Yah, it was in the papers. Three guys chased me down Marin, I was on skates. It was really scary. I don't think they knew what they were doing, just stupid behavior. Now I have to take them to court, I have a lawyer and sure enough they have a lawyer who is threatening me with a suit. It's so twisted, I was in danger, now I have to fight their lawyer. Frankly it gave some impetus to what we've just finished. I am pissed."

Kate's smile had a bittersweet twist. "It's my first taste of being a victim, I guess, and it's upsetting. But I'm learning from it, I will beat them in court. Anyway, old business, we accomplished something here so I'm glad."

She stood up wobbling. " Ouch, I really did hurt that leg." She flashed a broad smile. "Keep the faith. See you up on campus."

Tuesday morning dawned ever so normally for Alma May Morganfield. Up at 6 AM to begin bundling her two kids off to school, hoping for a few minutes over coffee for herself then on the bus, across east Oakland to Young Minds day care center. She had begun Young Minds five years before and in the past year received press coverage for the near heroic job she did in keeping it open.

Now things were pretty bleak. State and federal grants were about gone and most could not be renewed. A little money trickled in from the neighborhood but these were people without means themselves. Alma May opened up at 7:15 AM, turned on the lights, went to the ancient answering machine. She knew it needed a new tape but that required a trip downtown to find one and it wasn't in the cards. Two parents left messages, sick children and a third message from her bank from the day before to call. Sounded important. Two hours passed, she got a short break and called the bank.

"It's Alma May from Young Minds for Tory, she around?"

Tory picked up, "Alma May what would you expect your balance to be?"

Alma May shuddered. She thought she had a few hundred dollars left. Did she write a check she forgot? "Tory, honey, a little bit, few hundred, I hope. It's tight."

"Well, girl, you sittin' down? We got a deposit for Young Minds of $350,000."

Tory heard a croaking sound, then nothing, then a peal of laughter. "Tory, dear, you made a nice, fat mistake." The laughing continued. "Honey, you makin' my day if only in my dreams. Lord, I'd take one percent of that money." The laughing subsided.

"Alma May Morganfield, we traced it back, it was electronically deposited and that account is now closed at a bank overseas in the Cayman Islands. We sent them a wire message. They acknowledged the movement of the money and said 'thanks'. Alma May, at least for now this is *your* money. Now honey, what you plannin' on doin' 'bout this? As the closest thing you got to a banker I'm suggesting that you go get yourself a good cup of coffee and move on with your day, you understand what I'm tryin' to say? Right now you, me and one of the staff are aware of your little bonanza. If someone does something stupid like calling lots of people, well, maybe things will be different. Alma May, you hearin' me on this. Look, I'm just workin' in this place but if I were you, girl, I'd wait a good week and then start writing a few checks. I know you're dying for some new toys and books."

"Tory honey, what am I gonna say if someone comes in and questions me on this? That I expected this payment? Who's kiddin' who, here?"

"Alma May, you have an accountant, I know you do. You will call her up, tell her some money came in and that you want to make sure you are covered for taxes. Alma May, you got to pay taxes if required. You must. But after that, if we don't get any phone calls from the Cayman Islands, your little day care center just got real solvent. Now, one last thing, if I see any damn Eldorados or a Lexus drivin' around your neighborhood or parked in front of your little place I'm gonna be very upset with you. Or if I hear about that Morganfield woman is wearin' some new, very fancy outfits I'm also gonna be upset. But if life goes on quietly---Alma May, I truly hope you're hearin' me on this, girl---then life goes on. You get my drift? Far as where does this windfall come from, you look in the mail for a note or letter from some benefactor blessing your struggling little operation. And you know, there may be nothin' in the mail. Now I'm hangin' up and so are you. If we don't hear nothin' for a few weeks I'd start to breathe easier."

Alma May searched around for a pen and took a checkbook out of her purse. She carefully opened the check register to the current date. As she was about to begin writing she thought better about it and opened a drawer. She took out a pencil instead and carefully wrote in $ 350,000. She looked at the number and softly hummed a little tune her kids loved her to sing at nap time. Then she carefully closed the checkbook and patted it a few times with the tiniest smile on her lips.

Six days later Alma May found a letter at the day care center addressed to her. She looked at the envelope. It was handwriting she'd never seen. She opened the envelope. Inside was a short note.

"Dear Ms. Morganfield, we read about all your good work with kids in east Oakland. We are hereby donating a sum of money to Young Minds so you may carry on your efforts. With our best wishes, an anonymous party."

Alma May carefully placed the short letter back in the envelope. She held the envelope up to the light, turned it over, looked inside again. No return address, the postmark was hard to read but it appeared to be some country other than America. The postage stamps were colorful showing scenes in what looked like the tropics, places Alma May had certainly never been. Then she stopped to think. Perhaps she'd discard the note? Then she thought to keep it and discard the envelope? Then she placed them both in her purse, next she moved them to a desk, then back to her purse. Alma May afforded herself a quiet smile.

Across the country in Baltimore, Maryland two people running a walk-in health treatment center in a rundown neighborhood received a phone call. "Amos Setzer, this is Darien Johnson at your bank. How are you today?"

Amos never got called from the bank. There was little or no point as they had no money. The clinic existed totally off grants-in-kind from doctors and hospitals.

Amos had been up early, he was already tired. "Yes Mr. Johnson, what's up?"

"Amos, that grant you applied for just came through. Let's see, Health Grants Services, I guess that's a federal agency? Well, whoever that is just wired you $350,000. We double checked with the other bank, it's in the Barbados of all places. All clean and above board, the Federal authorities waved their hands over it. We wanted you to know your money is here and in three days, after we clear the deposit, it's yours to spend. But we think you should come down here and go over some procedures with us. We don't know much about your clinic, it's time we did, don't you think?"

Amos began coughing, bent over. He dropped the phone. His partner Shirley ran to his side. "Amos, Amos, what's goin' on here? You ok, sweetie?"

Amos pointed at the phone. Then he got back on. "Mr Johnson, we'll be down later today. I'm real glad to know our grant did come in. Thank you ever so much."

Amos looked at Shirley. "Shirley, honey, you ever play that Monopoly game when you were a kid? There's two stacks of cards you turn over one at a time. In the Community Chest pile is a card that says 'Bank error in your favor'. Honey, we just drew that card."

Amos sat staring straight ahead, one hand on his heart, the other on a desk. He concentrated on breathing regularly and then he began smiling.

CHAPTER FIFTEEN
KATE AND PETER BECOME AN ITEM

Time flew by, Peter Scalissi was finishing his second year at the University of Illinois, Champaign-Urbana studying Global Economics. His father tried to prompt him for a career in the foreign service or perhaps the FBI. Dad never made it down those paths, too caught up in lawyering and the Illinois political community but Daniel Scalissi managed to keep some connections to law enforcement alive. One of his old pals from Brown University now ran a super secret government agency dealing with the new field of data security in Washington and they talked frequently.

Aside from school Peter had one other thing on his mind: Kate McGill. She and Peter were certainly connected but not so they could talk about permanence. She had been in the news frequently, not always in the best light. She was quoted in newspapers defending hackers taking money from the wealthy creating an unpleasant bonfire of press activity, most of it decidedly negative for Kate. Kate was managing to struggle through the University of California, Berkeley but only by the scruff of her neck. Kate had two years to go at Cal and having come this far wanted to finish.

Peter struggled with thinking of Kate as his girl friend when they really did not get all that much time together. Peter dated, had no shortage of interested young women attracted to him but Kate kept re-entering his mind and life. He walked into a small barber shop off campus, sat down to wait for a haircut and picked up a popular fan magazine. On page thirty eight, there was Kate being interviewed with pictures of her on roller blades. Peter thought she looked so fresh and delicious, Peter thought, *I am attracted to her like a super magnet.* He studied her pictures and the text. Another student sitting nearby saw the pictures and said, "She is really something isn't she. What a totally cool chick."

Peter could only nod his head and smile in agreement. He wanted to tell this guy that Kate was his girl but that seemed somehow wrong. They weren't yet at that stage Peter and Kate had a distant boy friend girl friend relationship but nothing was written in concrete. They managed to see one another a few times a year, more during the summers but even then Kate traveled doing skating exhibitions, Peter had a summer internship with an investigation unit of the Chicago police which he found intriguing. They talked often but their closeness teetered back and forth as a true bond had not been finalized.

Helen smelled big trouble for her darling granddaughter. Handsome Peter, his self confidence brimming over, gifted with a good mind had to be sexual trouble for Katie, that's how Helen saw it. She just knew they were doing it like bunnies every chance they got.

The actual relationship between Peter and Kate turned out to be far more complex. Kate's downtime rarely coincided with Peter's, she came under constant pressure from school work, occasional performances, periodic media blitzes and now the federal government's hovering interest. But most critically, during two years of college when the stars did somehow line up Helen's granddaughter enforced a surprisingly tough policy with Peter on sexuality they both craved. It was killing him that his college friends were convinced Peter had Kate handing out her favors left and right when he knew his dream girl required careful, prudent handling.

Kate was not about to be his score or anyone's without stepping through a rigorous vetting process. Kate couldn't be more human having strong physical drives but she just knew there had to be genuine feelings---there had to be romance. She knew the romance was attainable and would be sweet with Peter, she found him unfailingly attractive and fun but it had to be right before it became outright sexual and that was that. Helen made it abundantly clear that Kate getting involved with Peter posed all manner of complications for the Harendt-McGill-Torpaydo clans. Helen could not know that Kate had no intention of allowing her grandmother or anyone to intercede in her personal life. Finally the summer before her junior year during Kate's ten city tour in the Midwest Peter's patience paid off. Kate made her decision, invited him into her hotel room, she reclined on the bed, sensually bathed him in kisses and in a smoky voice said, "My good pal, Peter, it's time we took the big step we both want."

Kate began seductively unbuttoning herself. "I've been waiting for this moment, let's make it wonderful!" Peter required no prompting and for both of them it was very much a pent up dam crumbling under pressure.

Fortunately the experience was not a letdown. Their shared lovefest prompted Peter to begin one new regimen back at school. One of his good friends noting the satisfied grin on Peter's face after returning asked him, "So was it incredible?"

Peter replied, "Awesome, wonderful but that girl is so damn strong! I will be lifting weights for the next six months."

Peter began appearing in a few tour photos circulated among the families involved culminating in "that picture", a snapshot of Kate wrapped around Peter, her idyllic smile pouring forth like the reddest new picked strawberries. Peter betrayed the "...oh my god, this is really happening, Kate is really with me..." look. Sarah thought Peter looked like a fourteen year old who just discovered chocolate malteds. Sarah also allowed herself the pleasure of seeing her only child in the arms of a young man Sarah respected and cared for. This also meant Kate would be off the hook with the phalanx of young and older men who lined up to attract Katie's interest. Kate had her first, serious boyfriend and Sarah began to relax. It had been too many years worrying how her daughter would get over that important sexuality barrier and become a young woman.

Perhaps most important to both young people was a deep, abiding emotional bond they felt for one another. They wanted to share experiences, be with each other, clutch on to each other's hands. Kate had never been a clinger but now she loved hooking her arm into Peter's, mussing up his hair and she finally got a chance to shave him. Kate always had a thing about shaving her guy but there had been no guy. It took almost an hour in a Denver hotel room, Peter explaining how he did it and then Katie studiously, carefully heating up his face with a wash cloth, applying shaving cream and then stroking across his handsome face. Peter became aroused with her straddling him in a half open robe while she shaved him but Kate slapped Peter on the cheek, "No way, hot stuff, I am going to give you the best shave you've ever had. That's the job here. Then maybe we'll see...."

The couplehood feelings emanating from Kate and Peter circulated all through their families. Dan Scalissi and his wife Lisa began talking about the affair which even showed up in two fan magazines. "Who is Kate's special guy? He's Peter Scalissi from Chicago, a student at the University of Illinois. She must be treating him right, he's always beaming. Look at that silly grin."

Lisa looked across the dinner table at her husband and asked, "So, what if these two kids get serious, talking about marriage?"

Dan's countenance darkened surprising his wife. She said, "Honey, our Peter married to that goddess with brains? Are you kidding, she is such a delight. I ate breakfast with Katie up in Minneapolis, she is kind, friendly, so funny and look at that face. Grandchildren would be perfect."

Dan nodded and smiled but was reluctant to disclose what his childhood pal Sal told him. Dan replied, "Honey, I love her like you but this young woman is such a handful, she's a powerhouse, not just her athletics, you've read the interviews with Katie. This is a truly committed person who has it in her mind to change the world and there will be conflict around her forever. Her feelings about defending innocent animals---just that issue can blow up anytime. She's serious, dedicated, deliberate---and I'm concerned that she will not back down even in the face of legal actions. As a lawyer, I know what this can lead to."

Lisa's demeanor altered. "Dan, are you saying Peter should not be with her, will this drag him into bad things?"

Dan stood up from their breakfast table and walked to a window, one hand in his back pocket, the other on a window frame. "Honey, Sal called me to pass along some scuttlebutt. So remember this is not verified and it's from a guy who has, well, you know, Sal's connections. Sallie has it on good authority that the FBI is on her case, they are tracking Katie because of some hacker incident when money was moved from a wealthy person's bank accounts. It went to a couple good causes but it's breaking and entering no matter who gets the money. Then there are these scumbag animal attackers who got the crap beat out of them and it was a woman who fits Kate's profile. This is scary stuff and sometimes the FBI can't just put it aside, they are obligated to act. It's the law."

Lisa shuddered, this was not the news a happy mother wanted to hear. "Danny, what do we do? I mean, this girl is so vibrant, happy, beautiful, a delight. Peter can't just walk away from her?" The look on her face made Dan terribly uncomfortable.

"Lis, listen. This is not a storybook romance. Our Peter must look out for his future, he could be implicated in some nasty business, his life could be ruined if Kate is out there pulling some prank, no matter how well intentioned."

"But do you really think Katie is actually beating up animal abusers? Is she breaking the law left and right?"

"Hon, Peter has confided in me that Katie has been seriously studying under a Judo grand master for seven years, this is not a young woman who gets scared. And he says Kate means it when she takes a position. Frankly she scares him sometimes."

Both the Scalissi's stopped talking and looked away from each other. Lisa was starting to understand the darker side of Peter's Kate.

CHAPTER SIXTEEN
HOTEL JOB

"So what do you know so far, Aggie? Look I'm a big girl, are you sure that Katie is even involved?"

Sarah McGill balanced uncomfortably on one leg on an outdoor bench in her home trying to replicate a yoga pose she learned at The Marsh, her health club. Somewhere out there her daughter was, apparently, running a school for social disturbance and Sarah thought it was going to crash around her ears.

Aggie Roemer was calling from mid-town Manhattan. "Sarah, let's not jump to conclusions. I know this much there's this big fashion show, real high end, Gucci, that other Italian company, Prada. Fancy, expensive stuff. Apparently rumors floating around, published in the New York Daily News, tabloids, all of that. They're saying this anti-luxury guerilla group is going to raid this show, turn it upside down. Now, I saw Katie two nights ago outside a restaurant with a few other kids and she mentioned this show. Maybe she's just going to attend?"

Sarah slapped her own forehead. "God, Aggie, you know from borscht about fashion. Prada, Gucci, that's what Kate is up in arms about. Pricey, real pricey, high grade stuff but it's skirts for $700, handbags for $500. Most of us think it's lunacy but women will spend that. And that's the low end, it gets lots more expensive. But I don't get why that show would get her so up in arms?"

Aggie was quiet. Sarah could hear car traffic, a few horns in the distance. "Sarah, it's not just fashion, it's also new technology mixed with fashion. Computer graphics mixed with models. Katie would know how to wire this up. She's really got this thing about networks, she spent most of last year at Berkeley figuring out network administration. I know she's doing that homework in depth. I am familiar with those concepts and when she talks about networking she speaks from knowledge."

The figure outfitted head to toe in a clinging grey bodysuit moved in total silence. She wanted nothing hanging loose or catching on objects. On her head, riding up on her hair she wore night vision goggles covered by a floppy hat. As she took steps her carefully padded feet made no noise. Her noiseless progress brought her to a small room bathed in nearly complete darkness. She reached into a pocket, retrieved a small cell phone and punched in a number. She rested her back against a wall in the sub-sub basement of the Sheraton Hotel. A voice answered.

"This is Abe, who's calling?"

"It's Eleanor. I'm here. Run me through it fast, ok?"

"Eleanor, give yourself at least ten minutes. There will be two NT servers, a Solaris workstation, mostly Cisco hardware on the network. I have no idea about cabling, none. But you don't care. I've been in, poorly protected. No firewall at all. This whole thing is just for the day, no thoughts of significant redundancy. You can do this from outside."

"No, I'll do the insertions and alterations here, they're small. We're only talking about some audio insertions. The graphics could be harder but it's just files. I have GIF's and some simple graphics. It will only be up there for a few seconds. Ok, I'm going. My mouth is watering. Thanks."

"Eleanor don't be a total surgeon. Just drop them in and get the hell out of there."

She clicked off the cell phone and pocketed it. She pushed on the swinging metal door which opened for her. Inside computers idled, network routers glowed. She heard disc drives kick on and off. She padded over to the NT server, touched the keyboard and the monitor lit up as she expected it to.

As she had been told, a small file contained the simple text document. The slides and graphics were more complex. She realized she'd need to examine each one, there were about 30. She computed the time, there was enough. Each graphic or GIF had to be examined carefully. She selected only four and substituted her own. The text for the teleprompter posed separate problems. After two minutes of scanning she selected only a few lines and altered them.

Footsteps approached the door. She felt panic rising. The room was dimly lit and she had not looked for hiding places. The footsteps were still coming. She remembered the night vision goggles and slammed it down over her eyes. The footsteps were nearly at the door. She scanned madly. One chance, a rack of routers standing tall enough to protect her. If they turned on the lights she was screwed.

She dashed for the rack. The door opened, a man in maintenance clothing entered and stopped. She prayed he wouldn't go for the lights. She reached behind her back and rested her left hand on the Taser gun. She knew it was supposed to stun but she'd never really used it.

He looked confused. Maybe this was the wrong room? She found herself praying for him to turn around. She'd never really prayed for anything, even success. The maintenance man was just standing in one spot. She gripped the Taser and loosed it from the holster. She couldn't understand why he was just standing there? She was sending thoughts that he should leave but, of course, she knew that couldn't possibly work.

The man's right hand shot up to his face almost involuntarily and then he was gone. She shook her head in wonderment. Was it her mental manipulation or just luck?

She rose from her crouch and padded across the floor. She went back to the keyboard. The files were listed in the system file manager. She could tell no one was paying attention to security. The only files in the file manager pertained to the show. She opened each one and scrutinized the content. She wanted to be sure her substitutions fit in the rhythm of the program otherwise they'd just shut it all down right away. Then she slipped a disc in the drive, scrolled to her companion files and made the alterations. The actual removals took four minutes.

She closed the various files. The sys admin, if there was one, would see nothing new. She buttoned everything back up and then realized she had overlooked telltale date and time adjustments. So she updated all the files with the current date and time. Now the admin would not immediately see there had been alterations. It took another precious two minutes but she erased her presence. Then just as she had been told she made her exit using NT Windows fatal back door. Studying all the NT security docs paid off.

She no longer existed.

The call from Women's Wear Daily to Rolling Stone caught the editor off guard.

"Did you see it yet?"

"I've been in meetings. Jann wants all we 33 year olds to act like 23, advertisers want this younger----."

"Jesus, you didn't see it or hear it did you?"

Silence.

"At the Sheraton, Prada, Gucci, all of them, blown away, just destroyed."

"What in the hell are you saying?"

"Listen to me. They're five, six minutes in, suddenly we're hearing '... the outfit she's presenting would buy dinner for two families of ten for nine days in El Salvador...' People thought it was planned, then a joke, then who knows? Then this graphic, should have been this gorgeous handbag, instead it's a picture of an old woman sewing, her face all wizened staring into this horrid light and the voice stumbling around but it comes out something like, '...she's almost sixty, she's infirm, she must work, that $480 handbag is her work, seam by seam. She earned less than six dollars....'"

"God, someone got in there. Oh, shit, there will be such hell to pay."

"More, then it's normal, the girls are out there, trying to look ok, you know. People start to breath again. They had no way to preview the multimedia stuff it's all on disc, just press start and it runs or that was the idea. So do they stop the whole show and check the disc? People were apparently just running around backstage yelling and panicked and you know the models who are so flighty are freaking. And people think maybe it's over. Then this canned audio, it was apparently supposed to be a series of short greetings from the major designers. Instead, it's this flat, toneless recitation about how much Calvin Klein earns, how much the Gucci people get, like that. And then this video, this was something, really something. It's this computer generated scene, a fashion runway, an audience, the girls strutting and this figure suddenly appears and throws this ax sort of thing. It was a take off on the Apple commercial back in '84. But it was so incredibly stunning. Someone gifted did this because it just captured the absurdity of all this overpriced nonsense. There was this groan like coming from inside all these people. This huge groan. Like someone took a meat cleaver and slit them wide open."

"So didn't they stop it?"

"How, where, when? The first couple things you really couldn't know if it was real or a fake or a joke or one of those Bennetton deals with the awful, grimy pictures. Oh, those pissed off so many people. Just denying any value to all these expensive clothes. No one has ever attacked the fashion industry at its core. No one ever broke into a show like this. It was most devastating because it wasn't like some smarmy protest. It was pure guerrilla theater all the way and really effective."

"So, then what?"

"Well, the video finished, oh, oh god, yah. So these last couple graphics appear, the girls are out there in the final outfits and suddenly this huge, monster sign comes up, took over the whole screen, most of the stage. It said, 'They're out there starving. And now it's your turn to stop this nonsense.' That's what it said."

"What did the audience do?"

"People left, they weren't talking, most of them. Some woman got up on stage with the mike and began lashing out at this infamy but even some of the important people just walked out, just wanted to get away. And within five minutes the room was nearly empty. People were embarrassed, confused."

"Is this an insider, is that possible?"

"God, who knows? But it was so inspired, really spare, not overdone. No signs, chanting, sixties bleeding heart shit. This was like a shiv in the chest. A blow, a real crushing blow coming out of nowhere. No warning. Just this straight shot."

CHAPTER SEVENTEEN
CORY MEETS KATE AT BEN BENSON'S STEAK HOUSE

Cory Madigan picked a restaurant she liked but which fashion people would never think twice about. It served steaks. Huge, juicy, delectable steaks so no model could even think about eating at Ben Benson's Steak House. But Cory loved the quality food and was amused by all the testosterone flying around. She requested and was given the furthest rear table. Cory hunkered down, read two reports, checked messages via a cell phone and waited. She was prepared to wait a long time.

But only a few minutes late her appointment showed. Cory knew it was she because at Benson's to reach the rear room one must travel along the long front side, make a turn and cross the entire main room.

The murmurs followed her like shark fins in warm water.

"Oh, Jesus."

"Good lord, who is that babe?"

"Oh my, just look at her!"

"Did she just walk in off the street looking like that?"

"Is this some kind of stunt? She's spectacular!"

Kate strode across the restaurant's aged wooden floor dressed head to toe in a form fitting shimmering purple body suit covered with a *GloryDays* top in rich grey which engulfed her breasts and shoulders glorifying every square inch of her femininity. On the bottom more *GloryDays*, body hugging pants in svelte black. Her longish hair touched her shoulders topped by a silver long billed baseball cap emblazoned with the slogan, *Spend Your Money On Nature*.

Cory's heart raced. This was her girl out strutting her stuff in New York and looking ever so grand. The entire dining room followed her progress including a dozen of the wait staff and half the bar who had to walk around a corner to watch. From one side of the room all the way across to the front door faces were eagerly peering at Kate.

"Nice entrance, this your usual style, Katie?"

Kate smiled smuggly. "Mom said I only have a couple years, might as well get the mileage. But here I'm getting the loudest wolf whistles from the women. In L.A. the women would not acknowledge my existence. Here, particularly the butch gals, a couple of 'em, literally cheered me on from across sixth avenue.

Cory took Kate's hand and squeezed it. Cory wanted to enjoy every moment of this. She could put 50 professional models in her clothes and not one would vibrate like Kate McGill. There wasn't one set of eyes in the whole house looking anywhere but right at her table.

Kate remained standing for a brief moment and then folded her form into the chair. Cory swore she heard the whole room of men collectively sigh. And Cory had to admit she'd never seen a woman exhude such pungent sexuality without pouting or posing. That was Kate's entire essence. She walked and her spiritual aroma trailed behind.

"I'm starving and my mom said I can eat side dishes here, it's all top quality. Mom knows her restaurants."

"You don't want steak or fish?"

"I'm a side dish freak, Cory. I want a few ounces of fish, the rest is salads, vegetables, soup if they have it."

"Tell you what Katie, I'll order fish, you take part, alright?"

For a fleeting moment Cory gazed at Kate and saw the eighteen year old kid. She could not imagine a young woman to be more enchantingly unaffected. Suddenly a terrible chill churned through Cory and her body felt caustically cold. Cory didn't have to think about this reaction, she had feared it for weeks since Kate became a possibility.

Cory feared exploiting this magnificent creature like taking advantage of an adolescent animal where the core was still forming. Cory wanted to believe that Kate's inner soul had settled, that Kate honestly was prepared to do battle. Cory had only a second to study Kate's visage.

Cory realized she still had Kate's hand and she was applying significant pressure.

Kate didn't look up from the menu. She leaned in just a bit to Cory and whispered, "Cory, I'm prepared. Don't be anxious for me."

That was it.

Cory felt her heart stop or so it seemed and then Kate looked up. Never had Cory seen such radiance in a smile. This young woman had the aura of a goddess.

Cory had to know what Kate knew?

"You heard about the show? Someone terrorized the fashion business. Broke in and supplied their own dialogue and images."

"I heard something on a taxi radio as I walked here. Something about interrupting some awards deal? Was that for the fashion people?"

Cory admired her cool. Like nothing happened at all. An awards deal, that's all it was?

Cory explained, "This was one of the important shows of the year and particularly because the Italian houses were fully represented. Someone apparently substituted some tapes, I don't quite know how it was done but the audience heard and saw things which said all this money could be a lot better spent."

Cory watched for her response. "Well, Cory, I'd say the fashion business is way overdone. Who cares what the latest styles are? Or, at least I don't pay much attention."

Kate began digging into the bread basket containing New York style rolls which she loved. A waiter came by and she ordered two appetizers, salad and soup. Cory let Kate soak up some food.

"Katie, you're in touch with computer people, isn't this prank the type of thing hackers might do?"

Kate was hard at work on her Bensons salad and third soft roll. "Not a prank, not by my standards. Pranks should be fun and make a point. This sounds like it just made a point. The computer side, ummm, depends on what was altered and how."

Cory was hunting for a truer response and Kate was backing away. Both women worked on their salads, Cory ordered a glass of Cabernet. A woman approached the table who Cory vaguely recognized.

Ms. Madigan, I'm Teddy Stoddard from the Daily News. Sorry to interrupt but I was curious to get a reaction on the blowup at the show today."

"Well, Teddy, I honestly don't know all that much. Our lines are pretty far removed from high fashion as you may know. Let me turn the tables, what actually took place?"

Teddy, a young reporter felt flush with news. "What we heard at the paper thus far was someone broke into a computer area in the basement where the multimedia equipment was stored and physically altered files. When they ran the program certain graphic images were changed, some dialogue was altered. I wasn't there but my office mate attended and she said the room cleared out like a bomb went off."

"Teddy, have they accused anyone? Cops find out anything?"

Kate looked up from her salad momentarily. Teddy now could see her face and a glint of recognition crossed her face.

Teddy replied, "Uh, no one arrested I don't believe. But there was a report of a person sighted near the room all decked out like a Navy Seal or something. You know, head to foot body suit with some kind of night vision gizmo apparently and no question it was a woman. That was a positive id."

Cory watched Kate from the corner of her eye. Kate waltzed through the moment putting away soup and rolls, saying nothing. But Cory swore she saw a tiny little response when the reporter mentioned the Navy Seal look.

"Teddy this is our newly signed rep for *GloryDays*, Kate McGill. I've looked for a person like Kate for almost four years so we're really proud to have her with us."

Kate put down her utensils, wiped her mouth and extended her hand. As Teddy shook hands she felt a twinge of pain in the handshake. Kate had quite a grip.

"Ms. McGill, I've seen you on VH-1. You were on talking about music and how you thought a lot of the current rap stuff lacked character. I was impressed to finally hear someone say something like that."

"Teddy, it's not all bad but it's not what I want to hear. I'll take Bonnie Raitt or old Aretha records, that's what I was raised on."

Teddy responded, "Well I know you have no shortage of opinions, that's why you're getting such an amazing reputation. What's your feeling about this fashion show and what happened?"

"I'm afraid I'm not the good source for comment. Sounds like someone tried to make a point for that industry. Sorry, I'm better on other issues."

Teddy asked, "Well as a reporter stumbling into one of the hot media stars---that's you right now like it or not, what do you like to talk about?"

Kate realized she was in for a dime, in for a dollar. "Umm, I have my couple interests: Preservation of nature, the environment and recommittment of personal wealth to better uses in the society."

"Hmm, sounds like you'd pretty well agree with the guerrilla intruder at the fashion show."

Cory felt the tiniest ripple in Kate's persona. That one hit home.

Teddy continued, "Kate, aside from those topics, I am curious if there are women or men who you particularly admire?"

"Oh, plenty. Uh, Bonnie Raitt for sure and Joan Baez. Both speak out and take stands. My mother because she made through both the 70's and the music business intact---big achievement. Toni Morrison, I like her writing. Here's one you won't hear about, Linda Scott. Gorgeous woman who drove race cars back in the 60's and later, drove competitively, looked great, now she flies as spotter for the crews in California when they're dropping water on forest fires. Really cool woman who followed her own sense. I think Brooke Shield, she's a good actor and turned out to be a neat person. I'm also a big Frank Lloyd Wright fan, his stuff is all over the midwest and I make my treks to see his work. You know when he was at the height of his abilities in his fifties, around that time in his life, he could not get arrested, oh, I mean he could not get any commissions. What an incredible feat to overcome that rejection and did his best work later in life. When most people retire and hang it up he's going strong. Whoops, got me going, I'll shut up now."

Kate returned to her salad.

Teddy responded, "Well, I'll leave you to eat. Thanks Cory."

"Well I had little to say. I really want to hear the facts about this incident anyway."

Teddy said good night and walked away.

Cory's curiosity finally got the best of her, "Kate, are you serious that you know nothing about this whole deal?"

"Cory, you think that was me? Do I have to hate high fashion couturiers?"

Cory nodded and accepted Kate's response while still having her doubts. Kate continued eating, looked up and smiled but had no further comments. Cory realized this was not a subject for further discussion. At least not now.

CHAPTER EIGHTEEN
CORY VISITS SARAH IN MINNESOTA

"Sarah, you have one remarkable daughter, I've never really seen anyone quite like her. I am very aware of her obligations attending UC Berkeley, that's a lot to bite off. Now that we're starting to see a few reactions to the early photo shoots with Kate I wanted to spend time with you and fill in more background, have a clearer sense of who she is. Over time we're planning to put her front and center in our campaigns. As a company we expect to work around her school year obligations but in the summers we hope Katie can be on the road promoting herself and our product lines."

Sarah McGill was trying to decide if she was flattered that Cory Madigan had flown all the way to Minneapolis from London just to talk about her daughter. Cory had just signed a major licensing arrangement for *GloryDays* in Europe giving her line of women's athletic and workout clothing a larger and very promising market. Sarah wanted to like Cory, they shared some Jewish roots, Sarah had always hustled to make things work and Cory was the personification of Jewish, New York hustle.

Cory started to wander around the small house in Wayzata, picking up Sarah's art objects acquired in her years of work on the road. "Sarah, what's this plastic chip over here?" Cory asked. "And this looks like one of those old fashioned radio microphones up here on the shelf?"

"The plastic chip is a guitar pick I got off the floor of the Stax Records studio in Memphis. It was used by Steve Cropper, the guitarist behind all the great Otis Redding and Sam & Dave records. A great player and he wrote superb songs as well. The microphone I also scored in Memphis at the Sun studio. One of the original RCA mikes used by Elvis, Jerry Lee Lewis and the others. I had to do some fast trading to get Sam Phillips to let it go."

"What did you trade?"

"Well, some memorabilia from England and, uh, I let him feel me up a couple times."

"I can see why, nature took good care of you. Your daughter, the same."

Sarah stretched a smile for Cory. Sarah regretted talking about her body, even to Cory. It was a lifelong issue being gifted with a bounteous body. Men ogled, women usually looked envious and Sarah preferred to deal with none of that attention. And Kate would have the same tradeoffs having inherited a great figure which she enhanced through exercise, weight training and martial arts.

Cory looked out Sarah's back window at the partial view of Lake Minnetonka. "Lovely setting Sarah. I bet in the fall you see the whole lake when the leaves drop."

"Well, I'm not on the fancy side of town but I have some view. Actually I love this little neighborhood, I'm a couple blocks from the library, I live very simply. When I'm home I nest like crazy."

Cory thought it was time to talk about Kate. "Sarah, I'm sure you know how important Kate may be to *GloryDays*. Our campaign would fill in slowly as we understand how our marketplace relates to the Kate presentations. We've already got the basic outlines of the first wave of advertising but having just returned from Europe and seeing the strong reaction to Kate just in photos, well, it was time to pay you a visit. I need to truly understand who Kate is, how she is likely to react to situations, who is this young woman?"

Cory reminded herself to go slow, this was Minnesota, although Sarah appeared quite worldly and very modern herself, this was Sarah's only daughter and Cory was effectively asking for Kate's total cooperation. Cory reminded herself not to "talk speedish", a permanent issue in her life.

"Sarah, I'm sure you've been hearing how wonderful your daughter is for years but never in my wildest dreams could I have imagined a young woman with her athleticism, her fantastic conditioning, her talent and her unaffected looks. She looks like the perfect young sorority girl, everyone's image of clean cut, innocent, dream girl looks, she could step off the cover of *Look* or *Life* magazine in the 40's."

Sarah knew she had a decision to make. How much to tell Cory about the real Kate McGill? This issue had been simmering for months since she and Kate had their heart to heart in the motel. Sarah had concluded that Cory needed to have a clearer picture of Kate and it demanded taking a few risks.

Sarah responded, "Cory, first, uh, I am going to ask for your confidentiality. I will let you know what Kate is about but I need to have your assurance this stays with just us. Is that acceptable?"

Cory felt a rush of adrenalin. *Where was this going, what did she not know about her new GloryDays model? Cory knew she had no alternative, she had to accept Sarah's terms.* "Sarah, of course, strictly between you and I. It stays in this room."

Cory thought, *Oh good heavens, I bet the farm on this girl. What am I missing?*

Sarah continued, "Cory, Kate is that gorgeous, wholesome young woman. But don't be surprised when she opens her mouth and starts talking about nature, the environment, her outrage over our diminishing natural state, her feelings about all the wealth that should be out working in the communities, those are the two big themes. She's a walking, talking advocate for social change in a prom queen package. Cory, by the way, expect the standard lecture about wealth. She found a way to check up on your financial holdings. Anyway, it looks like she can't wait to put on her cheerleading outfit for homecoming but Kate is capable of strong-arming bullies. She has no fear.. My daughter will confront anyone. If we're downtown and she sees some young punk toss garbage out of his Camaro she's on him in a flash, 'Hey, you gotta pick up your litter. What the hell right do you have to dump garbage on the streets?' And if the Camaro gives her lip she'll get right in his face and if that doesn't work she'll manhandle him."

Cory's mouth dropped. "What? She will get physical with him? Do you mean, uh, beat him up, threaten him? Are we talking about big, strong guys?"

"Cory, you must understand, I know you see the physical conditioning, the timeless honey blonde, the stunning athletic abilities and believe me, there is more. A top student when I was sure she'd crash and burn. One of those totally irritating young people who did not have to study much, just picked up on it. Has a real flair with computers, something I am totally hopeless at. Well, recently I began progressing some. Anyway then, she is such a warm kid, totally lovely around my couple relatives, has friends everywhere. Oh god, it's not easy being this child's mother but I've been handed such a gift, such a treasure and I can also be concerned about how she behaves."

"But Sarah, I'm trying to understand, you are saying? Kate walks up to some hot rodder and confronts him, even threatens him? That's, well, I don't know what to make of that. How can she do that?"

Sarah stood with both hands on the kitchen counter trying to stretch her back muscles. She had missed her daily stretch work at The Marsh and her back was complaining.

"When Kate was a kid we discovered by accident she could handle herself in a tussle. A young guy across the street was always following her. He's a big kid but sort of roly poly. One day he playfully grabbed her arm and she decked him."

"Decked him---meaning punched him?"

"The punch was part of it. His mother saw it, I didn't. She grabbed his arm, twisted it around, flipped him---he was around 220 then. In there someplace she wacked him as well. That was the beginning, when I first realized she had this innate capacity to manhandle guys. It was built-in, I guess. I've since seen her handle even bigger guys and a couple adult men. Along the way she began studying martial arts, particularly judo, she loved judo more than karate."

"Sarah, Kate goes around challenging them or what does she do?"

Sarah felt she had to give Cory a foundation about Kate's capabilities. "Men approach her, she's very nice, even deferential at first. If they keep hustling her she warns them. When she was younger this was just classmates. But she looks mature, obviously her figure attracts men like horseflies and then her athletic pursuits, especially all the amazing skating routines, that brings more, both girls and guys. But more recently adult men, mostly 20's, some 30's start hanging around. And because Katie looks like she does and has this extraordinary macho side men sort of assume she wants their company."

"Is this every day, how often does she get in dustups? I guess I should know this?"

"It depends, just depends. Kate did a state fair against my better judgement but they paid her and did a great job of showcasing her onstage. First rate. This was in Iowa. Well these farm guys can't believe her, she's from another planet. She looks like she stepped out of the 4-H showcase but that's not what's in her head. She argues with the 4-Hers about all the damage cattle do to the environment. Anyway, she does her show, kids go nuts as usual, after the show, normal crowd. Couple guys are all over her, trying to impress her. Hey, it's what young guys do everywhere I'm sure. She backs away, backs away, intelligent guys would get the message to give her some space. This one guy is really coming on, I'm trying to spirit her out of the backstage. This guy accidentally bumps into me and I hit this table, it hurt but I was ok. Well in one second Kate takes him out."

"Takes him out? That means..."

"He had no idea what was happening, suddenly he flies across the room. Her judo instructor said she had a keener sense of balance than anyone including his own grand master or whatever the guy was. She can use anyone's imbalance and send them flying. The guy crashes into some folding chairs, huge clatter and he is just devastated. Katie calmly goes back to finishing her autographs and looks over at him, 'You ok?' He did not know what hit him."

"Some day she'll get walloped herself, if she's the aggressor it's gonna happen, Sarah."

Sarah wanted to play this with a low key, casual approach. She shrugged and began polishing her countertop. "Tell me about it. I try to steer her around it but I'm not always there. Cory, my daughter is the handful of life and men can't resist her. So out of self defense Katie protects herself."

For the first time Cory began understanding the underpinnings of Kate's extraordinary skills.

"Cory what worries me is not young studs, it's the adult men who are extravagant real estate developers or, lord save us, big game hunters. We already hit the first category. Some guy is entertaining a group in a hotel in Detroit, this guy wiped out this forest to build gargantuan homes and Katie knows about these guys. She's got email pals all over the place. A local reporter is interviewing Kate and makes a reference to this developer, that this is the guy who environmentalists despise and there he is in the dining room."

Sarah reminded herself to soft pedal this side of her daughter but her immense pride in Kate's unusual committment to her causes overtook the need to be cautious. "Great, I know what's coming, the reporter leaves, Kate marches over to this guy's table and confronts him. God knows I should be used to it by now but there she goes. I can't hear what's said, only the reactions. She says her piece, comes back steamed up and then this other man comes to our table and says she owes the developer an apology. Kate tells him where to get off, he gets incensed, demands an apology, this guy's really incensed and begins yelling, she stands up and whammo! This guy suddenly goes sprawling. See what's so uncanny is it happens fast. She has these quick reactions and no one expects miss peaches and cream to send them flying. She walks over and says I apologize when the developer tears down those houses and puts the trees back up. Well, you get the picture, in reaction mode Kate is not programmed for win-win."

Cory started laughing self consciously and shook her head, "Yah, I should say so...I should say." The truth was Cory had not bargained for powerhouse retribution *Annie Get Your Gun.*

Sarah hoped she was packaging this side of Kate correctly and she was glad to see Cory losing some wind in her sails. Sarah liked Cory and wore a few *GloryDays* outfits---if the exposure was not outrageous. Cory had to know enough about Kate not to be blown away if Kate showed up in the papers for roughing up some bad guy. Sarah felt she had an obligation to front load the deal so Cory would know what to expect.

Cory took a seat at the kitchen table opposite Sarah. The small kitchen had a freestanding island, David Goines posters were carefully placed on the limited wall space. Goines drew detailed illustrations, a Berkeley based artist and printer who commemorated anniversaries at the famed Chez Panisse restaurant which Sarah adored. Cookbooks peeked out of cubby holes, the appliances were older and quite rudimentary. Sarah favored workout clothing when home, in this case she wore an older GloryDays outfit in cinnamon red which gave her a youthful appearance.

Sarah continued, "Since she began appearing on tv we get approached weekly for her to model, to endorse products. A Japanese company flew a team all the way here, sent a limo for me and did this unbelievable, elaborate presentation to ask if Kate would be their marketing image in the far east for a cosmetic product. They blew me away, they had collected every scrap of video footage, virtually every picture ever published, stories about Kate, all of it, utterly thorough research. It was such a totally Japanese experience, they were so dignified about it."

"Are you going to work with them?" Cory prayed Sarah said they would not. Cory wanted Kate all to herself but knew it was only a matter of time until some Proctor & Gamble, or worse, some fashion house stepped up with multiple millions and swayed Kate and Sarah into a deal.

"Kate's thinking about it. She's not really a cosmetics person, not yet at least. She uses a little eye shadow, some blush, nothing else. It's funny most women are really more envious about her face, not her figure."

Sarah began straightening up some cook books. After a moment she remembered one book had a recipe she had been looking for. She opened the book on the countertop and examined the recipe. Cory watched her from a distance. Sarah was charming and a real woman's woman. A female another woman could relate to.

"Cory, since my daughter was, like, 8, she has been capable of defending herself. Even before she began studying martial arts, Kate took care of herself. She was always fairly muscular, well built and very confident. Then she began training and training. I was driving her all the way out to hell and gone, east side of St. Paul so she could study with this tai-chi woman. Then we're up to, oh lord where was that, above Anoka? Up to this little town 40 miles up there to study karate with this Japanese teacher, he was fantastic and he showed her how to tie her natural acrobatic nature into the martial arts. She was a fish in water from the first time. Then, as she got more confident about her self defense she starts coming home with books about nature, the environment. Well, I'm in total agreement with her on those issues but this perfect young woman with the story book looks starts getting these attitudes. She gets so upset about loss of green space, killing innocent animals---that sends her up the wall. What's interesting is she did not get particularly pulled toward social protest. She hasn't been out marching although she might. What she'd really like to do is go head to head with the bad guys and they are almost always men who are destroying the natural world. Literally, if she could, she'd march into their office or even their houses and get in their faces. She'd go beyond that if it seemed possible."

Sarah paused to catch her breath. This was important for Cory to know about Kate.

" The summer she was sixteen, so that's just under two years ago when most Minnesota kids are up at a family cabin on the lake or off at camp Kate went off to her own camp. She found this guy who teaches approaches to survival, self defense and use of weapons. The guy was a Navy Seal and then was in some delta force, I don't quite know what it was called but they were like pros at hiding themselves in a population and did undercover surveillance and spying. It was tied into a federal program. This guy is in the back country in Michigan, I have no idea how she found him. So I drive up there with Kate. It's literally in hell and gone. You might have seen a few pictures of Kate with very short hair? She did that for the camp, this guy suggested it. That was after he called me twice and almost begged me to talk Kate out of coming. He said, '...these are rough guys, it's not a holiday, this is full on macho outbursts, I can't guarantee how they'll react to having a young woman here...' and he went on about it. Kate was on the phone, listened to the whole spiel. And then she said, 'Marty, you just talked me into it. I can take care of myself, I want this experience, I will sign whatever release you need now let's get on with it.'"

Sarah paused, drank some coffee and then continued, "Well we get up there and here's like a dozen ready to kill, honest to goodness commando types. I mean, these guys are scary but in the good sense. Very controlled, not strutting around, wearing camoflauge makeup on their faces, utterly focused, no drinking, only one guy smoked. These are serious soldiers and thank god some of them exist in this country. Actually they were all very friendly but these are definitely the types you want to walk you down that very dark alley. Brawny, built, rugged, you know, like Arnold with that kind of musculature and here's my daughter. Oh my god, it's a week in the wild. She is sixteen, gorgeous and here are these hulks. I almost died! Marty, he's still trying to talk her out of it. 'Listen Katie, this is rough, this is not always pleasant, this is definitely not Beverly Hills up here. These guys are all ex military and cops who want to dive in to the swamp, they're here to pump up their masculinity and relive military experiences Kate, we've never had anyone your age and certainly not female. I can house you separately but you gotta understand...' Kate lets him go on and says no, I'm enrolling, I'm ready."

"So what happens to her, Sarah?" Cory really couldn't quite believe what she was hearing but thinking of Kate it did fit together.

"Well, first, what am I doing? I'm up in armpit Michigan, am I sticking around for the week? This is not like sending your kid off to Camp Minawewe. And Marty offers to put me up. He's got a pretty nice cabin and he says, 'Here, Sarah, you take my place, it's not a palace but you'll be comfortable. I'll bunk with the guys, no big deal.' But Kate raises hell, 'Forget that shit, mom, I'm here, I'll handle this. You go home, I'll take a bus back to Minneapolis.' So what should I do? God, like I told you, being this kid's mom is not easy or simple. Well, I finally left. At that point our pal Buzz had gifted her with a satellite phone so she can call me anytime and she did. I also talk to Marty three days into the camp and he's like, 'Oh, hi Sarah. Well, Kate's doing, uh, really good. I told her I cannot give you special treatment, uh, these guys pay money to get down and dirty. Uh, honestly, you know this is kind of strange relating to you as her mother because your daughter does not blink, she is unafraid. Hell she is more willing to walk through these woods, climb through the obstacles than some of these guys. They are out in the woods, there is some hand to hand combat and she is completely comfortable taking on these other guys. Hey, they're not, some of them were cutting her slack and she starts yelling at them to cut it out. 'Treat me just like any combatant.' I gotta tell you, your Kate is a soldier, no fooling. Anyway, a few cuts and bruises but man your gal can drive anything. We have some old military vehicles, this ancient armored personnel carrier. One of the guys is trying to start it up, get it moving. She butts him out of the way, figures out the weird transmission and trundles off in this bucket of bolts. The guys are just shaking their heads.'

"Anyway, she took some hits but after this week with firearms and judo and survival courses she's all fired up. Two of the guys ended up driving her all the way back home and these are two bruisers, big, tough ex marines. They show up here at the house and one of them says, 'Hey, Mrs McGill, if I'm headin' in to trouble with bad guys I'll take Kate along. She can handle whatever you throw at her. We were out in this forest, it's all marshy and gooey, there are a few snakes, we're navigating a ropes course, it's really tough going and she does not give up, she does not ask for slack. She fell in the muck a couple times. No whining, no complaining, she pulls herself up, climbs a tree, gets back on the ropes, her hands were bleeding but she is really something!' And I'm thinking, God, can't my daughter just go to a prom or hang out down at the mall?"

Cory responded, "So Sarah, how do I take this? We'd have Kate in front of the public. What if she, I don't know, runs into some guys who are doing something bad. I mean, what would she do?"

"She'd rough them up. She'd kick their asses. My daughter is not a passive type. Martial arts are normally about keeping in balance, being essentially non violent she translates a different message. Kate is loaded for bear, she's ready to fight. Cory, you've only seen the public package, the skating and athletic person. She has this whole other side. She doesn't show it to most people, in fact, the scary part for me is she can keep this all under wraps. You'd never know she has this deep, concerned side and an attitude to go do some damage. *GloryDays* may have a tiger by the tail. It's one reason she has only done a couple endorsements to date. I had every manufacturer of anything to do with skates on me the last five years. She has been offered a percentage of the company by two of them to do the endorsements. And now that she's getting all this press coverage we're getting perfumes, toilettries, shoes, god, you name it. I got a guy in L.A. just fielding all these offers. I was told the chairman of Volkswagen, Piech I think his name is, he's hot for getting Kate because she's said she loves their cars. And they are talking about rich for life dollars. But we'll have to see,,,,"

Cory's heart sank like a rock. She asked quietly, "What is Kate's thinking?"

"Cory, my daughter is all these values that I frankly have not had the guts to fulfill. She understands ethics, she has very strong feelings about so many things and the temerity to stand up for what's right. I am principled but she makes me feel puny. Kate has inherited some virtuous person's soul and she means to change the world. I am scared silly that she will hurt someone or pull off some crazy escapade. That's another thing, we have an old family friend, Buzz Roemer. He owns a company that does business all over the world, he's well off, collects cars. Big hunk of a guy, a sweetheart but my Katie sees the bravado side of him. Buzz does chancy, scary things. He hires out teams to rescue people stuck in third world places. He loves completely unconventional approaches to solving business problems. Most of all, Buzz is a prankster and my daughter thinks his pranks are so fabulous."

"Pranks? What kind of pranks, Sarah?"

Sarah began slicing up some apples and put out some cheese. As she sliced she recalled, "Oh, Buzz Roemer is his own legend. Wayzata kids pass down this tale: A local guy had become a problem bully. He'd been that in high school, then he started a business. He had a bad reputation for pushing people around. He needed to hear the message to cool it. Buzz and a pal found out the bully was out of town and arranged for his small warehouse to be repainted pink and chartreuse. Actually, very striking, well done, good design. Buzz put up a sign to the effect that bullies should never wear pink. Of course the building owner goes ballistic. But it got played up in the news and the guy realized it could bring his business some positive reputation. I think he straightened out after that."

"A role model for Katie?"

"Yah, she follows his approach---Buzz is about rebalancing the scales. Kate first got that from him. He always had an angle and later in life he made serious money playing the angles. Buzz tried to have his pranks be meaningful. Another one, he borrowed these two huge caterpillar tractors, you know, the yellow things on construction sites. Didn't really borrow, stole. Anyhow, in a town right nearby they were gonna evict this old couple who had this cute little soda fountain, they couldn't pay their bills but kept trying to stay open. So finally some authority scheduled an eviction for ten AM. At eight Buzz and some big lunkers show up with these monster caterpillars, park them with those huge shovels up in the air wheel to wheel in front of this little shop, turned them off and walked away with the keys. They also cabled them together so they could not be moved with this industrial cable like six inches thick. So the authorities had to deal with that first. Meantime Buzz found some money, who knows how, enough to pay off their bill. On a simpler level he has his annual spring ice breaking contests. He'd have a few of his buddies out on the ice when it's breaking up, they're running around jumping from ice floe to ice floe, whoever stays dry the longest wins. Only hitch, falling in the lake when it's been frozen is pretty rough."

Cory nodded and chuckled.

Sarah added, "Cory, this was last year, Buzz is forty eight."

Sarah breathed a big sigh.

" Katie loves Buzz and it's mutual. He had her driving at age fourteen. Just in parking lots but he encouraged her to stretch her muscles."

"Fourteen? How could she?"

"Oh, no problem, she was big enough and she had the coordination. But it's not driving some Ford sedan. He has Porsches, a glorious Maserati, two Lamborghinis. One day I'm working in the garden, I hear this sound like a thunderstorm. I walk around the house, there is Kate, sixteen, just legal to drive. Buzz gives her this Lamborghini Countach. He trusts her to drive this 400 horsepower monster. 'Here, Katie, take the keys, have it back in one piece. Don't get crazy.' Oh, sure, smart Buzz. I wanted to literally kill him. Then Katie took me for a drive and she had it under control. She kept her cool. So then I only wanted to maim him." Sarah cracked a tiny smile at the thought.

Sarah continued her thought. "Well, Minneapolis is still a small town, that's what I like about it. The cops know who she is and she is always in the news here so lots of people recognize her. All the good Minnesotans appreciate the local girl making good. I mean, it's sensational, she's kind of bullet proof here, they don't bust her but I am worried sick when she's out of here. And she's got this ballistic approach to life. She has the pedal to the metal, well, not all the time. I can still take her canoeing and shazam! All of a sudden she's my daughter again, thoughtful, funny, really amusing, in fact, sweet as can be. She is a powerful package, Cory. There's a lot there. She's looked at your stuff, your previous campaigns. She likes your imagery and she wears your outfits anyway."

"Did she buy some here in town? We have only a weak representation here. We're working on Daytons."

"Well, I don't think you've got a problem there. Kate marched into some guy's office at Daytons corporate wearing this outfit of yours. She told me all about it. Sashayed right in, asked for him by name, '...tell him its Kate McGill...' It showed way too much curves for my taste but she looks so completely perfect in it and she says, 'See this outfit, you need to carry it. Women need practical workout gear that makes them look good and you don't have this stuff.' This was three weeks ago, your stuff is on the rack at Ridgedale. Oh, yah, Kate did a freebie little skating demo wearing your stuff, she, uh, used to skate through the place pursued by the security staff so she knows all the escalators. I saw it on the news, blasted it all over the news, Katie did this slide where she skates down the escalator bannister. You gotta see it, really something. The news lady said they cleaned out all your stuff in an hour. You didn't hear about that?"

Cory was having serious trouble containing herself. She was embarrassed that no one had told her about this windfall but she had been overseas. Now she would not rest until she had Kate's participation.

"Sarah, I am the perfect product line for Kate. Perfect! I don't have huge dollars but I'll mortgage my whole company to have her represent us. Sarah, my attorney cautioned me to never expose my whole hand, he's such a New Yorker and I guess he's right but the god's honest truth is I have got to have your daughter represent us. It means that much to me. The more you talk the more I see Kate as a *GloryDays* image worldwide. When we met at the Plaza in New York, I was just learning about Kate, I knew she was just fabulous but now that some time has passed I'm realizing what a bonanza she is. I have some female athletes in gymnastics, track and field and obviously we need them but I have been going nuts for three years looking for the perfect, correct young woman. Kate is that young woman partly because of that fiery spirit! I knew it the first time I saw her performing on skates on cable tv. She stopped me in my tracks. Sarah, I hope I'm not throwing too much at you but this is how I feel."

Sarah leaned against the kitchen counter top, one hand on a hip chewing on an apple slice nodding to Cory. "Cory, you know most of what you need about my daughter. Kate may do something that will embarrass your operation but she'll do it for the right reasons. You must be clear about that. Katie at eighteen is gathering ideas and feelings which will start maturing over the next few years. She is volatile, high powered, talented and the light of my life. I worry about her every day because she could do anything. Can you handle her, can you deal with all these desires and energies, Cory?"

"Sarah, I have to ask you, who is her grandmother, the one that does shows in Las Vegas?"

"No not grandmother, her great grandmother. Oh, that's a whole other story. Queen Royal Elixir. That's my grandmother and she's eighty one now. She does a show in a small cabaret in Vegas, she tells fortunes and kind of makes predictions. And then her daughter, Helen Aray, my mom, a self made business woman in L.A. Since you signed up Kate Helen will be involved. If you're looking for where all this toughness comes from, just check out Helen. I'm the wimp of the crew. Anyway, Queen Royal may have inherited some genetic predisposition that allows her to make predictions. It supposedly travels in the family, the gypsy side and it skips two whole generations among the females. So next in line is Kate. We haven't gotten to that yet."

"Predictions, like telling the future, Sarah?"

"Cory, that is the tale passed down in the family. In my case and my Mother's we never were visited by this legacy. It passed right over us. But in the last year Queen Royal began preparing Katie. It's a good combination, the great grandmother tutoring her great grand daughter. Queen Royal dazzled me when I was a kid, now Katie gets her turn."

Cory was trying to digest all of this. So now Kate tells fortunes or the future? All that Cory knew was she had to have Kate rep her product line. "Sarah, you don't know what I've done to get this far. I am not a spring chicken, I am certainly not some overnight success story. Every single inch of my progress has been paid for in effort, serious effort. I will make you this promise, with Katie on board with *GloryDays* worldwide I will try, best as I can, to think like a guardian, to act out of concern for her well being and to make no sacrifice of Kate's future for financial gain. Please try to understand, all these things you've told me this afternoon make it that much more critical to me to work with Kate. All her social concerns add greater urgency to having her with our company. And here is why: I couldn't buy those inner emotions, her desires, her commitments for a carload of money. Kate can help me fulfill a need of my own---to have my business also serve as a vehicle for some social contribution. I can write a check for some cause but having a firebrand like your Kate out there associated with my company, that is a literal dream come true for me. I hope this makes sense to you and you'll help Kate try to grasp this idea."

CHAPTER NINETEEN
KATE'S PREMONITION

Kate was now two years at Berkeley, she finally began enjoying the school and California but her yearning for home and Minnesota had become almost overwhelming. Against pressures to go back on the road all summer for *GloryDays* doing live shows she decided she owed herself at least a partial Minnesota summer. After completing her classes Kate took a flight back to Minneapolis, walked in the door at her Wayzata house and burst into tears.

Sarah greeted her at the door and realized something new was occurring. Kate looked fine but crying outbursts were not normal for her daughter.

"Honey, you don't look happy. Are you ok? What's going on?"

Kate made a beeline for the kitchen, made herself some iced tea, her favorite summer drink and plopped onto the big couch.

"Mom, I'm ok, really but I've never experienced such disruption, stress, whatever you call it. School is super tough, I thought I'm smart but these kids, especially the students from overseas have me beat all to hell. Now I see why it's a top school. I am seriously outclassed intellectually. Then there's all this media noise about me. I don't know, I can handle all that. I miss you and Dad, I miss friends here in town, most of all, I guess, I miss Peter. I had no idea a guy would mean so much to me. We talk frequently but I don't see him and it's two more years like this."

Sarah replied, "Honey, you have some money, you can fly to see him, listen, for that matter, if you are not happy you can move back to the midwest and finish at another school."

Kate had to stop and think. She remained silent for 30 seconds. "Mom, no, I can make this work, I started and it will be ok. I guess I had to say this stuff to you, that's all."

But there was one more issue. "Mom, these visions are upsetting."

132

Sarah's expression conveyed her concern. She already knew about the Harendt legacy from her grandmother Queen R. but now it apparently was happening with her daughter.

"Mom, it's stressful, it's these tiny visions, they show up but I had a string of them recently like in sequence and then they stopped. That's when I saw these people in a foreign country, in a marketplace and then they disappeared in a huge explosion."

"Kate, you saw this, actually witnessed it?

Kate nodded her head. "Mom, clear vision, it lasted for some seconds, then kaboom. I saw it like I was there."

Kate woke up in her own bed, in her own house, with her mother in the next room. She had not slept well. Her mind was in turmoil, emotionally she felt drained. She tried to walk through the situation in her mind. She had already talked to Buzz who said she should sit on this premonition because that was all it was, a mind guessing at an outcome. It was totally unproven. Pure speculation.

She tried to read but couldn't concentrate. Finally she slid down the bed and turned on her ancient tv set which she hadn't watched in years. It only received four channels, none of them clearly. She switched around, exhausted the possibilities and turning away from the set she punched the on/off button. When she turned back there was another image on the screen.

Kate almost stopped breathing. The image was the exact scene she had seen in her momentary vision. A man dressed in a long robe with a turban pulling a wooden cart with large wheels, he was laboring to drag it forward. And then a huge explosion. It lasted, at most, four seconds. Kate couldn't be sure the image had actually existed. She felt driven to tears. "What the heck is going on? Am I losing my mind?" She looked out the window, the sun was just coming up. She picked up the phone next to her bed and dialed Queen Royal's phone in Las Vegas where it was still the middle of the night. The phone rang and Queen R's sleepy voice answered.

"Queen R., I am so sorry, it's Kate, I just have to talk with you."

Queen R. replied, "Give me a minute, hang on. I need to get my mind working. Ok, I was expecting your call my dear. Go ahead, I knew we would need to talk. You're having some kind of vision or dream, am I right?"

Kate's astonishment was only exceeded by her embarrassment. "Oh, my lord, how can you know this Queen R?"

The phone line went quiet. "Honey, these are things I simply know. It's difficult to explain. Katie dear, please listen. When I was your age I had something similar, an urgent unexplainable incident. You need to tell someone about this, a person who can help you put this to work. Now, that's all I know my lovely Katherine. It's starting for you and this will change many things but you must proceed. Any questions?"

Kate sat dumbfounded on her bed shaking her head. When her great grandmother spoke it was always with such few words. But they always had useful meaning. "What, how, oh, God, how do I figure this out?"

Queen R.'s voice became luxuriously soft and comforting. "My dear, you will begin understanding eventually, now you can't. After you hang up walk out on to the back deck, take a blanket to keep warm and welcome the dawn. Your next life begins with this strange vision. Try to accept this step, even though this will be disturbing in many ways you must proceed, it is your calling. Now, I love you, I'm going back to bed. You are the princess of important thoughts, long may you reign."

Kate held the phone, now silent. She gathered the ancient blue and gold comforter off her bed, wrapped herself in it and quietly stepped onto the deck to be greeted by rays of the sun and two birds chirping.

Three hours later, having fallen into a deep slumber in the family hammock on the deck, Kate tiptoed into the house discovering that Sarah was up and gone to her exercise class.

She picked up the phone and dialed Aggie Roemer's number in Washington, D.C.

"Agg, it's Kate, I'm in Wayzata. Can you talk?"

Aggie sounded a bit sleepy, he often stayed up quite late reading and now with the internet, experimenting.

"Yup, go ahead, I'm a little foggy."

"Ok, in four days there will be a small nuclear explosion in Asia, I have seen this repeatedly."

Aggie was quickly waking up. "You know this, uh, how?"

"Agg, we've talked about Queen R's, visions. Now I caught 'em and she said I must proceed. The woman knows all, never seen her be wrong."

"Katie, what do you want me to do?"

"Call your pal Bart at, what is it, NETFODI? What does that actually stand for?"

"National Emergency Technology For Oversight of Damaging Intrusions. Terrible name. Gotta be changed. But he's concerned with the internet and what they're starting to call cyber space. What will he do with this?"

"Agg, you're the only route I have to someone in power. Can you tell him about this? I know it must sound crazy. I don't know where to take this, you're my connection to the high end of technology."

"Katie, I'll sneak it to him but there is no evidence. I guard that relationship, he gives me inside tracks on projects for my consulting business, I gotta be careful."

"Agg, I understand, I need to find another route for this, I guess?"

Kate hung up and stared at her Mom's small china cabinet. She loved the antique crockery inside she played with as a little girl. That seemed a long time ago now. She was losing ground on where to take the vision. She thought of Cory.

She called *GloryDays* and asked for Cory. "Katie, it's Damian, Cory is traveling, can I help you?"

"Damian, yes you can. Do you know a journalist, a gossip monger who would jump on a story but protect the source?"

Damian thought for a moment. "Yes, a woman I knew from Creem, a little fan mag for the music business, she has a big mouth and takes chances. Is this about you?"

"Damian, I'm not going to tell you this minute but if I'm right it could make her a big deal. Can I call her and use your name?"

Kate walked around the house, into her parents' bedroom, looked at the pictures of herself when she was very small, glanced at books on both of her parents' nightstands. Her Dad had a memoir about President Harry Truman. She sat on their bed and tried to stop thinking. Their room always smelled of both parents. Flowers and lovely aromas from her Mom, a cologne and outdoor scents from her Dad. Surrounded by their momentos, reminded about their lives was reassuring to Kate. She thought, *What would Mom and what would Dad tell me to do?* Finally she knew it was time to proceed.

"I'm Kate McGill, I work with Damian at *GloryDays*. He said it was ok to call you, Annie."

"Hi, Kate, I've seen those first photos of you, wowie zowie, you jump off the page. I know Cory is all fired up about having you with them."

"Thanks Annie, you don't know me so this will sound weird but by any chance would you be willing to take a gamble?"

There was a pause on the other end. "Well, I don't know, maybe. What's up?"

"In four days, specifically 94 hours and twenty minutes from now in Central Asia a bomb which resembles a nuclear device will be detonated. Can you find a way to leak that to a newspaper or wire service? The town is Sasovo in Russia. People there need to know."

"Kate, I work in the rock music biz, that's pretty far from my turf."

"Annie, this will happen, it could attract attention to you."

"Am I using your name in this?"

Kate stopped. This was it. Show time. No name, no story.

"You can say that I believe it will happen. Sure, absolutely."

"Alright, give me the details, I will use your name. I know a guy at the New York Times, he is always hunting for left field stories."

Kate hung up and felt herself totally freaking out. "What am I doing? This is insanely nuts!!! I'm going to be quoted, I will be a laughingstock."

She ran to her bedroom, threw on exercise tights and a top, ran out to the garage and pulled her old ten speed bike out, grabbed a pump, aired up the tires and started peddling madly down Broadway headed for the Luce Line bike trail. "I could have a regular life but, no, I have to be the wacko from Wayzata. What can I be thinking?"

Four hours later, totally exhausted from riding 25 miles west at her top speed Kate returned. Sarah looked at her, "Katie, you ok, you look like a madwoman? Maybe you should go shower up? Here's a phone message that was on the machine."

Kate showered, felt refreshed and called the number in 703. A man answered, "This is Bart, who's calling?"

"Bart, it's Kate McGill, did Aggie Roemer get you? I appreciate your call."

He cleared his throat. "Katherine, I need to ask you, how do you know about Sasovo in Russia? And I have to record your answer if that's ok?"

She replied, "Ok, I'm alright with that."

Bart said, "Do you know the New York Times just leaked a story saying you think there will be a nuclear explosion in that part of Russia. You are quoted."

Kate felt ready to cut off her own head. She regretted ever listening to Queen R.

"Yes, I saw a mushroom cloud. Yes."

Bart again cleared his throat. "Katie, you saw it? Like a vision. That town is 200 miles from Moscow, if you are right people in Moscow could be in danger. I'm about to call my counterpart in Russia, get him out of bed, I'm sure. You did have a vision? Do I have that correct?"

"Yes, Bart, I had a vision." Kate felt an involuntary rush of nausea. She was sure she would puke right on the kitchen counter.

Bart sounded quite cheerful given the situation. "Alright, this will be interesting and it's full steam ahead. Are you frightened?"

Kate's voice sounded a thousand miles distant to her. "Totally devastated, I can't believe I did this."

Bart laughed, "Katherine my dear, don't be. Life hands us opportunities. Aggie has talked about you. He said you're a very spirited and physically strong young woman. I saw you in a magazine our daughter subscribes to. If you're wrong, hey, life's unpredictable. If you believe this is real stick to your guns. Gotta run."

Sarah stood in the kitchen watching her daughter. "So?"

"Mom, I'm in such deep crap I can't even tell you but your grandmother told me to do this."

"Director, it's Bart Alliason. Been better. We just picked up something that I believe we must take seriously. A threat to use a small nuclear device. It appears to be in Sasovo in the Ryazan region of central Russia. We know little, very little."

Bart listened to an incensed voice.

"Director, I'm well aware of a potential panic reaction and no, I can't prove this is something tangible."

Bart had already consulted with an expert in the Defense Department about fallout. She told him it all depended on the size of the explosion, the makeup of the materials, placement, wind currents. Lots of imponderables that were outside Bart's normal purview. He made one more call.

"Hi, it's me. How's Danny feeling? Yah, I think it's a stomach virus. It should let up by tonight. Uh, honey, I think we need to do some planning. On wednesday evening, nine our time, I'd like to make sure the kids are home with you. I never operate like this but I am following a hunch. I'll explain soon. I'd rather they are with you if I'm not able to be at home. You know me, I'm not a worrier but we uncovered something."

Kate's foretelling of the explosion began triggering reactions. The National Security Agency, the Air Force and other agencies all took steps to examine what might happen if Kate happened to be right. However, no official felt comfortable taking the heat preparing for an event a teenager in Minnesota predicted would happen.

But in Sasovo in central Russia, at ground zero for the supposed blast the interest was very different. It took a few hours and then local media, such as it is, began circulating a story. It said that a young American woman had predicted detonation of an atomic bomb in their town on a specific date. That date was now less than 60 hours away. But a high percentage of the residents never heard this story communicated---those residents could not read the newspaper and did not own a radio or tv.

Fortuitously, this absence of readers, radio listeners and television viewers produced a result no one could have predicted. Residents in the supposed targeted town began going door to door, talking to one another. The story became distorted, now it was an American who would detonate the blast, or a Russian. But the precise date and time remained fixed. Within 24 hours nearly 90% of the residents were aware of the doomsday prediction. And some 20 hours before the appointed time people began quietly leaving their homes and possessions behind. People could only trust one another, no one trusted any government body.

The government attempted to intercept the growing line of emigres but no one had thought to come up with an alternate plan. So the residents continued to stream from the town. Most walked, a few had cars or trucks, others on bicycles. But there was little or no panic. People just left thinking that after the appointed date and time, if no explosion occurred, they'd walk right back to town.

The American intelligence services quickly noted the outflow of humanity and, for once, issued meaningful directives. American agencies tried contacting officials in both eastern Europe and Russia. Supplies were rounded up but the process terminated with a few trucks and train cars being loaded.

The young man in a flowing kaftan wearing a colorful head wrap and combat boots strolled through the marketplace. The sun had finally emerged, it had been unseasonably cool and foggy. He stopped to sample the first fruits of the season, he purchased a few items. He took a small pleasure in making the purchases and then promptly gave all but one peach to two young children. He checked his watch, strolling on further passing a school. He steeled himself to not think what that meant. He emerged from the market, passed down two long, dark alleys, and walked out into a large open square. The building, the one he hated, loomed opposite. Squat, hulking, modern, imposing and unfriendly, it represented intrusion by the government far away. What no one could understand was why the central government wanted to build this monstrosity in such a modest town? Off the beaten path, strategically unimportant, yet someone wanted this edifice built in the town's square, the place that many gathered to chat. Once it appeared, people began congregating elsewhere. It was, after all, the home of national security services. His town had certainly suffered more than enough. This was just more bitterness.

He again checked his watch. The man walked to a row of native shops and nodded to an aging vendor of hand made pots and pans. No words were spoken but the younger man tucked a small amount of money into the elder's hand and whispered a reminder that the man should close up and leave, then he slipped behind a curtain and began moving an aging wooden wagon.

As he heaved the wagon forward the young man wondered if he had properly constructed his device? He wanted a mushroom cloud. He needed it because the world would take notice of what he planned. If there was just a big bang it would never be important to the outside world. But if it made a mushroom cloud, that would get everyone's attention. That meant it was a nuclear explosion---even if it really wasn't.

It had taken weeks of painstaking research with primitive resources to get the proper chemistry for his cloud.

It occurred to the young man that the old vendor would never make it safely. He labored slowly toward a fountain and listened to the water play over the rocks. He thought about his mother lying ill in the hospital. His father had been killed in an accident. His brother, thank heavens, was out of the country studying in France. That was all he had. A few friends but they were not close. People didn't take him seriously. He was not able to afford any university but books were his endless passion. Between a few books in the science library, data from historical studies and carefully assembled ideas off the internet, when he could get the primitive computer to work, he had pieced it together. He pulled the creaky wagon seemingly full of handmade pots. It weighed more than he originally planned. The circuitry had been terribly difficult to assemble as he had no money, all the parts were begged and borrowed. The one learned person he could speak with, a man who attended college in America speculated that with such a limited amount of explosives available to him the blast could be just enough to level a few square blocks. That's all he needed, destroy the building and make his cloud. What happened to his own body, he didn't really care.

Moving the wagon was difficult. He'd haul a few hundred meters then have to stop. At this altitude everything was effort. He thought of the old man and hoped he had taken his admonishments to leave town seriously. By his calculations even being four miles away might be enough.

He checked his watch again. He wondered what it would look like when it was done? Would it be a crater? Only a few people were passing through the square now. He gazed up at the sky. White fluffy clouds gently swirled across the valley. He sent love to his mother and his dead father. He wished his brother all good thoughts. Two security guards were tracking his progress along the intimidating tall, iron fence. But he was at least fifty yards distant.

What if it didn't work? He squelched the thought. It would work. He realized onlookers might wonder what he was doing staring up at the sky. The two guards were still watching him. Now they began walking toward him.

It was time. He had moved the bulky wagon as close to the fence as he dared. He held onto the switch inside his kaftan. He took a last look around. This was better. His life would have had some purpose. He pushed the homemade plunger. For an infinitessimal second there was pain.

Two hundred meters distant two soldiers smoking cigarettes felt something very unfamiliar expanding in the air. They turned just as the flash occurred blinding both instantly and in under one second the energy wave reached their immobile bodies shredding flesh and bone like confetti.

A Russian airline captain some thirty miles out on a descent saw a sight he had only read about in school. The flash was exceedingly bright, then a wave of energy sweeping across a few blocks of the city. Then what appeared to be a small mushroom cloud emerged.

Thirty seconds later telephone systems in Washington D.C. and nearby Virginia were suddenly flushed with activity.

Forty seconds later a man ran into a staff meeting in the White House. The President stood up, excused himself and hurried out. No one in the west wing had ever seen the President run through the halls.

Across America communication devices of every description began erupting with messages. Faxes, electronic mail, phones but particularly cell phones emitted a wail of warnings. In inside two minutes the major news networks knew something had happened. NBC stopped their broadcast, switched to a commentator first in Washington, then in Ankara, Turkey. The Turkish military was taking extraordinary steps, reacting to something mysterious nearby.

In three minutes internet traffic began multiplying hitting peaks never before attained. In America over the next few hours in most major cities it became difficult to find an open phone line. All this activity was largely triggered by two separate video tapes captured from passing commercial jetliners showing some evidence of a small mushroom cloud. Electronic mail conveyed speculation everywhere and replays of the videos were carried on television.

Within half an hour, it was estimated, over 80 percent of the American public knew about the explosion but it was the mushroom cloud that attracted concern. However, the public had few details. Almost nothing concrete was offered through the media. So people began concocting their own scenarios. Rumors flew, speculation abounded. Within hours many were convinced more than one incident had occurred. A percentage of Americans, particularly those who had survivalist concerns began taking steps to protect themselves from atomic fallout.

The Atomic Energy Commission quickly released data claiming that fallout and long term threats were absolutely minimal. It was a very small explosion which leveled only a relatively tiny area. The public was told this was roughly equivalent to the damage from the Chernobyl meltdown in Russia.

Then the A.E.C. reconsidered. There did not appear to be radioactivity after all. But the first announcement remained in the public mind so there were fears of nuclear fallout. Gradually after two days the public understood that there had not been an atomic bomb detonated. Just a bomb that almost surgically removed one large building.

Slowly hard information was gathered. The American public was told a single individual, Hazeem Al Fayzol had built the bomb and died in the explosion. He was attempting to destroy a government security facility. He was successful, his home made bomb leveled the building and the surrounding neighborhood but the actual blast, while powerful was just a big bang. Just as its inventor had feared, once it became obvious that this was just a big explosion people stopped caring. But the small cloud did remain in the news for some time.

Then a video emerged in which residents of Sasovo talked through translators about their experience. It became clear these people wanted to thank the young American woman who spoke out giving them enough time to flee their homes. No one else had the courage, they said, to alert them. Kate McGill had become a legitimate international hero.

Kate's grandmother, Helen, watched the tv footage shaking her head. "My young Katherine, now the trouble starts."

Back in Minnesota Buzz asked his brother Aggie, "How big actually?"

"Buzz, they'll eventually have it all measured but small, quite small detonation. Leveled two city blocks. Actually, I'm told it was like a surgical incursion. Took out this one government building cleanly and the shock wave spilled over."

"God, how could anyone even think about using a nuke?"

"Buzz, that was the genius, it set off a cloud, everyone paid attention to what this guy had done and then it became a blown up building. Happens every day. "

"Yah, collateral damage, I guess."

"The press in Paris had this writeup saying the guy who built it was an overlooked young guy, kind of friendless, but real bright. He built it out of scrounged up parts. Can you imagine pressing the trigger?"

"Total guts or total fear, I don't know which."

CHAPTER TWENTY

KATE IS FORCED TO USE HER BOW AND ARROW

Helen Aray placed a call to Buzz Roemer. They knew each other, had met on family occasions in Minnesota but their relationship was entirely built around Kate. Now Helen intended to establish a more direct connection.

"Buzz, does your associate know I am Kate's grandmother? She seemed to hesitate before putting this call through."

Buzz was caught offguard. He had no idea his assistant, Marta, had tried to screen Helen. "I'm very sorry, Marta may well not know who you are so my apologies."

Helen allowed a beat to pass. She realized no one in his office likely knew her. "Buzz, don't worry about it. We have a few matters to discuss. First, you and I need to be on a steady talking basis. Katie trusts you completely, you have intervened for her, you are important in her life. Which also means I need to know you better. You and I don't have to be best friends but we are both vital support links for Katie." In typical Helen fashion she hardly hesitated as she moved through her agenda.

"Next, I would appreciate updates from you about Katie, I know you have certain important connections as does your brother Aggie. In particular and the reason for my call, my sources tell me Kate's little episode connected to that bomb blast in Russia or Asia, wherever it was, is bringing all the suspicious people out of the woodwork. 'Suspicious people' is my term for Intelligence or military or whoever may be researching her life, sticking their nose into her business or my business for that matter. I am constantly pursued by analysts, researchers and fast buck types who find my electronics products particularly fascinating. So you and I need to have an ongoing dialogue exchanging developments that may impact my granddaughter."

Having barged into Buzz's week, Helen now chose to let him talk so she stopped abruptly.

Buzz held the phone receiver away from his ear shaking his head. He thought, *Well, now I know why Katie talks about her grandmother like a force of nature. Ok, time to get better acquainted.*

"Helen, I'm all for a dialogue. Let me interject, I sweep the lines in this compound continually but that doesn't mean…."

In her usual style Helen finished his thought for him "…that the conversation is secure. I have a more severe precautionary system but I don't trust that either. Welcome to the swimming hole. I just assume everything is being recorded. If we have something of a critical nature to exchange I work with someone …"

Now it was Buzz's turn to cut Helen off.

"That has to be the Eshelmans from Israel, I use them as well. I think their services are top notch."

Helen rolled her eyes and thought, *Impressing the alpha female with your worldly expertise? Well I'm impressed, I thought they were my secret?*

Buzz continued, "Helen, what's on your mind?"

She replied, "After the news about Katie's little vision concerning the bomb with the mushroom cloud, her mother gets some odd calls, then through my government connections I get word that an unidentified federal agency believes she is being tracked because her ability to predict an event is so valuable. Tracked means potentially snatched and made captive. The next part I won't say out loud but there is evidence this could be an unfriendly foreign power. Now the stakes are obviously growing, so, they want to assign a protective person to Katie and I want you to sell her on this idea. If I merely open my mouth she reacts negatively. They will send this person to meet you first, that will be in two hours."

Buzz thought, *Helen you certainly are presumptuous. In two hours this guy shows up, what if I was in Illinois or Africa? Oh, she already researched my whereabouts I bet. Ok, this is Helen at work, I get it.*

Helen concluded, "Buzz, she needs a male figure she can lean on. Her dad, Paul, travels incessantly as you know. And I need a totally dependable source of information about her activities. In particular, I think you know this, the same government service providing her coverage has also been tracking her potential connections to a few incidents where animal abusers were beat up or maybe it's all this hacker nonsense. I am certainly not saying it's Katie but certain parties are likely to think so. Ok, I have to run, good talking with you, let me know how the meeting today goes, I gave your Marta my direct and private number already plus my secure email. Please use them."

The phone line suddenly went dead. Buzz smiled and said out loud to himself, "Welcome to Helen's world."

Three hours later Sal Torpaydo, Kate's maternal grandfather was summoned to the phone at his warehouse. He used this line for important calls which needed to be totally private. Ironically it was a pay phone which Sal had specifically installed as he was convinced payphones were far less prone to monitoring. He took the phone from Bruno.

"Yes, this is Sal."

"Sal, Buzz Roemer in Minnesota. Can you give me a minute, please?"

Sal nodded, "Absolutely Buzz, shoot."

Buzz went on, "I'll make it very brief, I just completed a meeting with a young man who has been assigned to cover your granddaughter. It's from a service I am guessing you encounter steadily, I won't say their name. This person, who I liked even though he was young, informed me that they are tracking a certain party or parties who may want to intercept our girl, borrow her for a few days, try to tap into her presumed talent for predictions. Am I saying this so you know where we are, so far?"

Sal felt a sharp jolt and replied cautiously, "Yes, I believe so. What am I doing about this? She is down here right now with her boyfriend Peter. I have someone loosely assigned to them but they are just kids, I don't want my guys haunting them."

Buzz responded, "Sure, understood. This party from overseas is going to make their move very soon, they apparently know she is there on a little vacation."

Sal reacted almost with an outburst. "Buzz you mean now? How soon, how many people are involved?" Sal rarely got upset but where Kate was involved he could easily lose his cool.

Buzz replied, "Sal, a few, not a threat to life, likely talk with her at a hotel or even in a van, then release her. Obviously that is kidnapping punishable by jail time but these guys are professionals, that's what I'm being told."

Sal grabbed Bruno by his very thick arm and pulled him toward the phone and motioned Bruno should not move.

"Buzz, so this happens soon and these are professionals at work? And this guy you met he's up there, they have no one on her down here in Chicago?"

"Sal, it just was uncovered so you and she are on your own. I won't attempt to tell you what to do on this but you haven't seen your girl in action, I have. Don't crowd her, just let her know to be on guard. I know that sounds cavalier but I trust her instincts. This girl is prepared to rumble. And she has to look out for herself, this is likely to happen again."

Sal hung up the pay phone feeling queasy and unsteady. He realized he was still hanging on to Bruno's arm and brought himself back to the present. "Bruno, take a few people, go to Peter's apartment, you know that place. Shadow he and Katie, don't interfere. Bad people are around, they may try to snatch her. No guns, these will be professionals but she could easily get hurt. I'm sending Carlo with more people to be available. Go quickly and be on your toes."

Sal turned around and grabbed a cell phone. He hurriedly looked up Peter's cell phone which he never called but had in his phone as a precaution. It rang four times and then Peter picked up.

"Peter, this is Sal. Don't say my name out loud. Is Katie with you?"

Peter normally didn't talk with Sal except by accident at his parents' home. This was by design, his father wanted to limit Peter's contact with Sal for legal reasons.

"Hi there. Yes, that's true," Peter responded cheerily. Kate looked up from her stretching on the floor. She thought Peter sounded a bit odd.

"Peter, someone is tracking you and her. They may have bad intentions but you need to go out and go about your business. You will have my guys nearby as company. Peter can you handle this ok?"

Peter suddenly felt a jolt himself. This was Sal Torpaydo asking if Peter could face up to some threatening bad guys. What else could he say but 'yes'?

"Sure that's fine, no problem." Peter was trying to modulate his voice so he sounded calm. Kate had her eyes closed in a yoga pose. Peter waited for her to come up for air. He tried to puzzle out his response. *Sal says go out, be careful. I'm not carrying a weapon and even so I don't know how to use it anyway. Sal will have guys watching us. God, is this what Kate deals with every day? But they might not hurt her? How the hell does he know?*

Peter watched Kate stretching and thought about his responsibility to her. *Ok, I got a plan.*

"Katie, I got an idea, how about we take a run over to Lincoln Park, it's not far, but let's do it on…(Peter walked to his closet and reached inside)… these! It will take like 45 minutes."

"Where on earth did you come up with those, Peter? Are those Rollerblades? That's a nice skate. You want to skate over to this park, what on the sidewalks? I'm ok with that but you can't bully people off the sidewalk, you know."

Peter replied, (puffing out his chest) "I have been in training, I can handle that distance, I can't do what you do but we'll get there. Bring your bow and arrow, I saw it in the car, you can teach me a few tricks."

Kate was quickly processing this last statement in her mind. *Ok, skate over but he's just learning. Sure. Skate on sidewalks and into a park. Could be fun. Why skate? Makes us mobile, gives me an edge, bring the bow and arrow. Peter's voice sounded weird before. Ummm. I smell a call from Sal saying something may be up. But if there is a problem what the heck does Peter do? Peter knows I can use the bow and arrow for defense but I bet he's not going to tell me anything.*

Peter was standing hands on hips with a quizzical look. "So, is that ok with you?"

Kate popped up off the floor, gave him a big smile. "Sure sweetie, we'll do it just like you said."

Peter replied, "Sometime before you leave I want to see you in that *GloryDays* outfit, the red and yellow super outrageous one. But it doesn't have to be right now. But I would like to be seen with the hottest girl in Chicago."

Kate was thinking, *Normally I'd just wear that but is Peter purposely trying to get me super colorful so I'm easier to spot? Man, life shouldn't be this complicated. Katherine, you do have a sinister bent sometimes.*

Peter watched her disappear in the bedroom. He grabbed his cell phone, realized he'd have to walk down to the first floor, then strap on the 'blades so leave shoes down on the landing, bring the jacket with the big pockets, bring the small baseball bat that fits into the pocket. He'd carried it before for protection but had no clue if he could use it?

Ten minutes later Kate was leading Peter down the sidewalk on North Clark Street headed for Lincoln Park. On the mid summer day only a few people were walking leaving sidewalks easy to navigate.

She yelled, "Ok, you're saying make a right, cross over to that street and we just head straight. Honey, you ok doing this on 'blades?" Kate pulled one of her little tricks and began skating backwards seemingly unaware of obstacles but she could see with two mirrors on her helmet and she could keep track of her guy. Peter was struggling a bit at curbs but Chicago had put in access ramps at most corners so they could skate smoothly.

Kate slowed for a corner and did a very wide sweep of the area. *Ok, do I see my good friend Bruno in that Cadillac down the block? Hi Bruno, ok, we're getting the Sal coverage treatment. What else do we have around? Well, looks like just Bruno. Oh, grandpa Sal, you're such a sweetie looking out for us.*

Peter found he had his hands full just staying upright but he assumed someone was tracking them after Sal's call.

The truth was, since Kate had been spotlighted on the news repeatedly for having foreseen the blast overseas she had begun feeling uncomfortable about the public exposure. Her mother, then Cory, then a press agent she worked with all brought up public reaction to her having "saved" a whole small town.

Kate thought, *I certainly did not save the entire town but I had a hand in it. Now I see why Helen has been telling me to be careful about public pronouncements. It's spooky that anyone would think I have some capacity to tell the future. I don't. But I did have that vision. And the one out in San Francisco. Thank god that got much less public coverage. Just this one incident in Asia is bringing weirdos out of the woodwork.*

In a few more minutes Peter was becoming more confident. He had done some lightweight training but he was certainly nervous trying to keep up with Kate who was almost blasé about urban obstacles. When she encountered cars crossing their paths she easily dodged around, sidestepped hydrants and mailboxes, just appeared to be out for a little, easy skate.

Kate called out to Peter, "Are we gonna hit that park soon? I can wear the bow over my upper body, it's not a problem. Just let me know if I need to turn left or right?"

Kate ran one hand down to the quiver bouncing off her right hip filled with arrows. Most were garden variety target arrows with blunt metal tips. Two were more threatening.

Kate paused at West Schiller and looked around more carefully. *Ok, Bruno is back there. That innocent Ford sedan, I know that car. It's Carlo's. He likes it because it sort of looks like a cop car. Ok, this looks like a green space coming up. That was quick.*

Kate waited for a light. Peter skated up, she put her arm through his and hugged him. She was starting to relax. Maybe this was just recreational skating and they could 'blade around the park and then shoot some targets. That would be fun.

She thought, *Kate tone down the suspicious stuff.*

Peter said, "Right up there is a nice path, it winds around in the park. I saw some hay bales with targets last week, maybe it's still there?" Peter also was thinking the quiet park looked great, he knew Katie did not care for noisy downtowns and hated high rise buildings.

Kate skated backwards watching Peter but also monitoring any uninvited company. Bruno now lagged back a few blocks as there were few cars around and Carlo seemed to have disappeared. Then a semi trailer truck pulled into an intersection and Bruno disappeared. Kate thought about it and concluded they were fine without supervision.

She sighed and relaxed some more. This was looking like a real walk in the park. She and Peter began bantering about where they'd go to dinner and maybe they should invite a few people. They both enjoyed eating out but as Peter was on a tight budget they went for economical places. The couple had agreed early on to split costs even though Kate earned very good money. But she did not want Peter feeling inferior for lack of funds so they ate modestly.

Kate turned around skating casually, almost languidly backwards. Her unhurried pace matched Peter's normal pace. She thought, *Ok, now I don't even see Bruno although he could be over behind that grove of trees. I really need to keep an eye on my darker thoughts. Not every phone call is from Sal about something threatening.*

Skirting around a baseball diamond Peter spotted the small archery range and pointed to it. They skated up and stopped. The targets were set up on the edge of a small paved lot so they could keep their 'blades on for now. Kate lifted the bow off her abdomen and pulled the quiver full of arrows off her waist belt. She fitted one arrow with a near blunt end to the bow, took aim and nailed the first target as a bullseye. Peter watched her. "So is it all bullseyes for you?"

Kate smiled, "I've been practicing archery since I was like ten and I've gotten real damn accurate. If you practice anything this long you should get pretty good." She rolled over to Peter, showed him the correct stance for his feet and then the proper way to hold the bow and level it with the target. She said, "Take your time, don't think about what I do, just make it your own, ok?"

Peter tried a few arrows and managed to hit the target each time but hardly a bullseye.

Kate laughed along with him and stayed out of the way. She backed up a bit and turned slightly when she noticed company. Two cars that had not been there had just materialized equidistant from she and Peter at ends of the parking lot, fifty yards away each direction. She looked for Bruno or Carlo but they were not immediately evident.

Kate rolled casually toward Peter as if to instruct him. She whispered, "Honey, we have company behind us, don't turn around. Could be nothing but I want to see who gets out of those cars." .

Peter felt his stomach bottom. He whispered back, "Katie, I got a confession. That was Sal who called. He said we might have company, someone perhaps trying to snatch you. I didn't want to upset you."

Kate took a short breath. "Peter don't worry, but if this is trouble you must follow my directions. I've had training for this kind of situation." She squeezed his arm. Her stomach was also churning.

Peter tried to make like he was paying attention to the targets but he swiveled to see one car, there were two occupants. Kate put one hand on his shoulder as if to direct him and she whispered, "The one to our left, it's two guys, the same with the other. So here's what we do. Give me the bow, you skate over and get those arrows. If they start moving toward us, we are skating away, but, Peter you must do this, we separate. If there is trouble it's me they want, I can get away and you need to take off. Don't be a hero, I'm in good shape here."

Peter did as she told him, went over to retrieve the arrows and looked at the two cars. These were not family picnickers, four men who had short crew cuts and appeared burly. Then the two on the right opened their doors and stepped out appearing not to pay attention to Kate and Peter. The two on the left did the same and purposely looked the other direction. Peter skated back.

"What do you think, Kate?" His voice betrayed nervousness.

"Peter, I am not getting good vibes at all. Here's the plan, we skate over toward that grove of trees, I'm pretty sure Bruno is parked there. I can just make out a car. If I'm right you skate directly for him, don't turn toward me. I can take care of myself, I'm armed and on skates. Please don't worry." She reached over and pulled him close giving him a big kiss on the cheek. Then she said, "We go now, look happy."

They began skating, advanced forty yards and both parties of men started walking and then almost immediately running to intercept them. There was no one else anywhere near them, Kate guessed they had been watching from a distance until they got the right moment.

One man called out with a murky Russian accent, "Ms. McGill, we came to meet you, our company wants to talk with you for two hours and you'll be paid."

Kate answered, "If you want me to take you seriously stop running now, I will give you a way to make contact with me but don't act like a bunch of thugs!"

The four men began running faster and were, at least, catching Peter.

Kate said to Peter, "Go, call Sal, tell him where we are, don't wait for me. Go Peter, please don't worry!"

Peter did as he was told sprinting as best he could toward the grove of trees his heart beating at a jackhammer pace.

Kate turned, reversed course to take the men away from Peter, began skating backwards fitting an arrow into her bow. As she skated she said to herself, "Keep coming, leave him alone, I'm the prize, don't give up your prize!"

She shouted, "If you don't stop I will defend myself, you are threatening my life, I can legally shoot each of you and I don't miss!"

The men began shouting to each other in what sounded like Russian to Kate. They began spreading out to surround her.

She again shouted, "Stop! Stop now!"

They were closing. She turned to her left, her best mobile shot, and dropped the man closest with an arrow in the upper chest, above his heart. He went down clutching his chest and screaming.

The man to his right couldn't believe it. She had taken out Churlov almost casually. He began questioning their mission. But their leader in a dark suit began barking directions in Russian, "Surround her, go that way, It was a lucky shot, that's all."

Kate looked across the parking lot and could not see Peter. Now she was free to attack.

One of the three remaining dropped back after seeing his compatriot take an arrow but he was reaching into his coat pocket. Kate assumed he would have a pistol.

She turned, taking a chance they would not attempt to shoot her in the back and took off at top speed away from the other three. She heard a loud bang, guessed it would be a warning shot, if any, kept skating furiously, then she turned. The men were all running for one car leaving their comrade writhing on the ground. Then she saw Peter in the distance apparently making a cell phone call.

Kate knew her only chance lay in leaving the park but that was some four blocks away and she had no idea how far it would be to other city streets so she set her course back the way she came. Glancing over one shoulder she could see the Dodge four door sedan accelerating toward her. Now she had to assume this was not a kidnapping, it could be life threatening. She could hope help would arrive but there was no guarantee.

The pursuing Dodge was almost on her. She turned skating backwards, brought up the bow now holding an Axis Full Metal Jacket Dangerous Game arrow which would do much more damage but now she needed an opening, an opportunity.

The man in the back seat was leaning out the window with some kind of rope sling in his hands. He was going to try and rope her. In fact, he began twirling the rope like a lariat used in rodeos. She waited and even waited a bit longer as she had been trained, she looked at the others but there were no guns yet.

Then she let loose the arrow often used to bring down big game by hunters. It entered his upper chest pinning his left arm, a move she was taught by a Special Forces veteran who was also an archer. The second man to be hit dropped his lariat and spontaneously plummeted out of the speeding car onto the roadway. The Dodge suddenly dropped back, the passenger leaped out, went to his compatriot's side and then ran back to the car giving Kate some time.

She turned and fled skating forward reaching a speed rarely touched by most skaters but still well short of anything a normal car can achieve. She knew she had only a few moments. As she skated she reached for a third arrow, dropped one, but managed to hold on to the next. She had only two more left and one was just for target practice.

Kate rounded a corner skating at her fastest pace. Up ahead a family of two adults and two small kids were walking across a green lawn. Kate could barely notice, her only thought being the pursuers. The father gestured toward Kate and brought up a video camera.

The Dodge was again catching up and she figured this time it would be with something far more deadly. Up ahead she saw the small stadium she and Peter passed on their skate in. Stadiums were a natural habitat for Kate having presented numerous shows in athletic fields over the years. She skated for the structure again looking over her shoulder at the speeding car.

She managed to career into a parking lot and saw a ramp leading up to the bleachers. She knew that would force the two men out of their car. Skating madly she headed up the ramp, her nervous system nearly maxed out from fight or flight. She immediately discovered the ramp stopped at a wall. She was trapped.

The pursuers slammed on their brakes, jumped from the car and this time seemed to have weapons. She had no place to flee. She brought her bow up with another hunters' arrow. She could take out one of them, there wouldn't be time for a second.

The men split up, one running up the ramp, the second approaching through some bleacher seats. The one on the ramp was coming faster, she had no choice. This time she aimed for the heart, a shot she almost never missed in target practice. The man fell screaming, the weapon fell from his hand.

She reached for the next arrow knowing she likely wouldn't make it. Her entire nervous system spasmed, she felt a terribly sharp shaft of light in her brain and the last man fell on the bleacher seats holding his head and neck.

There had been no gunshot, she shot no arrow, did he have a heart attack or stroke?

She looked up to see Bruno and Carlo with a number of men running crazily toward her with weapons drawn. They ran headlong for her from all sides and suddenly they stopped in their tracks. Two of them cried out in pain.

Kate was at a total loss until she realized her body felt paralyzed. Did she have a stroke? What had happened? She felt her body becoming nearly rigid. She might be dying from some brain aneurism?

Peter came running across the parking lot with a small baseball bat in his hand. He headed straight for Kate, stumbled and then yelled, "What the hell? Ouch, my head is splitting!"

Kate tried to look around although her neck felt stiff and unyielding. No one was moving anywhere close to her. She could see two men clutching their heads down the bleacher rows.

Kate felt paralyzed but she could also feel the spasm easing. A few men were starting to move but slowly. She tried to make sense of what happened. *The guy was running toward me and then he drops like a rock? What on earth? Oh...oh good lord, I felt something like that with Queen Royal. I bet my freaked out emotions triggered the Romanian Cold Hand?*

Kate spontaneously began laughing but her head and neck hurt so much she had to stop. She stood still feeling stupid but she was really unable to move.

In another thirty seconds her body began returning to normal, Bruno was now moving and walked to the fallen pursuer lifting him completely off the ground with one arm. The man was in a state of shock.

Kate could hear sirens coming from every side. She saw Bruno's men unobtrusively putting away their weapons. Bruno told a few of them to walk away. "Don't run guys, just head back to your cars if you can."

Now police in uniforms piled out of two cars weapons drawn. Kate stood wobbly on her skates. She looked down, she was standing alone on the ramp. Peter groggily walked to her side and embraced her.

A police captain with bars and stars walked toward Kate. "Uh, miss, we picked up some men on the road in here with arrows in them. Can you shed any light on what happened?"

She realized this could be gigantic trouble. She may have killed people no matter the reason.

Just then Sal's limo screeched to a halt, Sal jumped out of the rear seat and began running toward Kate. He called out, "Katie, you don't need to answer questions without a lawyer present."

Sal ran up breathing hard. "Hello Captain Corcoran. This is my granddaughter, she was being chased by a number of men who were attempting to kidnap her!"

The Captain looked over at Sal. "Well, Sal, nice seeing you again. So your lovely granddaughter left quite a trail of maimed men behind her. Now I know who she is, the young McGill woman. I've read about your prowess with bow and arrow. So, Ms. McGill, your grandfather is right, you can wait to speak with counsel present but it would be helpful to know, were you being pursued by some men?"

Kate felt she had to give him some answer. Looking at Sal she said, "My boyfriend Peter and I were out skating when four men in two cars began chasing us, we fled and they came after us." She stopped talking, utterly unsure what kind of trouble she might be in.

The Captain turned around and looked back where his car was parked running and shouted, "Bill, what shape are these men in, the ones you found?"

Bill shouted back, "Three men, only one speaks English, the others I think speak Russian. One took an arrow right next to his heart but he's alive. The others are badly roughed up but breathing. Two are headed for the hospital, the third in a minute. Someone is one helluva shot with a bow and arrow. Expert marksmanship!"

The Captain turned back around. "Ms. McGill, we will need you to give a report to this gentleman over here. We will wait, if you wish, for a lawyer to assist you. We know your grandfather knows a few attorneys. So make a call, please. You can just sit down on the bleachers and we'll take our report. Uh, off the record, if Bill says you're a crack shot I'll accept his reading. Sal, quite a granddaughter you have here."

Peter stood with Kate, one arm around her waist hugging her. Sal did his best to hide his grandfatherly pride in Kate. She felt her body slowly returning. Kate looked around. She thought, *Well, girl, no one died. Peter's ok, I'm ok. Did I get a free pass?*

Helen's private office line rang. She picked up.

"Helen, it's Buzz Roemer. Here's a little report about Katie. Some guys in Chicago chased her, she was on skates and had her bow and arrow."

Helen's heart began pounding. "Oh my god! What happened to her?"

"She took them all out, one is in serious condition, an arrow just wide of his heart. But the last one is interesting. Dropped in his tracks with no arrows. Kate must have inadvertently triggered the Cold Hand. That's what Sal told me. Sal said all the people who were near her felt paralyzed."

Helen thought, *Oh, God, that could have been just awful. I don't want this for Katie. But...she is a Harendt!*

Buzz added, "Uh, Helen, so she's ok, just emotionally shaken up. Unfortunately, 40 seconds of this is on video tape, a man with a camera was nearby."

"And?"

"He sold it to a Chicago tv station, it could be on the six o'clock news locally."

Sit in with Helen Aray explaining the Harendt legacy to Kate at www.katemcgill. com under "chapters".

CHAPTER TWENTY ONE

KATE TAKES THE FBI FOR A RIDE IN THE MULE

Kate was now putting the incident in Chicago behind her, the end of the summer was approaching, she had done a few small midwest tours promoting *GloryDays* but had enough time off for herself. She again missed Peter but he had an obligation in a training program in Chicago. Kate felt they had a good understanding of their relationship but it would still be some time before they were again together.

It had taken the incident in Russia with the bomb that discharged a small mushroom cloud to turn Kate into a much larger public phenomenon. Within days Sarah McGill called Buzz Roemer to report she was being shadowed or so she thought. Shortly thereafter Kate was informed first by Aggie Roemer then the FBI that the incident involving her premonition could put her in some danger. Kate herself was quite unsure how accurate the vision really was but crooks and intelligence sleuths could find her potential for envisioning a future event compelling.

Kate received a call from Bart Alliason at NETFODI. "Katie, you know the vision or whatever you call it is triggering responses. We believe you can use some protection, not a herd of agents, just one person to look after you for the present."

Kate's first reaction was to reject the coverage. It sounded grim and inflexible. But the Chicago incident changed her outlook considerably. "Bart, I don't really want this but I had a close call a few weeks back so I'm more open to it now."

Bart replied, "Katie, very smart. These people, whoever they may be, don't know if you can turn this little talent on and off or what? So those guys in Chicago were likely being told to bring you in, have you talk to someone. I'm sure they did not expect Robin Hood on skates with a bow and arrow. We found a young agent, a bit older than you, he will not be a problem. You'll like him, I think. I certainly did. His name is very unusual, Arkadia Ansil. A very competent young man and nice looking as well. Not that it will matter, of course. He can meet you at your parents' home in Minnesota."

Kate had to admit being intrigued about her own FBI protection. It was flattering but then she realized this "young man" might turn out to be stiff as a board and she'd be stuck with him. Would he be following her back to California? She had no idea?

Agent Ansil turned up at Sarah's wearing a suit, knocked on the door and waited respectfully back a few paces. The Minnesota summer was enjoying a delightful run of sunny days and higher temperatures. Kate answered the door wearing her favorite bikini, looked out and realized she was dressed quite inappropriately. Agent Ansil turned away shyly while introducing himself. Kate excused herself, threw on jeans and a polo shirt returning barefoot to let him in.

Agent Ansil had a preamble of instructions to present to Kate, what he could and could not do. He would follow her around, not ride in the car with her. He talked on for some minutes explaining the standard procedures. Kate pulled a knee up on the couch and studied Agent Ansil. Buzz was right, he was cute and so self effacing, he did not want to intrude. He was not checking Kate out at all which amazed her. She had not seen Peter Scalissi for five weeks with all her traveling and Peter's new job in Chicago. She found herself reasoning through her obligations. While she had no intention of trying to romance another guy this Agent Ansil grew quickly on her. Expecting a tough guy ex military type she was intrigued with his low key but very professional approach. After ten minutes Kate found herself having a little fantasy about her new FBI tail and then felt embarrassed at her own foolishness. This guy was assigned to protect her not have a physical relationship.

Sarah came in the back door, entered the living room introduced herself to Agent Ansil and began asking numerous questions. "Was he armed? Would he actually prevent someone from approaching Kate? Would he protect Kate back at school?" Sarah took some time to get her necessary answers. Meantime, Kate sat with her chin on one upraised knee and found herself dreamily fantasizing about this young man. The more Sarah talked the more vibrant Kate's daydreams became. Peter seemed far removed and, after all, they weren't engaged or even discussing marriage were they? It had been some time since Kate allowed the feminine side of her personality to take control and she was really enjoying the ride. While the world encountered Kate the aggressive skater or *GloryDays* model, the young woman herself had other very normal and mainstream ideas. She liked handsome guys and here she had her own built-in cutie.

Sarah finished up, Kate had only half heard the dialogue and wasn't really worried about it anyway. Agent Ansil stood up and approached both women to excuse himself. He would apparently be housed in a local motel in Wayzata. Kate began wondering if he could maybe stay in the spare bedroom in their house and then realized she was well down the wrong road with Agent Ansil. This was going to be business for him. She thought he looked pretty good in his dark blue suit, it could use some reshaping but not bad at all for an FBI agent.

The screen door closed and Kate had to shut down her dream factory.

For two days Agent Ansil tracked Kate McGill all over south Minnesota. She made no attempt to shake him off, he was her first FBI agent and he made her comfortable tailing her. He was courteous, had a sense of humor, didn't place himself in her line of sight and did his best to avoid gawking at Kate. He was, in fact, a fan of Kate's, had her two skating videos, knew her history and secretly admired her perceived reputation for kicking the crap out of animal abusers.

Kate thought Agent Ansil was incredibly cute. He had this funny way of looking a bit sideways at her. They were almost the same height so the few times they came in direct contact it was eye to eye. Kate liked men in strong physical condition and Agent Ansil was muscular, sinewy, walked erect and seemed agile.

Across town at Buzz Roemer's compound there was serious concern brewing. "It's Buzz Roemer calling, yes thank you. Director, I appreciate your talking now. Last night I received two calls from parties who had some interest in talking with Kate McGill, essentially trying to employ her to help, uh, foresee market conditions. It happens she's here in town but will return west soon. Then this morning, there was the mysterious full page ad in the Star-Tribune our local newspaper. I'll read it to you, 'Our company wants to sit down with Kate McGill for two hours. We'll pay her what is required. We don't sell products or services but we need her guidance and wisdom. We are not military in any form, we will not re-sell anything we learn and whatever we pay you, Kate, we'll pay the same amount to a legitimate charity of your choice.' There was no phone or email or anything. Instead it said, 'If you are Kate you'll know how to find us.'"

Buzz took a breath and said, "Yes sir, I agree, pretty cheeky of them. I'm calling because we want to protect her. Your agent Ansil is on duty, here, we know that. Ok, we're going to do our best to bring Kate's public profile way down for a while. This should blow over. That's our hope, sir."

Later in the day Kate arrived as requested at Buzz's offices where they began discussing how she could be better protected. Buzz was trying to sell a more stringent security profile possibly with a backup guard, using a driver, limited her public exposure even more.

"Buzz, listen, I appreciate everyone's concern but so far no scary guys are turning up at our door step in Wayzata and if they try to tail me I can shake them easily enough in the mule. I can live with Agent Ansil, he's a good fit but no more. I have a feeling there won't be a repeat of the Chicago incident." Kate had become very confident of her driving skills. This was upsetting her, all this threatening talk and she wanted her freedom back.

Buzz stood hands folded behind his back listening to Kate's discourse. He let her ramble for some minutes and then interrupted her. "Katie, here's the difficult truth. You have two shadows already right here in town. Did you know that?"

Kate stood up getting really steamed up. She resented this intrusion no matter how well intentioned. "Who, where? I'm pretty alert, there's no one on my rear end."

Buzz went to his desk and picked up two 8 x 10 black and white pictures. "We have someone tracking you Katie. This guy was parked a half block from your Mom's place but Agent Ansil scared him off. This other guy, we think, is just taking pictures for gossip magazines but either one could be much more threatening."

Kate lost it. "God damn it Buzzer, I really appreciate your doing all this but I am prepared to take my chances and that's that." Kate stomped out of the office.

When Kate walked out of Buzz's garage steamed up headed for the mule, it was Agent Ansil who she confronted. He parked unobtrusively outside the parking lot but she walked straight to his anonymous Chevrolet Impala.

"If you're following me today you'll have to drive fast, I'm really pissed off."

He gave her his best uncolored quiet response, nodding acknowledgement. She stood a few feet away, legs apart, hands on hips, her hair bound up in a head scarf, her frame poured into snug jeans and a dark blue t-shirt. Agent Ansil made a point of looking at her shoulders up even though the rest of him wanted to examine shoulders down. She watched his eyes and cracked a slight grin.

"Agent Ansil, you do a good job of keeping eye contact when that's not what you want to do, is it?" Now she grinned more. "So I won't tell J. Edgar if you sneak a few peeks, I don't mind." To make her point she did a little curtsy pointing her rear end out just a bit.

"Ms. McGill, I have your two posters at my apartment back home, you have a sensational, well, bottom, but I can converse with a woman and not look at her body if that's ok with you?"

Kate blushed a bit and felt embarrassed. For a fed he came off like a good guy.

She nodded and found her exasperation dissipating but she was still pumped to get crazy. "Tell you what, where I'm going is forty miles out country roads. Would the big Kahunas think badly of you rode with me? Then you can't lose me."

He stared out his windshield. The 27 year old guy part of him was going nuts at the opportunity but the Responsible Agent part was considering. "What are you planning to do, Ms. McGill?"

"Drive real god damn fast, get sideways, play music way too loud, get some thrills. Wanna come? Otherwise I'll lose you for sure. Where I'm goin' an Impala will be hopeless."

Then she turned on her heel and headed for the mule. Now he looked at her rear end but realized she was going away quickly. "What the hell...."

He locked the sedan and walked after her to reach the mule parked under a grove of low hanging trees.

She turned and watched him approach. It had been some time since she felt like looking a guy over. He was cute, walked sort of like a ballet dancer, light on his feet, his longish curly hair kind of bounced. She liked that.

Kate placed her hands against the roof line of the Audi Quattro and pushed against the car to stretch her calf muscles. She held a firm pose applying pressure to stretch her muscles. She looked down at the car door and the ground below. This was very different for Kate. She wasn't spooking him, he seemed so calm, well prepared.

She finished her stretching and lifted one leg placing that foot through the car window on to the seat. "You get in through the window, the doors don't open, they are bolted shut for rigidity. I gotta get them opened up. Anyway turn and slide down into the seat. You'll fit ok. Hop in."

They both slid in their respective windows and snuggled into the heavily padded and reinforced seats. She reached above him. "Here, drape these over your shoulders. Wait, take off that jacket, put it behind you. It gets hot in here, the engine heat comes back inside." She helped him remove the jacket and she draped it over the space where the rear seat had been. "Ok, snug down the shoulder harness, right, like that. You brace your feet in those two foot holds, right arm and hand over here, your left holds either to this bar or that one near the floor. Grab the helmet, hold it in your lap. You don't need it for a little while, I'll tell you."

She carefully checked his harness being sure to run her hand down his shoulders as she went. He looked straight ahead, said nothing but was enjoying her touch. She was enjoying the touching. He wanted to grin but held it in.

"Cell phones are not much good in here, interference from the electronics which are totally unshielded but you'll have fifteen minutes where the phone may work."

He watched her out of the corner of his eye. He thought she was really something.

A grey mat covered the floor and up the sides of the interior, a few lights blinked off and on as she threw switches, then she reached for a button on the dash and the interior overflowed with mechanical gear noises, a strange sucking sound and then the exhaust which made an intense ripping sound as she revved the engine. In front of her a couple instruments, a crude metallic dashboard, a bunch of unmarked toggle switches, Kate studied gauges, tightened her shoulder belts and glanced at Agent Ansil.

When she let out the clutch the mule dove forward and in moments they were flying down a narrow road toward a freeway. When she reached an entry ramp she shoved her foot down hard and the Audi Quattro screamed forward popping up through three gears, then two more. The acceleration shoved them hard back in the bucket seats and he grasped the grab bars hard. She rocketed up to 90, then briefly blasted to 120 to pass a few trucks. Suddenly they dropped to 65 and all the racket died down.

"Geez, this thing really flies!"

Kate nodded, was distractedly watching a gauge, ran the mule up two gears. "It runs way cold and it's hard, sometimes, to keep the plugs clean so I have to keep the revs up for a bit. You ok all belted in?"

He was stoked, this was more car than he'd ever been in including his brother's Corvette. "You obviously know this beast well?"

She smiled and settled in, both hands on the small rubber wrapped wheel. "Buzz loans this to me, looks beat to crap purposely, built to run from cops in Europe. Owned by a bad guy who thought the French or Italian police wouldn't recognize what the Audi Sport Quattro was capable of. This one was breathed on by a tuner in Austria, the big KKK turbo is not standard. It'll touch maybe 150 with this gearing, runs special Continental rally tires, major humongo brakes. You'll maybe see it spits fire when the turbo gate captures some liquid gas but it's exciting. Uh, if we, you know, roll, uh, tip over, just hold on to those bars. I had it on its head once, that's where the dents in the roof came from. The roll cage is super strong, the gas tank is a safety cell, you'll be ok. But get out right away. And haul me out if I'm not moving, alright?"

All his FBI training had not prepared Agent Ansil to roll cars into the ditch and he was aware that he hoped not to pee in his pants.

"Ok, helmet on." Kate paused the mule at a stop sign. She also pulled on her full front coverage helmet with "Devastator Babe" painted across the side. "You hear me ok? Alright, we'll go fast, I've done this road numerous times, I grew up driving out here. I just went over her end to end, every bracket and safety device, the gas tank cell, all checked out. Plug this line from the helmet in this box, now we can hear each other. If there is a police car, uh, tell me, don't get too excited. If you feel like you're gonna throw up tell me, I'll pull over."

"That happen to all your passengers?" He wasn't smiling now.

"Naw, just the pussies who get the jitters. Ok, time to haul some ass here."

Mechanical screams suddenly filled the interior, the mule went sideways and in seconds they were barreling down a scarily narrow road, sharp turns into a forest, onto a dirt and gravel road and now Kate brought the speed way up. Agent Ansil was already seriously apprehensive. She immediately had them at blinding speeds, the trees were seemingly inches from the doors. Most of all, the power slides had them sideways around corners. Descending a steep hill, flying literally half the way, she jumped all over the brakes and from 90 or 100 they were suddenly in switchbacks at 25 but she made the corners by yanking up on the hand brake between the seats momentarily. The mule's back end came flying around and Kate brought the revs up to 6000 and the car exploded out of each corner.

For ten minutes she focused in on dancing the mule between trees and bushes, sliding corners with the Audi Quattro's four wheels clawing for traction and Kate gunning the turbocharged five cylinder which responded with strange sucking and popping sounds. They were flying between 40 and 90 down the narrow roads, the acceleration throwing them both back against the headrests.

Suddenly a large farm truck appeared in the middle of the road 200 feet away. At 80 miles per hour she couldn't stop so Kate pointed the mule at a hillside and drove around the large truck swerving left and right to avoid the bigger bushes.

For another few minutes the mule crested small hills going airborne, they were partially sideways half the time, the mule's four wheel drive constantly grappeling for traction on the loose stones and dirt. Kate was attempting to be un-self conscious about this macho display of bravado on her part but dragging an innocent into it was wearing on her, much less him.

Cresting a steep hill, gravel spewing off all four wheels under power, the mule dropped in a metallic thud on the down side and Kate opened the five banger, turbo spooling up, side exhausts barking a guttural roar the speedo blasted past 130 and the needle pinned. For perhaps a minute she was able to keep the mule in a straight line but now she was doubting the wisdom of her course. She gradually lowered her speed. Agent Ansil felt an acid taste in his throat, his stomach churning as the Audi Quattro plunged crazily to the hill bottom which is where Kate blurted out, "Oh shit, this creek wasn't here. Geezuz, brace yourself!"

Brakes were useless hurtling toward 3 feet of creek water at over 70. He saw approaching disaster, no way out at this speed. Kate knew they were in trouble. Advice from experienced rally drivers flashed through her mind. No time to explain.

The mule was suddenly skidding sideways and Kate whipped the wheel applying all possible power, the motor shrieking, gravel flying every direction but a sliver of hope prompted desperation. Twenty yards short of the water Kate jerked the wheel sharply and the mule rolled sideways into the creek on its roof but the momentum flung the mule across the water, rocks crashing into the metal roof back onto its four wheels but the momentum carried it over again. As the mule hit its wheels for a second time Kate snapped the wheel hard right and the vehicle snapped back almost in a straight line.

A grinding, jangling metallic explosion followed by belches of shooting gravel and burning rubber and the mule spun 270 degrees stopping in a choking cloud of dust and dirt. Neither person spoke for 30 seconds. Kate thought to shut off the motor.

"I'm sorry. That was not called for. You ok, any bleeding?"

Agent Ansil stared straight ahead trying to master his breathing. He checked his hands and legs, reached up to his abdomen, twisted his neck gingerly and then exhaled like a wheezing old steam engine. "Was that planned?"

"Are you kidding? Listen, I am so really sorry. That was utterly stupid. I confused that hill with another one. I am such a god damn idiot. That's all I could think of. A veteran rally driver told me about that roll maneuver."

"Yes, I'll second that. The two rolls, that was interesting."

"Total desperation."

He was feeling sick to his stomach and he realized it might have been gas fumes and all the flames licking at the doors from the exhaust exiting underneath the passenger's door.

She restarted the mule and drove off at 40 miles per hour around a few corners, down another hill. Kate couldn't bring herself to talk and Agent Ansil was still wrestling with his involuntary temptation to throw up.

Kate pulled over and stopped. She unstrapped her helmet and began helping him pull his off. He was feeling a little less peaked. She put her palm on his forehead. He was damp and still queasy. "Come on, unbelt and we'll take a break. There a little stream under those trees. She pulled herself up and out the window in two fluid motions. She walked around and grabbed his shoulders. "Just push up, ok, now turn, grab the roof and pull yourself out. That's it." She made sure to hold on to him a little longer.

Kate was feeling overwhelmingly stupid. Her out of control driving embarrassed and diminished her. His saying nothing made it worse. "Let me apologize again, that was just so dangerous and foolish. I'm sorry I put you through it."

Agent Ansil simply said, "Yes, me too but I survived. It's ok."

Now she felt worse. Driving at 11/10's like that was the same as yelling at the top of your lungs when the other person is two feet away. It was over the top and not fun. He reached over just barely touching her shoulder with two fingers. "It's ok, you handled an emergency. No one was shooting guns, we made it through."

"Yah, but it was so out of control."

"Well, I guess that's you, isn't it?"

Kate didn't reply but thought about his statement as they walked. His observation hit home a little harder than she wanted. *He was right, I am out of control, aren't I?* She was feeling vulnerable and very un-gutsy. She liked his way of dealing with her poor judgment. Not accusatory, very down to earth. She glanced at him. He was an ok guy, no, more than ok. Nice, calm, quite masculine. Getting cuter too.

"Come on, it's just past this canopy of maples, well, and then through this short path." They walked for a few minutes and then emerged at the stream bed. She took his hand and pulled him across the small stream.

Kate motioned for him to sit on the river bank. Water gurgled quietly, a few birds cried out, sun played down through the trees. Two minutes earlier he was riding in a banshee of racket with flames shooting out the sides.

Neither talked. He sat cross legged dangling a hand into the water. She stretched out her legs and leaned against a tree stump. Minutes passed. He glanced her direction, Kate's eyes were closed, hands folded in her lap. She sensed his interest and opened her eyes momentarily. She smiled and closed her eyes again. His heart distinctly fluttered. Now she slumped into a nap. He stared at her. Her eyes overwhelmed her nose, wait, no, her mouth, particularly when she curled up the left side of the top lip. He scanned down her body but he returned to her face. Now he could see what made her fascinating. Her face had this way of looking strangely immature, almost kid like and then she got serious and this very strong adult emerged. He wondered what she looked like if she was, if she was stimulated, aroused? He caught himself thinking unprofessional thoughts. He was so enjoying the thoughts. *God, here I am with this babe, no, with this woman who people idolize. She is trusting me, totally. I could slide over there, I could take her hand in mine. Man, I'm that close. What would any guy do?*

Arkadia turned away, leaned back, dropped his head into some grass and exhaled. *Here I am, this is just ridiculous. I'm supposed to shadow her, now I'm having all these romantic and sexual thoughts. FBI training did not address this one.*

He felt like just letting go for a while. The anxious driving took its toll.

They both napped as the creek burbled away. She awoke first. She extended a leg over and gently prodded his lower leg. "Hey, Agent Ansil, Arkadia, cool name. Time to wake up." She left her toe there and prodded another time. He was awake already and wanted her to keep it up, then he smiled and laughed. She giggled.

"Ms. McGill, we were both out for 45 minutes. Wadda ya think?"

Kate sat up. "I guess we have this unresolved relationship deal don't we? Am I the prey, are you the hunter? You let me know, alright?"

He didn't really want this to stop, professionalism be damned. Arky thought this might be one of the sexiest moments of his life. *Her toe is touching my calf. Boy, raw sex!* Except that it was genuinely sexy and also endearing. He found her hard to really think of as a sexual babe. She was too valuable somehow, a person he could admire and find so challenging to understand.

Without warning she rolled over once and paused right above him, inches from his face. He felt her breathing on him. She gave off the faintest aroma of an elusive perfume. He kept his eyes closed. The combination of feminine assertiveness and trust struck him as so romantic, so intriguing and yet it wasn't clear she was coming on to him. Finally he opened his eyes. Kate was inches from his face smiling a crooked grin.

Kate loved him not grabbing her or trying to kiss her. She found it so enticing that she could be in this close and this guy maintained a discreet couple inches. Arky looked into her eyes, her left was ever so slightly grayer than the other, her nose up so close had a maddening little bend you never saw in her pictures, her teeth were quite white, the only part of her face that might be considered near perfect.

The eyes just bore in on him. Neither one wanted to move in yet and it wasn't even clear they would touch. Then she dropped her head and body on his chest, her mouth an inch from the bottom of his chin.

Arky felt honored she would trust him. He brought his right arm across and it rested on her back. She snuggled in a bit closer and that almost blew him away. It wasn't a sexual snuggle but it was so incredibly intimate. She was comfortable pressing her body into his.

"I'm not sure how I'll write this up for my report."

She blurted out a giggle, her face half pressed into his chest. He smelled sweaty but good sweaty, not nervous. Most men who got close gave off this jittery vibe. Arkadia was reserved, respectful even when she was almost offering herself. Not quite but close. She found herself feeling aroused and this was getting complicated. She wasn't ready to be sexual with Arkadia but the desire was beginning to spread. She delicately lifted herself off him, then thought better about it and sent him an unmistakable signal moving her upper body across his like a crawling snake and kissed him with some controlled ardor. She also came alert. That last move was a mistake if she wasn't ready to go.

"This is getting a bit hot for me, uh, correction I'm priming the pump myself….Arkadia. But this is not the right time although it's a very wonderful place. So I'll ask for a rain check, please. I don't want to be the temptress. But you're one handsome guy and I'm getting weak in the resistance department. I hope you understand."

He pulled her back down and gave her the best kiss he could muster. She felt her body responding very quickly and she knew holding back might be difficult. *Oh, this could get way hot right now,* she thought.

He lifted her off himself, her breasts collided with his face. He would have given anything to take that further but something kept his arms lifting her off until she found herself on her knees catching her breath.

"I hope we can meet again in such a lovely, quiet spot. I am getting up right now or we'll end up having very unprotected sex and that's not good. Oh, I gotta do something quick."

Kate turned and stepped into the little creek, sat down, fell back and was consumed by the running water. In a moment she resurfaced laughing. "Ok, that did the trick, I'm cooling down nature's way. Agent Ansil, we better head home."

CHAPTER TWENTY TWO

KATE'S NEW FAME AND
SHE MAKES A TV APPEARANCE

Kate assumed any endorsement relationship with *GloryDays* would lead to a few small opportunities, maybe appearances on TV or maybe nothing. She did find Cory's immense enthusiasm for Kate's first print ads infectious. If Cory thought this would lead to something, well, great.

Her experiences with Peter in Chicago were now retreating in memory. The police had been soliciting more commentary from her, Sal had appointed a lawyer to be her interact with the police. But it seemed the authorities were now satisfied that Kate had legitimately defended herself against attackers. Kate had been interested in what happened to her assailants and then decided it was old newspapers for her. The last she heard three of the four were going to be deported back to Russia for using visas that were not legit. Kate decided she didn't care, it was out of her hands anyway.

Some weeks passed, Kate had schoolwork overwhelming her, the GloryDays print ads made their appearances. She took a break from studies and walked down to Telegraph Avenue looking for a place to buy the issues with her ads. She walked into Codys Books, hunted through the magazine section, found one of the issues and stood there looking at herself on the printed page. A young guy walked by glancing over her shoulder.

"Wow, that's you, isn't it?"

Kate was delighted but really embarrassed. The *GloryDays* ad made no bones about her physical shape and Kate had to admit, she hadn't realized how on display she'd look. The male student collared a friend and dragged him over to look.

He said, "So, are you their new national image? My sister wears their stuff, it's cool."

Kate realized it was happening, she was now out there, no fooling.

"Yes, well, really, this is the first ad they've run in a couple magazines. Next week one more will appear in some magazine geared for men."

The second male student chipped in, "Are you kidding, they should run that ad in every magazine read by guys! You are sensational! And you're a student here at Berkeley? That's quite a surprise. Wait, you're the *GloryDays* Girl, they wrote about it in the San Francisco Examiner and I think Channel Two did a short story last night on the news. You're gonna be a big deal young lady! Here, I'm going to buy this copy, can you autograph the page?"

Kate obliged his request and the two boys walked away chattering clutching copies of the magazine. Kate stood in the aisle a bit lost. She was thinking, *Oh, my, is that a sign of the future? I hadn't really thought that photo shoot would be all that big a deal.*

Kate picked up a copy of Elle, a magazine she didn't love, but it also had the full page spread. She thumbed through the magazine and two girls her age walked down the aisle looking for magazines. Kate stepped back to give them room. The girls went hunting in the fashion section and then one of them noticed Kate had the magazine in her hands. The girl said, "Uh, are you buying that issue, we wanted to see...oh, good heavens, you're the girl herself aren't you?"

The second girl took the magazine out of Kate's hands to see the ad and then looked back at Kate. "That really is you isn't it? Wow they did a great job on this picture. Oh, that must have sounded awful. I'm sorry, I didn't mean you don't look great in person. But you just don't expect to see the girl on the page standing here in Codys."

Kate responded, "I just came in to see the ads myself."

The first girl said, "I saw in the Daily Cal that you attend school here. I was surprised such a hotshot would be a student just like us. Are you going to stay in school? I mean, you have this whole other life happening."

Kate replied, "I'm having to make some serious adjustments but I came here to get an education. So, yes, I hope to do all four years and graduate."

The girls looked back at the ad. The first girl commented, "I have to say, I've never seen anyone quite like you. Do you like being this *GloryDays* Girl?"

Kate looked at both attractive girls dressed in preppie clothes. "Honestly, it's just starting, I never thought much about it until now. But it's going to be different. It's strange but nice."

The next night she joined two girl friends at La Vals on the northside of campus. They ordered pizza and a pitcher of beer. Kate really enjoyed the camaraderie and was grateful to get away from all the news attention. As they dug into the pizza two guys passed by and one looked up at the nearby tv which was running the news. He said, "Hey, that's you up there isn't it?"

Kate looked up at the tv and blushed. It was her image once again, now on tv. A few of the guys nearby stood up and cheered for her. She smiled and raised up one arm in a little victory gesture. She thought, *Sometimes this is very nice. It can be fun.*

The next day Kate received a call from Cory. "Hey, Katie, we have some very interesting news for you. Those ads are now out there and our office is getting calls from press, from NBC, CBS even from overseas. Katie, they all want to know the same thing? Who is this new *GloryDays* golden girl? Our first campaign is heading stratospheric to the stars. In all my years doing this I never saw such a strong reaction. And we're opening up in two men's magazines next week because guys see you and go out to buy outfits for wives and girlfriends. Kate McGill, you are looking like a huge hit! Are you ready for this?"

Kate was standing in her kitchen in pajamas, it was seven AM, she had three classes that day and Cory is telling her she was a big hit! This was day two of Kate the media person.

"Cory, I'm working on it. People are relating to me very differently. I was just this student, now I'm in those magazines and I saw that image on tv last night. I'm learning."

But the pace was about to pick up in a serious way. Within a week four major magazines and numerous newspapers ran articles about the new *GloryDays* girl. Something about Kate's pose, appearance, visual attitude was registering loudly. And now guys were suddenly picking up on the *GloryDays* Girl as she was becoming known.

A small article with the ad reproduced appeared in the The Daily Californian and more reactions broke loose on campus for Kate. She had been a pretty girl in jeans and t-shirts who could easily fade into the woodwork if she wanted. In one class she walked in and a whole row of young men stood up and applauded. It was taking no time for people to wake up to the *GloryDays* Girl in their midst. Local fraternities sought her out to attend frat bashes and four sororities discovered the new girl who hadn't pledged so they came to her apartment to pull her in. Two tv crews tracked her down for interviews. Kate purposely walked across the street and stood in front of another apartment building. She could see her normal privacy was disappearing.

But these developments were minor compared to the impact of one reporter at the Wisconsin State Journal who concluded that the mystery woman who had been beating up men who harmed vulnerable animals might just be the *GloryDays* Girl. This reporter had made it his special project to figure out the potential connections even creating a chart showing the dates of incidents and Kate's possible location. Fortunately some of his research was flawed and the proof wasn't clear cut. It was all hypothetical but it spread like a fast moving forest fire. Within a few days Kate's *GloryDays* images were showing up in stories connecting her, possibly, to the Nature Avenger as the attacker was being called.

Kate was also relieved to find out the Nature Avenger might have an imitator. Some young woman had taken on two guys outside Tampa, Florida, a place Kate had never visited. Secretly she began cheering for more imitators to take the heat off herself.

Cory's next call to Kate was completely different. She asked if Kate was hearing about this new hypothesis, the connection between the Nature Avenger and Kate what did she think about the stories, would she like to make any public comment herself? Kate told Cory she would have no statement for now.

GloryDays had planned a huge second campaign with the first now a major hit. Cory initially hesitated and then realized there was no choice. Kate was their girl short of her committing something heinous. In any case, of course, the police would still have to prove it. *GloryDays* could not produce enough athletic garments to keep up with demand.

Cory hired a personal publicist for Kate to field all the offers rolling in from everywhere. The volatile mix of hit athletic model and sketchy, outrageous Nature Avenger were combining to create a volatile story.

Meantime, Kate lived in her second floor walkup apartment, her first living space on her own, attempting to make sense of the media outburst. She and Sarah began talking every day, she and Peter talked nearly every night, her dad Paul called from wherever he landed in his travels. But Kate was getting overwhelmed by all the attention.

Two months after the first ads appeared Kate's father Paul showed up on her doorstep just after dawn. She shuffled to the door barely awake, saw it was her dad and fell crying into his arms. They remained in that embrace for some time. All the media attention was far beyond what Kate had bargained for and she needed her dad.

She got dressed and they began walking toward the campus deeply engrossed in conversation.

Paul first said, "Katie sometimes we all need support and your mother and I are very concerned how you are dealing with this whole blow up? So I flew here for the day from Idaho, I have to leave tonight but we have the day, let me buy you some breakfast."

Kate hooked her arm through his and was totally grateful for his surprise appearance. She had been trying to keep it all under control but she felt herself cracking under the onslaught.

"Dad, I came here to attend school and figured maybe this *GloryDays* stuff would be a nice little sideline, help pay some expenses. Right now I can't walk across campus without attracting all kinds of looks, I get followed sometimes. So far nothing bad has happened it's just real different. Cory is saying she needs me to do a two day photo shoot, they rushed some new designs into production and I really can't say no to that. But I have to say, who could know a few magazine ads would create such a lot of noise?"

"Katie, as your father I only have one big question: Do you want all this on your head? If you are becoming too uncomfortable we just tell Cory it's a no-go. She can't force you to work. I already checked with a lawyer. It would be difficult but it can all go away."

Kate didn't answer her father. Seconds passed, then a couple minutes. Paul just kept walking letting his daughter think about his question. When Kate didn't immediately reply he added one more comment, "And honey, this wouldn't be nearly such a big deal if that Nature Avenger deal didn't come up. You know that. You could easily damp down that component."

Kate responded, "Dad, I can see you have decided I'm the girl doing those attacks. You know it could be someone else and that person could go on beating up bad men."

Now it was Paul's time to not hurriedly answer. "Katherine McGill, it's your father you're talking to. I'm willing to bet you could control that Avenger factor quite nicely. I'm very confident of what my daughter is capable of." Paul turned to Kate and gave her a proud smile.

Kate smirked and squeezed his arm. "Ok, Dad, here's the thing. I signed on for this college responsibility, I hope to finish it. And I also signed on for *GloryDays*. I was so utterly proud that Cory searched for years and ultimately chose me. That is a real honor. So, no, I don't want to bail out of either one. I think I can handle this, I want to be strong enough to follow through on both obligations. I need to stay with a standard, don't I?"

Paul hugged her arm. "Kate, your mother and I think your willingness to commit to high values is remarkable but we just don't want you to crash and burn out of too much striving. I'm not here to tell you what to do but I have this one observation. Katie if you are going to shoot this high be realistic about what you can handle. Be prepared for lots of stress and then look at any behavior that is likely to induce more stress. I don't believe you need a lecture on that topic but none of us can sit in judgment of others. If someone hurts an animal they must face legal justice in the courts. That's how our society works. Outside those courts one person meting out their own brand of justice is running extremely high risks. With all the attention the *GloryDays* Girl campaigns will generate you can accomplish a ton speaking publicly about issues that concern you. Lend your name to worthwhile causes but stop short of risking jail. That's all I can say, Katie."

They stopped below the Campanile bell tower on campus and sat on a concrete bench.

"Dad, from what Cory is telling me, this whole *GloryDays* thing is just getting started. Cory told me, 'Kate, you are about to become famous, I knew that might happen but now you need to make those adjustments.' I think I can handle all this and more but I just wasn't ready for where this was going and the speed. It's headspinning."

Paul looked out from the plaza below the Campanile, the symbol of the Berkeley campus, at the top of the Golden Gate Bridge in the distance. "Katie, life is decisions and these are yours. Do you continue with *GloryDays*? Do you associate yourself with this Nature Avenger phenomenon? Again, your choice. Do you choose to speak out on issues that concern you? That will start very soon, people are interested in someone who attracts public attention."

Kate stared at her feet and thought about his statements. Then she answered, "Well, I started all this thinking I wanted to be well known, a popular culture success. I know that. Now it appears to be happening. I didn't expect it but here it is. All the training and devotion to workouts on skates and in the gym were my choices. I gave up some normal contacts with kids my own age to be this devoted. So, I think I am ready. I can see this may get weird but that apparently will be part of the package."

Paul looked over at Kate as they sat on the bench. "Ok, honey, then that's your decision, now you need to be patient, resilient, determined, willing to tough this out. The further it goes, the less normal your life is likely to be. If you decide to present a certain set of images to the public that is how you will become known. Just be ready, it's likely an unpredictable ride."

Kate McGill walked onstage as a guest on the Danny Samuels show. At the time, Samuels was earning a reputation for honest, forthright broadcasting even though he was still only in smaller markets. Her dad lobbied to get her on the program for weeks even though Kate had turned down other much bigger name TV hosts. Paul's persistence finally paid off although Danny's staff insisted on plying him with information about how argumentative, combative, unrelenting and contrary she was likely to be.

Danny stood up in his stylish Brioni suit extending his hand.

"Welcome Kate, we're pleased you chose to join us today. I know you've turned down many other programs, some big names in there I understand."

Kate purposely chose her clothes with care. She knew the program might be heavily watched even though Danny was only now penetrating the bigger urban markets. So she wore a simple fitted long dress from Macys and a pair of slippers. She hardly looked the part of the urban warrior.

Kate nodded and smiled.

He continued, "I'm sure people are interested in why you'd say no to Jay Leno or David Letterman or even 20/20?"

Kate put her hands interlaced in her lap, legs uncrossed looking quite focused.

"I've appeared on a few shows and no one wanted to deal with actual issues. It was mostly how I liked modeling for *GloryDays* or how I liked my body or if I had a love life. I told your staff if we'd do this, it had to be on the issues."

Danny shrugged his consent. "Sure, well let's get started. There are headlines today about a massive assault by computer hackers against a number of prominent, wealthy individuals. What I read indicated this was like a hailstorm of attacks, never seen before. You know much about this?"

Kate stretched her body, crossed her legs, tried to not thrust out her chest on camera. "Sure, I have a pipeline to numerous people dealing with these types of attacks. First, why on earth is anyone thinking this is strange or totally unexpected? The list that appeared in today's Wall Street Journal included a number of people who I'd personally say are way off the curve in giving back after earning gazillions. People who have earned huge sums and never shown a willingness to participate in any charitable anything. That's who seems to be getting tapped."

Danny asked, "You think this is acceptable behavior?"

Kate replied, " I'm not sitting in judgment of anyone who earns the money or is now stealing it except to say now is the time when you will start to see this happen. The technology or rather the absence of protection in the technology makes it possible for really determined people to take actions like this."

"Kate, do you endorse this, think it's a good idea?"

"Danny it's happening. The imbalance is far too great, completely out of kilter. How many billionaires now exist due to someone inventing a new approach to some technology? There are thousands by now and far too many causes, deserving causes going underfunded or totally unfunded altogether."

Danny was surprised she would take such a position, "You say this is legitimate?"

"What do you want me to say? It's abhorrent, terrible? Nonsense, we're destroying rain forest at an astronomical rate and these technology or entertainment people are piling up untapped bank accounts. Well they do get tapped to buy a Ferrari or a house in Montserrat or Warhol paintings. But the money is frozen in assets which help no one except, maybe, a fortunate few. Look around at the decay in schools, the woeful plight of teachers who are caring for young children and earn low, low wages. Or how about nurses who carry much of the burden in hospitals and eke out a living. Is that fair?"

Danny was getting a little exasperated, "Kate, *you* are endorsing this wholesale attack on wealthy individuals aren't you?"

Kate clasped her interlaced fingers around one knee crossed over the other and gently rocked back and forth. "This is evolution, a form of progress, a rebalancing of the scales, forthright retribution. All of these and more. So far a few dozen individuals have had their financial resources tapped. The Wall Street Journal guesstimated the loss at something like $400 million dollars. Meantime, all around the world we are seeing reports of money turning up for useful purposes. This morning, the school system in Tuscaloosa, Alabama found two million dollars in its main bank account. The report I saw said the head of the school board ordered the money quarantined until they can figure out where it came from. Hey, it will take, what, six months to figure that out, then Tuscaloosa will shrug its collective shoulders and give their teachers a deserved raise, buy some computers and whatever else until the money disappears. I say that's sensational! Don't you think some little kid needs that money more than some billionaire? Sure that money may have been taken illegally but so are activities carried on all over the place that people don't go to jail for."

"Kate, you're sanctioning full scale theft. It's patently illegal in any country in the world."

Kate replied, "In the case of that city in Alabama it is not yet proven that the money they found in their account was stolen. It could have been but it's unproven. Some people believe that the right to earn money unendingly with no obligation to recycle the money back into needy economies should be illegal. But in a capitalist society it never will be. Our country is founded on the notion that you can create, earn and grow rich. No one ever said those billionaires would be left completely alone on their yachts off Corfu. You can own a Ferrari or fantastically priced piece of jewelry but now you may be asked to pay your share. Not just taxes but a proportion of the money you make over and above a certain threshold."

"Kate, you want the government to enter the marketplace and do this?"

She shook her head. "God, no. That's the worst solution of all. I think everyone agrees too many federal programs are grossly inefficient. I'd never endorse that idea under any circumstance. This is just the marketplace giveth, the marketplace taketh away. Do you see some creative programmer raiding the bank account of a family in Elk Grove, Illinois that gets by on $42,000 a year? Nope, the raids are only on the truly wealthy. I am endorsing an idea of 20 over 4 meaning if you earn over $4 million a year you donate 20 percent to charity or schools and the like. Done completely voluntarily, no government intervention of any kind."

A smattering of applause followed Kate's statement. Danny appeared uncertain what to do.

Kate stepped back in. "Let's look at it this way. Never in the history of the world has such massive wealth evolved so quickly. If you examine just the technology sector alone there are now hundreds and hundreds of genuinely rich people who even a few years ago appeared on no list, no roster of the mega rich. So we're seeing a flowering of wealth many times greater than anything ever seen in man's entire existence. Well, with that mushrooming has come a small reaction. A handful of determined activists are recovering a tiny, tiny portion of this vast, extraordinary wealth and redistributing it. And it's happening because no marketplace mechanisms exist, yet. Is it illegal? Yes, of course. Is it just, fair, a rebalancing of societal scales? The public will have to decide that. Let me suggest we're hearing about only part of this reaction."

Danny appeared almost shocked. "Kate, you're saying there's more?"

She shrugged her shoulders. "More to come, it's not hard to see that. Lots of people are picking up on the notion that endless wealth is wasteful."

"It's hard to believe a young woman, educated at a fine university is actually condoning, even encouraging such intrusions, such theft."

Kate nodded and smiled slightly. "Danny here's the dilemma: Will the world be better off with all the money in the hands of wealthy people or better off if a tiny group of disadvantaged children are allowed to enjoy a minute slice of that money? I'd say the kids deserve a better life."

Danny was clearly in disagreement. "How can you be sure that some amount, let's just use one million dollars stolen from some bank account or wherever will not wipe out the owner? What if some hacker does their homework wrong and steals from the wrong person? Then what?"

Kate nodded, looked tentative. "I'm sure my answers are not satisfying plenty of people. I have faith that these robin hood thefts will have symbolic value. I hope that the grossly wealthy will wake up and in a very public gesture begin increasing their donations to worthy causes. They could go on record that they can move money to needy people and causes. Is that naïve? Am I stupid to have these idealistic thoughts? I may be but having money tied up in pure splendor is ignorant waste. When talking about collectibles, artwork, fancy houses, gigantic boats, jewelry I say that kind of splendor is the new clueless."

Sit in as Cory Madigan battles it out with Helen Aray on how to best protect Kate. Witness how Helen stages a remarkable west coast dream scene for Cory's benefit. Visit www.katemcgill.com and look under the "chapters" heading.

CHAPTER TWENTY THREE

GREYSUIT ATTACKS IN BEVERLY HILLS

The two figures sat with their backs against a wall in a dark hallway, knees bent talking in whispers. One wore a head to toe grey body suit, the other was dressed in formal dress, a modified tuxedo.

Grey: "How long?"

Tux: "Three minutes, you'll hear them up above us, the stage is over that way maybe 75 feet but the sound carries down here. We're in a sub-basement. Listen, I'd like to talk you out of this completely. Given what's going on you should ----."

Grey: "Don't bother. Just don't. I'm on with this."

Tux: "Man, you're getting crazy, pushing it like this. How the hell close do you want the fire before you get burned. This is strictly heavy duty risk time."

Grey shushed Tux and put a hand over Tux's mouth. The hand held firm. Then the hand was removed.

Grey: "Understand this, I got something going back in my family, something I need to live up to. It means a lot to me in a world where it's all MTV and WWF. So just do as we said and walk away, got it?"

Tux carefully stood up being careful not to rub the formal wear against the wall and then turned offering both hands to Grey to pull Grey up to a standing position. They stood in silence as a musical soundtrack suddenly erupted filling the building with trumpets and pounding kettle drums. Tux surrepticiously took Grey's right hand and gently squeezed it. The squeeze was carefully returned. Tux turned and placed a light kiss on Grey's right cheek and then began edging down the hallway in the darkness. The only light emanated from a tiny glow in the dark toy Tux took from a cereal box. A door opened momentarily around a corner. For a brief second light flashed into the hall revealing stored chairs and janitorial gear.

The door closed and locked from the outside.

The Grey suit checked a glow in the dark watch pressing a tiny button and then slipped a timing device from a hiding place into a waist pocket. The figure began a series of relaxing, stretching movements in the pitch black lasting two minutes and then checked the watch again.

Three minutes later the figure uncoiled a mask which when in place covered the whole face and neck. A door lock snapped and the grey suited figure moved immediately to a ladder on the opposite wall, climbed twelve steps up and pushed on the door which gave way.

A voice on a loud speaker could be heard coming from the end of a crawl space. "...and gentlemen, John Galliano presented a similar full length chinchilla at the Dior show, now we see a glorious Marc Jacobs mink...."

The grey suited figure climbed another short ladder and could now look over a low wall to see figures moving up and down a runway swathed in furs. Five feet away a thick rope had been tethered to a velvet sash.

The music and commentary built in intensity, drum rolls, more trumpets and voices crescendoed as the narrator said, "...and we present for your approval a lavish Jean Paul Gaultier sable and our final Yohji Yamamoto mix of coyote and fox...."

The runway was now filled with half a dozen women strutting in the peculiar fashion dictated walk swaying lean hips, faces fixed in a near pout, head and shoulders thrown back unsmiling to faces shrouded in darkness.

When the figure appeared the onlookers were unable to separate models from the grey suited intruder swinging on a rope into their midst. One model flashed a flicker of recognition sensing something foreign in the air over her head and suddenly the willowy model found herself dangling in the air.

The audience predictably came to their feet and voices flooded the room as people tried to figure out if this snatching of the model was part of the presentation. Security people especially prepared for any problem dashed toward the runway.

Suddenly a crash and shout could be heard. Calls to bring up the lights were shouted and then the figure on the rope reappeared but two burly security people, one man, one woman were scrambling up on to the runway. The figure hanging from both hands aimed and kicked one guard accurately sending him sprawling but the second guard was ten feet away in the audience. Now other security people began running toward the stage. The show's organizers had been ready for any such intrusion.

Suddenly a blinding arc of light appeared and one model screamed in terror as something struck her back and the fur coat appeared to catch on fire. Moments later a second arc of light reached another model with the same screams. Both models instantly tried to shed the heavy coats.

Screams asking to bring up the house lights echoed through the hall. Instead two flood lamps triggered in the roof revealing a descending forty foot banner which proclaimed, "Living animals died for this madness. Give up fur!"

Voices in the hall became louder to turn on lights and shouts to rip down the banner were heard.

The figure reappeared once again leaping on to the stage, colliding purposely with a security guard who had lept on to the runway. The guard sprawled back into the audience as the grey suited figure ran toward a model who was shrieking to be left alone. The model struggled out of the coat which the intruder doused with a liquid and set afire. The fire became a white heat culminating in a muffled explosion. People nearby were knocked to the ground.

The figure ran for a doorway but was confronted by two security people who were shining extra bright flashlights at the person. Suddenly another flash and loud explosion occurred momentarily stunning the guards. The intruder lashed out at one guard feet first.

The figure ran for an exit, emerged into a brightly lit space where horrified patrons were colliding with one another attempting to exit the building. Police officers bore down on the intruder who disappeared down a stair well, turned a corner, descended another stair well and ran to a fire door.

The door was flung open into an alley. Hidden behind two trash cans the intruder pulled out a two wheeled electric scooter and yanked on the trigger throttle. The little scooter leaped forward.

The scooter accelerated to the end of the alley and shot blindly into a busy street full of Mercedes and Cadillacs. The intruder weaved in and out of cars, shooting up on the sidewalk, dashing down another alley heading off into a nearby residential neighborhood.

Police sirens filled the streets as the local police gave chase.

In two minutes the intruder turned into an alley behind a row of Beverly Hills homes. A Ford Taurus was tucked into a niche in the alley. The intruder removed a set of keys, popped the trunk, folded the scooter's handlebars flat and thrust the scooter into the car's trunk.

The now-driver dove in to the driver's seat and momentarily paused. The dark grey mask covering her skin slowly peeled off, the hood covering her dark blonde hair was removed and she pulled an old dark blue hooded sweatshirt over her head.

The siren screams were moving toward her.

Moments later the Taurus emerged on a side street driving toward Wilshire Blvd and back toward the scene of the fashion show. She purposely drove up Wilshire nearly retracing her prior route as two police cars with red lights flashing rounded a corner ahead, each one choosing a separate path to follow.

The Taurus now drove in front of the theater where police were attempting to corral patrons to question them. Behaving like a normal rubber necker the driver slowed, peered into the crowd. She momentarily caught sight of a young man in a stylish tuxedo apparently helping a young woman who was limping.

In five minutes the Taurus emerged on Santa Monica Boulevard, turned right and drove toward Hollywood.

As the small monkey awakened it's brain began transmitting signals which made no sense. Nearby two white frocked medical doctors watched the monkey's reactions. In a few moments the monkey's brain had begun collecting information. The brain could not control the body to which it was attached. By design, one of the nearby doctors had graphed the monkey's head onto another body but was unable to connect the brain to the spinal column.

The monkey, while still groggy, had begun understanding its dilemma. It no longer had a body, at least not one it could control. The monkey's face contorted into a series of agonies as the brain began dealing with its state of inhumane treachery.

The doctor followed the progress of the monkey's agony, noting certain reactions and taking notes where appropriate on a nearby laptop computer. Unknown to the doctor or his staff, the laptop had been invaded and the doctor was being monitored from a distance.

Some blocks away, a cell phone rang and was answered. "They're starting into the process, the animal has awoken. From what we know, normally the animal only lasts a short time before its brain circuits out from the agony."

"Try not to use those words, this will be hard enough as it is. I'm going now."

She couldn't help but think about the monkey. She began thinking about other animals that suffered. She recalled being in San Francisco with her mother and they visited the aquarium at the Academy of Sciences. She had visited a very large tank where fish swim right above your head. She remembered watching the sharks and feeling such a strong attraction for them. They were so powerful and scary but they were also vulnerable and could be easily caught. She hated the idea that people mistreated them. She recalled the Chinese tradition of capturing them and cutting off their fins to make soup. She thought, *That is so incredibly barbaric.*

The woman felt strong anger rising at that thought. Mistreating such beautiful, natural animals made her react almost violently. She had to calm herself down.

In the medical lab the monkey had partially lapsed into a semi-concious state. The attending physician made more notes.

The grey suited figure made her way up a set of stairs. The front door had been locked but her accomplice quietly violated the locking mechanism.

"I'm coming up with you."

"No, this is strictly and only my mission. And you can't see what goes on. Return to the car and wait. I'll be brief."

She waited outside the lab door, clothed head to toe in a Ranger's body suit, at her side a long club.

The doctor was not visible, then he reappeared from another room. An assistant also joined him as they considered some information.

She moved through the door padding noiselessly across the floor.

The Doctor looked up to see the menacing figure closing on him. He put up his left arm consciously holding back his favored right arm and hand. She knocked his defensive motion aside with one blow.

The intruder then extended one arm and clamped down on the man's neck with that hand.

The Doctor could not believe how powerful her grip was.

"You are a waste of intelligence. I should tear your body open and spill what passes for your guts on the floor. Instead, we'll see how you like your little treatment?"

The Doctor momentarily struggled thinking he could overpower the body suited woman.

"This club is an animal bone from Africa, an animal that was tortured to death."

She had intended to destroy his prime operating hand but just before she brought down the club her mind changed and she wacked his left leg below the knee.

He was completely aware she had made that decision. He stared at his hand, the hand that often performed the most delicate of his operations. The pain in his leg drove him to the floor where he continued protecting his hand.

The assistant had worked up the courage to shout. After one shout the intruder grabbed him from behind, whipped an elastic rubber device around his arms and secured it. She then stuffed a sock in his mouth and ripped a piece of gaffers tape off her leg to secure it.

"Shut the hell up," she hissed. She had practiced that move on a dummy hundreds of times. It went as planned.

She then locked a device around the Doctor's neck, similar to a neck tie but made of stretchable material. The Doctor recognized the collar, he had used similar ones to immobilize animals. She tightened the collar cutting off some air to his brain.

"You're choking me..." he gurgled.

Seemingly without effort she lifted him off the floor and tied him to a nearby table. On the same table the little monkey existed in a comatose state.

"I would prefer you conclude your life like this poor animal you have tortured."

The Doctor was turning blue quickly. She stood and looked in his eyes. Then she walked over to the monkey and in one swift motion put the animal out of its misery.

She realized this attack on the Doctor did not suit her. She felt compassion for him even while hating what he did to animals.

His facial skin showed signs that he was about to expire from lack of oxygen. But he was still conscious. Reluctantly she loosened the neck collar and he began gasping for air.

She had planned a few sentences to say but now that seemed irrelevant.

She looked at what her actions had accomplished and found it wanting. She turned and disappeared down the stairwell. At the ground floor she picked up a small backpack, removed a long scarlet woman's raincoast, removed her mask and hood replacing it with a large, wide-brimmed gardening hat.

Moments later their car departed. On the front and rear licence plate standards appeared placards from a nearby Ford dealer, in the rear window a white sticker from the DMV indicated a newly purchased car.

There were no license plates.

CHAPTER TWENTY FOUR

KATE ALONE IN BERKELEY

Kate woke up with a start from a deep sleep and had an upsetting thought, *Good lord, I'm missing the boat, I've been so focused on trying to change the world, be hyper athletic, be the glam model that the real life is passing me by.*

Kate sat up in bed shaking off sleep, trying to understand this notion. Was she really delusional trying to be so exceptional? She realized it must have been a dream that woke her up but now the dream had vanished.

She thought, *Am I being exceptional or just weird? Well, here you are back in your little apartment. Two days ago you're in Beverly Hills pulling off a few stunts, none of that was very normal was it? No and maybe I don't attempt any more visits to doctors. That was a bit more than I could handle. I'm better off with bullies. I'm the regular midwestern schoolgirl out there taking some awfully risky chances. If I get busted I could do jail time.*

Kate stood up and padded across the floor in her pj's she'd had since tenth grade to the window of her apartment. It was just 6 AM on a gray January day. She pulled aside the curtain and looked out on the street. *Hey, I am really in Berkeley, California. Is this odd that I like living alone?*

She wandered to the kitchen, opened the refrigerator, looked around and shut the door. She had forgotten the day of the week and had to think about it.

Do I have classes today, am I really that clueless? I have been back and forth to Minnesota, New York, the one trip to Europe, down to see Queen R. twice in Las Vegas, then twice in L.A. Where do I really live? Hey, this can be confusing, I'm human. Don't be so hard on yourself.

Sometimes I'd like to have a roommate but then I'd have to explain what I'm doing, if I decide to take off I have to cover that with a roomie. God, I miss

180

Peter, I miss my parents, I am always thinking about all these big issues like am I going to go avenge every criminal act?

Kate walked to a small book shelf, stood there looking at the books. She realized she was lost in her own thoughts. *What's wrong with me, I sometimes feel like I don't have friends here, I'm constantly so goal oriented? Well, wait, I do have friends, that's stupid. Man, I get so wound up with my life, last night I spent hours with those great girls next door, we had a blast, I even drank some beers. Go Kate, you need to drink a little, loosen up, come on, you can just have fun, girl!*

Kate decided she was up, she threw on jeans and a work shirt. Then she stopped, questioning this most basic of daily routines. *Now hold on, must I always wear this uniform? What am I going to wear, one of those GloryDays eyepoppers? I can't go parade around in those outfits. Maybe down in LA but up here, I look like an exhibitionist. I really need to go shopping at Macy's or somewhere and get more regular clothes. I want some cute skirts and blouses, all of that.*

Kate walked into the small closet and began handling clothes. She had segregated the *GloryDays* outfits in one section, she began picking them up, holding them up to her body, she walked to the mirror, then walked to a lamp nearby and added some light. She spent some minutes holding up outfits, shaking her head disapprovingly.

Good lord, these things all make me look like a girl who wants all eyes just on her. Oh, this one, Cory, dear, way too much exposure. This one, actually that looks really hot, oh yah, it makes my butt look, well, good. If you got a good butt you can put it out there can't you? But really, I can't go parading down Telegraph Avenue in these things.

Kate stepped away from the mirror, decided to hang up the *GloryDays* outfits, stopped and looked over some homework on her study table. *What the heck am I doing in Berkeley anyway? I'm certainly not a leftie, I often find myself conflicting with all this politically correct stuff, that's the new term. But I'm no republican either. So here I am, third year at school and I don't hang out with students all the time. No, I need time to myself, time to study, time for exercise. This can get confusing, I come back to school, try to put on that hat, jump on a plane and suddenly I'm a star on skates? I know those girls thought it off the wall that I had just done that tv show on ABC. Hey, that is your life Katherine, that's what you wanted.*

Kate paused to turn on a computer, stopped to thumb through a book about Unix systems administration she had been browsing. She realized how diverse her interests actually were. Technical software issues were actually quite interesting to her.

So there is also Katie the tech mind. Can't say I'm the deepest mind but I really do have a flair for sys admin work. The truth is I could actually do systems upgrades, cabling, I like that stuff. Whoops, doesn't fit well with the glamour image does it? You know I spend quite a bit of time with all those nerds and techies, and I'm comfortable with them, I enjoy those discussions. You know what else? I like how they accept me. Sure those guys are always giving me the eye but I can hold my own talking about TCP/IP, I'm not a slouch on that. These last three days, every evening was with fellow students. Oh my God, I'm behaving like a real student and I didn't even know it. Boy, I bet some of those guys think it's weird that I can talk about Unix little languages with them and then I show up in a fan magazine. That is so cool I can live in both worlds. But I gotta say, it can stretch me out pretty damn far. I go off to New York, I go off to L.A., in those places I could be a star. I come back here, to this place, hey, I'm Kate college girl, I can wield a screw driver, I can write some code alongside those guys, I'm not so darn clueless am I?

Kate felt proud of herself. She was realizing she had been overly self critical. She felt a nice rush of pride. She looked around, this was her life and it wasn't so bad. But another feeling emerged. She was definitely alone.

I really do miss Peter. Well he'll be here in what, ten days? What is today? No seven days. I am going to give him a major workout when he gets here. He won't mind, we're really good together. Really good. I love how he does that...hang on girl, not appropriate. Why not? It's totally appropriate. I better move on here.

Kate wanted to look more feminine so she decided to change clothes, taking off her jeans, putting on a mid-thigh skirt and then a pretty, light tan peasant blouse. She returned to the mirror, admired herself and smiled. She liked just looking girlish. Then she was glad it was Saturday, she could avoid school work, at least for now.

She cleaned up a few dishes in the sink, pulled out some school work she needed to finish, wrote down two notes to herself and then walked past the bathroom glancing again in the mirror.

Kate, if you look like you do and you're not afraid to show it, what's wrong with that? Yah, I could be showing a lot more, that magazine, according to Cory, was willing to offer me a helluva lot of money for no clothes. Oh, Kate, get real, you are not going to take off your clothes for anyone. Besides Peter, that is. Nude posing that's off the table. Forget it. But what if I just donate it to a great charity? Uh, naw, I can't live with that legacy. If Peter and I have kids, I can't have pictures showing up with me in the buff. Although Mom said she once did a photo session out in LA. I wonder, I never saw any of those? Anyway, I gotta have some standards don't I?

Kate sat down at the computer and thought she'd do some work but immediately was side tracked by email from Cory. Apparently a larger conglomerate was sniffing around Cory's company for a possible acquisition.

Kate shrugged, she was not yet much interested in business although she had to admit something about conducting business seemed appealing.

Cory's mail did make Kate come up short. Cory was realizing that her golden girl, as she called her, was becoming a runaway big deal. Kate sensed that Cory was subtly selling Kate on possibly leaving school, doing a tour in Europe, performing more shows. Kate thought, *You know, Cory has realized her hot model is in real life a college student and that could become a big drag for Cory. I can tell she wants me traveling more, doing more appearances. I did do that last summer but here she's mentioning Spain, Italy, even Poland. I guess they have good sales in those places? Down here she mentions Mexico as well. Hmmm, I could get into that. Boy, who would have guessed getting an education would be such a conflict for GloryDays? I didn't think about it but now it's for real.*

She read emails for ten minutes, she had a very active fan club and there were always notes from military guys and women. She began reading a few.

Whoa, I remember this guy, he sent that really cute note about his dog. But I gotta be careful, these guys are lonely, don't say the wrong thing. Hey, I'm lonely sometimes. Like right now. They are not alone. I'm sure people see me in a magazine layout and think I have the high life. Well, look around, I'm a struggling student, I have to study hard, this is certainly not glamorous. And my supposed boyfriend is 2000 miles away. He's so dedicated to his studies. Good for Peter, meantime, I get lonesome, I want intimacy, company, warmth. I'm not chopped liver.

Kate realized she was feeling sorry for herself. She momentarily thought about poor animals being mistreated, young kids with no place to live. *Ok, pity party ends now, Kate. Look at your life, you make money, you travel, you made a commitment to get a college education, that was going to be this priority, right? Yah, but that was more than two years back. Now I'm actually attracted by fame that's true, I didn't expect to feel such a strong pull. I like seeing my picture, I like doing tv shows, I like looking glamorous. I hadn't bargained on all that, I guess. But it's also like a huge magnet is dragging me to even up unfair scores, defend the vulnerable. That is so much more compelling. Man my life is really pulling two opposite directions. Over here fame, over there manhandle some clueless exploiter. Make some money, I like that, now get some wealthy bozo to contribute some money to a good cause. Whoa Katie, you may have a problem. Yes, it's true, I want the major recognition and I also want no recognition so I can be the redeeming score settler. Oh boy, never quite saw it that way.*

Man, what I need is exercise, not cute little skirts, I gotta dig out some exercise gear.

She opened up her only chest of drawers and took out tights, clean socks, a t-shirt and long sleeve shirt. She removed the skirt and wiggled into the tights. She always felt better getting exercise. She also liked not thinking so much but her thoughts flooded back in.

What the heck am I doing about Peter? What, indeed? He has to finish school, I'm supposed to finish, how am I going to make it through two more years? There are so many things I want to do, sitting and studying architecture or economics. Ugh, well, wait, all that econometric stuff I get that. It's intriguing and that's the future, girl. And really I enjoyed both courses on architecture. Yah, Bernard Maybeck he's the caliber of Frank Lloyd Wright. Don't turn your nose up at it. You know, sometimes I really enjoy school, Professor Litwack, his take on American history, that is fascinating. What a great teacher. Although I'm not sure I agree with his view of history in this country. He's more liberal than I am. Great, Kate, have a disagreement with a man who won a Pulitzer Prize, you're that smart aren't you? Tell him about your encounters with men who hurt animals or innocent women, that's your Pulitzer girl, I can beat up three guys at once. Those guys in Austin, that was a work of art. I wish someone had a camera for that one. If I say so, that was like ballet, that one guy, he could not believe a chick could take out three big bruisers that fast. Nice job kitten, you kicked their asses. Yah, and it felt good to do it. God, I wonder, did that girl who they assaulted finally nail them in court? I paid for the lawyer and it wasn't cheap so I should know. Man, my life moves so fast, I wrote him a big fat check and I really don't know what came of it. It doesn't matter, the girl finally got some justice, I know that much.

Kate felt hungry, she took out some fruit and yogurt and began reading the most recent San Francisco Chronicle. She turned immediately to Herb Caen's column in the paper. She adored how the writer turned the city into an utterly fascinating place. He was the true spirit of San Francisco for Kate, she vowed one day to meet him if she could.

Kate read the social columns in the Chronicle, then local politics, she had no real idea who all the people were. She skipped to the back pages, a story caught her eye. *Oh, man, what is this? This girl got assaulted AND her dog got hurt. I hate when this happens. Where is this? It's in San Jose. I could get there. So they don't name who did it but that takes some days anyway. If I send an email to that woman who sends me leads like the Austin woman I bet she'll track it down for me. Kate, maybe you need to stop this stuff? Really, maybe it's time? You've done some good damage, now maybe just back it off.*

Kate stood up from the little kitchen table, the sun was up but it was still normal Berkeley grey this early. She realized she actually needed to get dressed. She looked at herself in the mirror once more. *When Peter sees me his eyes light up. I love that, hey, I love when people look at me admiringly. Peter will be here soon, take it all out on him. Yah, he better be ready to work. Hee hee. Man I love that guy, I love walking into places on his arm, what a handsome package he is. But his mom, Lis, hmmm, she is not thrilled with me, she's afraid I'm gonna get him into trouble. Katherine, that could happen, you could be arrested for these little incidents. Yah, not so darn cool, buying difficult legal exposure. And Peter's Dad, the big time Chicago lawyer, I think he's even more concerned. Hey, I don't blame them, they have a sensational son, they should be protective.*

Kate walked back into the closet once more. She bent down to pick up running shoes.

Hang on, I get paid serious money by GloryDays, don't I owe them some public exposure? That stuff hangs in the closet. Ok, it's the weekend, time to show off Cory's goods. I can drive over to Golden Gate Park and hang out with the skaters. Where was that new purple outfit, here? Alright, you ready to go on display? I can wear a shirt over the top. What? Why wear any of this stuff if you don't show it off? But last time I did this that guy with the camera shot me skating and it ended up in the Chronicle. So? Isn't that the point? Ok, you'll stop some traffic in these duds but Cory is so delighted when I show up in the papers. Heck, so am I.

Kate has a mission to accomplish in Los Angeles but beforehand she encounters young actress Rebecca Almandor and her mother Rebel. Kate discovers connections to her own Mother in L.A. and attends a swank Bel Air party. Visit www.katemcgill.com and look under "chapters".

CHAPTER TWENTY FIVE

KATE MEETS ARNIE AT MORTONS

After a few more months of school in Berkeley Kate called her grandmother, "I'll be back in L.A., I want to raise some money for Israeli causes. A friend put me in touch with a group over there doing important environmental work." Knowing her grandmother's penchant for prying Kate thought that definition sounded innocent enough.

Kate turned 19 feeling an obligation to contribute meaningfully to important causes. Conventional non profit work held limited attractions for her. Edgier causes and real risk takers held definite appeal so Kate hid her actual intentions under the convenient rubric of environmental protection.

Helen told Kate she had to do some homework on an appropriate contact then called her back, "There is a guy who tried to get me involved in some causes. He's not a bad guy, Jewish to his toenails and might help you find some money for Israelis. His brother lives over there. I'll contact him but you better be sure of your facts, Katie."

Helen took a breath after hanging up the phone. Did she want to make this call? She knew Arnie through a few people in Santa Monica. Not her favorite type of person but she had a feeling that he would treat Katie with, at least, some respect.

"This is Helen Aray calling for Arnie, please." Helen waited abstractly scanning some business documents. She wanted this to be fairly quick but needed to make sure he was likely to handle this matter with some care.

"Arnie, how are you? Yes, I don't call but then you shouldn't feel left out, I am not the social, friendly caller. True to form I'm calling to ask a favor. Got a minute?"

Helen purposely made herself relatively unapproachable both as a public stance and based on her experience growing up. Being a woman of mystery came naturally to someone who operated purposely in the shadows.

Helen explained the favor to Arnie. "Please meet my granddaughter, see if you can assist her? Say no if you are not comfortable. I don't really know what all she is up to but I want her to have experience in approaching people on her own terms. She is not yet an experienced negotiator. Kate could become famous. Treat her right and she can be useful to you, perhaps? Make sense?"

"Well, sure, Helen, I'd be happy to meet her. Why me?"

"Arnie you are well connected locally and well thought of. And I trust you. Not too much but enough, got that Arnie? I have one granddaughter and she means the world to me. I am trusting you to look out for her. Clear? I know your brother, Arnie. He and I go back."

Arnie swallowed a bit. "Yes, Helen. I'll be a gentleman in every way. I'll take her to Mortons. What's she like, I've seen stories and heard the news?"

"Arnie, she's a young colt still in formation. Nothing surprises me about Katie."

Arnie couldn't wait.

Arnie Selznick's friend Martin Green who knew Arnie since grade school was trying to be helpful.

"Arnie, you must be on a suicide mission here. This Kate McGill would not be caught dead in any power lunch or power dinner or power snack for that matter. The very thing that is attracting fans, money and us is that she is a modern Marlon Brando who is not a poseur, not a fake. Arnie, this McGill woman downright hates anything Beverly Hills, Bel Air, Spago."

Just like Arnie, Marty had seen the pictures, the few videos.

Marty continued, "So Arnie you're bringing her here? Mortons?"

"Marty, her grandmother knows my brother and I want to be respectful of this relationship. Mortons is proper."

The two men hung out at the fancy, expensive, established restaurant, a watering hole for well off Los Angelenos. Mortons was a known to Arnie, he felt comfortable entertaining there. He wanted to be on solid ground for this Kate.

Arnie walked to the bar, ordered a tonic water, no alcohol and then walked to a nearby table. He had no idea what Kate McGill would be like? He heard she often made dramatic entrances. But on time, Kate appeared in the doorway alone, hands folded demurely in front of her, hair pulled back with quiet jewelry, in dark blue dressy slacks and red silk blouse. This was not what Arnie expected at all. Where was the bravado, the sex appeal the powerful physical statements?

She held out her hand saying, "You're disappointed?"

The look on his face told her enough, Arnie wanted some fireworks to start with. Dressed like this she could be any attractive young woman, not the outlandish skating star activist he'd been reading about. Not the hard body attention getter who did incredible acrobatics on videos.

She played him wrong, he wanted the public Kate, not the low key private person.

"Arnie, I'm trying to help an Israeli woman raise money to fight a specific terrorist. These people can do horrible things. I thought I owed you enough respect to not go parading around trying to look spectacular when I'm here to ask for your involvement in a serious and potentially dangerous cause. Since this skating stuff took off people expect me to be eye popping, I do that for cameras because I don't have a better way."

Arnie reminded himself that no matter who he wanted to walk through the door he had pledged a serious effort to Helen Aray.

"So, Kate, is that ok to call you Kate?" He wrestled with how to say what was on his mind. "Look, your grandmother asked me to meet with you. Frankly I was looking for a bombshell, that's why I agreed to this. Now I feel dumb. I didn't give you credit for having a serious mind. I'm just another putz who sees women for their bodies first, I admit it. Ok, so, I'll try to be an adult. Explain what's going on with you?"

Helen made Arnie out to be an oily semi low life. Now Kate realized he was trying to rise to the occasion.

"Arnie, you know I'm 19, I'm not the most mature young woman around. I even exploit myself, sometimes, because I want to make things happen fast. Good judgment may not be my middle name. So, don't apologize for being who you are and I'll do the same. Frankly, at times, I like looking spectacular, I use my physique to have an impact. So we're not all that far apart you and I. Ok? Now, let me prove I did my homework about you. You attended Brooklyn Polytechnic, served four years in the military."

Kate took a breath and reminded herself not to recite this like a high schooler.

"You had good grades Arnold Joseph Selznick and you played the violin."

"Jesus, no one knows that."

She smiled ironically.

"You were once thought of as a kind of mob guy but you walked away from New York, became a highly successful salesman in the apparel business, then took your money and invested in tv and films, made some real money. Am I right?"

Arnie was nodding, he could see she was trying to be serious and credible which he had to admit he appreciated.

"Arnie, how would you like to put your money to work doing something worthwhile? You're raised in a traditional synagogue, maybe even orthodox?" She raised one eyebrow.

Kate went on talking describing his youth, his upbringing even his family and she did it quickly. She built up the momentum, he could tell she had been rehearsing this pitch.

"I'm looking for 1.5 mill, the money goes to some Israelis and Americans working together to track a bad guy. He goes by various names but most recently Aashif. I'm told an Islamic meaning is courageous or bold. Heard of him?"

Arnie's total source of news was 15 minutes in the morning when he was getting dressed. He found most news to be such a bring down. "Kate I, uh, don't really know much in the news. I like the Dodgers, my wife is always on me to watch that McNeil and the other guy tv show. I hate all those talk radio people, blah, blah, blah."

His cell phone rang and he hit the button, "Marian, no calls. I'm in a meeting that is important." He felt that sent the right message to Kate. He was disappointed she was not showing off her chest. Then he kicked himself for the thought.

"Aashif is the next bad man coming down the desert road. Hates all the usual Americans, Israelis, Jews. But he even more hates the corruption of western technology, computers all of it even though he uses some middle range technology himself. Our guys are going after him and they need money."

She hit him unawares and she also hit him on a tender spot. Arnie's brother lived in Tel Aviv. Arnie visited once a year. It was the only time Arnie lifted the Rodeo Drive mantle and put it aside. No one in Tel Aviv gave a shit about finessing to get the appropriate table at Mortons or Michaels or wherever. His brother kept him honest.

"How do you know the ---."

"...money will get used for the right purpose?" she finished his question. "Because it will, because I've met them (she exaggerated), because they enjoy the one great luxury left in this world for people: The luxury of honesty. This is what they do. And they do not enjoy the trust of American authorities but they get some help anyway. Arnie, you bring in let's say, two fifty and help me tap some others for the rest?"

Kate knew Arnie would never pop for the whole amount but he was supposedly a master conniver. Kate was also well in over her head. She had never asked anyone for this kind of money much less so speculative and nearly impossible to verify. Buzz had started her down the road of asking for the outrageous to get what you actually need. He spun stories about his exploits finding money, convincing people his pitches were genuine. What he did not reveal to Kate was his consistent rate of strikeouts. Buzz would never talk about the failures, at least not easily.

She continued, "Arnie, American intelligence services have improved dramatically but no one can keep up with all these fundamentalist groups. They splinter by the hour. Our only hope is the Israelis and they are hard pressed to keep up. This group is trying to use American resources and Israeli common sense but they need funding. I need to count on you Arnie."

This was hardly what he expected. Arnie's network said she was tough, athletic, dynamic, attractive, a maverick, hell, a true rebel. But nothing about real world shit. Nothing about actual bad guys. Arnie encountered drug dealers---that was everyday. But not all this mideast stuff. Arnie was vulnerable on Lamborghinis, he owned one, on women who liked women if he could observe and his brother in Tel Aviv. His brother lived simply, believed deeply in this huge range of Judaic and Israeli values and was the closest Arnie got to hero worship.

So she had him. Arnie contributed to causes his brother told him about but this resonated about as deep as Arnie could go. She had him where it counted.

"You expect me to like write you a check on the spot? Make it out to *Stop the Crazy Islamic Bombers*? Like what do we do here and where are you thinking I'm coming up with another 1.25 mill?"

Kate wasn't about to let on that she had no idea how this worked. She tapped Buzz for 20 grand but that was different. This wasn't about slamming a volleyball or rollerblading down some impossible hill. But her instinct told her he'd be pulled in by intrigue. And she was willing to offer herself as bait. Up to a point.

"Get me in front of some others here in Beverly Hills. Let me do the pitching and I'll bring in a woman who actually fights these terrorists. Trained combat kill you dead babe. She leads a team. I guarantee she's completely for real. Will that make a difference?"

Arnie felt an almost uncontrollable urge to ask what she looked like and what would she be wearing? *God, if she only looked sensational and was a true killer.*

But he held himself back.

"I can get, like, three, maybe four who have bucks. I dunno, maybe a couple more. Look, Kate, now you're in my turf, this is the most superficial place on earth and I'm one of 'em. What we do, here I mean, what we do is posture, talk big, act like the assholes we really are, try to get laid at home and sometimes not at home and count the money. I grew up on the streets in New York. I didn't have money. Before my mother passed on she visited me and couldn't believe how we live out here. So you're dealing with *machers*, you know from *machers?*"

"Arnie, my mom is Jewish. I'm half and half. My grandmother speaks yiddish. *Macher* is a wheeler dealer."

He smiled and nodded. Kate was really getting to him. Quite a package. She even knows yiddish.

"How the hell can you be Jewish and look like that? Look, I gotta ask you, is that all you? Out here I don't know a woman who hasn't had a serious rebuild. Well, I know one but she's like from mars. God, what a body."

Arnie caught himself. He forgot he was around someone who might not appreciate all this focus on women's bodies.

"Arnie, you worried I'm gonna flinch or something? I'm a nice Minnesota girl but I got toughened up. Not too much fazes me now. Yah, this is all me. That will have to satisfy your curiosity."

She felt it was important to cool down Arnie's boyish fascinations. Kate didn't want him in too close.

Arnie squirmed in his seat. He had taken care to dress in an expensive custom made dark grey suit and hand made multi colored shirt with a flashy Countess Mara tie. Still confronted with this adventurous, chance taking young woman Arnie felt inadequate, overweight and unattractive. In his own world Arnie scored points by dressing expensively but somehow all his costuming meant little now. Here was this young woman who stood for something. Arnie couldn't remember the last time he was around anyone who stood for more than getting a woman to service them or driving his Aston Martin too fast on Santa Monica Boulevard.

He threw up his hands. "Hey, I'm a creature of habits. I see a woman, I look at her body. It goes with the job I guess. Look, I'll help you. You round up this soldier girl, I'll bring some guys with bucks. Uh, let's do it at my house. We'll put out a spread, make it nice. We need privacy right?"

Kate nodded. She couldn't help but like Arnie. He had a soul. It was just buried under many layers of Beverly Hills Jewish success.

"When is she available?"

"She's gotta fly here. They need money to do this. So we're not fooling around here, Arnie. I'm going to ask her to fly here from Israel and she'll do it if they can raise the funds. What do you think?"

Arnie nodded now. "It'll happen. I got a brother over there. I owe him."

CHAPTER TWENTY SIX

MIRIAM ARRIVES FROM ISRAEL

Justifiably nervous, afraid she'd be recognized and having to consciously pump up her self confidence Kate tried to decide if she had the courage to make this call. She had been wandering the neighborhood for half an hour with an uncomfortable pocket full of quarters. Finally she had to get on with it.

Kate made the call to Israel as instructed. She was asked three questions:

"How much can we raise?"

"Who are the donors?"

"When?"

Kate hung up the payphone in the back hall of a small deli filled with beat up chairs and mops off Fairfax Blvd. Somehow she figured it was more kosher to make the call from the heart of the Jewish district in L.A. And, she hoped, it would attract less attention if tracked.

She walked out on Fairfax and crossed the street to reach the mule. She glanced at herself in a store window. In Los Angeles she wore *GloryDays* outfits she never would consider in Berkeley much less Minnesota.. But today she wanted to look frumpy and utterly unremarkable in beatup jeans and a hooded sweatshirt.

It wasn't her appearance she was thinking about. *I'm now nineteen and I'm telling this woman to fly fourteen hours here on my say-so. I gotta be utterly nuts. Oh, God, forgive me if I screw this up, please forgive me. No...NO, don't let me blow this.* Kate said all these words under her breath.

The party overseas sounded so calm, so natural. Kate wondered if maybe something bizarre like this was normal for Israelis? Continued analysis seemed pointless, the woman known as Miriam was coming. The oddest little part of all this was the call itself. She put in country code, the Israeli phone number and it connected. Kate had very little experience making calls overseas.

When she called to confirm with Arnie he also sounded very grounded, "We're fine with this coming saturday, my place at 2 in the afternoon. Mayah in my office will explain directions to you, she's extension 23. She'll help you with anything, everything. Just don't explain the meeting, ok?"

Kate hung up thinking, *Great, he's fine, the Israelis are fine. The only person not fine is me and I'm a total basket case. Here I am playing the big timer, arranging this meeting. I feel like such a poseur sometimes.* But Kate also remembered Helen had encouraged her, told her you'll never realize your goals unless you just plunge.

Three days later Kate was waiting for the Israeli emissary at the busy intersection near Barneys Beanery on Santa Monica Blvd. in Hollywood. She had worked for three hours the night before with limited tools to unbolt the doors on the mule. Buzz had explained they were bolted to provide structural rigidity to the chassis. Then he admitted it was probably a dumb idea. Kate unbolted them. Now a woman in a skirt could make a lady-like entrance.

She was perspiring. She began mentally retracing the steps she needed to take once this woman arrived. *What am I doing sitting here? God, this is strange. I get myself into the weirdest damn situat----.*

BANG! SLAM! At first it felt like someone had run into the mule but then her recovering senses pinpointed the car door. Kate's nervous system just about flipped out completely. She realized someone had their hand on her right arm.

"Kate McGill, I hope."

Kate realized she was relieved. Her guest had arrived. Now it was showtime.

The face opposite was dark, intense and not overwhelmingly menacing. In a half second she realized the woman was not six feet tall. Kate had envisioned a full out sabra with menacing muscles. This one was medium height, dressed in an unassuming skirt and blouse with penny loafers. But the face had character---glorious full lips, and mysterious dark brown, almost black eyes, her face outlined by jet black curly hair close cropped. On second glance Kate felt like she almost knew her, there was a familiarity but that notion evaporated when she spoke.

"I am called Miriam. Is that ok for these people?"

Kate was completely off center. "Well, sure, if that's your name, sure that's fine."

Miriam dropped a small backpack under her knees in the front seat. "We want this to work. We need funding badly. I'll be Adolph if it sounds better to these men. Can we start driving? And please stop at a store so I can eat something. I haven't slept all that much but I'll be ok."

Kate obeyed, happy to have someone calling the shots. "What---uh, what would you like to eat?"

Miriam shook her head as Kate headed into traffic on Santa Monica Blvd heading west. Their meeting would be on the far side of Beverly Hills.

"Fruit and bread. That's fine. A little market where things are halfway fresh."

Miriam seemed so utterly unconcerned about anything. She busied herself rooting around in a small bag. Kate distinctly heard a clunk. Now she could look a bit sideways at this Miriam. Kate had expected a soldier, she now realized. Well, perhaps not in military mufti but this was just a plain woman. She could be anyone on the street. Miriam was invisible, so un-unique.

"You were expecting a someone different?"

Miriam was refreshing her makeup, what there was of it.

"I don't know. But you were probably expecting someone older, right?"

"I'm four years older than you. I got picked because, well, I got picked. We don't have a bombshell in stock. Is that what these men want?"

Kate realized Miriam was depending on her judgment. To have flown this far, Miriam needed to feel like it was worth it. Kate said, "Here's the deal: This guy, Arnie, has connections and that's who you'll be selling. I can't guarantee anything but I think they'll mostly be Beverly Hills Jewish men. The worst of them have a soul, that's what my mother told me. We need to grab them by the heart and the balls. Instructions from my mother, again."

Miriam gripped Kate's arm momentarily. "I'd like your mother."

Miriam produced the "clunk" from her bag--- a very techno looking device, punched in some buttons and looked at Kate.

"I saw videos of you playing volleyball. You're a real killer player." Miriam, if that was her name, had a slight Israeli accent or maybe it was New York. It hit Kate that Miriam could be just another Jewish woman from Brooklyn or anywhere. How would Kate know the difference?

Kate almost swallowed her tongue. "Th--thanks. Do you play?"

"Me? I work out every day, I did play volleyball years back. Well, I've tried it but it's for big women. The device beeped and Kate figured out it was a satellite phone. *Well they're not utterly broke, I guess,* she thought.

"My code is eleven twelve zero six on the ground, moving. Yes, she's driving. We'll be fine. I'm covered. Of course. Re-establish with you as agreed. Wish us luck."

Kate pulled over at a small market. When Miriam returned she said, "Yup, this is Beverly Hills. God this stuff is expensive."

Miriam watched Kate drive. "This car, it's quite utilitarian. Is it fast?

Can it handle difficult, challenging his speeds? You know how to drive at high speed?"

Kate eyed her. "You mean one hundred?"

"I mean when you're being chased at whatever speed."

"Uh, no, I'm pretty good but I've never had full blown evasion training. Have you?"

Miriam chewed thoughtfully on a carrot stick. "Yah, four of us were shipped off to Italy for three days. It was serious high speed driving along with other things. I'm ok."

"What's the other things, Miriam?"

Miriam opened a carton of orange juice. "Uh, defensive and offensive stuff. Work with a few weapons, some hand to hand and rudiments of identifying substances---uh, for explosives. Most Israelis receive some basic training. I got more."

Kate tried to look nonchalant but inside she was squirming. Miriam had done things, had been places, knew stuff. Miriam continued, "But I can't skate, I'm not on magazine covers, I'm not actually talented."

"Jesus, what are you saying? You've had all this military training, you're prepared, God that's awesome, Miriam. I'm the flavor of the week. It takes a bunch of me's to equal one like you that stands for something."

"Kate, don't be silly. The real heroes are all around you, the everyday schlump who raises a family or just goes to work. The dull, necessary, prosaic tasks require a steady hand and commitment."

"Uh, Miriam, are you actually Israeli?"

Miriam gave her a look. The look redefined Miriam's face. Not angry, closer to contempuous but just short of dismissive. "Let's get straight here. I'm here on business, back home I help run a small business with two relatives. I attended Columbia, I paid for the whole thing myself, I paid for my own plane ticket, there's no group with deep pockets. What you're going to fund is a handful of people operating outside the government channels. In Israel this can be dangerous to say the least. So to answer your question, I sure as shit am Israeli, so is my husband. Our country lives on the edge of non-existence every hour of the day. For excitement I learned how to shoot eight different kinds of weapons, I can defuse bombs, I can defend myself, I do not look like a Sylvester Stallone character. Actually that should be you. Why don't you become a soldier in Israel, carry a gun, train with our military, it'll change your self image over night."

Kate never felt much smaller. Miriam did the real deeds, Kate felt like a poseur again.

"Miriam you must think I'm a real nebbish. I'm saying nothing but you can----."

"...count on you. We know that. If I'm worried I'll let you know. I scream bloody murder. Meantime, you got us this opportunity. Even though our parents have strong links stateside none of them presented us with what you got."

Kate realized her English was virtually unaccented and momentarily froze, "Miriam, you have no accent, like, at all."

"Kate, with me get to the point. Why?"

"Because these men are likely expecting a genuine sabra sounding, you know, full blown Israeli woman." Now Kate felt about seven inches tall..

"Oh, vant dis sounding desert bitch in a khaki mini-skirt und matching khaki soldier's shirt unbuttoned down to here showing tons of cleavage toting two Uzis. Is that vhat they expect to stride in the door? Sorry, honey, I'm too short, I worked way too f-ing hard to erase the accent so some Islamic terrorist doesn't blow my ass away on a hunch I work for the Mossad. They'll have to grow up my dear. And besides, you'll have to be the cleavage for us both. I'm not into showing off my chest. Got it?"

Kate thought seven inches tall sounded powerful now.

"Kate, a sabra is merely an Israeli born woman. It's not a current term and there is no particular sound associated with a sabra but I am one nonetheless. Let me assure you that if we need to impress these gentlemen with something it can be arranged, alright?"

Kate replayed the situation in her mind, *Great, if they really do want cleavage and thigh high mini skirts toting Uzis, then what?*

Kate knew what, stopped the mule and got out to find a bag in the mule's trunk.

Then she dashed into a nearby store.

Miriam also got out when Kate stopped and just walked. Her body felt all kinked up from traveling so many hours. When she returned a different driver awaited her.

Miriam slammed the passenger door and smirked. "Oooookay, they'll like that."

Kate realized she may have just redoubled her own clumsiness but this was her decision and she was standing by it. "It's Beverly Hills, these should turn out to be typical Jewish macho power monger males so I'm today's featured T & A."

"You can say that lady. That outfit's really a traffic stopper, where did it come from?"

"I am completing a two year deal with *GloryDays* and they send me this stuff. Most of the outfits are appropriate for exercise and make you look great but a few, like this one, are more like costumes. They have paid me well and now, for once, it comes in handy. Arnie who organized this gathering was disappointed when I showed up in regular clothes. This will be my payback, he wanted me to look spectacular."

Miriam nodded her head and chuckled. "Hey, it's Hollywood, go native. We all have our jobs to do don't we?"

Kate headed up Doheny to turn on Sunset.

Miriam laughed, "Well you'll do the fantasy fulfillment. Actually I appreciate your doing this, it means I concentrate on drilling this home. I have to walk out of there with minimum half a million or we're dead horse meat. You have no idea how expensive it is to track this Aashif."

Kate checked her watch and brought her speed up.

As she drove Kate realized how little she actually knew about Israelis and the middle east. She thought she did but here was a real Israeli and there was no fooling around, Miriam was tough and seasoned. As she neared the Beverly Hills Hotel a tiny beam of light, Kate wasn't sure what it was, but something shot through her brain. It lasted no more than a second or so but it disturbed Kate's driving and she veered off the road. Miriam grabbed the wheel but Kate recovered instantly. Miriam said nothing. But Kate had seen a middle eastern man's face in that shaft of light and he was trying to enter Kate's unconscious. She knew that. He wanted her attention.

Ten minutes later they headed up Arnie's long driveway. Half way up they were stopped by two men in snug, expensive business suits. Kate guessed these were Arnie's little contribution to the intrigue aspect. These guys belonged in a Stephen Seagal thriller. Nasty looking slicked back hair, massive physiques, opaque sunglasses and menacing attitudes.

Miriam quietly clutched a small bag with one hand.

One man bent over the driver's side and looked in. "Which one's Kate?"

He admired her chest but said nothing. Then he waved them on.

Miriam commented, "Well, they'd last a micro second in our country. Maybe less. Every Palestinian teenager could drive a truck through that security."

Kate nodded. Her mind was on who Arnie ponied up for Miriam.

Miriam took in the sights as they plodded up the front stairs from the portico where Kate quickly head counted two 7 series BMW's, one Mercedes mini-limo, one Lexus GS 400, one Bentley and a Ford Taurus.

Miriam said, "You know what, I'll take the Taurus guy. He likely has more money and wants no exposure. Count out the Bentley, too much show."

Kate caught her reflection in a series of mirrors as they entered a gigantic portico, fully three stories high. Her regret for dressing like a harlot was only outdistanced by her severe concern over the the utility of their mission. *Can this possibly work, good lord....*

Kate also thought Miriam felt no such compunctions. She had flown 14 plus hours, they were entering a Bel Air mansion such as Miriam would never see in Israel. It simply did not exist but this opportunity might not reappear. Miriam only had something to gain. They traipsed down a long echoing hallway lined with expensive oils, sculptures and glasswork. Miriam could almost smell the money.

Arnie was waiting outside what turned out to be a living room the size of Kate's house in Wayzata. Inside waited six men. Miriam had been trained to do extremely fast takes with people, her life could count on it. She saw no threat, neither did she see a warm face. Arnie started an introduction standing just to the side of both women.

Arnie looked closer at Kate and grinned. For a moment a glint of mutual recognition passed between them. He got his spectacular babe. She wasn't quite sure if this was necessary but she supplied the hoped-for ingredients. She felt a little compromised and then concluded she was there to do a job. These were her working clothes.

Kate looked at the faces, the Armani top grade suits. Kate actually only knew the name but her father had taught her, once, about tailored clothing. Now she had a fair eye for good tailoring. So she gave the suits an Armani label for lack of greater knowledge. The suits looked back, mostly at her chest, then her hips and legs, finally at her face. They were still standing as Arnie finished. Kate concentrated with all her strength to not shake or wobble. All the bravado leading up to this moment, what got her to Arnie's with Miriam in tow now seemed distant. How the hell did she ever get herself into this?

Miriam and Kate barely had time to know one another much less to become sisters in combat. Kate felt the glare of great circumspection and she bore the load of responsibility having brought Miriam over.

Miriam had faced much harder faces but had no clue where to start. Arnie concluded and sat down leaving both women standing like statues. For perhaps five seconds there was dead silence. One man made a motion as if to make them welcome.

Kate said, "Arnie, the ladies are standing." With that Arnie snatched two chairs, handed one to Miriam and a second one to Kate. Kate couldn't be much more self conscious but decided to get over it, accept her fantasy vision and try to help get the money.

Someone who assisted Arnie had thought to write name tags so Miriam and Kate could identify each person. Kate was grateful for this touch, it would make the pitch easier.

Miriam dove in. "Gentlemen, we come for your money for a good cause. A man named Aashif and his last name is Khan has assembled a fearsome group of terrorists but this group far outdistances any group seen. Only a few carry guns, the rest tote computers. Unique as of this moment, a group of men and women, some Islamic, not all, who are hunting for your money. Mr. Habstein, I have numbers for your wife's account at the Beverly Hills Savings branch near your office. Would you like to know the number?"

Lenny Habstein, a self made movie producer and prominent Jewish philanthropist didn't stun easily, he had waded through two generations of offensive, aggressive hustlers to make his movies but her statement surprised him.

"Frankly I wouldn't know it if you read it but where did it come from?"

Miriam had no one's bank account numbers. She replied:

"Mr. Habstein, they have not only your account numbers, that's trivial. They can crack the alarm system on your house. So can I, by the way. Gentlemen, time is short, so we get to the point. This group is targeting most of you. At least Mr. Habstein and Jay Schlesinger." Miriam honed in on Schlesinger, her dark eyes holding his. Miriam had long since learned how to make that eye contact that did not immediately intimidate but certainly did cause a reaction.

Miriam continued, "Jay, you are on their list. You are prominent, with numerous relatives in Israel, one of whom is a known and outspoken zionist of the traditional stripe. They have no interest in killing you directly. They just want your money and holdings. What's odd is they may have the plan to do just that. Naturally security people in your government and mine are onto all this. Regrettably they are not properly equipped or not sufficiently. Our little group can accomplish what they cannot."

A hand was raised. "I don't know how you wish to be addressed, I'm sorry."

"Miriam is fine."

"Miriam how do we know they exist and you even have a group? Sorry if that is upsetting but as you want my money I want to know where it's going."

Miriam responded, "You are....?"

"Stanley Winogrond. I own the agency----."

Kate awkwardly jumped in, "...which represents artists in the newer television series on Fox that are so successful. And you also nearly singlehandedly created the incredibly successful campaigns tying technology into these various series."

Miriam shot a fast glance toward Kate who caught the motion and acknowledged Miriam's communication. Kate had help from a Berkeley hacker who seemingly could track almost anything if it contained actual data. But she prayed no one pushed her beyond the superficial.

Stanley Winogrond continued, "As I was saying, you both could be delivering information of vital import. Or you could be two hustlers. I grew up on the streets of Brooklyn, I've been hustled by the poor, the rich and the charming. Kindly prove what you're talking about is real."

The other men subtly nodded to one another. If there had been no bond between these self made Jewish men, at least a shadow of self defense might take hold.

Kate knew they were screwed unless Miriam had a trick up her sleeve. Kate now realized her own naivete'. She had thought the primarily male Rotarians who met at the Wayzata Country Club back in Minnesota were vaguely parallel to these six in Beverly Hills. But Arnie's friends existed in an intense, deeply competitive, unforgiving culture where winning remained paramount. Charity scored below gritty survival.

But Miriam was hardly finished. She began a slow stroll down one side of the table. Kate watched her movements. Miriam resembled nothing so much as a young college girl dressed in a white blouse and simple pleated skirt. As she moved down the room Kate realized how utterly vulnerable Miriam seemed. Kate stood stonefaced and frozen in place. Miriam was saying nothing and Kate felt terrible for both of them. The heads turned minutely as Miriam walked.

"Gentlemen I flew 14 hours to get here. I last slept Wednesday and then only fitfully as we were tracking two of Aashif's cohorts across Berlin. He grew up in Egypt, migrated with his family to Palestine, spent his youth in two refugee camps, barely attended school, watched his brother murdered by Israeli counter insurgency troops or so he has claimed. Eventually his family raised a little money and he actually made it to France attending a prominent university. He is the byproduct of a ludicrous wayward culture that has damaged tens of thousands of people, some Palestinian, some Israeli, Russian, Jordanian, you name it. It's a wonder every poor Arab didn't turn out like him. Jews too. Anyway, somewhere along the way Aashif Khan turned sour, then angry, then utterly bitter. But he also had a knack for finding sympathy from many quarters. In recent years the culmination of a life dodging security forces and finally the Mossad itself turned him into an embittered, combative guerilla. Not the first, nor the last in a long line. The difference seems to be he reads and absorbs voraciously. And he, nearly alone among the rabble rousers, caught on to technology as a weapon. He has two sons, one attended school at the University of Illinois briefly and took back knowledge. In this case, computer and software knowledge. Illinois has a top electrical engineering school and the son learned well enough. You may recall an incident here in Beverly Hills last week, it made the news I was told. A local real estate developer named Fishkin was in court defending various suits he could not meet his obligations."

Winogrond sat up straight looking shocked. "Ben Fishkin, sure, he belongs to my synagogue. Our fathers were best friends. What are you saying about him?"

Miriam had now circled the table and was starting her second lap.

"Your Mr. Fishkin donated to many causes publicly. More important, a dedicated zionist and forthright in backing the right wing in Israel. He spent liberally to support arch conservative Jewish causes in my country."

Winogrond suddenly stood up. "Miss, uh, Miriam, you're saying Ben was attacked by this madman?"

Miriam's pace never slowed, her facial composure remained bland, fixed, unaffected. "They took him out financially."

Winogrond shook his head. "That's impossible. He banked where I bank, I know his attorney, I went to NYU with that lawyer. He's brilliant. He would protect his clients from such intrusion, such despicable treatment. Something else happened to Ben Fishkin, I'm sure of it." Winogrond's demeanor suddenly had shifted.

"Let's understand something here. Aashif has rounded up some good minds and is bringing the fight to your doorstep, to your house, to your temple. These people are employing western tools and Islamic fundamentalist inflammatory rhetoric. They have no intention of fighting this out in Tel Aviv or Jerusalem or in the Negev. They are here, now. And he's no madman. We believe he is calm, methodical, logical and so utterly determined to wreak vengeance that it makes Saddam Hussein appear to be your ally."

Another of the group spoke up. "I am Emile Heller, I have interests in various companies, here and overseas. Miriam, you are saying this group is working here? Surely American authorities are working on this. Our FBI is hardly helpless. We have resourceful government agencies."

Miriam stopped at the far end of the huge room and picked up an expensive looking vase turning it in her hands absentmindedly. Arnie watched her with grave concern. The vase happened to be an original Torani worth thousands. Arnie knew this because his decorator made a big deal about the artist.

Miriam said, "Arnie, it's a Torani. Should be worth, umm, what? Fifty thousand, hundred thousand?"

Arnie stood up nervously. His insurance would never cover breakage like this.

Miriam held it both hands. "This vase would buy food for ten families for three years with plenty left over. People portray Israelis as hating Palestinians but in reality we are they, they are us. Lots of people doing without. Arnie, I came here for contributions. What am I offered for this very fine Torani vase?"

Arnie had no idea where she was going with this.

"Gentlemen, you live in a culture where elite capitalism is still encouraged. You can acquire to your heart's content. In the rest of the world things are very different. I don't begrudge you your success but now it's time to pay a few dues. Our group is on Aashif. We, alone, are pressuring them, keeping them hunted in country after country. You must understand, this is not some campaign to bomb American embassies. Operationally, their efforts are pointed at people in this room. And legally, even though you may have funds in banks which are insured, all of you have far more at stake. First they will crack your financial facade, then they will come for you."

Arnie realized she was closing but this was an uncomfortable close.

Arnie blurted out, "Miriam, you are making me a little anxious with that vase."

For the first time, Miriam smiled.

Arnie watched her slowly replace the vase on its pedestal. Then he said, "Miriam, you are trying to convince us this madman is here, is coming after us directly? There is nothing on the news."

"Lessons learned. You don't bring the fight to this shore and make a big splash. They want no noise, the guns are silent. They will find your enterprises and install troublesome, disruptive devices."

Stan Winogrond stood up once more. "Ladies, I need proof before I start writing checks."

Kate watched Miriam for a sign of wavering. Miriam played her trump card. "I'm sorry, by the time you have your proof you will have been had. I can offer this data only. And there is one opportunity, right now. I am not a slick sales person, I'm not even a decent *goniff*. If you let their momentum build it will reach beyond financial security, that is guaranteed."

Heads around the room shook in the negative. She had a thumbs down reaction.

"Going once, going twice, no help from any of you?" Miriam asked.

Winogrond still standing, hands in pockets shook his head. "I'll offer up ten thousand dollars knowing that I'll likely never hear what I just invested for, am I right?"

Miriam nodded. "Right, this money goes out, doesn't come back. You are investing for the future of yourselves and others. It is selfless spending."

Bodies rustled nervously but no one made an offer.

Miriam walked calmly to the door. "Your time is appreciated gentlemen. I'm sorry my presentation was insufficient." Kate turned toward Miriam and gave her an empty handed gesture. Miriam opened the door and left.

Kate looked back at the men around the table.

"You're going to let her walk away?" No one moved or talked.

Kate turned and also walked out.

The room was completely silent. The quiet was interrupted by a beeping sound. One man checked his pager. "It's mine. I need to call my office." He took out a cell phone and walked out of the room.

The men began conversing, offering reinforcement to one another for not offering to contribute.

Arnie's chef and staff began serving a mid-afternoon repast. Arnie broke out two of his prized Cabernets and his guest oohed and ahed. Arnie had spent thousands not only for the wine, the new cellar dug under the house but to be trained to say the words correctly and knowledgeably identify wines. Arnie was thorough.

An hour passed, one guest excused himself, the rest remained. Arnie served a fine feast. Stan Winogrond left the expansive sun porch to make a call. Two minutes later he returned looking stunned. "This seems too incredible but that was my accountant. Someone has damaged our financial files, funds have been transferred. And my wife received a threatening call at home."

"From who, Bernie?"

"They only would say they were recovering money for Palestine."

CHAPTER TWENTY SEVEN
KATE & MIRIAM RETURN TO ARNIE'S HOUSE

Kate drove the mule across Hollywood on Franklin. She gestured to an aging, stately apartment building facing the freeway. "That used to be the Scientology headquarters here. I think it still is."

"How do you know about Scientology? Are you involved, Kate?"

"No, but my mom knew Diana Hubbard, the founder's daughter back in the seventies. She worked on some recording project with her."

"Scientology hasn't taken hold in Israel. I think our culture is a bit too real but I don't know that much about it."

Suddenly first one then both of Kate's phones went off. Kate responded by laughing at first. "Well, nice to be so popular, right?"

Miriam checked her watch and recomputed time zones. "That should be our friends back at Arnie's place."

Kate shot her a quizzical look. "How can you know that?"

"It's 2 PM precisely, I told you we could put on a show. It's show time."

Kate didn't get it. She answered her cell first.

"Who called you? Arnie? Yah, I've got that number. Alright. Geez they must be pretty upset."

Miriam asked, "Who was that?"

"Uh, just, a friend. I have a line that can be carefully monitored. Whatever happened, it just triggered some shit."

Miriam nodded and smiled to herself.

"Miriam, you know what happened, don't you?"

"Kate, I really did not make this whole trek to be shut down cold. I'm getting some help. The deal was if I had not called in by a certain time the help started."

"Arnie, it's Kate McGill. I got messages you called. Alright, tell me.

All of them had something happen? Oh, just Winogrond and Heller. Oh, and Emile, what's his name? Right. Oh, ouch! Just waltzed in and helped themselves? That does hurt. So what do you need from me? Well, I can still get hold of Miriam, I think. Sure, I'll work on it right away and call you back. Ok, bye."

Kate grinned, then wondered if this was time to grin. "Well, your bretheren paid a call on Messers Winogrond and Heller. Or, more correctly some secured bank accounts. Shook them up badly. Heller went to the hospital to have his heart checked or something."

"It wasn't us. It was them."

"Them?"

"We passed over only two accounts to the bad guys."

"What are you talking about. Passed accounts to whom?"

"Kate, we operate in the shadows. In those shadows you must scrutinize your counterpart with great care. We know Aashif's people not by sight but by computing signatures. They have us outgunned financially right now, we have superior technical talent. But they are clever, resourceful and gaining on us. In the shadows, in what you Americans keep calling cyber-space, we trade little pieces of information. This is how we know who they are or at least can take a guess. One way to find out is to expose some data, see how they use it or if they use it. We traded Winogrond, Heller and one more. We received very useful leads, a few door openers. You recall our discussion, how you wanted to track down those two men who tortured those animals in, Florida, I think it was?"

Kate had the sinking feeling of being way in over her head. She was the sacrificial goat for these people. It was Kate who provided some significant data on these couple men. Not bank accounts but other data required to crack the security. This was weeks back but certainly not with the knowledge it would be used to injure them.

"You violated our trust by doing this, Miriam."

Miriam wasn't looking her way as Kate turned the mule around and headed back across Hollywood for Bel-Air.

"Kate, we play for keeps, we have no choice. Those accounts are almost certainly insured. They'll recover."

"But you handed money from Jews to Islamic terrorists."

"We demonstrated sincerity, offered genuine assistance, proved our value. This is the quid pro quo, you know that term?"

"I attend college, it's come up." Kate was trying to drive the mule and keep her composure. "You allowed your own enemy to rip off your potential allies."

Miriam decided it was time to raise the stakes. "Kate, now listen carefully.

You come from a safe part of a comfortable country. Americans may have their first taste of real terrorism but I guess it hasn't yet happened here. In my country we pass the terrorists in coffee shops and supermarkets every single day. We are brother and sister. I attend a synagogue, they a mosque but under the skin we share some commonality, certainly in a historical sense. And we share geographical space. I can drive across our whole country in 88 minutes. You'd spend that time entering a freeway and fighting traffic. We live in an exceedingly tight space with these people. One nuclear device and our whole culture is cinders."

"I'm familiar with Israeli geography, I've studied the history, I am half Jewish, I celebrate the high holy days, I know Ben Gurion, the war in '48, all of it."

"You don't live it, it's not your heritage, you're a visitor. We inhabit a hair trigger culture, it all can change in minutes, seconds. They can lob in a few Scuds and my family is non-existent. We know an enemy and we also know these same people could really be our next door neighbors. So, now let's get in synch as Americans like to say. You are being called back to Arnie's mansion to be confronted by the aggrieved businessmen who just got trimmed. So here's my advice: You go or take me and I'll tell them, 'Gentlemen, apparently Aashif struck already. He'll be back. Help fund our private effort to track these people down.'"

"Miriam, would you do it? Give the money?"

"I am neither wealthy or American. I see through different eyes."

"So Miriam, how can I trust what you say?"

"Tough world, Kate, tough world. Hard to know who you can trust. So let's put it this way. Help me get half a million. That is not all that much money in America. In Israel it's a useful fortune. Help me get my venture funding. Isn't that what you call it over here, venture funding? We will pursue Aashif and his offshoots of which there are presently at least two and we will be victorious. And, do me this favor, this mitzvah and I'll be your fairy godmother and grant you two wishes. One can be purely espionage, one can be force."

"Espionage and force? Explain that."

Kate steered onto Hollywood Boulevard but barely noticed where they were.

"Espionage, you know the term. We'll help you root out information. It can be an exhausting procedure but we have a few excellent people. That's how I got you your names for the animal killers. And 'force' means given some notice I can provide you with some muscle. They are here. Not right here but in this country. I need 48 hours minimum. There are two people, highly trained, skilled, virtually unstoppable. But you must be clear, turn them loose, turn around, walk way and do not look back."

"Killers? You have killers?"

"Kate you're a young, somewhat naive woman playing in a high stakes game. If you like, take me back to Los Feliz, you can drop me some blocks away. I will disappear, return to my family and start over. We tried. You are not yet skilled but your heart is right. No hard feelings, as they say."

Kate turned again onto Sunset Boulevard. The gaudy billboards advertising the newest movies, CD's and hottest stars paraded by. The fanciest Mercedes and BMW's swept past them, smoked out windows blanked off against intruding stares.

Kate thought Miriam must find this intriguing but terribly foreign. Kate imagined Miriam must miss her little son and daughter terribly. Miriam had talked about them on two emails and even mentioned them on the phone. Kate thought Miriam would be a tough, decisive mother.

"I believe you, Miriam. Is that your real name, Miriam?"

"It's close enough. It's what's on my passport. Kate, I'm the Miriam of your life. In other's lives I may be known by other names. It's unimportant. If something happens, you are questioned you refer to me as Miriam Levy-Sault. They will attempt to trace Miriam Levy-Sault and that will go where it goes. Now, we have work to do. How long to reach Arnie's from here?"

"Umm, 12 minutes. It will ease up in Beverly Hills. God, I do hate this place."

"Why are you here at all then? Don't you live in Berkeley? There are billions in the technology field. Why this?"

"I can't quite explain, partly some connections lead to Hollywood from my mother. She lived in California, spent a lot of time in the music business. Partly they are so utterly over the top here. Rodeo Drive, if you took fifteen minutes and cruised the stores. It's beyond description. Even my half Jewish side can't handle it. Makes you embarrassed to be Jewish."

"Kate, a bit of Israeli wisdom. That is the essence of being Jewish. You have brethren who have no concept of what is good and useful, tasteful and relevant. The absolute essence of modern Jewry. Some of them are launched into their own orbits but likely no worse than any other ethnic group. And then you have the good Jews. Who build cultural worlds, subsidize charities, contribute magnificently."

"Are you a good Jew, Miriam?"

"I have my days."

They rode in unsteady quiet, not quite icy, certainly not warm. Kate wanted to like Miriam, appreciate her, even be friendly. But Miriam's mission disallowed any thought of actual kinship. They were tied together by events and now the bond had become more serious.

Kate had been wondering about that middle eastern face that flashed by. *Could that be this Aashif that Miriam was ---*The shaft of light reappeared, no more than a half second, a dark skinned young man with a goatee and then gone again...Kate kept driving but Miriam picked up on her momentary bobble. Kate felt shaken but maintained her composure. *What was happening, who is this person?*

Arnie's driveway reappeared but now the muscle waited just inside the imposing wrought iron gates. As they cleared the first checkpoint Kate noticed two more men attempting to camouflage themselves behind tall rose bushes.

Miriam held a cell phone in her lap. As they arrived at the top of the driveway she punched numbers in, waited, heard a tone, then she punched in a series of numbers and ended the call.

"Calling in to the office?" Kate asked.

"We have our little system. They know where I am. They are nearby. Where I come from meetings sometimes need to be brief or they become dangerous. So we're on a timer, so to speak. Fifteen minutes, that's what I have."

"And if this takes longer?"

"Don't let it. You and I, let's not let it, ok?"

Kate did not answer. Her pulse raced, her skin felt flushed, her stomach felt uncomfortably close to cramping. Miriam was certainly borderline scary unless she was just bluffing---all talk.

Kate was glad she stopped and changed clothes. Now in jeans and t-shirt in running shoes she felt more prepared to take action if required.

Arnie waited for them near the front door. Normally agitated, Arnie actually showed trepidation. He zeroed in on Miriam, hardly taking note of Kate.

"I have two friends inside who are badly shaken. And they can't help but connect their conditions with your visit. What can you tell me before we go upstairs?"

Miriam played him stable, steady, unmoved. "Arnie, your friends were targeted long before I walked in here. Certain terrorists, as I told you, have concluded that bringing the conflict to your living room ups the ante, raises your discomfort."

Kate decided to let Miriam run the show. So far she had not lied in the strictest sense. But Kate was listening to every word. It also occurred to her that even if Miriam outright lied and deceived, Kate had no earthly idea what to do or say.

Arnie escorted them upstairs into a small study. Miriam's normal walking pace, urgent and directed slowed. They were approaching a new room, not the large meeting space. Arnie pointed ahead. "They're in there, the room is secure, has its own electronic connections, secured computer stuff."

Kate had the nagging suspicion Arnie might not know what he had paid for.

Miriam walked to the closed door and paused. "Arnie, I would prefer meeting these men out here, not in your secured room. I've had less than satisfactory experiences in such places."

Arnie stopped. His only resistance was that this was a bonafied occasion for using his hyper expensive secured space, something he had been aching to do for months. But Miriam had pulled herself against an opposite wall and her body language indicated she was stopped for now. Arnie quickly balanced his own self satisfaction against needs of his friends.

"Sure, sure. Tell you what, down this hall is a nice uh, what do you call it, a study, yah, study. I never use it, it's a great room, lots of books so let's go there."

They proceeded down the hall to the obvious study and waited. Kate checked her watch. "It's now 4 and a half minutes since we got here. How rigid are your rules?"

"Rigid. That's how we stay alive."

"Isn't this a bit extreme? I mean no one here is out for your skin."

Miriam replied, "We encounter problems constantly. This is our safety check."

The women heard voices, moments later Arnie and two of the men entered. "Miriam, let's get right to the point. Can your people make these fundamentalist nuts disappear? If we give you money, what happens?"

"I came looking for five hundred thousand dollars. You'll receive full charitable tax deductions through a front organization but in reality every dollar goes into defeating these people."

Winogrond and Heller looked at each other. "What guarantees can you offer? We both make a good living but you're talking a huge sum of cash here."

"I appreciate your dilemma, gentlemen. Your FBI and other services that you pay for with tax dollars would ideally be protecting you. But they are months, perhaps, years behind on this. The American public believes the threat from abroad will be explosives and shooting. But in many countries including Syria, Iraq, Libya clever people driven by a messianic fervor, words that really apply here, want to bring the war to your doors. Nearly impossible with conventional methods, but workable, as you've seen using modern technology. I do not have a guarantee. I am not stonewalling you, that is not part of our approach. I'm telling you what is so, that's it."

The minutes were ticking by, the men all had other, obvious questions. When would the money have to be transferred, to whom, in what form? Kate found an angle to place her hand where she could see her watch. It was under five minutes. The questions continued, Miriam parrying and thrusting with their concerns. Under three minutes. Kate cleared her throat to get Miriam's attention.

Miriam checked her watch. "Gentlemen, in two minutes thirty seconds I need to make a call that is urgent. Let me ask you both, are we any closer to a resolution? I recognize the validity of every concern you've presented. The truth is, we've found no better way to go on the offensive. We know who a few of these people are, we have a sort of relationship through a middle man. To make this more real, this man runs a small deli. He is half Jewish, but his mother comes from Arab and Islamic roots. He speaks to both sides. A simple, down to earth person, he happens to be well suited as a broker, if you will. This deli owner helps keep the balance between us and them."

Arnie spoke up, "Miriam, how do we know that there is a 'them'? Why couldn't it also be you? You and your friends?"

She did not blink. "It could be, the dividing line is nearly invisible. One of these people lives near my mother in Tel Aviv. He is her age, they see one another in the market, they even share a love for classical music. How much thinner do you want it? Gentlemen, I need to make my call now, in ten seconds."

"Miriam, we're struggling here. Just handing over so much money to a person we hardly know, it's terribly, uh, unsettling."

She punched in the buttons. It rang once and answered. "We're not able to reach a conclusion so I will leave now. What do you mean? This was not our agreement. I don't need that help. You listen to me, I can't work with these people under such conditions...."

Miriam glanced around the room. Her trepidation was clear.

"A mixup, unfortunate. They are coming in to rescue me. These are very determined people. I would suggest, Arnie, you use that room. Take your friends, go to the room and secure it. DO IT NOW!"

The three men ran from the room knocking over a chair in the process. Kate heard some noise, voices shouting, then two muffled explosions, then a third.

"What do we do, Miriam?"

"When they come don't move quickly. Just stay here. I'm carrying a device which pinpoints my location using GPS technology. They know where I am."

The voices suddenly became loud and one man was screaming. "Get out of our way, put down your weapons, we don't want you. We're here to rescue the women."

"They are fine, no one needs to be rescued!" another voice shouted back. A scuffle could be heard, then something that sounded like shots. But the blasts were again muffled, very small sounding.

Kate could not just sit still, she took a few fast steps to the doorway and looked down the hall. Two men dressed in athletic gear ran toward her. One of them raised something up in his hand as he approached her.

His accent was clearly middle eastern, Kate could not tell if it was Israeli or what?

"You are the McGill woman? Oh, there is Miriam. Are you alright?"

"We're fine, I did not need assistance."

"We came as instructed, that is our arrangement. The men, they are in that room?"

Kate strained to hear what was being said, the man had lowered his voice. The second man stood, legs spread, one hand on what looked like a weapon, the other carrying a walkie talkie. The walkie talkie crackled, Kate recognized hebrew words but it was said very fast so she only understood 'helicopter'.

The first man walked behind Kate. She started to turn and follow his path when suddenly she felt his muscular arm come from behind her. His other arm held her waist and in a split second she lost consciousness.

Miriam watched the man gently bring Kate's limp body to the floor. "Ok, we have a few minutes, you know your targets, we meet in back, on the lawn."

The two men ran back down the long hall. One stopped, removed a piece of art from the wall and expertly separated the artwork from the frame. His actions were precise. Miriam glanced momentarily at Kate, saw she was breathing and ran down the hall. She stopped just short of the entrance to the secured room. She knew there were cameras all over. She set off first one and then a second smoke bomb and the hall was quickly saturated with white and grey smoke. She turned, ran into a nearby room, removed two small art objects, then a framed picture which she inserted in her back pack into a package prepared for the artwork.

Miriam disappeared up the hall, exiting the mansion through a back door. In three minutes a whirling, chopping sound announced the arrival of a small helicopter. Inside the secure room Arnie watched it land on a tv transmission from the back yard. Winogrond watched as well, Heller was frantically trying to call out on his cell phone but the signal seemed to be jammed.

The two men accompanying Miriam met her at the copter, they boarded and in under two minutes the copter rose between the palm trees. Arnie lost sight of it at treetop level.

"Arnie, what do we do? asked Winogrond."

"Sit tight, police will show up in a minute. You're alive, we all our. We just got ripped off. Rather, I got ripped off. I saw one of them strip off that Chagall in the hall. They were common crooks. Well organized but just crooks."

Seven minutes after Kate was attacked, the effects of the chloroform abated, she woke up groggy. Her throat and neck hurt where the man's arm had crossed over. The hallway looked smoky and smelled like charcoal. She checked her watch. Almost ten minutes had passed. No one was around, the hall appeared empty. She stood up unsteadily and began walking down the hall.

"Hey there's the sacrificial lamb now. Too bad she trusted those people. I don't think they were Israeli, I think they were Arabs, likely Palestinians," said Arnie as he watched Kate move down the hall.

"Stop her, Arnie, she's going to get away,' yelled Heller.

"Nuttin' I can do, there is a timed release lock, it will trip in another five minutes. When we ran in here I hit that button. Just relax, the cops will find her or I will. I got a hunch she's just a naive kid who was tryin' to do something right. She sure doesn't look like a criminal."

"Great body, though."

"Yah, sensational body. You should see her play volleyball, it's a symphony of gorgeous flesh."

CHAPTER TWENTY EIGHT
KATE RETURNS ALONE TO ARNIE'S

It took Kate 15 minutes to recover from being knocked out at Arnie's house. Mostly she was upset over being taken in by these fake Israeli patriots, that's how she saw it. She drove through Beverly Hills and finally pulled over opposite the Beverly Hills Hotel. She shut off the engine and just sat. What to do? She found herself dozing off and finally gave in to that need to recoup and rest.

A ringing cell phone disturbed her nap. She checked the time. She'd been out for almost 45 minutes.

"Yah."

"It's Miriam. How are you doing?"

"Not too happy about fake Israelis. You totally lied to me."

There was a pause. "No, I did not. We are confusing the bad guys."

"Just how the hell are you doing that?"

"It will take time to explain and this is far too public. Name a place you know where you're comfortable I'll meet you there."

"How can I---uh, well, how can I do that? You screwed over these guys completely and me as well."

"Look, wrong time for that talk. Pick a place, bring a companion if you're more comfortable."

Kate tried to clear her head. This was asking to get screwed over twice. "Look, Miriam, maybe in your world this is what you do but not in mine. I'm sure I'll be arrested and these men who met with you in good faith will never talk to me if that's all they do. You screwed with all of us and I'm the idiot. I can't trust you at all. So no. Forget it."

"What if I told you that what happened was going to make a big difference in the future? What if I said we're inches away from pulling off a major coup to help defeat terrorism?"

Kate looked out the car window at some willowy palm trees behind the Beverly Hills Hotel. She felt very young and totally a victim.

"You cannot be trusted whoever you are. I cannot trust what you say." Kate increasingly felt like this was just another hustle and a bad one.

"Kate, would we have done what we seemed to do to those people and then called you on the phone? Does that make any sense at all?"

It did not but Kate disliked all this circuitous thinking. "It wasn't 'seemed to do'. You did do it pure and simple."

"No, wrong. Where does the video output of Arnie's secure room go?"

"How the hell should I know, Miriam or whatever your name is? Look we're done here. If I'm going to take outrageous chances I'll go my own way. I'm done talking."

"The video output went to a television transmitter, to a satellite, finally to a small town in Syria. It was all watched. It was play acting. No one got hurt. If that had been real there would have been bodies. We were on tv for our friends overseas. We were demonstrating that our alliance was real. I cannot go on about this on cell phones. I will be sitting on a park bench with a baby stroller in ten minutes where you and I stopped for lunch. Do you remember?"

Kate replied. "Yes, I do." The phone clicked off. Kate punched in new numbers.

"It's me, I'm having a problem."

"Oh, I already heard from two sources. My heavens, you're like a young boy who can't keep his hands off of it. You have plenty on your plate. Plenty, capital P. And someone has finally identified your animal you ride."

Kate had to think. *Buzz was talking about, oh, animal means the mule.* Her car was identified. "Shit. I will go to new, uh, I have a spare set of you knows."

Buzz did not know. "Spare set, oh, sorry, ok." Buzz figured out she had spare license plates. "From where? No don't say."

"In the last 96 hours you're done a fine job of dragging yourself into a whole variety of, uh, circumstances." Kate knew he meant dragnets. There were cops all over looking for her. Kate turned the mule into the network of back alleys in Beverly Hills searching for a hidden spot. She located a space behind a particularly high wall where people in the surrounding houses could not see her car, only someone driving down the alley. She tucked the cell phone between her chin and shoulder, popped the trunk and rummaged under two suitcases. The license plates from Canada were current, if stolen, when she passed through Toronto. She had learned to switch plates very quickly. It only took a minute to switch front and back. She then hurriedly removed four form fitting panels molded from extremely pliable, lightweight plastics and attached them to the mule's outer skin flicking bent metal clips holding the panels on each fender leaving new paint in key places. The panels were a form of plastic. The mule now smarted a clever two tone paint job, the fenders being one shade, the roof, hood and truck being a contrasting darker color.

"Ok, the animal is different." Buzz said nothing. One reason Buzz originally went to all the trouble to push the mule through the still existent grey market regulations was that it was built out with a variety of devices to give the car a quick change personality. The former owner periodically had to move contraband around Europe. He was still doing some time in Europe.

"I'm going to meet this person who just took that action."

"That is crazy, not good judgment. Wait until tonight, drive up the coast, get away. Go to your grandma's place."

"Right, I will. Gotta go."

Kate drove to a block from the park bench where she and Miriam had shared some lunch and then tucked the mule behind another wall. She removed her shoes and strapped on a pair of roller blades. Then she rolled the remaining block. Kate figured she had better odds on wheels if it came down to fleeing.

Miriam was sitting on the bench with a baby carriage. Kate had the image of an exploding baby carriage in her mind from the Paul Simon song but she kept rolling.

She sat down very uneasy about the carriage. Miriam picked up on her unease. "It's a prop, relax. Are you wearing any listening device? Of any kind? I can't really frisk you."

"Jesus, I should be frisking you, Miriam. No, I am not wired if that's what you call it."

"Listen to me, Kate, we have little time. I will be flown out in twenty minutes and will not return, Likely ever. When this started you were told there were high risks. Now you see that's true. We did that charade so that others back close to home would believe we were allied with them. It's that simple. We were Palestinian in that little play. We helped them arrange for the video feed to be piped back to their, uh, quarters. Do you get this so far?"

Kate nodded while she warily looked around. They were seventy feet from Santa Monica Boulevard, traffic was heavy, every other car seemed to be a Mercedes.

"Alright, I used you to get to those men. They are all prominent American Jews, precisely the group these others want to wipe out. So two things, the Jews are now on guard. That's where they should be. There is danger all around and it's much closer than they ever thought. Word of this incident will spread. That's appropriate. And my group were able to trade some information. We have located a person with their help who we want. Really want. Highest priority. That person is being attended to about now. It is the middle of the night back there. Now stay with me, this must be very fast. I am being pursued. A group, their name looks like this." Miriam wrote out the name Hamas.

"I know them, yes," said Kate.

"They are here, on the ground hunting and they are very clever, resourceful people. You have been brave, you did not blink when the incident took place. We would like to have you with us but that is not realistic. So, much was accomplished by our standard. You can go back to your men and tell them this. And, return these."

Miriam pulled the carriage toward her and lifted a blanket. Under the blanket were the stolen pieces of art and vases.

"Now, in thirty seconds I will be picked up, you must go away fast. We are sisters and I'm sorry to hurt you but we had a mission, that comes first." With that Miriam stood up and momentarily hugged Kate. "Oh, here, give this envelope to Arnie, ok?" Miriam then turned and ran to the street. A dark blue Audi A8, a long, very expensive sedan darted to the curb, the rear door opened and she was gone.

Kate examined the artwork more carefully. She wasn't sure but it looked genuine.

Kate skated back to the mule pushing the carriage. She changed back to her shoes and set out for Arnie's. She had no earthly idea how to handle this but she now believed Miriam or whoever she was. She turned on the talk station and listened absentmindedly as she wound through the streets.

"On a small farm near the Gaza Strip Palestinian authorities reportedly discovered the body of a man thought to be ill-famed terrorist Aashif Khan. Israeli forces apparently tracked him to this farm house and killed him there. Reprisals are expected by the Israelis."

Kate wasn't sure how she felt. Her promises likely resulted in the death of a person half way around the world or apparently that was what happened. Who knows if that actually happened at all?

Kate drove up the street to Arnie's house. The police were not in sight. Kate really had no idea what she'd do if the police were around. She drove up the driveway. No one stopped her. She parked the mule and lifted the baby carriage out and began pushing it toward the house.

Two men emerged from under a portico hefting very large guns. They couldn't have looked much more threatening but she kept walking.

"Stop right there. You gotta a lot of cajones to show up here lady."

"This is the stuff Arnie lost, I think it's all there."

"You gotta be kiddin'. You're shittin'us."

Kate shook her head to say 'no'.

"Boss, you gotta see what's down here in the driveway," one of the bruisers talked into a walkie talkie. Kate stood still with the carriage. She couldn't just turn around and leave. She heard loud footsteps down the long tiled staircase and then Arnie emerged toting a pistol looking disheveled. The look on his face expressed total disbelief.

"You, here? What the fuck? You gotta be crazy."

Kate said nothing but pushed the carriage toward him. He bent over and removed one of the rolled up paintings.

"You're shittin' me. I don't....The vases they're ok, the Renoir print, jesus. Is the oil in here?"

"That's what she gave me, you tell me if that's all of it." Kate felt a bit better.

Arnie looked at his possessions, then back at Kate. "You're a real trickster. A genuine slime bag trickster. You know the cops are lookin' for you big time."

Kate responded, "Ok, you know your secure room, it's got a video system. Get someone to detach the video output. It probably was supposed to go to a video capture like a tape deck or DVD."

"Yeah, for sure, piped to a tape deck."

"It's not, that signal went to a satellite, then to, uh, to, some people overseas. This was a sham, a play fake. Look in tomorrow's newspaper, a terrorist will be taken out by the Israelis. They traded you for that guy. I never knew what was happening."

Arnie stood looking at Kate then looked away, then back at Kate.

"You got some kind of major balls to pull this shit. Someone coulda gotten bumped off. Us, them, you, who knows?"

"I didn't know. I was helping them raise funds. They pitched me for weeks. I'm the sucker here, not you and your friends."

"So they didn't want our money at all, that was a sham?"

"Here, this is a note from Miriam, it's sealed up. You read it when you want."

Arnie took the note and ran his finger over the flap tentatively. Then he opened it.

"She says she's sorry for putting us through that, you too. Man she's got some balls too. She's askin' for money again. Says to send it to this address here. Man, they make 'em bigger than life in Israel. Ok, I'm callin' the cops, see if I can get them off your back. You got a lawyer if you need it, kid?"

Kate nodded and smiled. "Arnie, I'm sorry if that upset you or your friends. Life is not so simple any more. Uh, Miriam told me to tell you to be on guard. She said some of Hamas are on the ground here."

Arnie reacted in disbelief. "Here, right around us, those terrorists are here? Jesus Christ where does it end?"

Kate turned to leave. "Arnie, I don't think it ends ever. We just deal with it."

Kate turned and walked back down the driveway to the mule. She got in, took a deep breath and wanted all this to go away. As she started the mule another momentary shaft of light entered her mind. This time it was less threatening for some reason. She again saw a face from the middle east. Kate could examine the vision. It was a young man, perhaps close to her age, darker skin, black hair. He could be Israeli or Arabic. Then the face was gone again. Kate thought, *Why now, this second? Is this because of Miriam?*

CHAPTER TWENTY NINE

KATE JOINS A PICK UP
VOLLEYBALL GAME IN CENTRAL PARK

Kate had one day off squeezed between a *GloryDays* marketing meeting, photo shoot, two radio interviews and finally her first appearance on a network TV show. Having had only five days back in Berkeley after her bruising and disorienting episode with Miriam in Los Angeles, Kate now felt like she was stumbling through her life. Stepping out of the Hilton on sixth Avenue in New York, Kate had four hours to herself, nothing she had to do. Instinctively she headed to Central Park at a fast clip.

Dodging taxis and buses she headed up sixth avenue. Kate just wanted to reach the park. Feeling slightly lost and certainly alone, utterly unsure if she wanted her life to be unfolding in a chaos of media frenzy Kate looked for something, what she didn't know? Maybe the small zoo? No, animals in cages. No. She walked with greater urgency.

Into Central Park, up some sidewalks, then over two hills, around some huge boulders, through two empty playing fields and into a clearing. She finally hit some paydirt: Volleyball, three players and four players. *Now please let them be fun loving, solid players.*

She walked up to the game, gave them plenty of space, wasn't going to force it. She watched a nice pitched volley, good effort on both sides.

The ball rolled her way, she one-handed it in her palm and tossed it to the server with a solid, definite, accurate throw. Duly noted by the server. Kate sat down, hugged her legs, smiled. A second ball rolled free. She again one-handed it, tapped it up and then set it with dead accuracy to the other server. Again noted. They broke to change sides. *Please ask me in.*

A tall, spare young woman named Marnie with muscular shoulders and arms had been checking Kate out. A paunchy but quick guy named Greg who could set back over his head also had been wondering? Marnie said, "Are you lookin' for a game? What's your name?"

Kate replied, "Yah, love to play. I'm Kate."

Greg added, "Ok, our side, we're short one. You live here in the city?"

"I live in Calfornia right now. I'm in for some appointments." People nodded, introduced themselves by first name, two extended their hands and smiled. A hyper athlete, Marnie was adding up what she saw. This new girl is well developed, she reminds me of what I thought an Indian scout would be like. Wonder if she is good?

Play began, Kate fielded two passes, no bobbles, very smooth, she felt better already. She wanted to keep it simple, low key, just be dependable, don't drive it hard. More play, she passed and then began setting for a tall, athletic man, Tony, in his 40's who hit well with accuracy.

Kate thought, *Great, these are experienced players!* Now Tony could see she was a resource. Greg, the shorter man, took advantage of his lower height making a few fingertip saves. He realized this Kate could field the ball from almost anywhere.

Marnie thought she had seen Kate --- a few bells were ringing. Kate did not miss any balls, she deferred to Tony and also set for the other woman, Hendra, on their side who could do alright if sets were placed for her right at the net. Kate could set from the far rear with one hand and put it right in front of Hendra. The score was bending for Kate's team.

Marnie watched Kate. No wasted motion, extreme economy, delicate sets but Kate was not hitting, only setting for the others. Marnie smelled a ringer or just an adept player but this Kate was trying hard to stay way under the radar.

Kate thought, *I am here to play, New Yorkers. I just want to be a player.*

Marnie came down after a solid spike and was now sure it was *that* Kate. From her front line position, bent over, hands on her knees, sweating she gazed across at Kate in the same stance. Their eyes met. Marnie now knew it. Kate wanted to be anonymous. Marnie had seen her in *GloryDays* ads and some news story about the mysterious grey suited attacker out in Iowa. *Ok, honey, I got you pegged but I'll keep it to myself.*

Andrew, a burly young hockey player worked as a chemist never watched the news so he was clueless about her identity but he knew this woman could really play. Tony worked for Morgan Stanley, a talented quant and all he knew was Kate could set for him from anywhere and he craved it to continue.

Delilah playing against Kate, also quite tall, very strong, ex military, knew Kate could be a killer but why wasn't she hitting?

Andrew took a sharp hit from Delilah, fielded it ably and tried to pass but missed and Tony saved with one hand rolling on to his back. Kate in the front row saw it coming, wobbly but headed for her. Rising from the front row she sprang to the net and threatened to spike with her right arm but at the last second her left flailed across placing the hall hard to the far rear corner.

Marnie couldn't believe the play fake. The ball shot past everyone. Marnie shook her head. "Kate, alright!" A few other murmurs from others. Now Delilah knew. On the next serve Marnie set for Delilah who was just aching to have Kate meet her at the net and block. Kate sprang up with Delilah. In that split second you are allotted to fool the opposition Kate faked with her head, Delilah pummeled the ball like a madwoman but Kate put a hand on it and Andrew saved.

Delilah grunted, "You're something." Kate smiled, said nothing. Two more points then Tony picked up a hard hit nearly out of bounds and yelled "go girl". She had the near perfect position rushing the mid net from a corner and when her arm came around Marnie winced. Kate's powerhouse hit deformed the ball badly and it tore across to a rear corner. Her hit had both velocity and unerring accuracy.

Tony and Kate butted fists. Delilah whispered to Marnie, "She's a pro or a ringer." Marnie whispered back, "Neither, she's the hotshot skater in *People* magazine. Just let her play." Delilah slowly swung around. That would explain those thighs and shoulders.

Kate couldn't have asked for more. Good players and no one talking about Kate McGill. Players were exchanged, Kate now hitting against Hendra and Tony, Marnie playing jointly with Kate. The two women could block against Tony who adored trying to put it past the women. The game became more heated, power hitting, power retrievals, the jolt of great volleyball shared with eight people.

More heated exchanges then Marnie reached for a hard hit and it slipped off her forearm bouncing high into the air. Kate working off the back row saw it head skyward and the ball just seemed to go up and up. Kate backed up and then backed up again. The ball was absolutely out of bounds but it came off Marnie's arm so Kate had to play it. Kate took one look and realized the net was far away. She thought, *What the hell.* Kate checked her timing and then leaped far into the air. Marnie watched her rise off the grass and thought Kate would never touch it much less get it over the net. Kate and the ball met well off the ground and rather than just try to tip it back Kate went full power bringing her right arm down in a roundhouse. The ball flew across all her players, cleared the net and screamed into the ground missing Tony by inches.

Tony stood silently for a second shaking his head and yelled, "By all rights you never should have put a hand on that ball. Jesus, incredible shot!"

On break, Kate ran off to a bathroom near the zoo. The others took a break.

"She's a strong player", said Mel. Antonio chimed in, "I've seen that face somewhere and what a body, good heavens." Marnie replied, "Listen, I can tell, she just wants to be a player today. She's Kate McGill, that *GloryDays* outfit's media symbol and daredevil skater, she'll be on *Today* in the morning, I saw the promo. But know what? Don't blow her cover. Let her be, ok? She's got enough happening, I'm sure."

Kate trotted back, everyone stood up, new sides formed and the game began again. Joyous, aggressive, unrestrained hitting, blocking, wild saves and no one talking about the latest media girl.

With no one calling her out, Kate began playing a maximum strength, unbridled, go to hell in a handbasket game, reaching for the ball when she should lose it but didn't. Lots of laughing, yelling. Spectacular play that someone should have captured on tape. But that made it all the better, people playing for the sheer kick. An unbroken volley of twenty returns with every player nearly wiped out but just loving the competition.

Finally they called it a day. Everyone laid out on the grass catching their breath. Gradually each person began reconstituting their off-court life, picking up their belongings, hugging or shaking hands. People made sure to high five or butt fists with Kate. "We're here every week, same time until the snow flies. Put us on your calendar, you play righteous volleyball."

That finally left Marnie, Tony and Kate. Making small talk. Finally Marnie said, "Didn't want to blow your cover. You getting a kick out of all this attention? You're popping up everywhere these days."

Kate shook her head. "I'd gladly trade it all for these couple hours. I appreciate your keeping all that nonsense out of the game. This was just the best antidote for extreme media overexposure. It's becoming this job where everyone seems to know the answers before me. So thanks for asking. I'm learning how to deal with it."

Really wiped out in the best way possible Kate walked with Marnie toward Central Park South. Marnie wanted to quiz her, find out the real deal with this Kate. But she could tell this was downtime for Kate who needed a little company and no pressure.

"You wanna get some coffee?" asked Marnie.

Kate had an early breakfast with a new media advisor and then a meet and greet with a series of non profit fundraisers but she liked Marnie's company.

"Sure but nothing fancy. Just coffee is fine." After crossing past the Plaza Hotel they found a non-franchise coffee house and took seats. The rubbernecking started almost immediately. Kate had been in magazines, online, on one billboard with her face featured prominently. Marnie saw it starting and she switched seats so Kate faced away from the other customers which helped.

"This is all pretty foreign for you?" Marnie asked.

Kate nodded coolly. "I wanted it but had no idea what happens when half the world recognizes you and it hasn't even started. I grew up in a low key place, this is all such a wakeup call. Soon *GloryDays* goes with an online campaign and then billboards. But I'm getting tagged with this 'ranger girl in grey' business. The cops think I'm the one beating up men who hurt animals. It just happened in Iowa again."

Marnie replied. "How does it feel to get that exposure?"

Kate dug into a scone. "The beating up guys part, I don't know what to say, but the *GloryDays* part I need to put to work, something useful. Then it will all be worthwhile."

Marnie nodded. "If you'd like company when you visit New York, I'll give you my email or cell phone if you like?"

Kate smiled, "Sure."

CHAPTER THIRTY

GOING TO MEET BERNIE

After a challenging year at Berkeley and the run-in with Miriam in Los Angeles Kate was grateful to come home and do her version of collapsing in Wayzata. She spent two weeks bike riding on the Luce Line and swimming in local lakes. Finally she agreed to a fundraiser downtown.

Kate drove to downtown Minneapolis, the event took place on Hennepin Avenue, the main drag. A locally owned shop selling athletic clothing hosted, their small, funky storefront crammed in between high rise buildings. Kate sat behind a cheap card table loaded down with posters, *GloryDays* t-shirts and pictures of herself. A broad mix of teens and adults, male and female stepped forward asking for her autograph or a message. Kate patiently signed away with a pen or magic marker trying to keep some eye contact with each person. She agreed to this signing session if all proceeds went to charity and also as a kickoff for some new *GloryDays* gear Kate modeled in their latest print ads. The lines stretched out for two blocks.

Kate glanced up to see a short figure with dark hair. The person spoke to her in Spanish startling Kate and causing her to pause in her conveyor belt signing. Kate spoke back in broken Spanish asking the woman to repeat her statement and say it slowly.

Now Kate focused on the five foot tall dark skinned middle aged woman. She was dressed in a colorful central American serape. The woman shifted to English, "My name is Nora, I want to give you a package. Don't open it now, please. Read the letter, I'm sorry if my English is so poor. There is a book, it will help explain. And there is a small envelope. Please do not open this unless you want to help avenge my family."

Kate was trying to shift gears and understand what the woman wanted. She placed the package in Kate's hands. Her eyes burned so intensely it threw

Kate. "I have heard about the Avenging Angel. I know you care about helping innocents. This is where the Angel belongs."

Nora fled fearfully looking over her shoulder. Kate could not stop her assembly line signing. She put the package on her lap where it would not be lost.

At 9 PM she returned to Sarah's house and after greeting her mother Kate retreated to her bedroom shutting the door.

First, she read the letter written in broken, mis-spelled english. She read it three times very slowly. Nora was from El Salvador, a small village, her husband worked on a plantation, they had four children. When Kate got to the descriptions it made her ill and she ran for the bathroom.

Two of Nora's children had been brutally assaulted. The brutality was beyond Kate's grasp. And Nora's husband had been attacked but was still alive, Nora thought. The attacker was well known, a local businessman or grower or drug peddler on a global scale who was known to enjoy such atrocities but no one could prevent the attacks.

The attacker was Juerion Lasola. He owned property, controlled hundreds of vigilante fighters, owned the police in his region---this is what Kate got from the letter.

Then she began paging through the paperback book, *Salvador* by Joan Didion. It was the tale of Joan and her husband traveling through El Salvador witnessing the senseless brutality, Salvadorans murdering and mutilating each other, much of the violence apparently perpetrated by government troops depending on who you might believe.

Certain paragraphs were underlined or highlighted. Someone had written notes in the margins. Kate read the whole book in two hours. Then she went back and re-read Nora's letter. Now she understood why Nora found her. She wanted the Avenging Angel to find this Juerion Lasola and avenge her family's losses.

Kate went outside, Sarah had gone to bed. She looked up at the stars off the back deck, listened to the crickets, smelled the humid night scents and she rocked unsteadily on the wood planks. After an hour she knew she had to find out what Nora did not want her to look at. Kate knew this would be something terrible.

She sat down on her bed, turned off all but one light and cracked the envelope. There were five pictures, each had writing on the back.

"My two darling girls, this is what he did." Kate held the picture face down for many minutes and finally worked up her courage.

It was so much worse than she could have imagined. She shrieked and could not stop. Sarah rushed into the room. Kate was rolling on the floor crying hysterically. It took five minutes for her to explain between gasps to her mother with the letter, the book and now the pictures.

When Sarah sneaked a look all the color left her face, she could not catch her breath. The pictures were devastating.

Kate said, "There are four more, I can't look." Finally they did it together. One of her husband or what was left of him, another of the girls, another of two neighbor women. And the last picture was totally different. It was a man taken outside, apparently at a festive picnic. On the back was written, "This is who did these crimes. Please don't let him get away."

Kate did not sleep. She wrote in a diary, looked up information about El Salvador on the internet, sent email to friends and then cried until the tears were exhausted.

The next day at 1 PM Kate was knocking on a door at the University of Minnesota, a friend of a friend directed her to a teaching assistant in the Latin American studies program.

"Could you please help me find information on this man? This is a very important story and I need help in locating the right sources," Kate said to the T.A.

Kate spent two days in various libraries asking questions, making notes. Then she went home and started making phone calls. "Mom, I am placing calls to central America. You have that check from *GloryDays*, just take it out of there."

She called the American consulate, then an American aid organization connected to the government. Finally after fruitless calls she found a woman from El Salvador working in a government office. Over her own better judgment she helped Kate connect with an intelligence person who Kate would never know by her real name.

After four days Kate got what she wanted. Juerion Lasola was altogether very real, did control a province, owned various businesses, had the reputation for brutal behavior and the remaining description did match up with the woman's letter. Kate corroborated this research with a journalist familiar with El Salvador. It did appear this man was at least capable of the horrid acts depicted in the pictures.

Kate's cell phone rang at 4 in the morning next to her bed. She groggily answered. The caller hissed, "Do not attempt to pursue this man, you know who I mean. Those pictures are real, the same will happen to you." The caller added some disgusting details.

Kate tried to figure out how they got her cell phone. Someone she had talked to was connected to this beast. Kate never went back to sleep. She began studying maps of El Salvador.

Buzz Roemer's assistant rang on the intercom.

"Buzzer, you got company. It's Katie, she looks dreadful and she's gotta see you."

She did look pretty bad, hair pulled back tight, dressed in sloppy clothes, her face appeared to be puffy.

"What happened honey?" Buzz asked.

"I need a very, very big favor. You're going to think I'm nuts but hear me out, ok?" Kate told him about the letter and then handed it to him, then the book and then the envelope of pictures."

"Buzz these are atrocious, unbelievable, beyond comprehension." He finally got to the pictures. Buzz examined the images but betrayed no obvious emotion. He read each explanation but his face changed expressions when he got to Lasolo's picture.

"I've heard of him. There's a guy, Bernie, he's worked on a couple extractions with me in third world countries, former Army Ranger, did some time with espionage operations. I think he told me about this guy. Kate, you should not have to look at these pictures. And please don't tell me you want to be the arm of justice here. Kate, this is Central America, it's not Iowa. I'm sure this guy is heavily protected, out of the question, Kate, Let's be real here. No way."

After an hour he knew it wasn't going to stop. When she decided, it was just how long you wanted to hold out. Kate's entire being was committed to seeing justice done. She hadn't slept in 36 hours, she hadn't eaten, she was worked up to a distraught frenzy and she had PMS. Buzz was thinking about how to handle her mother.

Buzz called Sarah and started the discussion. He took her to lunch. Sarah was beside herself. This time Kate might not return and they both knew it. Sarah was trying to stay inside the bounds but she was almost over the edge. Kate could do that to people.

Kate finally crashed after another twelve hours and slept nearly 18 hours. When she awoke the first thing she saw was the envelope containing the pictures. She ran for the bathroom and wretched but nothing came out. She started trying to eat and finally managed to keep something down.

Buzz picked her up in his Lincoln Continental and they rode in silence for fifteen minutes. Then Buzz started. "Alright now, goddammit, you will listen to me. The notion of making this introduction is so nuts. Bernie is Bernard L. Ferguson. He is the meanest human being I have ever known. He has worked on assassinations, he's plucked people off the streets and abused them to extract information---I mean really abused. He does not have the restraint of a professional soldier, he was busted down various grades in the military at least three times. He did not follow orders, he followed his own urgings. This man can be unpleasant, violent, ridiculous. He does not believe in conventional justice. I worked with him once and he was like a one man posse out for blood, the jury, judge and executioner all rolled into one."

Kate nodded, crossed her arms over her chest and said, "Perfect. Does he speak Spanish, does he know central America?"

"Kate, I spent fifteen minutes asking him. He knows El Salvador, he worked there. I think he knows how to find this guy. At least that's what he says. Now, if you open this door the devil waits behind. Bernie is all these things and a mystery because I have no idea who he really is."

"Buzz can we trust him?"

Buzz looked across the highway, he adjusted his shirt collar, he stared down Highway 61 and finally said, "I believe so. I think so. Kate do you know how I feel about this? I hate bringing you here. I hate this. Bernie is not a regular uh, he is capable of really bad things, that's why I've used him. Kate, this is not volleyball or fashion shows or beating up people who killed animals."

"You convinced that's me?"

He didn't take his eyes off the road.

"Kate, I know your ways. It's got you written all over it."

She cracked the tiniest of smiles. But it only lasted a second as she glanced back over at Buzz. He wasn't smiling, this wasn't one of their little jokes. He had a totally different face on, one Kate was not familiar with. She knew the person but Buzz was not, well, Buzz. For the first time Kate felt a nasty chill. This man she'd known all her life had other sides, she knew that. In a stark, gut wrenching moment Kate felt a little piece of childhood slip away. Buzz was not telling her a laughable prank tale. He was not charming her with outrageous humor. She had never really seen a person she knew be this serious.

The big Lincoln drove down a dirt driveway, a mutt dog ran out and snarled guarding a dark brown cabin. Around the cabin a grove of maples created a circle of green. "Kate, you can just put those pictures back in your bag and this can be a social call. Bernie never has to know anything."

He was almost menacing and she was a bit frightened.

"No, let's go. Buzz, I can't flirt with reality, I have to live it."

He hated that about Kate. She was so damn grown up just when you wish she was still a silly little kid. But there was no turning back.

A man was on the porch dressed in military fatigues, one hand behind his back. His form suggested threat, big shoulders and back, bulky legs, mean face, dark eyes. This guy could scare anyone, Kate thought. But he cracked a quick smile and the whole picture changed. He walked to Buzz and embraced him.

"Buzzer, been a couple years, thought you were still mad over that incident."

"Bernie, I'm not thrilled but what happened, well...."

Kate stepped out of the car. She felt so un-girlish, dressed in a man's work shirt and jeans, boots, a heavy jacket but she was dressed for business.

"This is Kate, Bernie, she's got something to show you."

For the flicker of an eye Kate saw a streak of humanity from this hulking figure. It came from his eyes, it lasted only a moment but she knew it was there. This guy had a sweet side, she knew it now but then it was snatched back.

"I'm Bernie, Kate. Buzz tells me all about you over the years. What the hell you want with me? You should be havin' fun with other kids, not talkin' to me. I'm not your type young lady."

"Bernie, I need you to look at these pictures and read this short letter." She glanced over at Buzz realizing that maybe Bernie couldn't read. Her quizzical look was returned with just a simple, firm nod from Buzz.

Bernie took the package and pointed them to the cabin. Inside primitive furniture and ripe smells dominated the single room. In the cabin's center a thick wooden slab table covered with marrs and gouges was littered with books and magazines. Kate glanced across the literature. She felt better. This Bernie read, his appearance notwithstanding. If he read he was human and had a soul. That's all she needed.

Bernie plunked into an ancient easy chair and waved them to the table. He did not look up but plowed through the letter, then removed the five pictures and examined them carefully, his hands moved crudely but Kate noticed his touch was quite delicate. She was feeling more comfortable with Bernie.

Kate watched Bernie and started feeling curious about how he lived. She stood up and walked first over to a kitchen area where a stew was bubbling on low heat. She stuck her nose in the pot and it smelled scrumptious. Bernie's sleeping area, still in the same room, reminded her of cabins she visited in the north woods. The bedcovers were rather carefully arranged and clothing wasn't strewn around. Heavy duty looking pairs of boots were arranged along one wall. Aged plaid shirts hung on hangars in a makeshift closet. They were thick plastic not cheap wire hangars. She finally arrived at a far corner of the cabin where firearms were stacked up, manuals for guns occupied two wide shelves. She spotted a Thompson sub machine gun, the type that appeared on gangster movies. She wanted to pick it up but didn't want to interrupt Bernie's reading.

Finally he looked up, first at Buzz, then Kate, then back to Buzz and when he spoke it was first to Buzz. "I know this guy, this Juerion Lasola.

That's not his real name, it's much less exotic, something like Pablo Cortez but he adopted this half assed name. Doesn't matter. Full out killer, kills for pleasure, you can tell from these pictures. No woman should have to see such awful things, hell, no man for that matter."

Now he shifted his gaze to Kate. "I'm guessing Buzz told you about me. And this is what you gotta know. I live for re-balancing the scales, for evening up the score. Buzz and I share that interest. That's all I really care about. That and walking in my woods out here. I don't eat in restaurants or watch tv or see movies or socialize, I prefer the company of my two dogs. Am I telling the truth here, Buzz?"

Buzz sat arms folded across his chest. He nodded and there was no smile.

Bernie continued, "Now, Kate, Katherine, I prefer that name, you really want to walk this line with me because I am not playing with dolls, I am not fooling one little bit. I see what this woman wants---she wants this Lasola's blood. Katherine, she could be telling God's truth or lying completely. You will never, ever, ever know. You clear, girl, you could be on a terrible misleading journey. Once we go there it will be very fast, in, locate this thug, exact justice and out. We are there to kill a human being and you are sworn to secrecy for life. Make no mistake, if we take this journey you are in one hundred percent including your own death and they will not be nice. If they kill you they will take their time, violate you in ways you can't imagine and it won't be one or two men. Now you stop and think, girl, you want to be violated horribly and die in some God for saken hell hole in El Salvador for this woman you will never see again? Don't be nuts!! This is no game or charade! I have been face to face with scum of the earth. People so bad that Hitler looks good in comparison. A gorgeous woman taking revenge will be the most wonderful gift to these atrocious monsters if they get the upper hand. Now just drop the whole God damn thing!!"

Bernie's voice went far beyond loud. When he stopped talking the silence was a thunder clap. Anger married to dreadful thoughts made Bernie grow to an epic height and he took advantage of every inch. On top of it, he had been walking closer to Kate as he talked and now stood before her hands on hips, his weather beaten face twisted into a deathly stare.

"You go home to your life, Katherine, forget you've been here. Not worth it unless you are dyin' to re-balance the scales. If protecting the innocent burns in your veins it better burn hot and long. I've tortured people for pleasure. You want to know what that's about? I know who this guy in Salvador is. I've smelled his filthy breath because he lives in many countries. There are better ways to get even, less scary, just as productive."

Buzz knew Bernie would scare her shitless. He scared Buzz shitless.

She stood up inches from Bernie, her face just below his. "You're not scaring me, Bernie, I don't scare like that. I am the redeemer for these innocents." Kate literally had no idea where that line came from but it was real in that moment.

"I'm giving you one time to take that back."

Her face gave no ground, she was locked in and Buzz's heart sank. He was hoping Bernie would scare her out of this craziness.

Bernie even felt a momentary chill. Buzz was right, this girl had steel genes. "Alright, alright," Bernie said. "Buzz, I gotta travel, I need twenty grand or so, I need to rent a small military plane so we can carry weapons no problem. We'll need three fighters, one I know, two I gotta find. Buzz you don't go in, you're in Honduras with a plane and a chopper. You know nothing more than writing a check and booking aircraft. Nothing. Katherine, current passport, all shots, you will follow a dietary regimen for six weeks before. No one, NO ONE will know where you go. Once we start it will be very quick, hours. Buzz, she must be checked out on a sidearm, something good size."

She cut him off. "I can handle small weapons up through Uzi's."

Buzz's jaw dropped. "What? No, is this your God damn grandmother again? Uzi's? I will kill that woman one day."

Kate responded, "I beat on her until she did it. We were in L.A., she booked us into a gun club and I was checked out on a whole string of assault weapons."

All Buzz could say was, "Jesus Christ all mighty. What is she thinking?"

"Buzz, it's my doing, now shut up, please. Bernie, I can handle weapons."

Bernie took Kate by the hand and walked her sternly to the door. He reached into a cabinet and removed an army issue 45 and a strange looking machine pistol. He marched her fifty yards out from the house and stopped. They were on primitive rifle range with old tin can targets.

"Show me."

He planted the pistol roughly in her hand. Instantly she coiled into a shooter's crouch, flipping off the safety. The first shot missed the can, the next four hit four successive targets.

Without a pause he snatched the pistol and chunked the machine pistol into her hands. Kate had never seen this weapon. She rolled onto the ground as if she was protecting herself, rolled on to her back, bought three seconds to examine the gun, found a safety lever, found the cocking mechanism, rolled back onto her stomach and began firing at targets. The machine pistol laid out withering bursts of fire sending cans flying everywhere.

Bernie's arm extended down to her right arm and she felt herself lifted back to her feet. "Ok, not bad for a gal. I'm giving you some manuals, you read every page, every word. You may encounter some strange weapons."

They walked back to the cabin. Kate went off to find the bathroom.

Bernie said to Buzz, "That's as good as most special ops soldiers. I liked her reaction to the strange weapon. I'd prefer she can also handle a big knife. You told me she's an ace with a bow and arrow but that would never work down there."

Bernie paused staring down at the wood plank floor. "We're supposed to have visas to enter the country but on this kind of mission you can't possibly go through customs. So that could be a problem. I'm not telling her but I have a reason to go after Lasola myself. It's so strange she turns up here with his picture."

Buzz asked, "Why are you even agreeing to this?"

Bernie replied, "Like I said, I have my reasons and for now it's better to tell her it's possible. That can always change. I'll be ready by the fourteenth. Meantime, feel free to talk her out of this nonsense."

CHAPTER THIRTY ONE
PREPARING TO ATTACK IN EL SALVADOR

Buzz stared out the two bay windows facing onto the broad flood plain surrounding the St. Croix River outside Minneapolis. For two days he slept little, his inner thoughts all focused on his own stupidity.

He put both forearms on his wide desk, continued staring out the window to the expansive view far onto the horizon but the stupid feeling would not abate. He thought, "Roemer, you are just a total messed up ignoramus, how the hell can you introduce Katie to Bernie? Bernie has the good judgment of a matchstick."

Buzz considered calling Sarah and spilling the beans. He realized she would not only chew him out, she might stop talking to him, something that would break his heart.

When he heard the voice it shattered his pity-boy reverie.

"Bernie won't have to talk me out of it, you'll be happy to know." Kate sounded cheerful, optimistic, charged up. Buzz wheeled around in his chair. Wearing a t-shirt with the sleeves rolled up, baggy military style shorts, her leather carpenter's belt loaded with a cell phone and tools, hiking boots, oversized sun glasses and a base ball cap with "love those firemen" emblazoned on the front, Kate looked typically sassy.

"Why, Katie?"

"I drove back out to Bernie's and he took me shooting on his assault range."

"Assault range, Katie?"

"Yah, it's cool, it's back out beyond the target range. All these targets and figures and fake mine fields, trip wires. I had to run the whole shootin' match in under two minutes. I didn't make it, got blown up four times."

"Blown up?"

"Not real blown up, Buzz, you hear this compressed explosion. Anyway, I ran it three times and never made it through. I blew away all these pursuers but I got tripped up by wire traps and mines. Man, it's so incredibly tricky."

"So, what happens, Katie?"

"I finished the fourth attempt, Bernie sits me down. He has this kind of irritating but compelling way of talking. He goads you and taunts you and makes you examine what you're saying. Anyway, he turns to me while he's disassembling this machine pistol I was using and says, 'Ok princess, you're quick, agile, smart, totally determined and dead. Four times dead. If we go into El Salvador, I know where this Juerion Lasola's compound is, actually he has two. We go in with maybe three others heavily armed, two hours before dawn with night vision goggles, well prepared and run right into what you just failed at four times. Lasola has been raping and pillaging for two decades. Everyone hates his guts. You don't think he's well protected? He's no fool, he knows someone's father is coming after him. And he'd just love meeting up with you. Even if we do all the homework he's got the field advantage.'"

Buzz reminded himself to buy Bernie the biggest steak at Ben Benson's. He could see she was tipping away from the assault idea.

"So, I got Little Stevie on it, Buzzer. And my guys back at Berkeley. Lasola has a monumental ego. Monumental. Big enough that someone talked him into a web site. Supposed to promote his business interests I suppose. Naturally it doesn't talk about killing villagers or stealing their livestock. It claims he's a kindly paternalistic landowner, progressive, respected, all that bullshit. He's showing off his legit side but tucked way in an obscure corner we found a reference to an American accountant. That eventually led us to his banks outside El Salvador."

Buzz ran his hand back and forth through his buzz cut. She always did this. Start from next to nothing and she digs in and then redoubles her effort and builds on that. How could anyone be so ridiculously determined? "Katie, forgive me, this means what?"

"I'm going after him. We're going after him. About five people are involved now and we have not broken one law. I was ready to fly down there and tear him out of his hideout but it's not practical. Beyond what I can muster. I let Bernie know we're holding."

Buzz thought, *Ok, we're getting a little more mature and realistic, Katie.*

She continued, "We smoke him out, get access to his funds and cut him down to size. It's the same story as Wealthgate but this time we're ...."

Buzz held up both hands and shouted "Hang on! Katie I don't want to know anything about it. I've been through this twice in your behalf. Last time I had authorities digging around for two days in this office, I got nothing done, total waste of time. So don't tell me nuttin', alright?"

Kate's compatriots steadily interacted. The conversations took place always on public phones, never on cell phones. When calls had to be made they rode bikes across town, sometimes even driving from Berkeley over the hill to Orinda or beyond. The weak link, really the only exploitable connection was from Lasola to his accounting firm with an office in Houston. Lasola hated even that limited exposure.

The planners were not even sure why he had an American accountant? There was no requirement in El Salvador.

It took nine weeks to narrow down phone numbers in El Salvador and Lasola's people seldom used phones and he never himself picked up a phone, not even to to speak with his own family. He might employ a satellite phone but only rarely and then only for short conversations.

Every night Kate withdrew the now creased and bent manila envelope, momentarily reviewed some but not all of the contents, reminded herself why she kept prompting and prodding her compatriots not to give up on this quest.

After weeks of work she ran into an immovable wall. Kate hated to admit it but this whole idea was heavily flawed. Her five compatriots said Lasola was too protected, you can't bust thirty years of paranoid defenses in a few weeks. And he purposely had virtually no electronic communications, their strong suit.

Kate felt terribly let down by her own willingness to capitulate. But everyone she trusted told her this was not realistic or even possible. You can't beat a pro on his own turf heavily defended and with local law totally on his side.

She went back to her school work dispirited and unhappy. Kate always managed to overcome tough odds. With all her big talk she had finally failed. In her own private thoughts Kate began entertaining significant self doubt. Success in athletics had ill prepared her for going up against a hard core bad man with immense resources.

She talked with Buzz who strenuously argued there was no percentage in pursuing Lasola. Instead he suggested she try lobbying American Intelligence services, perhaps the CIA could have an impact? Espionage was their business, let the pros take over he argued. She consented.

Weeks became months, Aggie Roemer found her a connection at the CIA who surprisingly demonstrated interest in researching Juerion Lasola. For a few months Kate fielded repeated calls from actual government spooks. She got excited, these people clearly did know the grave pitfalls of operating in a foreign country. Kate talked Aggie into taking her to El Salvador with the understanding it would be a cultural visit, no thoughts of violence. They traveled for four days in rural El Salvador visiting San Miguel and San Carlos.

Lasola had plantations and farms in that region. Aggie spoke fluent Spanish and made a few inquiries. Their last night someone knocked on Kate's hotel door. Two men carrying sidearms in paramilitary uniforms faced her. They told her she would be leaving the country in fifteen minutes, to pack her suitcase. Four more men dressed in the same dark tan uniforms carrying sidearms brought Aggie from his room. Aggie began asking questions in Spanish and an imposing, unfriendly man carrying a large wooden truncheon which he repeatedly rapped into his hand while talking told Aggie to shut up, they were departing, there would be no talking until they boarded their plane. Kate felt genuine, unvarnished fear, this was a clear message from Lasola.

The men drove her and Aggie to a local bus which serviced the national airport. Two jeeps loaded with uniformed men carrying firearms drove in front of and behind the bus to the airport. Six men rode on the bus with them. Four men walked Kate and Aggie to the ticket counter and stood with them until they were ticketed.

A man from Salvadoran customs stood at the counter, checked their passports and visas, stamped them and walked away. They were told they would not need to pay the normal exit fees. Gratis from a friend.

Finally one man took her and Aggie each by the arms saying, "Don't fail to board your plane for America and don't think about returning. You are not welcome here."

As they waited Aggie noticed soldiers in completely different uniforms on duty in the airport. Those soldiers appeared to not even see Kate, Aggie and their escorts. Aggie figured out those were real Salvadoran soldiers who did not acknowledge the paramilitary forces shepherding Kate and Aggie.

Altogether 8 paramilitary men who Kate would later describe as "goons" accompanied them to the flight lounge and waited until they boarded the plane.

Kate looked around inside the plane. She and Aggie were the only passengers. Their escort waited until the plane was ready to leave the gate before they also departed. Kate and Aggie sat together surrounded by dozens of empty seats. They had barely spoken since the knock on her hotel door.

Finally Aggie said, "Ok, message received, Lasola controls everything, he got this airline to take just you and me out of the country, those were certainly his soldiers and you noticed they were armed even in areas that were supposedly secured in the airport."

Kate nodded and tried to control her anxieties. She was caught completely offguard. She now had experienced terrorism firsthand, albeit controlled, calm terrorism.

They flew to the West Houston Airport where their bags and possessions were inspected at length and then they were driven to the main Houston Air terminal.

Kate and Aggie sat facing one another over a small table in a restaurant.

Kate was totally demoralized, Lasola had taken over their lives for a few hours. She said "He plays for keeps, he could have just bumped us off, I guess?"

Aggie looked removed and glassy eyed. "Yup, we just had the Lasola Red Carpet Treatment. Katie, if I were you I'd let this be the wake up call. This guy is not to be trifled with, not at all. Go back to school, do your studies, let it go."

Kate wearily nodded her head. She was beaten.

CHAPTER THIRTY TWO

FLYING IN TO LASOLA'S COMPOUND

After arriving back in Berkeley Kate gave in to the inevitable and buckled down to her studies. She tried to put aside the experiences in El Salvador, it was too overwhelming. When a week had passed Kate decided to call Buzz.

Kate started, "Did Aggie fill you in on our joyous reception down there?"

She wanted to inject a little humor into the call but Buzz was having none of it. "Kate, Aggie told me every detail. You're just lucky Lasola didn't wipe you off the map. Now do you see what you're up against? I should never have agreed to have Aggie accompany you. Now we're done with this guy Lasola. Finito." Buzz stopped just short of hanging up on her.

The next day on her way back from class Kate walked across an athletic field on campus pausing to watch a young woman in a wheel chair who was struggling to climb a very small hill. Kate walked over offering to help. The young woman in the chair looked up and said, "Thanks, but I have to do this for myself. I lost the use of my legs three months ago in an accident. My life has become an uphill battle learning how to cope with all these new challenges."

Kate stepped away and watched the wheelchair bound woman push and tug until she finally made it up the hill. It was only a few feet difference in elevation. She waved thanks to Kate as she pulled away.

Kate sat down on nearby bleachers looking out over the fields to downtown Berkeley beyond. A cool bay breeze was blowing, the sun shone with its customary warmth. Kate was disconsolate, she had failed, she had been intimidated, Lasola had flexed his muscles. Wrong triumphed over right. With her hands interlaced on her knees Kate started crying out of frustration.

Power had won out over righteousness and it hurt like hell. "I am not letting that terrible man beat me. I have to rededicate myself."

Some days later when her phone rang late one night she answered it reluctantly. The caller said, "You met my mother's sister, my aunt in Minnesota. Nora. She gave you some materials about a man from my country who she despises. I also have reasons to see justice served with this man. He badly harmed my two brothers. I live nearby, I work in a restaurant to make ends meet. Would you talk to me? I need your help."

Kate was not about to rush forward with any offer. "I'll meet you in a public place on campus tomorrow. Right now I don't trust anyone from your country."

He replied in somewhat broken English, "I understand. I am Javier. We have an opportunity occurring within two months. Meet me tomorrow, please." Kate chose the Faculty Glade, a park like setting with plenty of foot traffic. Surrounded by old growth trees the Glade inside the UC Berkeley campus was a sylvan escape from the outside world.

Javier was waiting for her on the bench she described, his face looked honest and pleasant but she was trusting no one. As students hurried by and diners entered and departed the Faculty Club they talked.

Javier told her, "I know what happened to you in El Salvador. Lasola has his tentacles everywhere in the country. He assaulted my two brothers. They lived but he is a heinous murderer. I can't take revenge alone. I lack, uh, resources. This is why I contacted you. In just over two months he will briefly step into, how you say, an unprotected zone. He created this picnic and awards ceremony and then he gives himself awards which proclaim he supports the villagers. Given who he really is it's sickening. But for a couple hours he walks around just like all of us."

Kate responded, "What, no body guards, no defenses?"

"No, no, he has protection but far less. Much more important, he is not loved and adored. His own soldiers often get abused, he has little regard for anyone so if someone attacks him most of his protection is likely to melt away."

Kate said, "What do you want me to do about this?"

Javier looked around warily, students were passing near their bench. He waited for a lull in the foot traffic. "Help me get down there, I will take the corrective steps, not you. And I can't go in to El Salvador through the front door. His people will find me in a minute. There is a man named Bernie who you know in Minnesota. He also has a reason to settle up scores with Lasola. His friend had big trouble down there as well."

Kate was astonished, "How do you know this about Bernie?"

Javier replied, "Bernie and one of my brothers were very close, Bernie married someone in our family, a cousin, who Lasola beat up, nearly killed."

Kate asked, "I know Bernie, he has no wife that I know of?"

Javier replied, "No, they separated, Bernie is a tough man, he would not talk about this but it's true. I know this is a lot to dump on you but I have to finish this business. Please help me."

That evening Kate called Bernie's cabin. He answered, "Yah, this is Bernie."

"Bernie it's Kate in California. I met a man named Javier today."

There was a very long pause and he cleared his throat. "I wondered if he'd find you. Yes, Javier and I have a connection. It's time for the picnic down there, it's once a year, is that why he's talking to you, Kate?"

"Bernie, is that such a big deal, this picnic?"

"Realistically it's the best window for settling up scores. Is he asking you to help him get there?"

"Yes, in two months. Would you help him?"

"Kate, do you understand what he's asking? This is such a high risk proposition. You're not thinking of going on this are you? You and August Roemer had a close call in that country. Are you seriously considering returning to El Salvador?"

She steeled herself, this was leaping off a tall building. "Bernie, I am."

Again there was a break. "You need to consider this carefully. I can't tell you not to but this is so risky, so ugly if it fails, I don't understand your thinking. Well, maybe I do, but you have to be just crazy to get involved."

"Bernie, would you do this? Javier thinks you have a score to settle?"

Another long pause. Then Bernie's response was uncharacteristically low key. "I do have unfinished business with that beast. Javier and I have talked about this previously. For many reasons we put it aside. I'd go in with him, he would need help but your being part of this is unnecessarily risky."

Kate let Bernie's statement sink in. She began talking and the emotion in her voice grew as she talked. "Bernie, Lasola bullied me and Aggie, awful intimidation, it's exactly what I hate. I don't want to kill him, that's not my deal. I just want to embarrass him, to show him up in front of Salvadoran people. I don't know, I just can't let him get away with all this. I hate someone using their power to frighten or kill!"

Bernie had never heard her speak with such vehemence. He replied, "Kate, I'll give you ten points for originality. How on earth do you plan to insert yourself in a confrontation and embarrass him? That's a new one, I have to say."

"Bernie, this is not rational and logical. What I know is this exploiter deserves to be beat the hell up and tossed off a bridge, some kind of retribution!

He is going around killing and raping and the most terrible things and no one is stopping him. It's got to stop!"

Bernie thought she sounded pretty damn serious. "Katherine, if I journey to that country and go after him you can't rule out the ultimate punishment. Your idea of embarrassing him, well, maybe both could happen?"

Kate had packed only the most limited possessions and caught a flight from San Francisco to Minneapolis. She realized if she showed up at her parents' place there would be a million questions so she called Bernie and asked if she could stay out at his cabin. She put up the money to rent a plane and gather provisions. She could not call Buzz.

Anticipating what she was not sure of Kate had spent the intervening time gradually building up her regimen of study, dietary shifts, physical exertion, spanish language practice, fashioning and rigging clothing, packing and repacking one backpack, writing a long letter to Sarah and Paul. She made a short call to Peter in Chicago but couldn't bring herself to explain her real plan. So she fudged the truth and said she had some business to handle and would let him know when she returned.

When Bernie saw her walk up to his cabin he almost did not recognize Kate. She walked differently, her hair was cut short and lightened, she wore makeup that re-shaped her face, gave her features a latino flavor. Her pants and shirt masked her body almost completely and Kate greeted him in Spanish. Bernie spoke his own brand of Spanish and Kate said they must converse only in that language. With typical Kate determination she now was reasonably fluent and could alter her dialects.

Above all it was her walking gait. Kate had learned how to walk more or less like a man. From a distance Bernie thought she'd pass easily for a man.

She entered the cabin, tossed her gear up on a bed Bernie set up in a small second room. He had been cooking his favorite stew which she loved. She sat down at the communal table in the center of the cabin. A few minutes into eating she heard a car pull up. Footsteps walked up the stairs onto the wide porch and the door opened. She turned to see who was arriving.

Buzz stood in the doorway dressed in old army fatigues with a shotgun slung over his shoulder. In an almost defiant tone of voice he asked, "Were you planning to do this without me?"

She didn't know how to react. She had no intention of telling him as she assumed he'd be utterly negative on the whole idea. "No, I wasn't going to. I thought you'd just chew me out and tell me to forget it."

"You're not doing this without me. I established your connection with Bernie. Do I think this is a good idea? Are you shitting me? It's a terrible idea but I will be there, if I didn't go and you die I could not live with myself.

Kate, you know, this can result in your death, Bernie's death. Are you clear about the potential results?"

She turned back to her stew. "Yah, I'm clear. I don't need a lecture, I've thought it through. Are you hungry? Bernie makes the best stew on earth. Some of this is venison he hunts himself. Sit down, this may be our last enjoyable meal."

Wearing heavy boots Buzz clumped over to the table. Before sitting down he bent over and kissed Kate on the top of her head. She responded by lovingly hitting him in the arm with her fist.

"I'm glad you're coming, Buzzer."

Javier met them at the airport in Mankato, Minnesota dressed in clothing that a native Salvadoran might wear to work in the fields. Baggy cloth pants, a loose not exactly clean tunic shirt, old, dirty boots. He wanted to look like the kind of peasant no one even notices. He had altered his appearance also, with a beard and longer hair. Javier hugged Kate like a brother before they stepped on to the plane.

The B-200 Super King Air climbed through the spring skies and set a course for El Salvador. They would stop once for fuel. Bernie booked a plane that had been partially rebuilt for carrying cargo so only a few of the regular seats were installed. In the air Bernie sat opposite Kate in a sling harness and began showing her disassembly and reassembly of five different weapons. They ate military rations and some fresh fruits and vegetables. Kate had been consuming foods most like what they would find in El Salvador.

When Bernie talked as they flew he had to half shout to be heard. "Now listen, first, you will be Raffo, Kate. It sounds more male in Spanish. We will only speak in Spanish from here on out. We refuel in Mexico, no one leaves the plane. We will land at an airstrip, two men will join us, both are natives, one I know. We will go directly to a pre-arranged meeting point, then two hours to a small village. Buzz and this plane will drop us and then later land near our target village. We would attract far too much attention if we flew in nearby. This will all be surprise, nothing else could possibly work. We are alone, that's safer. If you are captured...Do you want to talk about that?"

Kate thought about it. "No, not necessary. I know what to do." It was likely the only time in her life that Kate outright lied.

Bernie proceeded to walk through the planning. " Javier carries only that old shotgun and his shivs. Javier show her your stuff."

Javier silently reached for a beatup army shoulder pack from world war two, maybe earlier. He began removing objects and placing them with precision in front of Kate. She realized they were all knives of varying sizes.

Javier gathered them all back up placing them with great care in specific slots in the bag. "I had a completely different identity before I emigrated to the states. These beauties were my stock and trade."

Kate thought it pointless to ask what that trade might consist of.

Bernie continued, "This is how it will be. Raffo, you only discharge your weapon if threatened. Otherwise you are an observer."

Kate's first reaction was to go ballistic. But after a brief reflection that was what she would want anyway. She had no desire to be a killing anyone. Lasola might be a different issue.

"These are my rules, you protect yourself and...AND you protect Javier and me. You protect us. Raffo, got it? Cover us. This goes down one way only. We will enter the village where they hold this picnic. It will be early evening so we will have some cover of darkness.

"We are there tops, twenty minutes. We handle him, we defend ourselves. We leave. Time on the ground is precious, we have to avoid the authorities. You, me, Javier will all be there illegally, no customs or proper visas."

Bernie then spent two hours assiduously poring over maps, diagrams, outlines, repeating procedures four times at least and then asking Raffo to say the procedures back to him. Javier sat on his haunches Vietnamese style and listened. He had already memorized every instruction.

"Finally, if you see a video camera, a still camera, any camera look away at all costs. Do not allow your image to be captured. Now sleep."

Buzz sat up with the pilots monitoring their progress. As a licensed pilot he needed to be conversant on how this particular plane was flown.

Kate thought in Spanish, "Right, sleep now. Ok kid, sleep."

Some ten hours later they landed in El Salvador on a beat up airstrip. Two vehicles approached. Bernie waited until he saw the right faces. "Raffo, meet Juan and Greeges. This is Raffo." They shook hands. Kate thought she'd never seen two such tough gauchos. Javier walked over to Greeges and embraced him. They had known each other previously and shared a distaste for Lasola as well.

In ten minutes they left the airstrip.

Kate was so frightened her body was shaking but she controlled the fear as best she could. Thousands of miles from home and safety, Kate was struggling not to be terrified. She knew quite well Bernie would not stop and say, "Now Katie dear, don't be worried, I'll handle all this, you go down by the beach and take a little walk. We'll call you when it's all done."

The Toyota Land Cruiser and aged VW Thing stopped in a clearing. All piled out. Bernie explained the plan. They were three hundred yards from the picnic site. It was late afternoon, in the jungle sunlight crept down through the trees. The temperature was in the nineties, everyone was sweating profusely.

Now Javier took the lead. The others crowded around him as he drew a crude map in the dirt. In Spanish he said, "We are here, all of this is forest, over here, maybe 200 yards is a clearing. The picnic is held in a primitive park, there are two shelters with roofs, on the far side is a small, elevated stage. When he's here, Lasola will walk in from this side, he will have guards but not many. He only spends an hour at this event, he goes onstage for a few minutes and speaks. It could be different this year but I've been to three of these. Lasola likes predictability in everything. We wait until he walks onstage. His soldiers hate that part as he proclaims he is a great man. Usually the mayor gives him an award and Lasola is likely to have been drinking cervezas. We come in from behind the stage. Now listen to me, when we attack you shout, yell as loud as you can, 'This is for Nora and Jesus.' Kate met Nora, Jesus is her husband. Keep saying it. His troops know who that is. When it's done we leave at that instant, do not wait around."

Bernie was armed with two machine pistols, stun grenades, two small bombs.

Bernie held up his hand, grabbed two packs and disappeared for a few moments. Kate could see him down on his knees apparently preparing something and then he ran back to the group.

Bernie added, "We find him, pull him out, do the job. We're gone immediately."

Kate realized that Bernie was saying they were going to kill Lasola. That thought had not quite become internalized in her mind. Now it was likely to happen.

The two teams moved swiftly encountering a few obstacles such as fences in the jungle nothing solid stopped them. No guards, no lights, no resistance, no sentries.

Juan and Bernie split up, Greeges went another path. Kate followed Javier who moved very quickly until they stopped short of the clearing. People were gathered around two large fires, recorded music played on cheap loud speakers. The insurgents remained stationary for ten minutes until announcements were being made from the stage.

Kate clutched on to a machine pistol used by the Israelis, the IMI Micro Uzi. She avoided thinking about what it would be like to actually shoot someone. When Bernie handed her the Uzi he said, "Try not to spray the bullets indiscriminately. Concentrate your fire." Twenty feet away Bernie and Greeges also waited, Javier crouched next to her.

A voice could be heard from the stage announcing Lasola's presence. Kate had memorized a very brief statement in Spanish which she hoped she'd have the opportunity to say in front of Lasola.

From their concealment they could see a phalanx of men arrive apparently covering Lasola who then stepped up onto stage and began speaking. Kate could only catch part of his remarks in Spanish but the tone was acceptance of an award for being the village's protecting spirit.

Kate could now see him reasonably well as there were lights shining down on the small stage. He looked almost innocuous, certainly unremarkable---a short, stubby man with a large pompadour dressed in a shiny orange suit sporting a prominent mustache. As he spoke he also glanced around seemingly looking for potential problems. His retinue stood behind and to the sides, their weapons at a casual, relaxed position.

Suddenly a young man dressed like a field worker burst from the crowd screaming at Lasola, "You killed my father, you ruined my family and took our little farm from us!!" His voice resonated across the gathered throng.

Kate had been preparing for this confrontation for almost ten months. Her emotions ran from pure anger to total non comprehension. Journeying this far twice with threat of incarceration or death had numbed her to normal feelings. But seeing this man stand up to Lasola with full risk of being killed on the spot triggered a response she had not expected. She came on a mission and now it was time to act.

Kate stood up and began walking toward the stage. Bernie and Javier sprang up in total surprise, she was supposed to be the observer. As she walked she removed the floppy hat covering her blonde hair and shook out the hair. She began removing an old jacket Bernie had given her. Underneath she wore a sleeveless tight dark blue t-shirt that made no secret of her form. Now from the waist up she looked totally out of place, a blonde beauty striding toward Lasola. She hoped the incongruity of her appearance might slow down reactions.

The man who shouted from the audience now stood frozen near the stage unsure what would happen. Lasola turned toward his guards and began cursing them for not taking action, "You imbeciles, this man would kill me and shoot that yankee bitch, shoot her!"

Bernie stood up, aiming his SR25 Crane marksman rifle at Lasola. He shouted in Spanish, "Lasola, if they raise their guns you are dead!" Juan and Greeges raised their rifles as well aiming them at guards surrounding the stage.

Kate kept walking slowly. Lasola was screaming more loudly at his guards. The crowd of 100 or so villagers began standing up riveted by the unfolding drama.

Lasola watched Kate approach. In Spanish he said in a firm voice, "I had you thrown out of our country, I know you are McGill, I should have had you killed. I can order them to shoot you now!"

Bernie advanced steadily toward the stage, his rifle pointed directly at Lasola as did Juan, Greeges and Javier.

Lasola turned toward his troops as Kate stepped onto the stage. In Spanish she said, "We are here for Jesus and Nora." The troops reacted at the mention of their fellow villagers. Their weapons were slowly, surrepticiously lowered pointing down to the stage.

Bernie walked next to Kate his weapon pointed directly at Lasola's head. A glint of recognition passed between the two men. No one spoke. Kate would remember later thinking it was like being in an airless chamber---for a few seconds.

In Spanish she blurted out, "You owe all these people an apology. You are an embarrassment to Salvadoran people." An instant later her inflated bravado suddenly collapsed. She was in grave danger and that realization crowded out any other thoughts.

Detente ended in a flash. Lasola suddenly grabbed Kate around the throat, turned her like a human shield shouting, "I am Juerion Lasola, I control this country. All you gringos will die!"

But Javier had been correct, Lasola's body guards looked at each other and momentarily did not raise their weapons. In numbers there was safety. If Lasola lived they could claim to have acted together.

Kate's years of physical training did not fail her, she grabbed his arm around her neck and in one swift motion threw him over her head, Lasola flew twenty feet landing on his back with a loud crack. In a flash Javier moved to Lasola's side unsheathing a Turkish assault knife.

Bernie ran and took Lasola's other arm but he realized it was unwise to kill Lasola with all these witnesses. They had to pull him into the darkness.

Javier and Bernie together picked up Lasola and began dragging him from the stage. Running together they dragged Lasola for hundreds of feet while behind them the guards were now aiming their weapons. But shooting at the intruders could entail killing their boss so they hesitated.

It was incomprehensible to Lasola that these gringos could foil him. This was his stronghold. He kicked and struggled as they dragged him. Worst for Lasola was the shame he felt at being overpowered on his own turf.

Javier ended the thought for him. Javier had a surgeon's professional interest in "the operation" and his knowledge of physiology saved his victims from any pain.

Lasola indeed felt no pain but he could sense his life spilling into the dirt. He gradually slumped to the ground.

Bernie yelled, "Now, we go!" Bernie grabbed Kate by the arm, Javier was already running from the picnic ground. Juan and Greeges fled as well.

Lasola's troops now began firing at the fleeing intruders.

To Lasola's right Kate's crew were escaping, to his left his own troops were running toward their crumbling leader.

Lasola descended into a painless emptiness unlike so many of his own victims. His troops were firing wildly at the fugitives. Bullets kicked up the dirt all around Lasola. His boys had never really trained as marksmen. Lasola was bleeding but not all that fast. The mis-aimed bullets altered that condition. Three slugs tore into Lasola. Mis-aimed or purposely aimed?

Kate easily outran all the men arriving at their two vehicles. They piled in the two trucks and in seconds they were bouncing back down the road. A chain of pre-set charges Bernie arranged behind their path began detonating. The pursuers were stymied for the few precious minutes the Americans needed to reach the airstrip three miles distant.

Bernie unceremoniously dumped Kate into the Super King pushing on her bottom, head first where Buzz caught her and tossed her into a web harness. Buzz yelled to the pilot to begin taxiing.

The others piled in leaving the Range Rover and VW running. As the plane taxied at top speed Bernie could see the first pursuers in a beat up Chevy pickup bouncing out of the undergrowth at a crazy angle. Bernie calculated the distances. The Chevy could stop them.

"Get behind me, hold me steady!!" The plane was halfway into its takeoff. Bernie aimed an AK 47 and began zeroing in on the pickup's windshield. The Chevy was catching them. Bernie began firing, the windshield shattered but they were still coming. He went for the tires and sparks flew but the Chevy was gaining. Bernie kept gunning for the driver but somehow missed.

Tad Malabar drove a Chevy side tanker pick up back in Wayzata and he let Kate drive before she was 16. He let her drive thinking he could at least touch those boobs but she insisted on driving at scary speeds from the git go. He yelled, "Don't let this thing hit something right behind us, that's where the gas tanks sit."

From behind Bernie Kate yelled, "Bernie, it has side tanks. The gas tanks are outboard. Shoot low right behind the door, it's right behind the passenger cab!" He began firing and the AK 47 emptied of ammunition. Kate yanked a 9mm Glock out of Bernie's belt, threw off the safety and lept up to the open door. Steadying herself against the wall she gripped the pistol with both hands.

On the fourth shot she got lucky and hit home, the Chevy caught fire as the plane broke free of the ground. Buzz was holding her by the waist of her camouflage army fatigues as she emptied the pistol.

CHAPTER THIRTY THREE

KATE ON ICE

Buzz tromped into the kitchen of his parents' home in St. Paul covered in snow. Aggie sat next to the ancient woodburning stove warming his hands. Aggie asked, "So, what do we know, anything?"

The two brothers had been up long into the night trying to understand what was happening. Kate had shown up with no warning in the dead of winter in Minnesota. She had been living in California for three years, reappearing in Minnesota during the summers. Locals were beginning to think Kate was treating Minnesota, her stomping grounds, as fly-over territory. Buzz and Aggie were always in touch with Kate but she had dropped out of sight after the trip to Central America. Her mother said Kate was taking her studies at Berkeley very seriously. She adopted a much lower profile in the media, stopped doing interviews and seemingly had pushed aside her former interests.

Aggie said, "I talked with her two weeks back, I know she had been down to Las Vegas twice to spend a lot of time with Queen R. All she would tell me is that Queen R. was tutoring her, helping her learn new skills. That was how she talked about it."

Rubbing his hands next to the fire, still wrapped up in a parka and furry hat, Buzz nodded. "I know, Agg, something happened after El Salvador, it changed her, made her more serious I guess. Honestly, I don't like it, I think she is in training, preparing for some test or trial. I don't know, maybe I'm reading into it too much. I just know when we talked she sounded older, some of that joy was missing. She talked like a soldier in training, that's what I heard."

Aggie stood up to make some tea. He heard Buzz's cell phone ring and Buzz grunted a hello. When Aggie returned Buzz was listening intently on the phone, saying almost nothing. He just kept saying, "Yah, I know. I know." Aggie felt he should give Buzz some privacy. Minutes passed. The talking stopped and Aggie returned.

Buzz didn't look happy. Aggie didn't really have to say much, he could tell something was wrong.

Buzz stood up, took off his fur hat, rubbed a hand through his thick brown hair while staring at the floor.

Finally he exhaled and said, "She's here, she's been here for a couple days staying down with Bernie."

Aggie exclaimed, "Bernie? What's she doing all the way out at his place, why not at her Mom's place in Wayzata?"

Buzz replied, "She is flying way below the radar, didn't even call her folks until now. That was Bernie. She's been in training with him, firearms, cold weather preparation, he says working on this Cold Hand stuff, this is why she dropped from view."

Aggie was confused, "Why? What happened?"

Buzz wearily said, "Bernie says the FBI confirmed Juerion Lasola is alive and headed here in the dead of winter. I told Bernie that sounded almost humorous bringing central Americans here in a bad cold snap. There was no laughing from Bernie. He said disabuse yourself that Salvadorans can't shoot straight or handle the weather. These are scary banditos being well paid to find her and finish her. On top of that, Lasola apparently may have some inoperable liver condition so he just doesn't give a shit."

Aggie nodded, "A suicide run, salvage his injured pride it sounds like?"

Buzz replied, "Bernie said the FBI got wind of Lasola tracking her, they told Kate. They've had someone tailing her for months. So Bernie thinks the FBI told her, 'Look he's coming, we'll protect you but you must stay underground.' She told them back, 'I don't hide. Do this, pass the word I'll be especially exposed on a visit to Minnesota, not in California. I want to deal with him on my turf in the winter.' So that's what the FBI did. Kate is working with them but Bernie says the only way to end this is get Lasola totally exposed. Apparently they sent word to Lasola through some third party his best opportunity would be when she's home never expecting he'd show up in the winter climate. I must say, it's smart, he thinks he'll get the drop on Kate. Meantime Bernie thinks she holed up with Queen R. to get her working tools in shape."

Aggie shook his head, "I spent time with Queen R. in Las Vegas. She told me Kate has learned the Cold Hand? Man that's crazy, she can't stop a madman with some old Romanian mind tricks."

The phone rang again, Buzz picked up and listened. Then he clicked off.

"That's Bernie, he's saying he just talked to her. She's hiding in plain sight. I can't believe this. This Lasola, he's on a suicide mission, he doesn't give a crap. Death is relatively trivial compared to a woman showing him up directly in front of his own people."

"Sitting there in public?"

"She is armed to the god damn teeth, putting herself out there, this is so Kate. She's in downtown Wayzata drinking coffee so he can find her. I think she's laying a trap for Lasola, the FBI have a team backing her up. They'd love to capture Lasola, he's wanted on all kinds of charges here in the states."

Buzz added, "Bernie says she shipped the mule back here and now it's equipped with two of those *Aray Powersource* amps."

Aggie rolled his eyes. "Well I know what they're supposedly for---to extend the power and range of human thought. The CIA owns dozens of them, maybe hundreds. Those are Helen's secret weapons, designed to supercharge someone's brain waves."

Buzz shook his head, "Come on Agg, that can't be real."

Aggie looked at his brother. "Buzz, *Aray Powersource* sells something like $90 million a year in those unreal amplifiers. Either Helen bamboozled a lot of intelligence people or maybe they actually work?"

Kate was sitting in the Northern Lights coffee shop on the main street in her hometown. She finally had called Sarah who was stunned that Kate just dropped in unannounced. But Kate refrained from explaining any details and just said she'd soon be home to be with her parents. People passing by gawked at her as they shuffled through a recent snow on Lake Street. Though a big, local celebrity Kate did not often just hang out at the coffee mill. She looked up. A man in a strange amalgam of clothing approached Kate as she drank coffee and wrote letters. He was clearly wearing body armor, an all black outfit festooned with protective panels and pads. He was awkwardly shielding an automatic weapon. He held a black helmet with a face shield under his arm.

"Mind if I sit for a moment?" he asked.

She smiled and gestured to the chair at her table.

He said, "Do you know that we have major out of town company and our crew is assigned to protect you?"

"I've been briefed by the three letter guys. I know there is a ring arranged around me and we have company from central America. But I still need to pull him in close before the ring can trap him."

The man in military gear said, "I should not be out here dressed in body armor but this is absolutely killing me to watch you sit here defenseless. Why don't you come with us, we have armored vehicles parked in the parking garage. We can make you safe."

People passing by on the street and those in the coffee shop were glued to this odd couple with his blatant body armor and Kate awkwardly hiding the Uzi machine pistol Bernie loaned her keeping it in her lap as she fiddled with pen and paper.

One man said to his wife, "Isn't illegal to brandish one of those guns? Is she filming a commercial or some crazy video?"

"Merv, go outside and report her to someone if you're that upset."

"I can't, that's Kate McGill, she's one of us. If she's armed there's a reason."

Kate was staring at the male soldier at her table

"I need to sit right here for a few more minutes. My pursuer needs to think I'm a sitting duck. What's your name?" Kate asked.

"Colonel Answar Rosen. I am an officer back in the Israeli army. Your government asked me to come over temporarily to help. I am a specialist at protecting people in my country. Look there is almost no time, we have reports they are closing in quickly."

Kate replied, "Yes, in about two minutes I have to move out of here. Colonel, I made this decision, I'll do it my way and maybe pay the price. The guy who wants to punish me, I can tell he's somewhere around here."

The Colonel knew better than to look around but her statement was stunning to him. Like this Salvadoran criminal was right near them?

"You can see him?"

"Kind of." She did not look up.

She continued, "It's Lasola's people, they won't shoot me, he wants me alive. I'll walk to that mail box on the corner. Then I'll get in the beat-up Audi, drive up the block, make a left, another left, then a right onto the main street and two blocks down a left. I'm going to take a little drive out on Lake Minnetonka. It's a trap for Lasola. On that frozen lake I have a field advantage. I know where every likely pressure crack in the ice will be."

The Israeli man stared at her unsure what to do or say. How could anyone predict pressure cracks in frozen ice?

"Colonel, have you heard I can sort of see somewhat ahead of events?".

"Yes, I never knew if that's true."

She got up slowly picking up an old heavily laden backpack.

"Well it is and right now I'm ahead of him and all the others. Colonel, help me out here, I've been drawing you a hand-made map. The X is where we are in Wayzata. These are the peninsulas that stick out in the water. Avoid them. Avoid these two other areas, they are mostly likely to have open water. I want Lasola and everyone else out on the lake. He will try to snatch me and you can take him out ."

Kate turned and walked quickly to the mail box and then more quickly to the mule. It fired up noisily and in seconds the guttural growl of the turbocharged five cylinder rebounded off the walls of nearby buildings.

Moments later three vehicles began turning attempting to follow her up a short hill. A lone siren began wailing. Three blocks away inside two more Chevy Suburbans radios squawked in Spanish and men brandishing weapons fell in a short distance behind.

Bernie was calling Buzz. "Buzz, she's just so loonie, she's dragging them all out on the lake. It's 5 degrees above zero, I don't think there's open water or not much as it's January. But even old hands go out cautiously."

"Bernie, with any luck she'll gain a small edge on the lake. Listen, you remember where Spirit Knob Point is? Head that way, it's only a mile out. I'll meet you there."

Kate's Audi Quattro snorted and blatted through town, slid sideways across a parking lot and disappeared down a short hill at the Wayzata marina out on to the ice. Momentarily a quarter mile in front of the mule lit up like daylight as Kate used her rallying headlights to illuminate her way.

Then she shut off all the lights completely. Kate did this for thrills back in high school but then it was an old '62 Buick she conned Buzz to loan her. Now with a well prepared rally car she could hit 70 or faster on the ice with no lights touching 90 miles per hour flipping all her lights on for an instant.

Kate knew the disadvantage of this trick. Your eyes could not adjust quickly enough in the suffocating dark. In five minutes she penetrated the dense dark on the lake and headed for the approximate center of Browns Bay. She came to a halt, did a fast donut to face back toward Wayzata. She hesitantly shut off the engine but double checked the ignition ensuring it remained on, then she reached down and re-secured the DC converter which, in turn, was driving two *Aray Powersource* 91 amps mounted on the car floor. She carefully threw the two switches to "on" and the amps glowed red.

Kate very nervously settled back in her seat.

When she looked up headlights were bouncing crazily off the ice as various vehicles appeared to be following her. Kate controlled her breathing, tried to relax and sidestep the anxiety of how she could ever get this pack of hyenas off her back. She could elude them one place or another but they would never stop their pursuit. This was the place and time to ambush Lasola. On her turf.

Kate knew they would initially miss her even on the wide, flat, white surface as she parked behind a large bank of ice but inevitably they would locate her. Her head set crackled with Buzz's voice.

"Hey princess you out there?"

"Yah, hi Buzz."

"I'm headed out but I don't see you moving. You can elude all these jokers but you better get moving."

"Goin' with Plan B. I don't want to elude them. I've been in training with Queen R. Remember when we were on the plane and talked about that Russian defense mechanism, the one that causes people to stop cold, to avoid you? I'm employing the Romanian version and this one freezes him in his tracks."

"Yah, it was always rumored to have been used in Leningrad."

"Queen R. has been instructing me for months in the Cold Hand. This is perfect, no obstructions. I've experimented. With buildings it's hard to keep the focus properly. And Grandma loaned me a couple of her supercharger amps. I'm as ready as I'm going to be."

Buzz was not about to say it but he wondered how this 19 year old girl was about to stymie a totally bonkers Salvadoran mad man hell bent on her destruction?

"You used it where kiddo?"

"I used it Buzz, that's all. If it fails you and Bernie stand up for me will ya?"

Kate shut off her phone. When the Russians employed this mental repellant it was against German soldiers with bayonets. Kate hunkered down in the mule reaching for an elusive mindset.

Inside a dark blue Chevy Suburban five men from Central America were attempting to figure out how they could snatch this girl while nearby were a handful of soldiers assigned to defend her. Lasola yelled at them, "I don't care who else chases her. I must have her! Just get her for me! GET HER!"

His paramilitary soldiers, more thugs than fighting men, were terribly uncomfortable chasing her on this frozen lake. Nothing in El Salvador froze ever. And if that wasn't enough, other vehicles bounded off the snow banks diving and dodging on the frozen surface also trying to locate Kate.

As they neared her hiding place suddenly one of the Chevy Suburban's containing four more Lasola hired guns drove up a snow and ice bank, lofted airborne momentarily crashing back onto the ice. Its front end came down hard and broke into the ice floe. Shards of ice flew everywhere and the long SUV became wedged into the ice. Then the two ton wagon dropped lower into the ice. It was sinking into a huge ice hole. All four doors flew open and the occupants tumbled out in utter confusion, one man fell into the icy water and began screaming.

The other Suburban with five Salvadorans holding various weapons sat idling fifty yards away with its headlights aimed at the sinking vehicle. All five men watched in disbelief as the one man tried to save himself but he was up to his shoulders in near frozen water and his compatriots were scrambling across the ice, away from the drowning man.

Kate strained to keep her concentration. She could hear some people yelling in a foreign language. Kate's focus did not include any of them. Instead she kept her mind on a sort of mental barrier. Kate had worked for months, hours at a stretch reaching into mental recesses as Queen.R. suggested. At times painful, other times boring, Kate had done her homework.

Kate felt the barrier level out and take shape but she had no idea how it would impact anyone. She just had to hope.

Driving out onto Lake Minnetonka Lasola bounced off the seat glancing around at the totally foreign snow banks. Driven by an urgent need to recover his pride and have some measure of revenge Lasola attempted to pay no attention to the winter conditions. He had paid thousands to supposed advisors and tens of thousands more to arrange this mission. Venturing onto a frozen lake was totally outside his experience. Inside his body an increasingly virulent pain throbbed in his liver. He had only limited time.

The driver suddenly veered off into the dark and made a strange noise like a laugh but intensely agitated. Lasola screamed in Spanish, "No! That way! Over there! You're going the wrong direction!" Lasola could see Kate's parked Audi eighty yards distant but his driver headed away from her.

Lasola brandished a pistol and screamed again but the driver appeared unable to respond. Having come such a distance and under impending threat of his own mortality Lasola had banished normal fears. He pointed the pistol at the driver's leg and pulled the trigger. Blood flew and the vehicle stopped abruptly.

The sinking Chevy Suburban did register in Lasola's mind however. The other Salvadorans were strangely quiet. He shouted, "What's wrong with all of you? This is nothing, NOTHING! Stop this thing. I'm going after her. Stop!!!"

Lasola pushed open a door, pulled out a shotgun and looked across the ice. It was frigidly cold, he had never experienced such temperatures. He paused to catch his bearings. Suddenly a back door flew open and one man jumped out and began running. It was Frietas. Freitas who enjoyed torturing women.

Three hours earlier Lasola had stepped off a private plane inside a heated hangar at a small airport near Mankato. His English was spotty so the advice from his security consultant barely registered. Lasola knew he was running immense risks skirting American customs. He had been informed '...you land at the airport, we'll drive you to intercept this girl, take care of your business. We'll create a diversion but you must depart within two hours, three hours at the most, no more.' Lasola had received expensive outdoor clothing, it was placed in the rear of the Suburban. But once they felt the intense cold his men had divvied up the gear between themselves.

He felt the jarring cold when the door opened. His instincts were telling him this was not a good idea. What had he been thinking? The penetrating frigid blast drove into his brain. *Is this what this cold feels like? I almost can't function.*

Kate counted on his unfamiliarity with winter to play in her favor. She was correct, Lasola could not tell the difference between icy temperatures and the Cold Hand's paralysis.

Lasola thought, *All this way to fail? No, unthinkable. I have overcome more difficult problems. I've killed hundreds, she is just one more.*

His troops were useless, realizing he had no other options except surrendering Lasola jumped out wearing a Yves St. Laurent suit, an expensive winter overcoat, white shirt, tie and dress shoes. He had been advised to be well dressed in case someone tried to stop him. He began running toward Kate and immediately fell down on the ice. His face was smashed into the freezing surface. He arose, pulled his jacket closer, cocked the pump action shotgun and began walking but his expensive patent leather dress shoes had almost no traction. He had been told to wear the dressiest clothes possible, his hair was done over, he had on makeup. He looked almost like a cartoon version of himself. The people he hired to advise him were primarily concerned with his not being recognized The same advisors thought it would be obvious to Lasola he would need boots, gloves, a hat, and parka. Lasola thought he would be on the ground less than two hours. Since he began leading his small army of bandits he was accustomed to things working out like he demanded. He had hired a venal private detective who paid people to tell him how to find the McGills.

Kate was, herself, somewhat frozen but not from cold. She had already felt the intense paralysis the Cold Hand could induce. But this was different from prior experiences. She was surrounded by dozens of people, a number of vehicles, the cold and snow and all these factors caused the mental process to behave very differently. She was locking into a sort of focal trance and like her grandmother told her, she was becoming part of this repellant barrier. Kate found herself locked down by her mental state. She was finding it hard to move her body.

Next to her the two *Aray Powersource* amplifiers pulsated sending waves of energy beyond the mule. These two amps, model 91's, were new, more powerful than Kate had experienced. Kate brought them along as an insurance policy. As she sank into the paralysis she had her own epiphany. *This is not logical, trusting my safety to the Cold Hand and these amplifiers. But Queen R. said I must remain focused and positive.*

Kate did not see herself in a shootout with Lasola and his troops, it ran counter to her instincts. That would make her no different than criminals.

Vehicles filled with police and FBI agents now circled Kate's mule and the two Salvadoran vehicles. Lasola could be seen crossing the ice or attempting to as he slipped almost with each step.

Watching his boss creep across the ice in the impossible cold, one of Lasola's soldiers pulled the bleeding driver from behind the wheel, jumped in and began driving back toward Wayzata. Lasola turned to see his trusted troops fleeing. It wasn't Kate's beam of fear, it was the sinking Suburban. When you grow up in the tropics dying in a frozen lake is more overwhelming than anyone can imagine.

Kate found herself being sucked down by this mental state. She had never experienced anything like this. It was taking her down into some strange unbreakable trance. She felt her body vibrate and shudder like a motor was driving her. The very fear she was broadcasting turned on herself picking up momentum, her body began vibrating viciously.

Lasola found himself floundering but his determination was such that he was willing to crawl across the frozen lake to have his revenge. He could see the girl was still in her car. He looked across the ice, he could see men with rifles and pistols dressed in military gear. Lasola fought the cold, the mental repellant, his own internal pain, the knowledge there was no escape. He managed to keep crawling, then stopped and tried to stand up on his feet. He struggled to a standing position now brandishing the shotgun. He was thirty feet from her odd car. Now all that mattered was pulling the trigger. He steadied himself, held the shotgun level. His finger rested on the trigger. His body cried out in pain from cold, his throbbing liver, the Cold Hand's paralysis. Still his dedication to this last act remained steadfast. But his finger would not pull back an inch. He screamed in frustration.

"Go get that guy on the ice, soldier. That's Lasola the butcher."

"Commander, I can't explain this but I can't go over there."

"Soldier, it's an order, shoot him first if you're worried, just get him now!"

"Commander, something very weird, I can't go that way. He's between us and the girl. I can go THAT way, like back toward the shore. I know this sounds, God...."

Commanding officer Eliot Robinson began moving himself but he felt a burning sensation in his head like a spike driven into his brain. He wilted, fell to his knees. He wasn't in danger, he just could not move his legs and now the cold became a penetrating force of its own.

Bernie had driven out on the ice as well and now stepped out of his aging

Subaru wagon. He felt the drilling fear, he knew what was going on and he also was impacted. He picked up his cell phone and hit the recall button.

"Katie, what's happening to you?"

She couldn't answer or lift a finger.

The Suburban was now up to its door handles slipping slowly into Lake Minnetonka. In this other worldly tableau some twenty people were seemingly frozen into inaction by their fears.

"Katie, can you hear me at all?"

She knew there was a call but it seemed unreachable. She managed to slip one finger toward the phone in her lap. It was taking forever but she inched it to the "send" button.

Bernie heard her respond.

"Katie, break it off, just break it off. Stop thinking."

She was thinking, *I'm not thinking. I don't know what I'm doing?*

Inside the sinking Suburban its vertical position caused a metal shovel to crash forward and bounce into the steering wheel. For a moment underwater the SUV's horn honked twice.

Kate felt something cold crack the frozen veneer. It was the car honking.

Now what to do? Kate was sure this fear mechanism would cease when she emerged from its grip. She moved her face and one arm very slowly, very carefully. Queen Royal's warnings were returning. "It can control you and your enemies. You must learn to control its impact on you."

She could see the man with the shotgun literally frozen into place.

The bizarre scene before her appeared as frozen as the lake. Nothing was moving. The SUV was nearly swallowed by the icy water. Kate realized she had to unkink herself. Her only instinct was to flee. There was no rationality, no logic. Just flee.

She could almost move her arms and legs. Lasola fell over and stopped writhing on the ice. Kate attempted to stretch one arm. It took forever. She reached down and started the mule. She reached for the rallye lights and suddenly the whole scene lit up like daylight. Able to move a bit more Kate reached over and switched off the *Aray Powersource* amps. The wave of fear began abating. She turned the mule and headed for Excelsior shutting down the lights as she drove. She moved up to third gear and began making time.

Commander Robinson felt the fear threshold ebbing. His troops were coming back to life. Two soldiers emerged from their SUV and walked across the ice to Lasola's now rigid form. They picked him up and dragged him to the rear door of their Jeep. Other agents began tracking the disappearing Audi Quattro.

Bernie felt himself coming back to normalcy. He blurted out, "Jesus Christ, she figured out the Romanian Cold Hand..."

A phone rang in Bethesda, Maryland. "You need to hear this General. Are you awake enough to hear me?"

A groggy voice said, "Yah, go."

"I'm right now on a frozen lake. Bitter cold. There's something like twenty of us, we got a few central americans, you know....we got their director."

The groggy voice became animated, "You, you mean, Lasola! You telling me the guy from, oh shit, this is so stupid, I can't say the words. El Salvador, that's it!"

"Yes, him, he's completely rigid, may be gone. He took some serious exposure wearing a flimsy dress suit. It was almost a comedy. Wait, listen, yes we got that bogey but more important, much more important. She, you know the she I'm referring to?"

"Yes, her. Go!"

"She apparently learned, I don't know if your people talk about the Romanian Frozen Hand?"

"Romanian Cold Hand. Absolutely! You're kidding, you saw it used. Did it impact you, your people? Really?"

"Froze us all. The outside temperature was nothing compared....well, it's hard to describe. It's a sort of fear that removes your will to take action."

The Commander grew quiet. "You know, there's a lab, well, it's not important where it is. There are hundreds of millions of dollars tied up in isolation rooms, sampling devices, small supercomputers, all of it. Creating weapons which avoid physical harm to stop someone. Dozens of scientists. And this broad has it goin' on already with only her mind. Wait! Do this again, you're telling me you experienced fear, inability to act? It lasted how long? And it's only her?"

"I'd say it was upwards of five minutes. I couldn't move, I'm telling you she froze everyone. And unless there was a second person concealed it's all her."

The general was now fully awake. "Jesus Chriminey, Robinson, you see where this goes now? She had big value before. After this, she's got the Romanian power tool, now she's more valuable. Five times more. Can you imagine what happens if she can teach our people the technique. She learned it, we can learn it. You walk into downtown anywhere, Baghdad. Twenty guys just freeze the bad guys block by block. No more killing, totally immobilize their asses."

Kate hunted down a boat launch and drove the mule up the ramp off the lake. She drove a few blocks and stopped. They would come looking for her car. She drove a few more blocks. Where to go? Then she remembered the aging Carson family warehouse one block over. It was still intact, she slid open an ancient sliding door and drove the mule inside. She sat and breathed feeling her muscles starting to unkink. To describe the experience as unpleasant didn't do it justice. She warily emerged from the Audi and unsteadily walked onto the main street. She craved food and knew at this hour the frozen yogurt shop would be the only place open in Excelsior. She wore glasses, a silly hat, a formless down parka, boots. She just wanted to be left alone. Kate stood in a short line, ordered yogurt and some toppings, then slid into a corner chair turned away from the windows.

She finished the yogurt and ordered a second one. The woman behind the small glass counter didn't look directly at her but said very quietly, "You need help? You need a place to go? Do you remember me? I was at Wayzata High, I'm a year behind you. Look down at this ice cream. Don't look up. I'm Mayzie, you knew my brother Steve."

Kate did as she was told. "Yah, I remember both of you. Are they out on the street?"

"I'm pointing at different flavors, follow me down to the end. See the door, walk through it, there's a bathroom, go in. I'll come get you." Somehow Kate knew this was correct and did it. Minutes passed, Kate heard a soft tap at the bathroom door.

Mayzie reached in, took Kate by the hand and pulled her outside pushing her into an older jeep. Mayzie walked around and slid into the driver's side. "I got Dwight to cover for me. I just live a few blocks away. You must be a hot tamale right now, they're crawling all over this place."

Kate slid down in the seat and peeked out. Mayzie was right, cops and soldiers everywhere. There had never been soldiers in quiet little Excelsior, ever. Mayzie drove a few minutes and parked just off the bike path that cut through town. She came around, opened the door and took Kate's hand hustling her around behind a house and into the back door. Inside she almost ran Kate down in the basement. "This is my sister's apartment but she's over in Italy. What the hell you been up to? I never saw uniforms like that anywhere?"

Kate half collapsed on an old couch. She looked at Mayzie. Now she could place her. Mayzie Dundee, six feet, solidly built, a perpetual frown but also a great smile. "You were the one who tried to crack men's wrestling, right?"

"Man, I'm too big, girls can't do this, yah da ya da ya da. What the hell can I do? I'm a killer on the mat but the guys hated wrestling me. I watched you and watched you. I have always admired you so much. And then you get this shit happening, the modeling, the skating, the clothing, then magazine covers. Jesus, girl, two People covers! Two! Then we see you on tv and you are kicking ass. God, I cannot believe I saw you in the halls in my school. Do you know how much you mean to all of us? She's Kate, she's totally unstoppable, you are a hero bigtime. Then beating up these animal cruelty assholes. Oh, man, you just go girl ...."

Kate held up her hand. "Mayzie, I get that way too much. Give me a break. Right now I need to deflate. Can I stay here, right here, on this couch, this is perfect. I'm one of three females in the entire world that likes basements, midwestern basements. Is that cool with you?"

Mayzie hugged Kate. "It's all yours, I live upstairs, it's not much but there is a good music system, it's secluded. Stay however long, you're makin' my year just sitting there. Pillows here, blankets there, bathroom behind that door. I got a little portable stereo. I got CD's. Lots of food, I like eating, tell me what you want and I'll bring it back."

Kate just said, "Thanks kiddo. I need to crash right now." Mayzie walked up the stairs. Kate punched in her mom's phone number, a cell they only used in emergencies.

"Hi, I'm good, I got rescued by an old classmate. I'm near where Dad used to live, got it? I'm layin' low for a few days, we'll get together."

Sarah replied, "Uh, you did something on the lake, right? Buzz called me."

Kate answered, "I froze a few with your grandmother's recipe."

Kate heard the sharp intake of breath from her mother's end. "Oh my god, you learned it didn't you?

Kate, her mother and Buzz found themselves riding with two very quiet young men in a five year old Buick sedan, a car that no one would ever notice passing by. It had taken a few minutes for Buzz to convince Kate this compromise would work.

"Katie, you know full well that your little escapade on the lake is going to attract everyone from governments to the military to whoever else. You've had heat on you for 18 months now and it's not cooling off. It's taken your grandmother, myself, a couple law enforcement people, Judge Reitenhause and ...."

"Buzz, who is this Judge?" asked Kate.

Buzz glanced at Sarah. "Katie, there were FBI agents camped outside your place in Berkeley and your mom's place here waiting for a court order. This has been all about protecting you. This Judge has now twice stood up for you, kept the authorities off your back, he's a real stand up guy. He understands that you need..."

"Buzz, why is this the first I've heard about this Judge?"

Sarah interjected, "Honey, there are now at least three people who are working to keep you walking the streets, preventing unnecessary legal actions, protecting your rights."

Kate looked nonplussed. "Honestly, protecting me?"

Buzz added, "Katie, it's you, it's your mom and now that the media are all over these stories about the animal abusers getting kicked around you're both under suspicion. We are paying a lawyer monthly to advise us."

Kate looked stunned. "You mean if this weren't happening I'd be in jail or Mom and I together?"

Buzz shook his head. "Not jail, protective custody. Yes there are a few sheriffs who want to nail you for these animal abuse things but you have federal officials who are trying to guard you, protect you. And the feds are pulling rank for now but who knows? Anyway, I cut a deal with a military guy with ties to the highest office. You accept a loose cordon of protection and they try to leave you alone. Katie, dear, this is an excellent deal and we're officially out of alternatives for now."

"So you're saying, I have no choice?"

Buzz and Sarah nodded.

Aggie visits with Queen Royal Elixir when she reveals her suprising connection to one of the century's most admired women. Go to www.katemcgill.com, look under "chapters".

CHAPTER THIRTY FOUR

KATE ENCOUNTERS DA HIJ SILBI

In many months, this was the first Saturday that Buzz Roemer was not preoccupied with the Harendt family. In truth his brain had overloaded with Kate's recurrent borderline behavior and the Harendts' four woman floor show. Buzz walked around on the deck overlooking the St. Croix River with no phones ringing, no one with panic in their voice and appreciated a placid, unspoiled sunny but chilly afternoon.

He had not heard from a federal government agency in over three weeks. His brother was somewhere cross country skiing with friends. Not one tv channel called asking questions in over a month. And Lasola was finally in custody.

Cory Madigan sent him a cute postcard from Aruba but no phone calls, no manic interruptions. He went inside, sat down in his favorite chair and began drifting off listening to John Denver.

His cell, the one that only Aggie usually calls starts to vibrate.

"Yup, who's this?"

"Mr. Roemer, we've met but I am not important in this. Your brother did me a favor and this is my way of returning it. I work in one of the three letter agencies, ok?"

Buzz knew from lots of experience not to waste his breath asking who was talking? Better just to listen.

"For complicated reasons one of our country's important people arranged to underwrite a person in the middle east. The resources were made available because it appeared this particular young man would surface as a counter force or offsetting balance against certain Islamic powers which appear potentially threatening to American interests. It's 1994, the middle east is changing rapidly to say the least. This guy goes by a weird name, Da Hij Silbi. He has been quietly gathering followers quite peacefully along the very lines this VIP had hoped for."

Buzz waited and waited saying nothing so far. Now he said, "Ok."

The voice continued. "This young guy seems to have a showman's flair. He has repeatedly gathered groups of young men together for rallies in a few Arab countries. No one can get a handle on his background so far. He speaks a few languages including Arabic but English as well. There is a little footage of him doing magic tricks of all things but mostly he seems to have a way of leading young men."

Buzz was waiting for a punch line. "Ok, with you so far."

"So, here is why I'm calling you. This young Da Hij is hoping to meet Katherine McGill. She is the one western woman that has established ethical and moral behavior he admires."

Buzz asked, "This Da Hij, what does he want from Kate?"

"Simply to meet her and speak with her. Very reasonable. No special meeting conditions, she shows up and they talk."

Buzz thought about this idea for a moment and responded, "Well, I don't know much about this guy but I'll certainly broach it with Katie when I next see her."

"Mr. Roemer, uh, this is all happening, as they say, in realtime. This Da Hij Sibli has a few thousand young Islamic men standing around in a desert location. He is making this request now, presently and in a few moments you'll see the results. As it were, the American government response. We hope you can help. Your federal government is thanking you in advance. Good bye."

The phone clicked off leaving Buzz holding the cell phone. He held it a few more moments and then realized it was no longer needed. He shoved the phone back in his pocket and shook his head.

Buzz knew this had to be heading his way but he indulged the remainder of his vodka gimlet, turned on a ball game, turned it off, thought he heard more than one car arriving out in the parking lot, then he was sure. Moments later the first of them appeared on the back deck led by a soldier dressed in battle gear. Behind trailed General Spike Drake, the military man who served as chief liaison for the President. Buzz knew this would be the unequivocal end to his formerly relaxing afternoon.

"Buzz, we're intruding, a bunch of us but your country, your President needs you and I'm afraid there is no time to lose." General Drake tried to appear apologetic but he really wasn't.

"Ok, General, shot my lovely afternoon all to hell. What's up?"

The General took Buzz by the arm, led him to a corner of the porch and turned his back on the accompanying soldiers and retinue.

"Two months ago the President was briefed on an unexplained, really baffling phenomenon that occurred in Minnesota southwest of here. There were reports of...."

Buzz smiled and finished the General's thought, "Ooh, yes, reports of an unexplained huge airship southwest of Mankato, I bet. Then masses of ground troops mysteriously turning up in some farmer's fields."

The General nodded and then withdrew two pages of paper from his breast pocket. "This is a short quote from a report given me two weeks back."

Buzz took the paper, scanned it and replied, "Yes, I've seen this a few times about the Harendt Illusions as they now seem to be known."

The General paused to catch his breath. "Buzz we know now this unexplained display of military might was tied to this Harendt family, can I say, fooling around? Can you explain what occurred?"

Buzz leaned against a railing on the porch holding what was left of his vodka. "General, first, some intelligence guys were all over me for a few days after that so it's in various files I'm sure. The four Harendt women, Kate's family, spent a few days together on property southwest of Minneapolis. It was likely the first time in their collective lives all four had spent that much concentrated time together. Specifically, the first time Kate the youngest and Haddassah the eldest could comfortably explore their shared mentalist gift passed down in the family. Anyway, all four of them were fooling around enjoying themselves when Kate insisted they try an experiment. The army had secretly been monitoring Kate because of these reports she had some potentially useful talent for mental projection. They had a crew of three in a very well equipped mobile laboratory very close to the house the Harendts were using. Kate's grandmother Helen Aray brought along brand new amplifiers her company has produced. That equipment may also have amplified those images. No one really knows. There have been rumors Helen's amps have this capability but I certainly have no idea."

Buzz stopped momentarily, drank the last of his vodka and then continued. "Kate had never tried experimenting with what images, if any, she could project. She used military pictures because she had no investment in planes or tanks which allowed her to objectify them easier. She pulled her relatives in to help her. That rolling lab apparently used certain computing software which could enhance observations on a battlefield. The newest systems could allow field commanders to seize on certain activities and magnify them for closer inspection. More careful review indicated that these systems may have somehow latched on to some image Kate was manipulating and made it many times larger. That discovery did not come out until six weeks later. So General this is not guaranteed to work under battlefield conditions."

"Buzz whatever happened out there it showed up at the Pentagon and later the White House. And here we have a situation where it may really make a difference."

The General's cell phone rang. "Yes sir, we're here now with Mr. Roemer. I'll have information for you in thirty minutes. Yes sir, without fail."

The General admitted, "The Boss is under real pressure. That's why I came here. We have a problem not easily solved. And our normal planned responses are coming up far short. In the middle east, the perennial headache, we are seeing what began as a few hundred young men massing in Iran but then also Syria and now other nearby countries apparently preparing to march toward Israel and Palestine. A young guy has emerged as a leader and he is urging these groups to coalesce and march to Israel."

"Is this Da Hij Silbi? Do I have that name right?" asked Buzz.

"Right, a mysterious guy but he has somehow captured the imaginations of way too many young men, a festering sore of dissatisfied youth. You just can't have masses of leaderless men heading for Israel. That country will defend itself and the Israelis have appealed to us to help quell this growing problem.. The fear in Washington is that Arab dissatisfaction with the Israelis is now getting stirred up by this Da Hij. We believe there are thousands of young men on the move heading toward Israel and we need to turn them around. So some bright bulb at the NSA who had seen the report of the Harendts little military display suggested we ask them for help. And here I am. We need your cooperation in putting the Harendts to work."

"General, you want them to put up some kind of threatening military images, is that the idea?"

"Buzz, we can't fly troops into countries like Iran or Iraq can we? But if we do nothing these kids and young men will show up on Israeli borders and it could be a massacre. Da Hij Silbi might implore them to sacrifice themselves on Israeli bayonets or the equivalent."

"General you're telling me I need to round up all four women but particularly Kate and fly them to where?"

"You don't have to do that. You simply convince them to cooperate, we'll put them in a very comfortable private jet already contributed by a wealthy and concerned party, they'll dine well, they can sleep. We land them in the middle east, they will have full military escort in comfort to a specific location we're working out presently. They do their thing, so to speak, hop the jet and return. Very simple."

Buzz responded, "Uh, General, the oldest of the Harendts is not a young kid, she's up there in years and she does not like to leave her home in Las Vegas."

"We've made arrangements for a medical doctor and nurse on the plane, she will be well looked after."

Buzz had to admit they were covering their bases.

The General and company trooped back off the porch and Buzz recovered his drink. Buzz reached under a wooden table and brought up a satellite phone. He punched in a series of digits. The ringing sounded like a small navy klaxon.

"Agg, having fun skiing?"

There was a pause. "Yes, Buzz, great time. I hope you're not about to end my little reverie."

"We have a problem brother dear. In the middle east."

Twenty four hours later two military air transports and the private jet landed on an improvised airstrip in the Negev desert and began disgorging four vehicles loaded with equipment. Special arrangements had been made with Israeli air defenses to allow the planes to land on Israeli territory. In under an hour people and equipment arrived at a carefully chosen location thought to be two miles back from the Israeli border with Jordan.

The Harendt women were shown into an air conditioned trailer where an Israeli commando was waiting to give them some instructions.

"Ladies and gentlemen, welcome to Israel. I am David Gannon, I grew up in America and emigrated to Israel. I want to give you a very simple orientation. We are presently a few miles from the Jordanian border and not too far from the Dead Sea. Our country has been negotiating with various parties including the Jordanians as it appears this March of the Innocents as it has been termed will come across Jordanian territory. We are sure the Jordanians, really no one, want this mass of young men to be crossing their country but it was considered more politically acceptable if they were in Jordan. At present the marchers are some miles from us traveling slowly. Hopefully the Arab parties who are attempting to negotiate a sort of armistice and keep these people short of our border will be successful. But there are now something like 6000 marchers, far too many for Israel to allow them to cross our borders. When they approach maybe 3 miles out from Israel we are hoping whatever you can do will be employed to stop them. If it appears your efforts may not be sufficient we will evacuate all the Americans by air and Israeli troops who are stationed immediately behind us will move forward to their border. That is not what anyone in Israel wants but will happen if required."

Kate asked, "Commander, will that be a military confrontation with the marchers?"

He replied, "Yes, most likely and our government has warned any and all interested parties of the measures we may need to take. Believe me, it's the absolute last ditch approach if all else fails."

Helen then asked, "And this Da Hij, where is he in all this?"

David replied, "Our intelligence people are attempting to track him now. We believe he will likely not appear in the confrontation. But he can cause more than enough trouble by appearing on television exhorting these thousands of people to continue their march toward Israel."

Aggie Roemer sitting with the Harendts asked, "Commander, are these marchers saying they want to cross your border? What if they stop short? What happens then?"

"Officially, if these marchers remain in Jordan or even Syria which is not all that many miles away it's the concern of those countries. That's all we know presently. If they don't try to cross the host country will have to deal with their needs which are considerable. Having a few thousand people stand around in the desert creates some fairly monumental problems."

Kate then asked, "How soon do we attempt our procedures?"

General Drake stood up. "You have perhaps an hour to get situated. This process will be very delicate. We have ways of monitoring the reactions of these marchers from a distance. There are military and civilian parties in Jordan with the marchers. The Israelis have stated that a group of concerned citizens will be looking on from this site. But no one has mentioned who is in our party or what steps will be taken. All of you which includes the four Harendt women, the two Roemer brothers and six military guards accompanying you may be asked to pick up and move at almost any time. If we detect any kind of intrusion coming towards this location we'll hustle you on to a military helicopter for transport back to your plane. There will be absolutely no heroics. If your attempt is successful we stay out of the way. If we believe you and we are threatened by any party you are removed quickly. Those rules cannot be broken."

The Israeli commander then asked, "We need to understand your setup. Aside from chairs and some food and water all we can see, so far, are boxes of what appear to be some type of electronic amplifier. Is that all you want or need?"

Helen Aray now stood up to be heard. "I'll answer that question. Those are actually non solid state amplifiers my company builds. We have experimented with them and the tube type amplifiers may enhance our efforts. How much we don't yet know? We had only one opportunity to get all four of our family together with these amplifiers in a real world test."

The women decided they wanted to be seated under a simple tent close together. They were surrounded by the amplifiers which travel in hard shell carrying cases. Otherwise they had no other tools.

Twenty five minutes later General Drake walked into their tent and stated, "Alright, folks, time to get started. We have one rule in this case, if I or one of my staff walk in here and ask you to break off your attempt there will be some potential urgency. And from what I've learned, you can't just drop everything on the spot. It takes you time to wind down. We'll give you notice, as much as we think is safe but you must follow our orders strictly. Alright, we'll leave you to your efforts."

The Israeli Commander reappeared. "Ladies, they are now approaching our location traveling at something like one and a half miles per hour. We cannot have you sitting here past a certain point. You will need to be moved. So you have something like an hour to work your magic. Good luck."

Kate had first found all this attention flattering and stimulating. But now the base reality began intruding. Her country, these soldiers, the President were all looking to Kate McGill and her family to be miraculous and Kate had emotionally arrived at the end, at least temporarily, of being the miracle girl. As she sat there with people essentially leaning on her Kate felt like looking for the door.

Kate turned to her family members, "How could Miriam not show up for this crisis?" That was upsetting Kate. "We're all supposed to be in this and for heavens sake this Da Hij guy is 'her' guy. I honestly don't give two craps about Mr. Da Hij. And what is really confusing is Miriam described him like a scary, malevolent criminal. What gives? This guy is threatening peace it sounds like?"

Haddassah observed, "Don't worry about Miriam, she has her reasons I'm sure. This Da Hij is out there exhorting his brethren to follow him. Let's give our best effort and summon up a few images that may cause this big group to turn and walk away."

The four women gathered, held hands and began concentrating. Their tent was three quarters surrounded by soldiers but standing back some forty feet. In front of the Harendts an empty desert of sand with remnants of broken glass and trash extended out for miles. The women tried concentrating together for half an hour. Nothing happened. It was like whatever talents Haddassah and Kate together could amass---were adding up to nothing. They redoubled their focus but after fifteen more minutes they gave up.

The General returned to see the four drinking a local favorite coffee in demi tasses. He tried to control his emotions. "Ladies, Kate, what do you think?"

Kate replied, "General Drake, as we've said many times this isn't a light switch you throw on. We're trying, really working at it but maybe it's the setting or all these soldiers or the mass of young men marching right for us.

Please know we didn't come all this way for fun. But we're stuck for now. We're very sorry. Do we need to move out of here?"

General Drake's mind was racing. They were almost completely out of time, their best estimates being radioed down from aircraft put the marchers now under three miles out. He knew nearby Israeli shock troops equipped with all the latest weapons were awaiting orders. "Folks, we need to move you back, this may not be a safe place so please follow the directions of our staff, we'll move you toward your aircraft. Thank you for all your efforts." The General hurried off. He had no news for military commanders back in Virginia.

The Harendts picked up their few articles, took their last taste of the marvelous coffee and walked dejectedly toward the two Ford station wagons. Kate felt embarrassment, the Harendt secret weapons had crashed and burned. She began wondering why they drew such a blank? That had never happened.

Haddassah stepped over to Kate, wrapped her arm around Kate's arm and pulled her close. As they slogged through the sand Haddassah said, "Katie, it's such a human, frail power, I often found the whole idea maddening. People may expect you to just snap your fingers and bingo things appear. It's not at all like that. When we were just fooling around in Minnesota we were enjoying ourselves, we were all utterly relaxed. This is nothing but anxious people, who the heck can blame them?"

Kate squeezed her arm back and said, "I really understand how this is just so ephemeral, so momentary. When I was out on that frozen lake it had to happen, I had to make it work or else. But here, I don't know, it's not our deal to begin with. We're hired actors today."

Haddassah laughed a bit. "Yah and we didn't get the parts. I'm guessing the Israelis will have to confront this army of disaffected young men."

A woman in military clothes stood nearby attempting to attract Kate's attention. She had the bearing of a soldier, wore a sidearm but from the neck up she was exquisitely made up, her hair carefully styled. She was not saying anything but her body language spoke loudly. Kate re-angled toward her. The woman said, "I cannot officially talk to you but you're needed in here." With that she took Kate's elbow and muscled her firmly up the stairs into a mobile communications lab filled with blinking lights, tv monitors surrounded by heavily armed soldiers.

The so far unidentified woman said, "We need your help in here but we don't officially exist. Your family was imported by some brass and maybe the President, we're totally under the official radar."

Kate scanned across ten video monitors. Almost all were showing video feed apparently shot from a distance of the mob of people mostly dressed in native garb and robes. She focused on one monitor which brought the images of the mob in close. No one looked particularly angry, no guns were evident. In fact they looked pretty happy.

She asked, "Have they been like this, you know, just standing around? No one's yelling or raising hell."

One of the soldiers turned to the side and said, "I'm Major Tedeschi. You must be Kate?"

She nodded. He continued, "Were you briefed on why they are out in the desert?"

Kate replied, "Kind of. Well, not really. We knew they were threatening to march this direction and our family were hopefully to persuade the mob to march, well, elsewhere. We're the shot in the dark option. That's all I know."

The Major responded, "Kate they are not out here on a whim. A particular person has been persuading all these young men, there are no women to speak of, he is known as Da Hij. He's the motivator, the arm twister. He's in that mob of approximately 5000, it could be even more. What happened when your family tried to, uh, summon up whatever it is you do?"

"Nothing, it's never been like that. We got nothing."

"Could you see people, the mob, anything?"

"No."

"Well I'm here to… Let's see, alright, I'll just spit it out. I'm a psychological profiler, I work on contract with American intelligence services. Over here, this is Marie Balthazar. She's a….Marie, you tell her."

The elegantly coiffed and made up woman, her military uniform pressed to match her makeup stepped forward with a very worried look on her face.

"Kate, I'm a Captain, I train Rangers to spot trouble, I help prepare our best trained troops to see a problem before it gets to them. Problems like people who want to cause a fight. You get the idea."

Kate replied, "Ok, why didn't we talk to you first?"

Marie replied, "Long story and right now we have almost no time. Kate we hoped to pair up with you because we have a problem. We can't find this Da Hij. He's there, that's our belief, we have camera coverage from the air but no Da Hij. Not anywhere. We're all here to spot him, no one here has footage of him, if he exists at all?"

The Major added, "And we're being told your family has to clear out in three minutes. We can't reorganize that fast and be effective. We commandeered this mobile lab last minute, all of us are here as essentially volunteers. The military just didn't quite know how to respond to this mob in the desert. It's no one's fault, this just doesn't follow any pattern. Mobs are in cities, they have places to hide, out here, well, it's a damn desert. Marie and I think this Da Hij, whoever and whatever he is may be important to diagnose, uh, understand. He got these men to march for days with absolutely no support system. There is limited water over there, little food, no beds. He is demonstrating he can persuade large numbers of Arab males to do anything. That's his goal."

Kate replied, "Now what?"

"We need you to be a volunteer...like us. We'll have some help---we think."

Major Tedeschi looked at Captain Balthazar. He added, "I know this sounds weird but as far as Washington, the military chain of command all of us standing here right now are not recognized. We don't exist. This is all off the map and completely unofficial. Uh, what do you say?"

Haddassah had been eavesdropping at the doorway. "Kate, you can help here, we'll be fine. Stay if you want."

Kate turned back to the Major. "You want me to try and find him in that mob?"

Captain Balthazar replied, "Kate, he needs to be neutralized as well but not killed. Immobilized temporarily but no drugs, no stun guns. We need to take him out of commission, so to speak, briefly. But all unofficially. Americans on Jordanian territory."

Kate expressed surprise, "I thought we were in Israel?"

The Major replied, "Uh, this is actually Jordan, right here. You walked exactly 150 yards, 137.16 meters. There was a little misunderstanding about precise location. We are on this land only long enough to finish this task then we are airlifted out. The Israelis will momentarily defeat their air defenses to get us out."

Kate was trying to follow this line of thinking. Then the Captain added, "Alright, Kate meet Captain Arrias and Captain Montaine, respectively Syrian and Jordanian armies and Captain Devlas, the Israeli army."

Kate looked around in bewilderment. The Major added, "None of us is actually here officially. We all walked into this encampment strictly by chance. That will be our story if it comes down to it. Let's just say there is some real interest in this Di Haj from many quarters. Now we have no time, let me show you a few things, Kate. Sit here, look at this monitor. This is our very best magnification available."

The Major steered Kate to the seat before the particular monitor. Then he said, "We think Da Hij is likely to be in this sector based on some intelligence gathered by Captain Montaine. You see, no one wants this person mucking around, goofing up an already terribly tense situation."

Then Captain Arrias said in perfect English, "In various religions and cultures there is a concern for a savior, a leader materializing to guide the masses. Christianity calls this person Jesus, for instance. Muslims have their own definition. You get the idea. The thinking is that Da Hij will be presented as a figure of redemption, a Jesus like figure returning to earth. Our problem is this massing of the Innocents as it's being referred to looks dangerously like the religious figure making an appearance. While the Syrians and Israelis have numerous disputed issues we share a concern, a wish to see no wild card savior showing up here on the borders of these countries. Not now. Make sense?"

Kate nodded a bit dumbfounded. Her history of the middle east knowledge from college was being sorely tested.

The Major now said, "Kate, please, I know your family encountered problems together. Can you apply whatever skills you may have to help us locate him? We may have only minutes." The Major's face reflected his serious agitation.

Kate began studying the monitor. Behind her one person surreptitiously clicked a stop watch. Outside the mobile van various armed men stood essentially back to back watching the nearby horizon hoping to see nothing and no one moving.

Kate asked, "As no one has a good handle on his appearance, why might I recognize him?"

The Major replied, "Because you're who you are. That's our hope."

Kate nodded. "Ok, great, I'm the designated hitter. Please show me how to increase magnification?"

For three minutes with help Kate gradually scanned the amassed men. She paused.

"I have to be among them. You can't feel the essential human energies this way. With all these people you can't differentiate well. I need to walk out there. Who will accompany me?"

None of the assembled military people were prepared for this. Captain Balthazar replied, "Kate, no one can protect you. If we send you with soldiers, that will be unworkable." The Captain looked around helplessly. All the various officers looked at each other. There was no actual solution if she waded into the gigantic crowd.

Kate shrugged and stood up. "They are people, I'll go alone. Just give me a phone of some kind. And if I find him or think I find him, what happens?"

This time all the officers knew what to do. The Syrian Captain replied, "Just show him to us and then walk away."

Kate smiled, bemused. "Anyone know where exactly I go at that point?" The various military officers looked at each other nonplussed. They all knew there would be absolute hell to pay if something bad happened to the American girl.

"Captain Balthazar, we have company coming over the sand dunes." The various officers quickly exited the van. Voices could be heard as they discussed their options. Kate returned to the monitors trying to figure out what to do next?

The American Captain and Major re-entered looked harried. "Ms. McGill, there are a couple thousand walking towards us, you must leave right now. We can put you on a chopper and …."

Kate was glued to one monitor she had overlooked. "Folks, here's your guy. I don't know how I missed him, it's obvious. Look."

Officers streamed back in. Captain Balthazar asked, "How can you be so sure? It's just a guy in a robe standing on a sand dune. He looks the same as the others."

Kate shook her head, "I guess you'll have to trust me on this. Here's why it's him. He has an extremely extended aura or prominence, all the others skirt him at a respectful distance, no one is approaching him. Most of all, he sends out very distinct energy, quite heightened."

The officers looking on shrugged their shoulders. They clearly had no better idea than Kate. She jumped up. "Let me take that ATV out there. Just me and our pal Da Hij. He's off by himself and from the looks of things, the masses are moving away from him as well." Kate walked very quickly out the door headed directly for the brown and grey Kawasaki ATV. "I need a working phone or walkie talkie."

Two soldiers rushed over holding out walkie talkies. "Miss McGill, there's a pouch right on the front for two of these. Just press this button, we'll pick you up. It's good for five miles in this configuration."

Kate accepted their offer, looked down found the key and pushed the starter. Moments later she hot-shoed it away from the van heading into the late afternoon sun.

Cameras instantly re-directed to the disappearing ATV and moments later the officers in the van could see her heading across a large dune. This had not been anyone's idea of a good plan but she moved so quickly no one could stop her.

They heard her voice say, "Ok, I can maybe see him out there. All these men are kind of headed away from him. It's almost like they want to get away from our guy?" Two lines of armed soldiers had now surrounded the small encamped van Kate was leaving behind. The masses seemed to be heading away from the soldiers also but no one could tell what all these young men were attempting?

Kate brought the ATV up to thirty miles per hour traveling up and down a few dunes, winds and heat waves distorting her vision. To her left a mass of people in native dress shuffled slowly toward the west and the Israeli border. They seemed almost hypnotized, no one acknowledged her presence some 100 yards distant.

She crested a sand dune and 100 yards ahead stood the lone figure arms crossed, unmoving, his robes being blown in the desert winds. Kate stopped the ATV, stepped off some forty yards from the lone man. Then she noticed some dozen men gathered a distance behind him standing together, not obviously armed, not moving towards her but seemingly protecting the lone man.

She walked with a sense of purpose but not quickly. She was dressed in jeans, a long sleeved dark blue work shirt, boots, a broad brimmed dark tan hat and sun glasses. It seemed oddly quiet.

He unfolded his arms and extended his hand. "Welcome to Jordan Ms. McGill. I heard you might be nearby and always hoped to meet you. I am Da Hij Silbi. I assume your Israeli and American friends have you on camera?"

Up close the dark skinned, medium height, goateed man around age 23 or 24, Kate guessed, appeared to be similar to most middle eastern arabs. His eyes projected no particular penetrating gaze, his smile actually seemed friendly, he carried no obvious weapon and his followers some 30 yards distant made no move towards Kate.

"Do I call you Da Hij?"

"Sure, why not?" He smiled broadly. His English accent sounded almost Midwestern American.

In a momentary flash she recognized his face. He was the image that visited her a few times in past months. This was apparently her mentalist visitor for whatever reason.

"Uh, Da Hij, you have a lot of people quite nervous. There must 3000 people or more moving toward the border with Israel. That may be a difficult confrontation, don't you think?" Kate asked.

"It's actually almost six thousand. There are more over that tall ridge. Did your Israeli and American commanders ask you to ask me if I would call off the dogs, so to speak? I went to school in Illinois, I'm a non naturalized American. What do they think will happen with the March of the Innocents?" He still smiled and kept a steady gaze with Kate. She wore sunglasses, he did not. She decided to remove her glasses.

Da Hij said, "You have the most gorgeous grey pearlescent eyes. You should never wear sun glasses, at least with me." The comment was innocent enough but Kate detected the unmistakeable self centered bias.

She smiled back.

"Da Hij, what will happen when they get to the border do you think?"

He chuckled, "I believe they all need to get their passports validated. Sorry, a little joke to lighten things up." He paused, looked up at the sky momentarily. "Well Kate McGill, what would you have me do with these Innocents? What would be your suggestion?"

274

Kate was acutely aware of the circumstance. She and Da Hij stood facing one another in an almost empty desert being scrutinized by any number of airborne cameras. She guessed numerous powerful observation devices including satellites were likely trained on the two figures sending signals back to listening posts across the world.

This time she smiled. "Well, Da Hij, ask the Innocents to stop, turn around, head back into Jordan and avoid a nasty confrontation at the border. How does that sound? If it would help I will request supplies like food and water be made available in trucks at the border. I know some preparations had been made to offer food supplies to the mass of young men. Did you have any supplies for them yourself?"

Da Hij nodded and smiled again. "Well, I had no supplies. That was purposeful. It gave you, the Americans an opportunity to assist us. Here's what I propose: You and I walk together just beyond that group of my followers. We shoot a video, the two of us. I have a camera crew waiting. You say what you just said. I will agree. We will shake hands and I will ask my Innocents to stop their progress. I'm sure they will welcome the food and water. But no American soda and you know alcohol will not be appropriate. I see you have some type of phone or walkie talkie. Tell your crew what we're discussing so they can begin moving trucks to the border. How does that sound, Ms Kate?"

She paused for a moment. She wondered how exactly he communicated with this large mass of people? "Da Hij, no objections, you're ok with the Innocents turning around?"

He bowed slightly toward Kate. "For you Kate McGill, I will gladly turn the March of the Innocents away from Israel. I know you are relying on your powers of the mind to assess my credibility. Isn't that the case? Do I seem ok to deal with?"

Her mind raced forward and back. What else was there to do but accept his offer?

"Da Hij, I'm a civilian, not a soldier. What are you after, why would you ask all these people to walk across the desert? That is certainly unusual." She was trying to pick unloaded words.

He momentarily did not answer as though he was preoccupied with some task. "Yes, good question. I wish to demonstrate to westerners and to people in our world that I can command others, I can ask people to join me in demonstrating our faith and power and this can be done peacefully. No one is carrying firearms in our March of the Innocents. That's all, here we all are gathered. Now that you have asked in such a nice way I will turn the Innocents around and we walk back to our homes." Da Hij was taking obvious delight in flexing his cultural and organizational muscles but seemingly had no intention of causing a problem.

Kate thought this seemed altogether too simple.

"Da Hij, surely there must be an easier way to demonstrate your leadership in the middle east. This is a lot of people standing around on the sand."

For the briefest moment she caught a flash of resentment but he caught himself and returned to his serene state.

"In this world we go out and take a walk. Not one drop of oil has been wasted. We're also not asking for anyone's help and we're not making demands. I can guarantee you Ms. McGill, in the coming years this approach will be greatly appreciated in retrospect. I know you and your relatives have been hard at work summoning up the Romanian Cold Hand. Pity it did not work."

"Why do you think my family were here in the desert?"

"Ms. McGill, please. I have researched your family, your personal history for months. You have become lady of the hour for preventing dangerous incidents. I know all this. Dates, results, I know all this information. Are you surprised? I will need your help and, in turn, I will show you a productive resolution. In our future there will be far greater and more critical moments to contend with. You are my counterpart in the west. You should be flattered."

"How is it you know so much about me and my family?"

"I have no other choice. I must know. That should be obvious to you, I would hope. Much is expected of you Ms. McGill. I will test your will in this matter. Oh, but I have accidentally tipped my hand, have I not?"

Kate could hardly get comfortable but she realized this guy was parlaying this whole border incident into world class political exposure. Now she was becoming curious why? Certainly he wanted to be recognized?. Is he a complete charlatan, does he have real mental powers, why are people willing to follow him? Who on earth is this man anyway?

Again she felt a strong chill. Staring at Da Hij she realized there was an uncanny resemblance to someone. Her mind flew to Navood Dassur, the Sinbad in Superman Comics. No. Jesus? No. The Russian Rasputin who was claimed to have powers to influence others?

Da Hij passed his hand over his goatee smiling. "Your Romanian powers, that did not work today. It's because you and I were meant to meet. That is my belief. As your family is from Romania, do I have that right, Romania?" She nodded. He continued, "My family from Lebanon and Jordan also had a gift of sorts. We are to either combine our talents or have them clash. Today they combined. Another day may be different. I believe you would be a formidable foe. And I can tell you, I would be a truly difficult foe. But let's enjoy our little day in the desert with my submitting to your suggestions. I am turning my little army around as a favor to you! I had planned that we should meet like this. I had created my little army, my Innocents for this special occasion. So you know I have followed the growth of your popularity in America, and elsewhere. In Japan you have quite a large following. Now, I will have my following. We both will have our adherents. Anyway, better communicate this back to your commanders. Your government will be immensely relieved that you turned the tide here in Jordan. A spectacular success for Ms. Kate McGill!"

She watched him intently. Kate had met a few extraordinary people but this Da Hij did send out a sort of hypnotic power.

"Kate, I needed to achieve some prominence. You will enhance my standing, the gorgeous western girl who defends the vulnerable and innocent. You have delivered my Innocents from danger and saved the day. Sometimes we are the hammer, sometimes the nail. Today I am the nail. In a few years the west will see Islamic men very differently. They will be frightened of us. Today they see us as peaceful, calm, controlled. I will be remembered as the peaceful Islamic leader."

Da Hij turned and walked a few steps away gazing toward the horizon.

Kate was utterly flummoxed. She was wondering if this would all work out so easily? She walked back to the ATV and picked up a walkie talkie. "Is someone listening out there?"

A man's voice said, "We were able to monitor your conversation via satellite. We are rolling a fleet of trucks with supplies to the border. Are you ok, Kate?"

She felt this almost an out of the body experience. "Uh, what can I say? Let's hope this works like he said."

The voice said. "He wants it on tape. We'd say go ahead. Our cameras are showing the Innocents are stopping and some are turning around. Tell your new friend we're sending the trucks across and they will be parked. He needs to supply drivers."

"Ok." Kate walked back to Da Hij who still remained alone. "Da Hij, the trucks will be parked at the border. Can you find drivers?"

He turned back to face her. "Yes, our tribe will pick up the trucks and bring supplies back to the Innocents. When you talk to them say our drivers will bring the trucks back empty to the border in a few hours. Come, let's make the video." He reached over and very gently took her right arm directing her to the cameras.

He spoke first, "I am delighted that with Ms. Kate McGill's help we worked out an arrangement to bring food and water to our March of the Innocents. They will soon be returning to their homes. There was never an angry confrontation as apparently had been feared in some quarters. We are certainly a peaceful people."

He paused and looked at Kate. She had a sinking feeling that she might eternally regret standing in front of a camera with this man but she proceeded, "And I'm delighted this large group of young men will get supplies. I'm gratified there was no disruption or violence."

She turned to Da Hij, extended her hand and they shook hands for the camera smiling.

As she turned away, after the camera had been turned off, she glanced towards Da Hij and for what could not have been longer than a mille-second she saw a face made up of jagged, stone-like elements with extended teeth, yellowish intense eyes and a facial composition resembling an Aztec death mask. She knew this face had appeared but no camera could have captured the image.

Kate thought, *"Did I just project that image on his face? Did I really see that stoney mask? He's definitely spooky."*

Da Hij said, "Our work here is complete. I look forward to our next meeting with great anticipation." She had no response but kept smiling.

As he began walking toward the now stopped assembly of young men. Kate remained almost paralyzed by the thought of the bizarre face. Da Hij, paused, looked back and asked, "Ms. Kate, in the future you will need to bring your strongest resolve. For one so young you demonstrated great composure. My compliments."

Looking off toward his returning Innocents Da Hij casually commented, "A nice little adventure today. Next time I'll try to bring a few hundred thousand of my adherents. They will go where I ask."

Kate wanted one more shot, "Da Hij, what was your name when you attended college in Illinois?"

He smiled broadly. "Nicely done Ms. Kate. Always good to know your counterpart has done some homework. Well I've had a few other names in the past. When we meet next I'll tell you those names. As they say in America, God Speed."

Da Hij walked off and the crew of nearby followers fell in behind him. Kate walked to the ATV and rotated the key. She turned the ATV back toward Israel riding off at a slow pace. She looked across the horizon where thousands of figures in robes now shuffled back toward the east. The whole tableaux seemed totally surreal like a scene out of "Lawrence of Arabia".

CHAPTER THIRTY FIVE

KATE TRAVELING IN FRANCE

Cory Madigan finished watching the 7 minute video that had been splashed over tv news shows for the past two hours. CNN somehow obtained three different views of the scene between Kate and Da Hij Silbi all shot by helicopter or satellite. Cory tried to digest what this might mean for *GloryDays*? The footage was both bizarre and dramatic. It showed Kate approaching the lone, robed figure but footage of the thousands of young men shuffling across the sand gave the whole scene an epic biblical appearance.

Damian appeared in Cory's doorway. He said, "Can you believe this? I mean, really, if our P.R. office dreamed this up it still would not involve so much drama and mystery. This strange guy who commands thousands, the American girl sweeping in to stop the March of the Innocents. What soap opera perfection! Kate had a big name but now she's an international savior, the girl who saved lives and stopped a potential nightmare at the Israeli border!"

Cory nodded but looked distracted. "I wish she had been in a GloryDays outfit when it happened. I guess that's a bit much to ask isn't it? But we can run a congratulatory ad in a trade mag. Like, picture her in the desert with a tag line, this could be perfect: There was a German general who commanded all their troops in the desert, Erwin Rommel. We could borrow his nickname for Katie. How about, 'Hats off to Kate McGill, our own Desert Fox!'"

Bart Alliason walked past the Washington Monument with General Spike Drake. Bart had an urgent thought, "General, I don't want to put a damper on this moment but we have to be thinking ahead. So you just met with the President, it's a great success and Americans were clearly thrilled this young woman walked into that mess and solved it. It's been about 48 hours, my staff are picking up some rumors. This guy, Da Hij Silbi, he is very clever, for such a young guy he operates like a veteran. He was ready with a little campaign the next day. He publicly thanks Kate and even thanks us for not interfering. This whole thing is a planned charade, Katie got set up by this guy. Fortunately nothing bad happened but he used her to satisfy his own ends. My people say it's not over, this Silbi, he will not leave the stage so fast. This adopted name he goes by, are you seeing what that is supposed to mean? I feel stupid we didn't figure this out before. Da Hij, that's the Islamic term for an emotional campaign, but backwards. Jihad, it's what those Muslim soldiers refer to as their cause. A jihad, that's the struggle, it's defending Islam against enemies. And Silbi, Buzz's brother spotted that one. Again backwards, it's an Islamic reference to the devil. Iblis. Their name for a devil or the devil. It appears in the Koran, their bible. So he's taking two powerful words and turning them backwards. We need to be very cautious about this guy. He had his dramatic moment before the cameras. Now what happens next? He waged a campaign and he represents the devil. It may not be a good combination for us I'm afraid."

It had all happened in such rapid fire succession, Sarah assumed Kate would want to return back to America immediately after the desert incident. As they boarded the private jet for home Kate stopped. "Mom, I have some unfinished business with a woman named Miriam in Israel. And now with what happened here, I want to disappear. Just evaporate. I can see already I'll be treated as this high priestess of conflict avoidance. I just want out. Look, can you tell them to drop me in Tel Aviv at the airport, I'll be fine, I have my passport, I have money."

Helen overheard Kate's comments. "Katie, dear, you are going to be hailed as an international hero after what you pulled off. Don't you want to...."

Kate held up her hand. "Grandmother, I'm serious, I want out of all this. I can see what's coming."

Helen responded, "But honey, everyone, the media, I'm sure the President will want to welcome you home ..."

"No, not now. Maybe in a while. Maybe never. This was not what I bargained for, I want a life, a real life. I'm glad I was able to help but now it's my turn. I want my freedom and going back to America right now is all wrong for me. I'll be fine, I love bumming around and I am so totally ready to see places, be a regular person, ok?"

Helen tried to intercede, "Katie, after what happened, you can't just be the average citizen, you are not average, you're incredibly special and ..."

"Grams, the decision is made. I've got some clothes, With email, we can all communicate. I'll buy a phone card. Get them to drop me at the airport. Can we go, please?"

Kate was brought into the terminal in Tel Aviv and wisked through customs with all the gravitas of a visiting dignitary. The Israeli officials stood watching her walk away with a small satchel and large backpack. They knew she was some kind of big deal but no one from the government, no one at all was waiting for her. She walked out of the terminal in beat up jeans, an old work shirt, a full brimmed canvas hat, boots and quietly boarded a bus.

Damian rushed into Cory's office. "Guess what, Kate just disappeared in Israel. She was photographed by a tourist in the airport boarding a bus dressed in the same clothes she had on in the video. She's not coming back, not now."

Cory couldn't believe it. "Oh my lord, how can she do this? I'm sure the White House, the press, us, we all want to welcome her home, make a big deal out of this surprising success. And she's walking away? That is so her, so Kate."

Sarah walked to the library. They had installed the first public personal computer that allowed access to the new internet. At Aggie's suggestion given Sarah's abhorrence of learning new technologies here was a free and easy way to email with Katie. In Sarah's inbox was an email from her daughter.

"My dearest mom, this is just what I wanted. No one tailing me, taking pictures, I cut off most of my hair. Everything single thing I need is in this backpack. I'm down to just the most necessary possessions. I'm free, I'm so happy. I'm in a library in Tel Aviv. Just like you I'm sending my email. I would be happy to share this wonderful time with you as we had discussed. I need some time to just cool out. Let's think about meeting in Paris. With all my love your daughter Katie."

After her few days in Israel Kate flew to France and began traveling by train or bus and occasionally thumbing a ride. It had been six glorious, unbroken, unbothered weeks bumming across Western Europe. Kate was totally in heaven. For days at a time she went unrecognized, often slept on someone's couch, even a few wood floors, the dilapidated sleeping bag she purchased in a youth hostel threatening to give up the ghost. Farming families willingly helped her with food and water. She swept up at a tiny family winery next to the Seine and would have stayed much longer but she got spotted twice and suddenly cameras began popping out.

Kate bought a used bicycle with a rack and occasionally traveled back roads.

One French family gave her a bedroom for a few days and Kate was delighted they had two young border collies they had rescued from a farmer who wanted them gone. She spent hours walking them to a local park, watching them romp in a field. She realized she was most totally at peace with animals. People were great as well but with animals, almost any animal, she felt a strong kinship.

Sitting on a bench Kate realized the two border collies were wandering away and she thought, *you guys need to come back here.* The two black and whites stopped and looked over at her. *That's odd, I felt like I communicated with them. Come on Kate, get real, dogs can't read your mind.*

The dogs trotted back and lay down at her feet gazing up adoringly. She reached down and petted both dogs. *These are such smart animals, they just seem to know what I'm thinking.*

This was not brand new, she had strong feelings about animals cooped up in zoos. They needed to be somewhere, she guessed, but she could put herself in their place, stuck in a cage. That bothered her. The notion of ever actually being jailed nearly enraged her. She could never live in a jail.

Kate found herself in a tiny café in Bois Le Rois an hour from Paris scrupulously paging through a French newspaper, her back turned to the compact Citroens and beatup Renault farm trucks in the adjacent cobblestone street. She felt an obligation to learn the local language as her conversational French was limited.

Inevitably her number would come up as it did this early morning over coffee and croissants. The voice said, "Pardon me, I think a lot of people are looking for you." The mature woman's English had thick overtones of French and maybe German, but she was understandable. Kate had a decision to make. Admit her true identity or try to fake her way out of this? Kate turned slightly to see the speaker and realized the woman was almost certainly a local dressed in farming clothes, dirt on her hands.

Kate smiled. "I'm hoping they don't find me. Can you help keep my secret?"

"You are the girl, Kate? My daughter has your poster up in her room. She thinks you are *incroyable!*"

Kate turned more directly toward the speaker. "What is your name? I'm sorry I struggle with speaking French.

The woman looked in her late forties, definitely rough hewn, her face showing signs of sun exposure, a simple handkerchief tied around her forehead, dressed in an aging workshirt, jeans and workboots. "I am called Grace. My daughter is Angeline."

Kate replied, "Your English is excellent, far better than my French."

Grace's face lit up. "Merci, I work on my English every day, I want Angeline to know your language well, it is the future but we can still speak French. My daughter goes a bit crazy over you. I can't believe you are here, right here in Bois Le Rois."

Kate felt comfortable with this simple French woman.

Grace said, "Come to our house, we're just down this little road. Maybe you would be happier off this street?"

Kate thought about it. That sounded appealing. They stood up and Grace lead Kate away from the town square. They walked for five minutes and Grace pushed on a garden gate entering a hand tended garden. Kate loved the tiny house with flower boxes below the windows and a very robust broadleaf tree standing guard over the two story home.

Grace called out, "Angeline, we have a guest you would like to meet." Moments later a fifteen year old dressed in jeans and a t-shirt worked her way down the narrow stairway. When she entered the tiny kitchen Angeline stopped, the color left her face and she stifled a scream. Holding one hand over her mouth she stood almost paralyzed utterly unsure what to do or say.

Kate stepped toward her, extended her hand, "Angeline, I'm Kate, your mother says you know of me."

Angeline could only swivel her head in total disbelief. "You, uh, you are really her aren't you? Oh, my god, this is completely, uh, I don't know…." She began crying.

Kate said, "Angeline, if we're to be friends you must stop all this nonsense. I'm a girl just like you. Can you just be yourself?"

Angeline looked up, realized how this must look and putting both hands on her face nodded her head and said, "I'm sorry, that is foolish. Why, uh, how did you come to our town?"

Kate laughed, "I'm here, that's all, I'm traveling around, just sightseeing."

Angeline nodded. "You know everyone is looking for you. This Da Hij wants you to go to Egypt and meet him there with lots of followers."

Kate sighed, pulled out a chair at a dining table and sat down. Grace thought Kate didn't look too well. She walked to her side and put one hand on Kate's shoulder. They remained like that for a moment, Kate staring straight ahead, Grace standing solicitously at her side, Angeline standing nearby still digesting how Kate McGill ended up in their kitchen?

Kate looked at the Mother and daughter and wanted to remain in her travel revelry. "Ladies, we have a sunny day. How about we go over to the river Seine. This will unfortunately be my last truly free day and I'd love spending it with the two of you."

Angeline inquired, "Kate, why is this your last free day?"

Kate stood with her hands on her hips stretching side to side. "Because tonight I will make a phone call I would love to avoid but it's inevitable----you know, it must happen."

After an unfettered, delightful day meandering along the Seine and into the surrounding forest, Kate regained her balance. She said to her companions, "You are so incredibly fortunate to have this vast forest next to your house. What a delight!"

Back at the house, Kate waited impatiently while a bi-lingual long distance operator attempted to connect her with Buzz's private phone back in Minnesota. After nearly ten minutes Buzz's familiar voice answered, "This is Buzz, who's calling?"

"Buzzer, I know all your pals in DC are trying to locate me. I'm prepared to be available but only if I am absolutely required. Don't ask me to meet this strange guy again unless I'm the only person possible."

Kate's initiating the offer took Buzz by surprise. He knew she had the strangest feelings about this Da Hij.

"Buzzer, what happens now? What would be my obligation?"

Buzz had to collect this thoughts. What would she have to do? Actually no one really could say what Da Hij wanted or needed? All he had said was he wanted Kate to show up once again. More specifically now he was pointing at Paris, the Champs Elyse', one PM four days hence.

"Katie, let me make some calls. Just give me your number there. It will be a couple hours." Kate spelled out the French phone number and hung up.

Kate slouched in a kitchen chair with a displeased look on her face. "Da Hij just wants the American girl to show up and bless his show of thousands or whatever the numbers are. I'm incidental, nothing more."

Buzz got Bart Alliason at home. "Bart, tell me literally, what does this middle eastern guy want? And why is anyone caring? He's not wealthy, he has no army, he has no influence, what's the deal here?"

Bart cleared his throat. "Buzz, he's important because he can motivate young men to show up for a rally or whatever you want to call it. He did the first one last September, then a couple more and always far larger."

Buzz responded, "Why, I mean, why the hell should that matter?"

Standing in his library stacked with full shelves of books, Bart replied, "The Israelis are very concerned but cannot touch him. Other local governments including Jordan are concerned about this guy lining up mobs of young men. It's dangerous. Within our circles here in the concrete mausoleums in Washington the word is Da Hij could be a flash point. He's a problem, he can cause danger. His name connotes bad guy. So one way or another, he's got to be moved to the side or controlled."

Buzz responded, "So what will you do?"

Another pause from Bart. "It won't be termination. Money will change hands, I'm guessing."

Buzz thought this whole tale very strange. *This guy is holding them for ransom! What a clever, deceptive little mongrel.*

Two hours later Buzz's phone rang.

Sounding tired Bart said, "We found two pictures, him with not just oil shieks but two prominent Russian financiers and another, Da Hij with Chinese emissaries in Saudi Arabia. We got the Chinese people id'd. Top level trade people who don't leave China unless there's something shaking. If he's in some conclave with serious Chinese diplomats someone is grooming him."

Bart continued, "We're thinking he's gotta be someone's close relative, a son of some muckety muck to be mixing it up like that. We wonder if he's being developed by middle eastern players to be a home grown pied piper?"

"Bart, so you're getting pressure to sort of match this Da Hij with Kate? What the hell is she supposed to do? That meet up in the desert, I mean, she got lucky, she took charge but she's not politically aware, she's this girl who cares more about animals, not politics."

"That's the point, precisely. She's from a neutral corner, she has no axes to grind and most important, this little guy with the swagger thinks Kate McGill has her own swagger and he likes being seen with her. She is his power-broker girl friend."

Buzz took a deep breath. "They want her to put out a fire. That's it, isn't it? That's why all this hoopla, that's why they put serious military and intelligence people in the desert with her. She's the poor man's power defuser. She costs nothing but a plane ticket, no troops, no arms, she walks in and all these marching feet stop and turn around. I get it. She saves them time, money, if she fails America is no worse off."

Kate told Bart she'd agree to be the American sacrificial lamb for this bizarre meeting on one condition: She wanted to meet Da Hij alone beforehand. Knowing this might be absurdly unlikely she went further requesting he meet her off big city turf where she was staying in the tiny town of Bois Le Rois. From Paris it would be no more than an hour by train. She insisted he must be totally alone, no hangers-on, security, nothing and she the same. She fully expected to have him turn down her request. The French papers were full of scuttlebutt about the new March of the Peaceful, the latest name. The Paris police announced plans for closing down an entire section of the city surrounding the proposed route of the march. The American Ambassador to France made a public statement, news crews from all over the world were being flown in to capture the event.

At the appointed hour three days before the supposed March of the

Peaceful at 11 in the morning Kate sat alone under two trees on a somewhat isolated park bench near the river Seine. She could hear the water gurgling under a bridge in a tiny tributary river, some ducks were quacking and a mother and her very young child were happily chattering away in French at the river's edge.

Kate could see down the park path almost to a street, there was no other approach to her bench. A person entered the park dressed in an African looking dashiki and dark blue pants. The temperature had been rising, Kate wore jeans and a t-shirt. As he drew closer Kate could tell it was Da Hij. She watched him approach and wondered if he had handlers hovering close by? He ambled, seemed in no real hurry, actually looked around in the trees and paused at a water fountain for a drink. He looked up at Kate and smiled as he approached. She rose to greet him, extending her hand which he accepted. They stood shaking hands almost like two old friends but she felt considerable reluctance about meeting him. In a few days much of the world could theoretically be watching their public meeting over television and satellites. Kate was totally astonished that he even showed up and alone at that.

Kate had to completely flush all her prior thoughts about this young man from her mind. She found him scary, disarming, confusing and she could not shake the image of the stone face icon she saw momentarily in the desert. Yet, here he was looking average, nicely dressed, innocent, un-aggressive, friendly. What on earth could this be? Should she not trust her instincts?

She bade him join her on the park bench. She momentarily glanced around, they were alone except for the mother and child and two ducks that were waddling slowly toward the bench. In the perfect sunny French day nothing seemed out of place.

She began, "Can we speak English, my French is not good."

He smiled almost shyly and replied, "Sure, that's fine. This is a beautiful little town, I took the train to the local station and followed your directions here. You were right it took me twenty minutes to walk it."

Somehow she had imagined he would have handlers with a car driving him around. "You're comfortable on the train? Your face has been splashed all over newspapers and television. No one bothered you on the train?"

He gave a little laugh. "I take trains and busses everywhere in Europe. It's only in the middle east I need to be more guarded. Not because of danger but I've been mobbed a few times. Did you think I would have an entire entourage? I think maybe two people recognized me and even they said nothing. People in France have left me totally alone. I was walking around Paris yesterday, I walked the route of the March. I wore sunglasses and a hat but I was nobody. People are too busy to look at you."

She realized her perceptions of him could be incorrect. "Well, you've become a real phenomenon recently."

He looked briefly away. "No more than you. Did you think I would turn down your request to meet here alone?"

She nodded, "Yes, frankly I was not sure you'd even respond. I hoped to get to know you before this huge public event. I really have no idea who you are or what you want from me or even the public."

He nodded also and gave her a relatively shy smile. "Who do you think I am?"

She threw up her hands. "Honestly, I don't have any idea at all? I read somewhere that you may be related to a prominent Saudi family. You had your picture taken with some diplomats, I know that, you may have attended college in America but you are a true mystery, at least to me."

Da Hij watched her carefully. He had longish curly hair, clean shaven, no beard, dark brown eyes and a prominent nose. Kate thought he was nice looking, nothing exceptional. His body build was slight, maybe 140 pounds, his hands seemed slightly expressive but he certainly had no remarkable physical characteristics and yet Kate clearly recalled out in the desert he had a large, very prominent presence almost like a totally different person. But she was also under enormous pressure, totally unsure what would happen so she may have ascribed all kinds of misleading qualities to this guy. She realized he had no beard, a common mark of many Islamic men.

"Why don't you have a beard? Isn't that common for most Muslims?"

"I am definitely not like most Muslims, my father would tell you that. He thinks I'm much too individual and unwilling to follow the traditional ways."

"What does your father do? Does he live in France?"

Da Hij now looked away. "I don't see my father frequently but he is likely going to show up in Paris. He lives, well, he lives in a few different countries. Unlike the rest of his family he is not settled, he is figuring out his mission in life. He has a few wives as is a Saudi custom, he has a few other children."

Kate had the feeling as father and son they may not be close. "Da Hij, you must have a regular or given name, can I know what your real name is?"

He hesitated. "Not yet, I am Da Hij for many reasons, let's leave it at that. What do you want to know from me?"

"What is your mission, what drives you? You must have a special gift as young men are apparently willing to follow you. Do you have a goal you can explain to me?"

"It's very simple, I wish to be a respected leader of youth. I decided that was my mission in life. I have certain issues in mind. It's not restricted to Muslims or any religion, I want to lead, I can, I have certain special qualities.

But this is not complicated. I see my mission being fulfilled if people will follow me, it's really that simple."

When he spoke his face became animated but he hardly seemed larger than life or dramatic yet in the desert he absolutely commanded your attention. Here in the little park by the river he seemed to be an unassuming young man most people would never notice. Kate could not be comfortable with this dichotomy; it didn't make sense to her.

Kate said, "People back home tell me things and they said you have raised money, you have backers who are giving you funding. What is that for?"

He seemed unconcerned about the question. "It costs money to stage a march, I get help from two sources in Saudi Arabia, uh, and now one in Iran. They think the image of a peaceful gathering is important and useful. So do I. Islamic men are so often portrayed as marching in politics. I am completely apolitical, I don't back anyone for anything. That's why I noticed you. Because you don't talk politics. Isn't that right?"

Kate took in his statements. She thought, *I wonder if he has no political agendas? Why get all these people marching if he doesn't? Just to be peaceful?*

Kate responded, "No I don't back candidates or parties. I care about animals and useless wealth. Those are my issues at this point. So what do you think about Israel?"

Da Hij stretched, twisted his upper body momentarily. "I actually don't talk about Israel. I avoid the subject because it's very controversial. I am trying to build up my presence, you could say I'm out campaigning for peace and getting my name out there. I have no plans to be a politician at all. I guess that sounds odd to you but I'm more like a talk show host or even a comedian on a stage. I want to attract attention. This is sort of my mission or path. That's the truth."

Kate thought, *He is not so wise cracking now. He had this big guy presence in the desert. Now he's almost humble.*

She said, "When we met briefly in the desert you had a totally different presence. You demanded attention. You're quite different now."

He replied, "Why is that so different than you, Kate McGill? When we met in the desert you also had a large presence. The men around me saw you coming almost like a huge bird descending from the sky. I could hear them talking, being agitated. Why am I different than you? Right now we're both just ourselves, there are no cameras, no soldiers. We're just sitting quietly on this bench listening to the river, watching the two ducks waddle around. You're asking me about my mission as though it's so extraordinary. I heard about you in the news, the media for two years. Your skating, your interviews, you appeared in dozens of ads for that athletic company, you were on magazine covers. You, in fact, inspired me. I saw what you accomplished."

He continued, "You are physically attractive which I am not and you certainly turned yourself into a media figure. That looked like fun, a challenge, something to accomplish. I am not gifted with hardly any actual talents but I feel I can lead, the term in English, I believe is 'galvanize'. I want to galvanize people in our age range to take charge of their lives, seek out something of importance. That's as far as I've gotten but that seems desireable to me."

Kate was softening. His vision wasn't really much different than her own view. And he wasn't talking about beating up animal abusers, in fact, he wasn't talking about violence in any form.

"So the March of the Peaceful, that is meant to help young men find a mission?"

Da Hij nodded. "Sure that would be good. I am not, what is the term in English? I am not messianic, I don't see myself as some religious zealot, I'm a guy who can lead. I ended up in Las Vegas. I saw visions in Las Vegas of entertainment, media, spectacular displays that had never occurred to me. I found that exciting but I wasn't going to be an entertainer, I can't sing or dance. But I can talk and have an audience listen, particularly younger people. I have a facility for magic, sleight of hand. Just fooling around I could perform simple tricks. In Islamic cultures magic is not well thought of. It's not sinful but is regarded with suspicion. I learned sleight of hand as a young child, I had to practice under blankets and in closets. I enjoyed the challenge. I have gradually built up my talents and I now can perform illusions, large ones. I got that experience in Las Vegas working in a couple large scale magic shows. That is where I first heard of you. I went to your great grandmother's childrens' show, she is wonderful, entertaining and terribly clever. They made me sit in an isolated booth, I couldn't be in with the children. She talked about you in her show with these kids and I was intrigued."

Kate couldn't quite believe this. He was a bit like a stalker following her around, learning who she was. If he was in Las Vegas it would be no surprise if he stumbled across Queen Royal. Sure why not? She was trying to figure out a way to get him unguarded, vulnerable. Maybe she would see his true inner person?

Kate asked, "Did you talk with her?"

He nodded, "Briefly after her show, she was very involved with the younger children but I shook her hand, we chatted momentarily. You can definitely learn from Queen Royal, she has very interesting knowledge."

It occurred to Kate getting him involved in a mental experiment might open him up?

On the same wave length he said, "You know, there could be something we would try together. Queen Royal talked about your family trait, the ability to see into the future. It is certainly mysterious and hard to grasp. She talked about you and sharing that talent and she said it's possible it could be shared with other people as well. We could try that."

Kate momentarily froze as Helen's words about never revealing her mental abilities to anyone came rocketing back. *I can't just not talk about this stuff with him, he already knows about our family.*

Da Hij knew Queen Royal, apparently had studied her. Now he was suggesting they try to combine their mental abilities. Her defenses went back up. Why would he want to experiment like that? But she realized that would be her opening to see more of him.

Da Hij could sense her reluctance. "We don't have to but I'm interested in any talent of the mind. We could just experiment for a few minutes right here on the park bench if you want?"

She decided to feign innocence first.

"I don't know, that's something private in our family."

He smiled, "That's fine, I just thought it might be interesting. Talents of the mind are intriguing to me."

She decided it was worth the risk.

"Well, ok, we can try it," she said. She thought, *Ok, let's see what is revealed?*

Da Hij said, "Let's think about my March of the Peaceful and what might occur. I can certainly use any knowledge possible."

Kate thought about it. "Ok, we can try that."

They both tried to get comfortable on the park bench which was unyielding but in a few minutes Kate felt herself relaxing. She felt some images forming then suddenly the images took dramatic and clear shape. She could see thousands of young men walking in Paris but with a sharpness and clarity she had never experienced. It was like seeing a movie but in graphic dimensions. Individual faces, clothing, were all evident. She became aware that Da Hij had to be experiencing these images, she could feel his presence in the images and now his imagery became stronger, more forceful but not really threatening. Kate became distantly aware that the mother and child by the river picked up their things and hurried away. The two ducks stopped quacking and disappeared into the river.

She thought, *Good lord, it's exactly as Queen R. explained it. I have some strange gene in me and this is really possible. I've been thinking all along it's some dream, some made up trick. It's not, this does happen.*

Kate still felt ok with it but the drama was becoming a little unnerving.

Kate had no real comparison, no yardstick. Her experience with the Romanian Cold Hand was completely different than this sharing. She and Da Hij were surrounded by some energy they could control but neither one had any idea how to exercise that control.

Only a few minutes had passed but it felt like much longer, almost years.

For a brief moment Kate felt she and Da Hij were rushing headlong into the future but at a furious, unstoppable rate. She became aware of certain figures who appeared to be politicians or leaders who were speaking but their words took on some monster resonance. She could see waves of people behaving just like a giant tide sweeping thousands of bodies toward some unknown destination.

She glanced at Da Hij. His face appeared normal. Then it happened. That face emerged. The stone face with the jagged teeth. There was no question, that side existed and it became stranger and more threatening. It only appeared momentarily but this time she was sure this was not her imagining it, that was his face. Or was it? Was she simply projecting something scary on him?

Finally she felt compelled to stop the imagery, it was becoming too much.

She found herself yelling for them to stop and in moments images began decaying but were not entirely disappearing. She looked at him. His face had taken on a very different appearance. Now he looked much older, like he had aged fifty years, like she was sitting with him as an old man. He seemed momentarily upset or frightened. She looked down at her own hands and they were weathered, aged as well.

She forced herself to break this set of images as somehow maybe he could not.

For a moment neither person moved or talked. Warm, fragrant summer scents wafted up from the river flowers. Kate realized it had happened again---the genetic gift was at work. She disliked her lack of control but the power was undeniable.

Then it all was a memory. She looked at Da Hij. His face reflected concern, not so much fear but he definitely had been shaken by the experience.

He rubbed his face and forehead, then ran a hand through his hair. "I never realized what might be possible like that? Your family has something extraordinary."

Kate was trying to recompose herself. "God, I've never felt anything like that. You added some intense power I've never experienced."

Both of them were having trouble digesting what had happened. Kate knew she saw a frightening image but did that mean the person was malevolent, violent? Could it just be a side any person had in them?

Da Hij realized he had just tapped into some reservoir of amazing strength but had no idea what it all meant.

Kate looked over at the river and the ducks were returning but she swore they had an odd look like they were upset or offended.

Da Hij stood up and walked to the Seine, kneeled down and put his hand in the water. He didn't move for some time. Kate was trying to put the experience in some perspective. She realized her breathing was somewhat labored and she took some deeper breaths. He finally stood up and walked back to the bench and said, "That took me totally by surprise. What Queen Royal talked about with those kids, you have that in multiple dimensions. When I watched her work with young children you could tell she was able to reach out to them and stimulate them. That is a true gift."

Kate realized they had tapped into something amazing but had no idea what to make of it. They looked at each other. Kate knew that never could have happened if they met in a busy, distracting place. This calm quiet little park had allowed them space to find a common vision. But now she had a clear take on Da Hij and one that was difficult to figure out. She knew she had to show up in Paris at the March. Wherever it took her she had to go.

He said, "What just happened here, that is astonishing, at least to me. It felt like this hidden storm swept us both up and carried us off in a wave. I wish we had been able to just sit here and try to control it. I have had hints of something urgent, mysterious, uh, intriguing but alone I could never come close. But with you it was like putting it into some high gear and we just took off like a jet plane."

He sat on the edge of the bench, holding his hands together shaking his head. This was not a flippant, boyish kid. He clearly had been impressed and dumbstruck by this brief experience.

Da Hij stood up but had no idea what came next. "We just touched something that I don't think we'd have found alone. I know for sure I never could have found that by myself. It took both of us and I am really confused. I came here because you are the only person I've encountered who seems similar to me but you are further along a path. Being very honest, I have relied on bravado, on bluffing to convince people I had something when I have never been sure. I bet you're the same except you can actually physically intimidate men. You have talents I don't. But what just happened, that was a revelation."

Kate nodded. "Yah, that was a revelation. But what do we do with it? You can't go around lighting that fire and not controlling it and that would take weeks or months or who knows how long?"

Da Hij also nodded and quietly admitted, "Yes, it would need time for real control but it could be useful as a tool to convince."

Kate did not answer. The word "convince" had overtones she was not comfortable with.

Then she said, "That could be terribly dangerous, I can't go there. Not without practice and discussion. I just can't."

He acknowledged her statement in body language but he did not comment. He turned and walked to a few feet from Kate extending his hand. "I need to go back to Paris. I hope to see you in three days at our meeting place off the Champs Elysee. Will you be there?"

She looked at him. "Yes, I'll be there."

He extended his hand and she took it. They were not best friends, she really had no idea what they were but now they were apparently in this together?

CHAPTER THIRTY SIX

KATE ONSTAGE IN PARIS AND
THE VANISHING SHEIK

On her last night at Grace's tiny house in Bois Le Rois Kate awoke at just after 3 AM and realized she had an appointment to keep. Without hesitation Kate stepped out of the double bed, dressed hurriedly and collected Phillipe who slept at the foot of her bed. She tip toed down the narrow stairs and headed out of the house. She knew exactly where to go, it took a half hour on foot with Phillipe happily tagging along. Grace's house was 300 yards from the storied Forest of the Kings, thousands of acres planted for the pleasure of the upper class back in the 1800's who visited Bois Le Rois as an escape. As she took long strides across the moonlit landscape she did think it was a bit peculiar to wake right up for an appointment in the middle of the night.

Kate arrived at her destination, what she termed "my sitting rock". She found it the first day in a clearing surrounded by tall trees and again bounded right up to the top of the rock formation where she had discovered a perfect sculpted space serving as a surprisingly comfortable chair. She sat down feeling utterly at home. She had arrived in her spot.

Now at 3:30 AM the night or actually morning was luxuriously warm and resplendent with wonderful scents of leaves and plants, some smells of animals mixed in. Kate also realized she could sense their physical presence. Best of all, a full moon illuminated the clearing with silver and blue light. Kate felt completely at peace in this natural space with Phillipe snuggled up on her lap.

Then images began appearing in her mind. Kate knew she was meant to keep this appointment to seek guidance. The whole affair with Da Hij had been upsetting, she could not shake the feeling that dark forces were gathered near him even if he himself was not evil. The stench of manipulation seeped everywhere around Da Hij starting with his name. She knew the name had been created for some purpose. She found herself wondering why she had been pulled into this March of the Peaceful, it was definitely not her concern. But having come this far she had become resigned to stay with it.

Kate tried to put all this far from her mind but the images came hurtling back and finally she stopped denying them. Having opened the floodgate, images of next day's March of the Peaceful began spilling out.

For the first time Kate could discern forces behind Da Hij. Not in total clarity but at least one man who controlled or directed Da Hij was evident. A few images from the March itself appeared and she realized disruption would be lurking around the event. Strangely the threats seemed normal, almost predictable as if they had to happen.

Kate marveled at these revelations. She thought, *This is how this Harendt legacy might work. I can see tiny scraps, slices of images but never the entire picture.*

Then the images dissipated and were replaced by one more set of images, actually more of an intuition. Kate could foresee a path for herself. Not surprisingly it involved nature and animals and took her further from human conflict. She had one clear revelation: the Romanian Cold Hand was not for her. Repelling people and scaring them lay far from her natural center no matter how useful or powerful it might be.

Finally Kate understood one last insight. What the Cold Hand encompassed, its potential could possibly be realized in a very altered form. She only knew it involved turning that power almost upside down. Hidden in her inheritance from Queen Royal was another more promising energy which apparently she would have to discover.

Then all the imagery seemed to drift away. Kate felt a sense of quiet, not peace but almost emptiness. And then in an instant the empty space began refilling with colors, bright, sparkling, almost shocking. The colors had no definition at first but they came flying from all directions and Kate realized what it meant. This was the replacement for the Cold Hand and this was also her mission. The colors congealed and swirled then stopped. For a moment a face appeared, part human, part animal and this face was smiling with the power of the sun. It is that smile she would see for months afterward. The smile could only mean one thing to Kate: Your job is to turn the Cold Hand into a positive, good over evil. There was no doubt, no equivocation, no waffling, the job was taking this gift and doing something good with it.

When she "awoke" the forest was still bathed in moonlight. She looked at her watch, 20 minutes had passed but it seemed like hours. In fact Kate felt like she had lived in another life momentarily. She stood up from her special chair, took a few steps and turned around. Kate knew she would likely not see this place again so she bent down and touched the rocks. She intended this goodbye would last only a moment but she found herself still kneeling a few minutes later like she had been glued in place. During these minutes Kate felt like she could sense the life around her in vegetation, animals, the huge trees and even living in a nearby tiny stream. The sounds became amplified, the scents of flowers seemed more intense, the sheer size of the trees grew in dimension. Even in the dark she could see purples and yellows and a wave of warm energy poured over her. She felt nature was saying goodbye.

Then she was released by the forest. She giggled to herself. *What a silly notion that the forest could wrap me up like that.* But as she walked home through the forest still bathed in moonlight she knew it was true.

Kate arose in the morning feeling completely refreshed. For the past months she rarely awoke feeling energized and she had to work at pumping up her spirit. The trip to her sitting rock had rebalanced the scales. Kate dressed, packed her bags and went down the narrow stairs to say goodbye to Grace and Angeline. Grace looked up at Kate over her morning newspaper. "You look much happier today, Kate. You must have slept well."

Kate smiled, "I figured out a few things for myself, I feel much better, thanks." She gave both women hugs and Phillipe a big kiss.

Kate waited to get off the train from Bois Le Rois to Paris, reluctant to jump into what she knew would be a situation that was complicated and messy. But she reminded herself she was now on a mission that required fulfillment. Finally she collected her beatup backpack and tossed her favorite leather satchel over the other shoulder. She avoided leather for the most part but the satchel was handed down in her family from her father's father. Wearing a floppy hat, jeans, a t-shirt and sun glasses she slid out of the train car hoping that nothing and no one would be waiting. She had the address of the apartment where she'd be housed.

She peeked out, no one in sight, the platform at Gar de Lyon was nearly deserted. Kate ambled down the platform headed for the street. A dark haired, svelte, well dressed woman in slacks and blouse stood alone waiting for someone but Kate did not recognize her. The woman watched Kate approach and said, "I am Cherise Laroche, I'm a police officer from the Paris police and I'd like to accompany you. Is that ok?"

Kate brightened. "Did they send you to find me?"

Cherise replied, "I did a little digging, I knew you were out in Bois Le Rois. I've been here on my own time hoping I had it right. I've read about you and you will need some assistance I thought."

Kate liked Cherise right away. "Sure, but I'd like to walk, I need exercise."

Cherise smiled, "I walk everywhere I can, it took me an hour to get here but I walk very fast. *Tres vitesse.* I can also run quickly. I'm licensed to carry a firearm I speak four languages and understand a few more. I can assist you."

Kate thought, *Well you're certainly perky, friendly and informative. Did my vision last night put me in ultra positive land? Good heavens, sometimes being so cynical is a bring down. I like this woman.* "Your English is excellent, pardon my limited French," said Kate.

"No mind, I speak passable Arabic which is what your pal Da Hij likely grew up with."

Kate noted her perceptiveness. "I welcome some help. Can we walk to this address?" Kate handed her a slip of paper. Having Cherise waiting for her made the Paris visit more welcome for Kate. She took it as a sign that things might go better.

"Sure, it will take maybe a half hour. Here, give me that leather bag, you take the backpack."

The two women began their walk at a fast pace. They chatted and got acquainted with Kate wondering if the police had combed their ranks to find a useful matchup in Cherise.

They arrived at a four story apartment building three blocks from the site of the March. Kate picked up a key from the doorman as she was instructed. When they entered the apartment Kate had a surprise waiting.

"Aggie!" she exclaimed. Seeing Aggie Roemer was not a total surprise, he traveled constantly and had extensive connections in France.

"Katie, I've been researching your pal Da Hij and you need to know what I'm uncovering. Who is your friend?"

Kate replied, "This is Cherise, she is with the Paris police and has offered to help me today." Cherise smiled at Aggie.

Aggie stood up and shook hands with Cherise and then gave Kate a warm hug.

Aggie said, "I would think this is relevant for the police to know as well so let me fill you in."

Since her experiences in the forest Kate had begun seeing things more in black and white, dark versus light. She knew Aggie was here with news from the darker realm even before he began talking.

With wire rim glasses, a small peaked hat, dressed in his usual corduroy jacket, dark blue cotton pants and button down shirt, Aggie always looked like an academic right off a campus which in a sense he was. But Aggie cultivated sources in the Intelligence community and was an inveterate snoop. He always wanted the truth of why events took place. He turned this curiosity into a profession providing information to companies in areas of security and technology.

Aggie motioned for them to sit down on the two couches. Kate looked around the room which was furnished in an old fashioned style with heavy wooden furniture, elaborate water colors on the walls and bookcases stuffed with hard cover books. Two french doors opened onto a patio which overlooked a few square blocks and the Tuileries gardens could be seen nearby.

"Ok, this Da Hij, he's not some young guy who just showed up in the desert with a few thousand of his friends. He has backers and handlers. In particular my connection said his mentor-teacher and controller is Sam Nasser, a Lebanese deal maker who talks to Arabs and Russians and Americans brokering oil and commodities deals. But in this case he has been grooming your friend Da Hij for three years or more. What I'm told is he anticipates Islamic fundamentalists will be on the rise later in the '90's so he somehow found Da Hij and helped craft a young leader who would bring a message of peace. This is good for Nasser's business connections."

Kate nodded her head. "Well, anything wrong with that idea? I mean, what I know of Da Hij that may be totally true." Kate had decided to surrender her threatening instincts about Da Hij. She needed to give him a chance.

Aggie continued, "Nasser works all sides of the aisle, he talks to capitalists but also talks with Islamic people who want to foment uprisings in places like Pakistan and Iraq. He is respected and feared. The Lebanese have always been wedged between the west and east, the Israelis and the Egyptians, Beirut has long been a watering hole for the wealthy and a sink hole for the impoverished."

Kate listened intently. "Ok, he's a power broker of some kind. If Da Hij brings a peaceful message what am I missing here?"

Aggie turned quite serious. "Kate, I am told he is being used by this Nasser to bring naive rootless Islamic young men together in places like France and across the middle east. The historian Arnold Toynbee believed Islam will be a far greater threat to the west than communism ever was. He believed the western nations had dismembered Muslim nations and Islamic forces would rise against the west."

Kate interposed, "I'm not overly surprised by any of this. There's always been a dark shadow hovering over him."

Aggie continued, "Da Hij becomes a harmless, friendly Pied Piper leading young people to the river. At the water the message will change. Instead of peace and sharing it will become preaching the rise of Islam to take over the world. Nasser apparently can talk to both sides in every conflict. So Da Hij becomes the organizer, the magnet, the symbolic leader and he can innocently bring Islamic masses out into the open. Even America will applaud the peaceful gatherings. In fact there is American money flowing to Nasser to set up Da Hij."

Kate responded, "Aggie, you're saying this is like a first step getting Islamic youth to gather and know more about their culture? Then someone will step in and whip them into an angry mob? Well possibly but so far I'm not seeing that mob whipping part at all."

Aggie replied, "Katie, you need to be careful that you are not attached to this Pied Piper. He will be thought of as misleading youth, herding them together to be turned into mobs of dissatisfied, angry radicals."

Kate stood up and shook her head. "Agg, I have to deal with right now, today. You're saying Da Hij is being manipulated. I don't know, is he? I can't see the evidence yet. He and I met, I'm not uncomfortable with him and we share certain commonalities. So what am I supposed to do? Should I stay away because some manipulator may turn him into a screaming radical? I'm sure I get manipulated by powerful interests constantly. It's the way of the world."

"Kate, the sinister forces are the invisible people pulling the strings. I believe this Nasser and others mean to sell him out to whoever bids the highest. That could happen to you as well."

"Aggie, the only money I take is from *GloryDays*. I hope I'm not some dunce for people who mean to wreak havoc."

Aggie got up, walked to the window and stood there with his back turned. "Katie, the same sources told me that his handlers are not comfortable with how Da Hij is evolving and they are concerned about you being involved."

"Aggie, I didn't ask for this at all. Bart Alliason and your brother both pushed me toward him. I was supposed to keep him calm, kind of tone down his loud music. When we met in the desert, well that all changed but we stopped the march."

"Kate, there is danger for you, that's all I care about. What happens to this Da Hij I don't care. I would stay a distance from him. I would prefer you don't even appear at this March of the whatever it is."

"Agg, a little late for that I'm afraid."

Less than two kilometers away in a rented apartment also close to the Tuileries Gardens two men faced each other across a large wooden dining table. The apartment was sparsely furnished in a modern style, it had been rented for just two days and one night but it cost a month of rent. A corpulent, bearded, dark skinned man in his sixties dressed in casual slacks and a blood red shirt faced a spare, somewhat innocent appearing young man the world presently knew as Da Hij Silbi.

"Sam you have offers for me, here, now?"

Sam Nasser restlessly adjusted his place on the dining room chair. He had rented this apartment to ensure he had a quiet meeting place with Da Hij.

"My young friend, I am looking out for you. We'll talk about the offers in a moment. It costs money to organize all these people. Your people in the desert, we provided trucks and buses outside Amman, Jordan. You're smart enough to know these followers of yours don't spontaneously show up. We have people walking neighborhoods, handing out paper flyers, we offer them money to show up for your rallies. We provide buses or subway tickets. It all comes at a price. Now, in the process the world comes to know you, sees you as a positive guiding force."

"Sam, where is this money coming from? As you know my father and I are not that close but he told me an Islamic group desiring radical ends gives you funding. Is that true?"

"My friend, I talk to everyone. At any given time I may take money or support from conflicting sides. That's why they like me, I'm connected to everyone. And, your American friend McGill, she doesn't know it but there is money from their intelligence agencies, she may be receiving money from a company that kills the very animals she wants to save."

Da Hij recoiled inwardly but had learned to keep Sam's barbs at a distance. Sam had definitely helped him progress but his tactics were constantly suspect.

"Da Hij, you must know, I am always strategizing. The very name you use that I helped you find, it's constructed to confuse all these Islamic forces. Are you for them, against them? All they know is a young man has followers, he is very different, he talks of peace but most important, people show up for you. That's what your backers pay the money for."

"Sam, I have heard you plan to bring Sheik Awahdi to my March of the Peaceful. I read things, he is in favor of violence. I don't want him there."

"Da Hij, if Sheik Awahdi is present it indicates you can bring even a radical Islamic leader to your event. That is an achievement, indicative of your powers to persuade."

"Sam, I have needed your help but we often disagree on many things. You need to listen to me sometimes. All these young men come because I offer them a peaceful option. That is what got me started in all this. To talk peace."

Sam shifted his weight in the chair, looked past Da Hij out the windows to the Tuileries. "You are not in a position to dictate to me my young friend. I gave you support and guidance, it can be taken away very easily. You said you wanted public prominence, I have done that for you."

"Sam we have done that together. They are not following Sam Nasser, they are following me, I am the March of the Peaceful and I mean to keep it peaceful."

Da Hij was getting upset and anxious. This happened almost every time he and Sam talked. They once argued about the color of a shirt Da Hij was to wear.

Sam allowed a silent beat to pass. Da Hij had grown but with it had come a bigger ego, feelings that he had done all of this without much help. Sam anticipated such problems. Da Hij was not the first young leader he had supported and funded. Sam had an eye for them when they are just starting out. Not all of them were successes but establishing the control early guaranteed Sam leverage if his prospects became prominent.

Sam's facial expression darkened but only slightly. "Now, we will have some expenses here in Paris. Da Hij Silbi is a new name in this arena so we spent liberally in the outer ring of suburbs where your followers are stashed in those ugly high rise buildings. As usual buses are required but in Paris the underground works well so we spread out money for Metro tickets. I have made a deal for you to give away a wonderful food supplement from the stage. They are putting up substantial funds. You don't need to sell anything, just give these bottles out from the stage, ok? I am working on a funding arrangement with a large country bordered by numerous smaller countries with large Muslim populations, you will certainly like that money. Finally I spent more than usual for robes and special robes just for you. The followers, we have nearly 50 this time, will be robed in all white and you will have shining red robes as befits the leader. I rented a first rate sound system, your American friends who like your message also brought in two experts in live outdoor shows to ensure you have a good experience and there will be backstage food, better than anything you've ever seen, Da Hij. You'll enjoy this event."

Da Hij had been becoming wary of Sam. But without his support March of the Innocents and three prior events never could have happened. Having thousands trudge across the desert in Jordan turned out to be laborious for those marching. There were complaints by the second day. Sam made sure dollars, always the favorite currency, found their way into the many hands, but still there had been complaints that walking in the sand was difficult. Sam liked the masses crossing the desert images but it had become obvious there would be problems. So he paid to have trucks with food and water along the way but well out of sight. Sam reminded himself, no more desert marches.

Sam also reminded himself that the true payoff was in sight and having come this far he needed to keep Da Hij positive and engaged.

Kate had a phone number for Da Hij. It was now a few hours until the

March of the Peaceful was to commence. She called and he answered. "It's Kate, I think we should talk before the event. Can you talk now?"

He hesitated. He was sharing the apartment with Sam who had three people in for a meeting. "No, not here. But I can walk outside, hang on."

Kate heard him descending some stairs and then traffic noise. He stopped and said, "Ok , I can talk."

Kate asked, "I am being told you have a handler and he is taking money from everyone under the sun to pay your expenses."

Da Hij tried to make a joke, "No, not everyone, just half the planet. Sam has connections to anyone with a stake in Islamic relations. He once invited two men to a meeting who were completely opposed to each other's positions on Palestine and I was stuck in the middle. Fortunately they weren't armed. Sam makes me nervous."

"Da Hij, I am being told you may be in danger. That very well could mean I'm also in danger. I wouldn't trust this Sam."

He responded, "I don't trust him but he's come through for me each time. I don't like feeling uneasy but without him I'm, uh, back in Las Vegas working for Mr. Nash the illusionist."

Kate replied, "So, would that be so bad, working in Vegas?"

He shrugged. "It was ok, I enjoyed the work and I have a flair for it. But here I am hoping to make a big difference in peoples' lives."

Since arriving in Europe Da Hij had been thinking about unpacking his two small trunks that contained all his illusionist gear. It had been three years and he'd been hauling the trunks around with him.

"Da Hij, why don't you show the audience some illusions. Everyone could use a little entertainment."

He shrugged, "Sure, I've been thinking about that. In fact, since the desert meeting I made some time to prepare a whole introduction for the all American girl. You'll like it!"

Kate thought, *Da Hij, you can be a bit over the top. I hope I do like what you created.*

They talked about other issues for a few minutes but time was pressing both of them.

Having settled nothing of consequence it still made Kate feel better about the event. They were definitely in this together.

The French police were on notice that certain French groups could be planning to protest the event. When Da Hij was in the desert no one thought of protesting much of anything. But the Muslim population expected to turn out for the event was a restless, unsettled population which made many French people uncomfortable.

Sam Nasser had tapped into this group who begrudgingly remained in France for the work but received only the most limited lip service from the French government. They were coming out of the woodwork for this March of the Peaceful. As Da Hij had only scant knowledge of Paris he arbitrarily chose the Avenue Champs Elysees as a route but people began gathering in the hundreds taking buses and subways from areas far outside Paris. The March had turned into more of a concert setting. Now they were essentially standing around in the Jardin Des Tuilires and there were a few hours yet to go. Then paramilitary troops, medical resources and dozens of buses began appearing. No one had been prepared with a plan for such a gathering. To the dismay of local Parisians, a sizeable crowd had been forming in the much loved Jardin de Tuileries which connects the Louvre to the Arc de Triumphe on a straight line to the Champs Elysses and Concorde square. This historic park and walkway embodied much of what makes Paris so remarkable and the last place Parisians wanted mobs of people hanging around.

Kate turned back into the apartment. She was grateful to have the place almost to herself. Besides Cherise and Aggie only one policeman in uniform had been assigned and he waited outside the door.

Kate had to remind herself she had a mission but how to implement it was a different issue? She asked Aggie, "What is this setup like, have you seen it?"

Aggie replied, "There is a stage facing an audience. We managed to get two veterans from Bill Graham's concert company over here in a hurry, they worked out things with French authorities. There is a stage and sound system."

Kate's thoughts were interrupted as Cherise had a two way radio which was now crackling in French but Kate couldn't really understand.

Cherise listened and turned to Kate, "That's the gendarmes network, it goes out to anyone authorized to carry this radio. They believe there is some kind of counter march heading toward the Tuileries. Lots of French people are not happy about this gathering and apparently mean to protest. So the police are scrambling to be ready for any conflict but because of the jammed up conditions police can only move on foot."

Aggie looked up from his computer. "Kate, Da Hij's handler is Sam Nasser, he will be there. He is large, heavy, from Lebanese extraction and wearing his trademark dark red shirt. I bet you can spot him."

Kate checked her watch, "I need to be backstage in a half hour, let's go into the Tuileries." She and Cherise descended the apartment's stairs out into the street. They began walking at a fast pace. Kate was delighted here was someone who could out run and out walk her. They arrived at the backstage area after clearing three levels of security using Cherise's official badge. As usual people were darting about, yelling instructions. Smoky smells from nearby food stands drifted across the stage. When two officials spotted Kate they snared her and brought her to a backstage room where she was essentially isolated which she hated. As soon as they departed so did Kate with Cherise in tow. They began exploring the backstage area.

Kate stopped to look around. Young men in long white robes were gathering to one side, security was tight. Music began playing and someone began announcing a welcome to the March. The music continued, people began clapping in time to the rhythm, the mood was festive and light.

An announcer began speaking in French and then switched to Arabic as well so Kate could not really understand what was being said. She did hear her own name. She asked Cherise to translate. Cherise listened and then said, "He's saying welcome to this March of the Peaceful, uh, there will be music, a local leader will speak, you were mentioned, Da Hij Silbi will soon be out here. You will enjoy the entertainment."

Off to one side of the backstage something was happening. A wave of people were entering, all dressed in white except one person dressed in purple and red. Kate had a hunch that was Da Hij and sure enough he was swept up toward the stage and directly to the microphone. He began speaking, first in english.

"Welcome to all the peaceful warriors here in Paris. Our purpose in being here is to reaffirm our commitment to peace, to peaceful expression and enjoy each other's company, Islamic brothers and sisters together."

Kate scanned the audience. Not too many sisters, she thought. Kate listened and Da Hij seemed to be piling platitudes on top of cliches, nothing really registered with Kate. But from what she could tell the audience liked listening to him. Then Da Hij switched to Arabic. Now Kate was utterly lost and Cherise could only catch a few words.

Two uniformed police were close by, Cherise stepped over to them and inquired what they had heard about the counter march?

She returned to Kate. "They said there were people gathering outside the gardens with protest signs, they are being orderly but the police will try to separate the protestors from this audience. That may not be easy."

Kate thanked her. Da Hij was talking and finally returned to English. Kate tried to hear his words which were slightly garbled due to their location backstage. The tone of his words sounded calm and reassuring, that was what mattered. She checked her watch, they were just over a half hour out from the start time. Kate took Cherise's arm and said, "Let's find a quiet spot back here, maybe we can go back to that room they gave me?"

They found the isolated room. Kate wanted time to think. Now a new speaker was talking and the public address system was piped in to Kate's room. In a few moments some musicians began playing. So far, nothing difficult was occurring.

Kate was thinking, *All this buildup, all this planning, I'm off on this sideroad from my path. I must learn from this experience to choose my involvements more carefully. Back in the States all these government types are leaning on me to be here, to help Da Hij but it's his trip, not mine.*

Half an hour passed with more music and two more speakers in various languages. The audience mood remained upbeat.

Cherise walked off to find a sandwich and offered to bring food back but Kate had no appetite. Kate attempted to meditate and collect her thoughts. Cherise returned with a French equivalent of a hot dog and some iced tea for Kate.

Cherise's radio crackled in French. She listened and then translated. "They said the protestors are trying to push their way into this gathering. They are objecting to having all these people in the Tuileries and want them to leave. They are being disruptive but so far no violence."

Kate now heard various voices on the radio, they were sounding excited and concerned. She could tell enough from their tone of voice, she thought. Then people were shouting on the radio sounding stressed. That didn't help Kate deal with added pressure.

An announcer introduced another person who Kate had not heard of, Sheik Awahdi who began speaking only in Arabic. Cherise attempted a rough translation. "He is telling these young people they have a responsibility to pay more attention to traditions of Islam and...I can't get all the words but he's condemning youth who go off his path, he's not a happy guy..." Even looking at the audience Kate could see their faces darkening as they listened.

Kate knew it was time to act. She took Cherise with her and found Da Hij backstage. "Da Hij, whatever this man is saying it's not good. I can tell just by the inflections in his voice."

Da Hij replied, "Yes, you're right, he represents a difficult interpretation of Islam, he preaches violence, I didn't want him here but Sam said he'd offer something useful. This was not my idea."

Da Hij finally worked up the courage to act. He walked out on stage and stood next to the Sheik who looked at Da Hij angrily. They exchanged words and the Sheik stomped off stage in a huff. Kate realized Da Hij may finally have exercised some influence in a positive way.

Da Hij began another introduction then the sound system was filled with a swelling, exciting music. Kate cringed, she hoped he was not putting up some splendid show biz illusion just to introduce her.

"She met me in the desert, a truly unique young American woman is joining us today, she stands up for causes she believes in I respect her commitment to important issues...Ms. Kate McGill!!"

Kate was about to walk onstage when colored lights began flashing across the stage, then voices in many languages began speaking all talking about peace and then to her surprise, images of herself began appearing on two screens followed by images of people marching together in a parade and then illusions of women running in a large group in athletic outfits cascaded across the stage. The whole show went on for nearly two minutes. Kate had expected some razz matazz for 30 seconds. She had no idea he had the resources to generate such a big deal.

The audience stood up applauding responding to the show on stage. Finally Kate walked out onstage dressed in her most glamorous *GloryDays* outfit. She felt she owed Cory at least this much.

"Hello, Da Hij invited me to join him today. Da Hij and I want to try an experiment with all of you gathered here. We are going to silently create a vision of peace and we need all of you to contribute your thoughts and feelings. We will gradually build a ring of protective calm around our gathering with your help. Da Hij will now translate what I said into French and Arabic."

She stood back and tugged Da Hij forward who did his best, she hoped, to translate her words.

Then Kate told the audience, "Take the hand of people on each side of you, you'll find this experiment interesting and rewarding." *Oh please let me be right about this.*

Then for Kate the smiling part animal part human face appeared in her mind. With all the confusion around her she could not forget what she saw revealed on the sitting rock. She needed to turn the Cold Hand into good over evil. Somehow.

At the back of the stage a technician attending to sound equipment reached over to a control unit running four amplifiers labeled *"Aray Powersource 93"*. He flipped the switch to "on" as he had been instructed.

Kate felt a surge of energy and the vision, such as it was, became amplified reaching further back into the audience and across the backstage area.

Kate said to the audience, "Now, we're here to affirm good, positive feelings, you are here to remind yourselves and the world you have an important role to play on the world stage."

Kate had never attempted any mentalist vision with four Aray amps working near her. She knew the devices could theoretically enhance a vision but her actual experience with Aray gear was limited and the last experiment in the desert failed.

Holding hands with Da Hij and a young woman in a white robe onstage

Kate reached a starting plateau she understood, the same place she had reached attempting to create the Cold Hand. Now the emotional inputs were different. She soared past that plateau in seconds and found herself in uncharted territory. An initial vision multiplied on levels she had not encountered and connecting with hundreds of adults and then the larger audience behind them amplified the emotions and visions dramatically.

People in the audience felt their spirits lifted as well and began shouting in a number of languages. But the language hardly mattered, their spirits combined and a few thousand people found themselves webbed together sharing a group induced euphoria. Any bystanders including police and safety personnel were similarly impacted.

Kate recognized this was a radically expanded experience. What she had learned from Queen R. had not touched on group happiness jags. She also had no real idea how it might end? Like everyone present, Kate found herself projected into a state of euphoric abandon which felt quite wonderful. *Good lord, did those amplifiers really kick this up so fast?*

In the midst of this joyous experiment Sheik Ahwadi found a microphone and began preaching in Arabic from the side of the stage. His strident tone contrasted sharply with what the audience were feeling. And then something occurred that no one could have prepared for. The Sheik's harsh words conflicted with a larger shared vision and people apparently did not want to hear his message at that moment.

Kate looked over at the Sheik and thought, *I'm not against your having your say but you have definitely picked the wrong time to be lecturing these people. Maybe you need to go?*

Like a wall of churning water a wave of collective energy swept from the audience in reaction to his jarring demands. Kate may have temporarily harnessed the Cold Hand but she couldn't completely control it. The Sheik found himself engulfed by a powerful opposing force and having no experience with all the joyous vibes he reacted by trying to harangue the audience more angrily to follow his dictates and be good submissive religious followers.

Kate felt a powerful rush. She thought, *Oh man, what the heck is going on?* Then the unleashed Cold Hand overwhelmed the Sheik who was swept from the microphone and disappeared from the stage.

Kate glanced sideways and thought, *Did he walk away, was he snatched?* She only knew he was gone. The shared vision continued building and then seemed to peak. Over the next few minutes the audience found themselves returning to a more normal state of mind, the shouting and cheering gradually abated and then a collective hush.

They found the Sheik or the physically altered version of him a distance from the stage in a storage area still alive but looking quite different.

Kate was curious what happened so after a few more minutes she walked backstage. Medical people crouched around someone. Is that the Sheik? She moved closer. Kate thought, *Good lord, what happened to him? He instantly aged, is that possible? He was, like, forty years old. Now he looks seventy. Is this just temporary? How could that be?*

They bundled him on to a stretcher and took him off to a hospital. Kate stood watching shaking her head. She looked around at the quickly emptying back stage area. Cherise walked up and put her hand on Kate's shoulder. They watched the ambulance leave.

Cherise said, "Well, that was very strange. They'll look after him and we should get going."

Kate hunted around for Da Hij but his entourage had departed. But she did encounter Sam Nasser in his deep red shirt carrying a heavy leather satchel. When he recognized her his face turned slightly angry.

In a heavily accented deep voice he said, "I am Sam Nasser, Da Hij's director, I arrange all his marches and appearances. He seems to believe you have great powers of persuasion, your appearance in the Jordanian desert was certainly, ah, unexpected."

Kate couldn't tell if he was upset. She extended her hand and he paused before shaking her hand. " Are you upset with something I did, Sam? Da Hij and I have a relationship, he would tell me if he was angry, I hope. What are you saying?"

Sam responded, "Certain parties feel you overstepped your place stopping the march in the desert and now ejecting the Sheik."

Kate realized this was a no-win situation. "Sam, I hardly ejected anyone, that was poor judgment inviting that man to a peaceful gathering. Thousands of people wanted him gone, it's that simple. As for the march in the desert, it had a positive ending."

Sam considered his options and surprised her. "Ms. McGill, I have vast connections in the middle east and Europe. I have substantial influence. Perhaps we should discuss my representing you as well?"

Kate gave him a pretty smile. "Thanks for the offer, I'll consider it. Right now I'm taking early retirement, I will not make any more appearances for a while. Please tell Da Hij I wish him well and for yourself also."

Sam watched the two women walk away arm in arm.

Kate departed with Cherise and true to her word made no more public appearances for almost two years.

In another hour the Jardin de Tuileries was nearly empty leaving only a cleanup crew and technicians taking down equipment.

Aggie was making a call from France to his brother back in Minnesota.

"Agg, how's it going with Miss Twinkletoes in Paris. I know she was supposed to appear with her soul brother Da Hij today."

"Well Buzz, it started off like a garden variety political rally. A few speakers, some music, Da Hij talked collective peace. Then Katie shows up and it all went nutsy. The audience were getting carried away, like this incredibly positive, joyous feeling, it made no sense intellectually, how did that even happen? So then a few minutes passes and this Sheik hijacks a mike, and starts yelling at the audience. One moment he's on the side of the stage and then shazam, I swear, he just disappears. Like apparently just plucked right off the stage by some invisible claw. He turns up way at the rear of the backstage in this storage shed."

Buzz reacted, "What? He just flew away?"

Aggie replied, "I don't know about 'flew away' but he was definitely gone, I saw him when the medical people were bringing him out on a stretcher. He looked like he'd aged 30 years! This Sheik knew it, he could see his hands were aged and he was freaking out."

"That sounds crazy, Aggie."

"Buzz, say what you will. I saw the guy. He became an old man. Kate saw him and was totally shocked. She lost color in her face, she was utterly dismayed like she had caused it. She kind of blurted out, 'Aggie, I tried to turn the Cold Hand upside down. What happened to this guy? I've never seen anything so strange!' She and I are standing a few feet apart as they carted him out."

Buzz was having trouble processing this thought. "What a strange tale."

Aggie replied, "So a minute after she's gone these two guys come running up to me after I was talking to Katie. They said they were Special Ops guys, they flashed credentials. They were assigned to this event in case she used the Cold Hand. These two were totally flipped out by what happened. They saw the transformation in the audience, the exuberant reactions, and then they also witnessed the disappearing Sheik. One guy told me, '...one second he's onstage preaching up a storm, the next moment it's an empty space...' He could not believe it. Man that is the true weapon of choice. Take the opposition out with sheer delirium."

Buzz was thinking, *Our friends in Washington will be very interested in that euphoria reaction. That's even better than a wall of fear.*

Aggie added, "Equally strange, I think, were those *Aray Powersource* Amps and what role they played. I don't know what exactly they did but I can tell you just as soon as the amps were shut down two uniformed guys packed them up in special reinforced shipping cases and out the door they went. I watched them, they were quite protective of those babies. I was told Helen had them shipped special all the way from California for this march."

CHAPTER THIRTY SEVEN

HUNTING THE HUNTERS

Count Adrianno Falacci sat facing Tom Wisani, a wealthy real estate developer from Texas and self professed big game hunter. The Count had invited Tom along on a hunting expedition in Zimbabwe meant to be kept strictly secret. The two men arrived along with two professional hunter guides, Ali Servo and Henny Derasmus who grew up in what had been the Union of South Africa but spent years hunting across Zimbabwe, Namibia, Botswana and Mozambique. Most important, Servo and Derasmus knew all the steps required to hunt big game across all these countries obeying laws which were unavoidable and sidestepping other restrictions which could be glossed over when necessary.

Both guides served their time in the South African army, they knew weapons, and how to avoid observation when essential. A rough hewn water buffalo look-alike, Servo could be counted on to react, fight and overwhelm adversaries be they animal or human. Derasmus preferred not to fight whenever possible using his nimble brain to outwit foes. A keen shot, an expert with a knife and avid chess player, Derasmus outlived other hunters and professional soldiers by being smarter.

Tom Wisani made more money in a month than both the guides earned in five years. He had virtually no patience and only the most limited appreciation of sportsmanlike conduct. His reputation back in the States for rapacious, ugly behavior in meetings or night clubs traveled before him. He had 24 hours to bag at least one white rhino, the relatively rare breed prized by so many big game hunters. It bothered him not at all that only a few white rhinos still existed. "Well, let me be the proud hunter who takes a white before they're all gone." Guides and bearers went out of their way to avoid any outing with him. Tom Wisani's name was synonymous with bullying his way through

310

predicaments and he would not tolerate being told his goal could not be accomplished.

Count Falacci and Wisani had traveled ten hours to reach a hunting ground near the border of Zambia and Zimbabwe. Hunting was still not approved in Zambia in 2003 but was expected to reopen. Wisani had planned his trip months in advance only to find that in early 2003 hunting was still not officially legal. His guides and the tour company were naturally communicating crazily to find an alternative. Zambia had been Wisani's first choice for reasons likely known only to himself.

Finally Wisani put down his foot and demanded some hunting, he did not care where but it had to happen or he was stiffing all of them. He then said, "Look, money is not the concern with me but time is an issue. So we're here, you are all saying this country is not really tracking hunting parties because it's illegal. I'll fly in a small plane to remove any carcass that we take." Servo turned away momentarily and rolled his eyes to his partner. Wisani then ranted on about how this had to occur instantly and then he added a financial bonus. The incentive to go forward was now so high that Servo and Derasmus finally caved in. Servo in his stiff Afrikanner accent said, "Alright, Mr. Wisani. I know a place two hours from here, the game will be gathered there as they have had no hunters pursuing them for some years. But we must get in and get out quickly. And you need to know there is danger, they can arrest us if we're bagging big game."

Wisani showed a petulant, little boy face, "I have cash, we'll buy them off if we have to." The two professional hunters knew they were taking an immense gamble but Wisani was willing to enrich them with an extravagant and characteristically American cash bonus.

As the helpers and guides ran to and fro packing up firearms, food and water a native woman filling in as a last minute cook surreptitiously crept away and quickly removed a beatup camouflage brown metal box. She reached inside, threw two switches as she had been shown. She pressed two more buttons holding down the last one. The box emitted just one weak beep. Her "yes" or "no" message had been received.

By eight the next morning the hunting party arrayed themselves around a large knoll topped by trees and not far from one of the few water holes.

Derasmus led Wisani and two gun bearers out 200 yards near a much smaller dirt mound overlooking the veldt and watering hole. Large animals began gathering near the water as the sun rose and temperatures climbed.

Count Falacci accompanied Wisani, Servo and Derasmus led the two men, Servo lagging slightly behind watching their backs, scanning the horizon and even the blue green sky. Now Servo began walking facing backward. Two native bearers trundled behind hauling a few supplies, water and two sling chairs. One, Alsa, had years of working hunting expeditions, he knew the routines and normal demands. He walked hunched over favoring one hip and occasionally stood up and glanced around. With three mouths to feed Alsa avoided conflicts or disagreements at all costs. His seemingly passive manner happened to suit this party with bulky, ignorant male egos being flexed constantly. But Alsa had his feelings

Servo was starting to relax, nothing moved, no vehicles, nothing so far. The party stopped, the two experienced hunters stepped forward to watch the game, Servo motioned to Alsa to keep an eye out but nothing seemed untoward. The hunters began conferring with Wisani.

Five minutes passed, suddenly Alsa moved quickly toward Servo wishing to attract his attention but Servo was now dealing with the interesting and challenging part of his job: Identifying the appropriate targets, lining up the firearms, directing Wisani who was eager and very ready to go.

Alsa again begged Servo's attention. Servo shooed him away, then thought better about it and separated from Wisani for a moment. Alsa whispered hurriedly, Servo looked over his left shoulder and froze. He asked Alsa a question and then attracted Derasmus. He could barely be heard. "It's her. I can't believe this. How the hell could she find us?"

Derasmus yanked up a pair of Bushnell binoculars and tried to scan the horizon without disturbing Wisani. After a few seconds Derasmus uttered a simple, "Shit." Wisani now realized something was happening and his instincts kicked in.

"Servo, what the hell is going on, we're here, we need to move on this."

Servo looked at Derasmus. Speaking in a mix of English and Afrikaaner accents he told Wisani, "We have company. Not police, no legal danger. Have you ever heard of this woman who hunts hunters? She is experienced and dangerous. She hates what we do, what you're here to accomplish."

Wisani suddenly seemed terribly curious. This rang a bell, something he read in an airline magazine back when he still flew commercial. No not an airline magazine, it was an email from a hunting friend. They exchanged thoughts about her, what if she attacked a hunter? The hunter could defend himself. That appealed to Wisani immensely. The truth was he could prefer hunting a person rather than animals. This American woman, then she might have been in her late twenties or early thirties? She stalked hunting parties in Africa trying to scare them off but willing to attack and never with a gun. Only a bow and arrow.

Wisani's hunter instincts were turning 180 degrees. He grabbed the binoculars.

"Where, where is she?" He began scanning the horizon. Servo walked over, hesitated, then carefully raised his right hand up to Wisani's right arm and gently directed the binocs 45 degrees to the right. "Mr. Wisani, please understand, this may not make sense but you don't want to be looking for her, at least not yet."

Wisani felt anger boiling up, "What do you mean, I can't see her, I can't look for her? This is crazy!!" He was starting to get loud.

Servo began pointing southwest indicating an arc of space where their unwanted visitor had popped up momentarily. "Mr. Wisani, please listen to what I have to say. We don't know if this is her but Alsa has great experience, he believes it might be her. If this is her you can be in great danger. She doesn't care about us or the bearers, she only wants you and the Count. She is experienced, clever, resourceful and incredibly strong."

Wisani predictably said, "Does she look amazing? That's what I was told, she is an incredible looking hot bitch. Have you seen her up close?"

All conversation stopped. Servo glanced at Derasmus, both men looked at Alsa who kept his eyes averted. The Count was becoming visibly anxious. Dealing with wild game was his cup of tea. Being hunted, he had heard of this woman before, had no appeal to him. Scuttlebutt in hunting circles was she killed diligently.

Wisani now was unalterably tuned in. That email began coming back to him, the presumed history of this woman, her talent for tracking her prey, her ability with a Martin bow, her weapon of choice. He had to know more.

"Listen you two, I will double your bonus, she interests me far more than some damn rhino. But give me the correct information. Where is she, where do I look?"

Servo had been well trained in the South African army, not much got to him but Wisani's talk was totally crazy. "Mr. Wisani, I will show you but you must listen to us. We believe when she appears it is because she is tracking someone. It's you or the Count. We are known to be seasoned guides and, as you are well aware, we charge high prices for our services. She knows that also, we believe, so she may be tracking us as well but we know she has less interest for me or Derasmus."

Wisani shot back, "Why? Why do you say she has no interest in you?"

Derasmus replied, "Because I have encountered her. Two years ago, with a client named Hooper in Zimbabwe. Like you, wealthy, determined, loved killing rare animals. Loved it. We were tracking a certain beast, Hooper cornered this animal, a very rare one, he began closing in and the animal could not escape. A certain kill but definitely illegal which we don't care for. We normally honor the local laws."

Wisani could barely contain himself. "What? What happened?"

"Hooper raised his weapon, it was a sure kill. He had this animal, the gun fired but Hooper suddenly keeled over. One arrow through his left shoulder and then almost instantaneously a second one through his neck. Mr. Wisani, it was a perfect shot slicing right through his juglar vein. Perfect. It prevented Hooper from making the kill."

Wisani had trouble slowing down his heartbeat and breathing. "And, And??"

Derasmus continued, "We looked all around. No one. Not a sound except Hooper's dying gasps. A few minutes passed. Then she appeared, we couldn't figure out where she had been hidden. Even the bearers had no sense of her presence which is unusual. She strode toward Hooper quickly, efficiently, no wasted energy. She came right to me, put one hand on my firearm, looked at me eye to eye and said, "I hate what you do but I don't kill your kind, only these rich assholes. Don't trifle with me, do you understand my English?"

"I told her in English that I understood her. She went right to Hooper, tested his pulse, then his heart. She stood up, looked around more carefully. She strung another arrow. She said, 'Take this envelope. This pays for his funeral.'"

"I told her Hooper was immensely wealthy."

She replied, "Then spend it for something useful, just not guns. I've learned about you, hunters respect you, find something better to do with your skills. She looked around and then began backing away cautiously. A young white South African suddenly sprang at her with a knife in his hand. I can't even tell you why he did that. In one smooth, unbroken movement she caught his arm, he was strong and fairly tall. With just one arm she took his knife arm, twisted it so he cried out in real pain, shook off the knife and threw him to the ground. She never ran, never showed even the slightest sign of concern and then disappeared. We waited a moment and I ran for the closest jeep 200 feet away in the woods. I jumped in, turned the key, the engine started, it ran five seconds and died. She had somehow poisoned the petrol supply in all three vehicles. We walked four miles back to a village."

Wisani was awestruck. "Wha...what did she look like?"

Derasmus was dismissive, "Mr. Wisani, she is a tall, muscular blond woman in her late twenties, no more like early thirties I would guess. I am well trained in martial arts, firearms, I have no desire to mess with her. It's not worth it. She was intimidating."

"But how did she escape, you're miles from any town...."

"We think a quiet dirt bike. No four wheel vehicle. She stashed a lightweight dirt bike."

Derasmus walked to Wisani, handed him binoculars then grasped Wisani by the shoulders from behind, turning him 30 degrees toward the northeast. "Next to those two large rocks, focus there and be patient."

He focused on the rocks. Nothing moved. He remained fixed. Nothing was moving. Then she appeared bow in one hand, her own binoculars in the other. After a moment Wisani felt like they were both locked in on each other. It may have been the single most exciting moment even beyond hunting big game or having sex he would experience. She stood almost six feet, her body was difficult to make out but she definitely had a shapely rear end. He didn't care what happened for a moment. He could not take his eyes off her. He believed she lowered her glasses and may have, Wisani was not certain, but he thought she gave him the finger.

He couldn't believe his luck. She was the ultimate big game.

Servo glanced at his watch, checked the sun. He could handle risks, if it was the Animal Avenger as she was known he wasn't overly fearful but if authorities tracked them or...? Derasmus judged distances and rather casually sidled closer to a thick bush, not behind it, just closer. There they remained, Wisani increasingly keen and excited, the bearers very on edge. Wisani lost her or so he thought. She had been standing full height, not hidden, bow in hand, glasses trained on him. He loved being her target. He wished he could remember what the email had said about her?

Another two minutes passed, now Wisani became concerned, he could lose her and the white rhino if this all evaporated.

Her voice surprised all of them. A deeper sonorous voice than anyone expected but most curious was her location. She stood behind all of them, even the native bearers who normally could not be easily flanked when dangerous animals were involved had been taken by surprise. Alsa felt a strong concern. She had easily moved around all of them and now, most strangely, she stood only fifty feet from the rhino. Alsa knew animals, their habits, rhinos typically would not allow any human to approach that closely. When Alsa turned there she stood in safari gear, tan top and shorts, tall boots, her blonde hair bound up tight under a hunter's hat with a long bill. Her bow and arrow were in readiness but surprisingly she didn't seem tensed up.

Wisani drew his rifle up closer but not so close she would be alarmed. Alsa watched her carefully. Why was she not preparing her weapon? It takes two movements to use a bow and arrow, Wisani had a powerful rifle, he could kill her before she could get off an arrow.

Wisani said, "What is your name? I like to know my adversary's name." She smirked a little. Wisani realized she had reangled her long body, her free hand on her right hip in an unmistakeably suggestive pose. This feminine sexual taunt, however subtle, made this standoff even more alluring for Wisani. To bag a wild animal would be exciting, to go up against this near legendary huntress when she was clearly presenting herself as a target transcended any normal safari experience.

He was utterly thrilled, she did not look frightened, this would be the highest point in his life if he could bag her. His heart was racing also throwing off his timing and judgment however minutely.

For a second he realized that he would have witnesses. Wisani said to Servo, "Get away, all of you, don't be here, you get that?"

Servo started to talk and then realized he wanted no part of this anyway. "Alsa, go back to our vehicles, Derasmus and I are also leaving. Go now!" Alsa had no hesitation. He began walking behind Wisani, glanced momentarily at the woman and then the rhino. He walked quicker. Servo and Derasmus began backing away, never taking their eyes off both the woman and the massive animal.

Alsa's last image was of the woman quietly sliding closer to the rhino. Now they were alone, the hunter, the woman and the white rhino. Wisani swore she could communicate with the animal as it had not moved when she edged closer.

"My name is unimportant but it's Katherine."

Wisani replied, "That's it, Katherine, Kate McGill, that's it isn't it? I've heard about you."

She did not reply but in a flourish brought the bow up in one clean and very quick motion. Now she had the advantage.

"Mr. Great White Hunter, you can have me or the rhino. But I hope you'll take me, there are still a few thousands rhinos left in the world but I'm the only one of me. So let's make it just you and I. And now it's time for us Mr. Brave Big Balls. Bring up your firearm, it's time."

She motioned up with her bow and arrow signaling that he raise his rifle. He was thinking this really should be a piece of cake, his powerful gun should take her out. Now her right arm began cocking backwards but as she prepared the bow she also took one large step toward the rhino. Wisani was befuddled, she seemed to be scaring off the animal. He brought the gun up resolved to beat her at this game.

He watched her eyes, she was turned slightly away, he thought to aim a bit higher when her arrow let fly penetrating his left arm and emerging in his right chest. The blow staggered him and the pain nearly knocked him unconscious and then he saw his prey coming at him. She had frightened the rhino and it began trundling toward him. In a flash the rhino picked up speed. He tried to turn the gun but she had made that impossible, his arms would not turn toward the onrushing animal.

When the rhino's horn entered him in his lower intestines he didn't actually black out, he realized she had planned this whole ----.

His last vision was of the rhino's massive head driving down and the woman standing 50 feet away watching.

It lasted a few moments and then the rhino shook off Wisani's body and continued on its way into the veldt.

Servo heard the sounds but could not tell what happened. She appeared laying a new arrow on to the bow. "Your customer will require some assistance. Take him with you, do not go near those other animals. I'd be delighted to take you both out."

She then walked backwards to a hillock and leaned against a large rock watching them. The men ran to find Wisani, she heard some shouting, the hunched over native ran to them, then ran back to find a tarp. Moments later the men carried the dead body past her. She waited. There was loud swearing as they discovered one of their vehicles would not start but the other did. They drove off due north leaving most of their supplies strewn about.

She walked at a fast pace to a grove of trees, retrieved her sound deadened 4 cycle Honda dirt bike. It kicked over obediently. She slung a leg over and remained astride the idling cycle, looking around. The small pack of rhinos had sauntered out of the water and were tracking into a nearby grassy field. Wisani left blood on the ground.

She had learned to consider her alternatives before departing. Finally she decided and began riding southeast. From this spot she would be exposed for, perhaps, 20 minutes before entering more rugged country where her presence would be far less obvious. She brought up her speed, sometimes riding standing on the pegs, her bow slung over her shoulders. At higher speeds the hot air penetrated her clothes streaming across her body.

She didn't feel particularly victorious but there was one less of his type destroying precious wildlife. She wanted to smile but it wasn't something to smile about. She had committed herself to defending such important animals. An ancient, undiluted form of natural justice seemed fair and reasonable.

But it did occur to her that this brand of justice was becoming increasingly dangerous to pursue.

Author's acknowledgements for Kate McGill Romanian Cold Hand

Kate's book came to life when our family lived in Wayzata, Minnesota from 1991 to 1995. Kate was never in a rush to be discovered.

Thanks:

First to my wife Laura, our daughter Jessie and son Gabriel, all my deepest gratitude for being a sensational family. The best moments of my life have been shared with the four of us. Also to our border collie Scuba, as old now as the development of this book. A devoted friend at my feet as I've written about Kate.

To my brother Alan for reminding me to get on with it and finish the book. To our sister Gail who we both miss and our late parents Ernestine and Samuel without whom nothing could have occurred. Our Mom's ability to articulate thoughts and ideas lives on in both her sons. My value system was handed down and defined in conversations with our parents.

Mandi Studler in Minnesota has helped me critique and understand the characters in R.C.H. as well as stimulating book promotion. Thanks also to Angie Griffith who connected us and was the director of photography on Gabe's movie.

Bianca Bisson, daughter of my friend Barry Bisson at about age 17 digested the very imperfect book that existed and sent me a dead accurate, totally useable critique of all the flaws written succinctly.

Editing, proofing, spotting problems, thanks to Kathleen Lawrence, Eileen Simard, Carol McKegney, wife Laura, Jessie and Gabriel. While I've been finishing Kate, Gabe was editing his movie, "My Suicide" which won over 20 international awards. In our family both children are big stars. General assistance and encouragement: Dick and Trudy Herman, Chris Davidson who helped me understand the mother-daughter dynamic.

Were it not for the sixties and the music business I might have had a career in public health beginning at the University of California, Berkeley. Thanks to the nice people at the graduate division of the School of Public Health who had to put up with me.

Book cover graphic design by Gabriel Sunday and Toby Auberg. Execution by Toby Auberg. Photography front cover Cameron Crone. Special thanks to Jacquelyn Zook.

The illustrations of Kate which appear on the website www.katemcgill. com executed by Mozart Bautista, www.mozartbautista.blogspot.com. The delightful animation graphics on the website itself designed and executed by Arvin Bautista, www.greasypigstudios.com,. Strangely they are not related.

You can send email to katemcgillskates@gmail.com. If you write a note about the book it will likely appear on the website. Kate reads her mail.

My Background

I also created "This Is Your Brain On The Internet", a collection of techie ironic humor published in 1995 by Ziff Davis Press. In the sixties and seventies I worked as an Artist & Repertoire Producer at CBS, Capitol, Vanguard Records and my own company, Waterhouse Records. I produced or served as the executive producer for album projects with such artists as Leo Kottke, Minnie Riperton, Redbone, Phil Austin of the Firesign Theater, Harry Shearer & Michael McKean (Spinal Tap), Henny Youngman, slide guitarist Roy Rogers, songwriter Alex Harvey ("Delta Dawn"), Diana Hubbard (L. Ron's daughter) and the Hoodoo Rhythm Devils.

An added thanks to the Joker Steve Miller who helped me get started in the music business along with Jack Leahy in San Francisco and Ed Denson now of Garberville, CA. Thanks also to my two mentors in record companies, the late Don L. Ellis at Epic Records and Samuel B. Charters at Vanguard Records who both opened important doors for me. Also thanks to Jim Peterson, Randy Levy and Gary Marx in helping establish Waterhouse Records in Minneapolis.

After the music business, for nearly thirty years, I worked as an executive recruiter focused primarily in technology and financial services. I live in Petaluma, California with my wife Laura. I'm an avid bicyclist but never in spandex. I advise people on financial survival and career longevity, www.pyfnow.com.

Your comments are invited to www.katemcgill.com.

Trade or Service marks:

GloryDays
Aray Powersource
Queen Royal Elixir
Katherine Harendt McGill
Audi and Quattro are trademarks of Audi of America, Inc. and are used with permission of that organization.